Isabella's Not Dead

Previously Creative Director at RDF Television, Beth Morrey now writes full time. Her debut novel, *Saving Missy*, was a *Sunday Times* bestseller and longlisted for the Authors' Club First Novel Award.

Beth lives in London with her husband, two sons and two poodles.

/BethMorreyWriter

@bethmorrey

@bethmorrey.bsky.social

www.bethmorrey.co.uk

Also by Beth Morrey

Saving Missy
Em & Me
Lucky Day

Isabella's Not Dead

Beth Morrey

HarperCollins*Publishers*

HarperCollins*Publishers* Ltd
1 London Bridge Street
London SE1 9GF

www.harpercollins.co.uk

HarperCollins*Publishers*
Macken House, 39/40 Mayor Street Upper
Dublin 1, D01 C9W8, Ireland

First published by HarperCollins*Publishers* Ltd 2025
1

A catalogue record for this book
is available from the British Library

ISBN: 978-0-00-855531-3 (HB)
ISBN: 978-0-00-855532-0 (TPB)

Set in Sabon LT Std by HarperCollins*Publishers* India

Printed and bound in the UK using 100%
Renewable Electricity at CPI Group (UK) Ltd

This book contains FSC™ certified paper and other controlled
sources to ensure responsible forest management.

For more information visit: www.harpercollins.co.uk/green

For my friends, past and present

Yes; I was tired, but not at heart;
No – that beats full of sweet content,
For now I have my natural part
Of action with adventure blent;
Cast forth on the wide world with thee,
And all my once waste energy
To weighty purpose bent.

'The Wood', Currer Bell

PART ONE

1

I was on my third gin and tonic and thinking about sneaking off for a bath when Rachel produced the Ouija board and Amanda announced she was leaving her husband. She'd been building to this decision all afternoon, drowning her marital sorrows in a bottle of Rioja and moaning about his endless business trips. There wasn't much I knew about Christian Simmons – he worked in construction and in Amanda's Instagram photos he always looked painfully sunburnt, but neither of those things necessarily marked him out as a matrimonial disappointment. Mind you, there wasn't much I knew about Amanda either, not having seen her in the flesh for several years. Nowadays, she was much blonder, and self-consciously moderated her northern vowels – she might have changed in other ways, but they weren't immediately apparent, and we were only on the first night of the weekend. It was clear no one wanted to get into Mrs Simmons' impending divorce, so we all turned our attention to the Ouija board instead; the lesser of the two evils.

The cottage was a converted pub, tastefully renovated. Art prints of various lakes on the walls, wipe-clean leather sofas, a welcome Kendal Mint Cake and a complimentary basket of logs for the fire. There was a big kitchen with two dishwashers, and four double bedrooms with beds that could be re-purposed as twins. Perfect for get-togethers, if you didn't mind sharing, which I wasn't sure about. Even though I'd officially known my roommate for forty years, co-habiting wasn't much fun when you were fifty-three and a restless sleeper.

History repeating itself, Rachel was revelling in her role as the rebel of the group, having brought hash brownies to the party, plus twenty Marlboro for old times' sake. The brownies were actually a traybake, which I appreciated as a middle-aged twist on misdemeanour – Martha Stewart meets . . . well, Martha Stewart. Never mind drugs; I was pretty sure the Airbnb was strictly non-smoking, but as we worked our way through the booze, rules went out the window, along with our coughing exhales. I'd had two fags and I'd never smoked before, not even in school. Chloe (my roomie) had already been sick, and it was only ten thirty, though long past bedtime for all of us. Eight former schoolfriends fuelled by various hormones, herbs, chemicals and tipples. It was a messy regression.

Rachel Lloyd, Amanda Simmons, Chloe Coulson, Min Chiu, Erica Stanley, Holly Griffiths, Bhavini Gupta and me, Gwen Mortimer. Our Lake District idyll had cost £1800, plus £500 for a highly alcoholic Ocado order, which meant I'd spent nearly three hundred quid on a weekend I felt deeply ambiguous about. We'd kept in touch intermittently over the years, through an email group called 'Harpur Harlots', which was what we'd named ourselves when we were sixteen and playing in a hockey team together against the nearby 'Bakewell Tarts'. It seemed funny at the time.

Why had we kept in contact when so many other friendships had fallen by the wayside? Probably due to Holly, who did something glamorous in PR, was aggressively social, and had established a tradition of round-robin emails between us every Christmas. She'd also organized the whole weekend, finding the cottage and cajoling everyone into booking. Seeing her name flash up on my phone a few months before, I'd answered because it was such a novelty to hear the dry rasp of her voice after all that time, then couldn't think of an excuse on the hop. To get eight out of the original eleven team members together was quite an achievement, really. Danielle Seitzman wasn't there because she lived in New York. Gracie Wagstaff couldn't get childcare. And . . . well, eight was good. An even number. It would be fun, wouldn't it? Apart from weddings and big birthdays, many of us hadn't seen each other in years. Hadn't got together as a group in decades.

'We're in our prime!' Party girl Rachel had shrieked, doling out the cigarettes after we'd eaten Bhavini's chilli. But we weren't, really. She said it again when she got out the Ouija board, and it sounded like she was protesting too much, but it turned out I hadn't heard her correctly, and she was actually saying 'Amazon Prime' in reply to someone asking her where she got the board. It was a flimsy wooden thing, with the alphabet in a semicircle across the top, and numbers in the straight line along the middle. In the top two corners it said 'Yes' and 'No' and at the very bottom it said 'Goodbye', which I supposed gave the spirit world its way out if it got a better offer. Even fuelled by gin, I wasn't sure I really wanted to strike up a conversation with a bunch of dead people, but the alternative was marriage counselling with an increasingly maudlin Amanda. We put our fingers on the planchette and looked to Rachel for further guidance.

'It says you just ask it questions,' she mumbled through Lindor, a chocolatey finger tracing the instructions.

'Don't we have to open a line of communication?' pondered Chloe, who'd made a miraculous recovery and was back on the whisky sours.

'How do we do that?' Bhavini, swigging on a can of mojito, was simultaneously patting Amanda's heaving shoulder in a comforting manner.

'I'll create an atmosphere,' said Chloe, and went round switching off lights. Everyone then grumbled that it was too dark, since Min was deaf and relied mostly on lip-reading, but Chloe was set on the drama. Commanded by chief coordinators Rachel and Holly, Erica lit candles, grudgingly, because she was still pissed off with Rachel for bringing the hash brownies, which had eclipsed her straight carrot cake. Tall and rangy, one of those 'natural beauties', Erica fancied herself as a bit of an earth mother – not the kind of woman who would actually wear an apron, but maybe one of those Toast smock-dresses to signify rusticity. She'd bored me rigid earlier talking about her chickens, and her cake tasted vegan. But maybe I just felt guilty because I hadn't brought anything to the party, physically or emotionally. Not so much as a tea loaf.

When the atmosphere had been created, a silence settled, and we all stared at each other in the candlelight. It softened our features, briefly, and I could see the girls we'd been, before life took over and gave us the lines and sags of middle age. Rachel still looked good, probably because she hadn't had children, plus she was leggy and had big hair. Min had also aged well, her blunt fringe framing a youthful, open face. Amanda's blonde princess-prettiness was as brittle as the balsa board, but then my own pixie-ish, scrawny look was increasingly difficult to maintain without looking pinched and haggard. Erica was kind of ageless – she could be thirty or sixty, like a smug nun. Chloe had just been sick so wasn't at her best, but usually she looked well groomed, like a show pony, thick brown mane swishing whenever she told one of her tall tales. Holly was still sexy in her mussed-up, grubby way and Bhavini was beautiful but had allowed her hair to go completely grey which made her seem older than all of us. When I thought of the ancient photo Holly sent along with the house details – us in our kit, lithe in shorts and bibs, flushed and carefree and so goddamn *young* – I felt depressed. We were that much closer to the spirit world already – did we really need to be striking up a conversation with it?

'Are you there?' intoned Rachel.

'Is *who* there?' barked Holly. 'Who are we talking to?'

Rachel shrugged. 'Whoever's about. On the other side.'

'Shouldn't we have someone in mind?'

'Elvis?'

'Marilyn?'

'Mr Fogarty?'

We all made sad noises. Mr Fogarty was, or had been, a favourite geography teacher, kind and gentle. He was also the last person I'd imagine would be hanging about in the hereafter waiting to talk to a group of drunken, middle-aged former pupils.

'Princess Di.'

'Geronimo the alpaca.'

'Bambi's mum.'

'I want to talk to my great-aunt Verity,' piped up Chloe. 'Ask her why she never put me in her fucking will.'

'Let's just ask the spirits who's there,' said Rachel firmly. She cleared her throat. 'Erm . . . who is there?'

'Why are you talking like that?'

'Like what?'

'All sing-song.'

'I'm not.'

'Yes, you are! "Whooo is theeeerrrre?" Like Madame Arcati.'

'Who's Madame Arcati?'

'Philistine.'

'Look! It's moving!' Chloe shrieked, nodding frantically at the planchette. Sure enough, it was shifting slowly towards the letters. I couldn't feel anyone pushing, but obviously that was what someone was doing. Having a laugh, stirring things up. Intrigued, I leaned forward for a better view. The little plectrum inched forwards until it came to rest with its circle on the letter 'I'.

'Oooh!' said everyone, and I managed not to giggle, imagining what my husband would say if he saw us.

Then, with a jerk, it set off again, right along to the letter 'S'.

'Verity, is that you?' whispered Chloe.

Briskly, the planchette moved back, down the row to the letter 'A'.

'Amanda, it wants you!' Bhavini hissed. Amanda looked up, her face tear-and-mascara stained. As if to contradict her, the arrow headed straight for 'B'.

'I . . . S . . . A . . . B . . .' spelled out Rachel.

I felt myself stiffening, amused grin turning rictus. Surely not.

'Isab . . .' intoned Holly. She didn't need to go any further. We all knew what was coming. There was only one person it could possibly be, though it couldn't possibly be that person. We watched, breathlessly, as the planchette moved inexorably to 'E', 'L', 'L', and finally 'A'.

The muscles in my back spasmed, prickles running down the nape of my neck. One of the candles blew out, and Bhavini gasped, putting a hand to her mouth. The room felt suddenly cold, despite the fire we'd lit to ward off the spring chill.

'Holy shit,' murmured Min.

'Who did that?' I demanded, pulling my hand away.

A series of denials.

'Maybe . . . Isabella . . .?' Chloe gestured towards the board.

'Don't be stupid,' I said. 'She's not . . . she's alive.'

'Yes, obviously,' murmured Holly, clutching her throat.

'Are you *sure*?' said Rachel, in a stage whisper.

'Yes, of course,' I snapped, but my own throat felt dry and I could feel a guilty burn beginning in my cheeks as they all turned towards me. 'She's . . . just . . . you know, kind of AWOL.'

'But *where*?' Chloe breathed, the candlelight of scandal in her eyes. 'None of us have seen her in forever. She never replies to emails. She's not on social media. She's just . . . gone. What if she *is* dead?'

'She's not,' I said, stubbornly, taking a slug of gin. 'We'd know if she was.' It was true. There would have been some sort of sombre announcement, somewhere, and the news of it would have trickled down to us, some of us, one of us, eventually. Me. I'd feel it in my bones.

Though really, she'd existed in a weird limbo for so long that maybe the Ouija board was the only way we would be able to contact her.

'Well, you should know,' said Amanda. 'You were her friend.'

It hit me like a body blow, another light snuffed out. I blinked back whatever was swilling around my eyes and tried to smile.

'You know how it is,' I croaked. 'People drift apart. She moved away, I think. New job. She . . . wanted to make a fresh start.'

Everyone was staring at me sceptically as I choked out my nonsense, all the while thinking of that hockey snapshot – Isabella at the end of the row, head back, laughing, young and lovely, with no contemporary version to challenge the image. How had *she* aged? Was she crumpling into her fifties or fending it off, was her hair grey, did she have crows' feet, bumps and lumps, a partner, children, hopes and dreams that weren't dulled by the years? My memory of her was unlined but faded, like a sepia portrait.

'I tried to track her down,' mused Holly. 'For this weekend. Drew a total blank. Gave up in the end.'

'How long's it been?' Rachel lit another cigarette, and blew atmospheric smoke over us all. 'Since anyone saw her? Ten years?'

'More like fifteen,' I mumbled. The length of time was startling. How had it been that long? The blink of an eye, and a huge gulf. I needed a drag of Rachel's fag, but my lungs were too old.

'Is that you, Isabella?' demanded Erica, turning back to the board. Chloe giggled nervously, winding a lock of hair around her finger.

'Don't be stupid.'

'She's just messing,' said Rachel soothingly. 'Of course, Izzy's fine. She's just MIA. Could be any number of reasons.' She handed me her Marlboro and I took it, my fingers shaking.

'What about Chloe's aunt… who was it? Emily?' asked Min. Her gaze darted nervously between me and the disgruntled descendant. 'You could ask her about the money?'

Chloe snorted. 'My great-aunt Verity. She was such an old bitch! My gran hated her. We could talk to them both, see if they're still having a go at each other.'

And then someone pushed the planchette again, and everyone screamed and they started trying to make contact and the little heart-shaped plank moved this way and that, occasionally veering off, but I had no idea what messages we were receiving, because I was gone, to my own nether world, remembering and wondering and tipping between anger and guilt with a great blanket of fogginess enveloping it all. Like someone waking from a long sleep, groggy and disoriented, waiting to snap out of it. But that might have been the hash brownies, which were potent and unpredictable. Isabella Harris was obviously not contacting us from the other side, someone was just stirring, and I should just forget about all of it. When I finally tumbled into my single bed, parallel to a comatose Chloe, I'd drunk just enough to muzzle the sound of Izzy's laugh in the photo, that dirty cackle I longed to hear again.

The next morning, jaded and grumpy, directed by a brisk Erica, we waded into the freezing Lake Windermere together as fifty-something women must, holding hands and shrieking as the water reached our waists and then plunging in, washing away the excesses of the night before. As I swam, I kept my eyes fixed on the horizon, a resolve hardening under the bright April sky. The lake wasn't really a lake at all, it was a 'mere' – shallow in relation to its size – which meant the depth I sensed beneath me wasn't that significant. Nothing to it.

When we got back to the cottage, I texted Angus my previously arranged coded message, then waited in a frenzy of irritation as he failed to read it. Finally, he called.

'So sorry to interrupt your lovely weekend,' he read like a robot. I'd had to write it out for him or he would have forgotten, so uninterested was he in my plight. 'But I've broken my toe and you have to come back.'

'You've broken your *toe*?' I raised my voice slightly, so everyone in the kitchen could hear.

'Well, that's what it says here.'

My policy was that the lie had to be simple (for my husband to read) yet unexpected, but also, I couldn't be bothered to try too hard because I fully expected this would be the last I saw of the Harpur Harlots for a while. At our current rate of reunion, we'd be on the other side of the Ouija board before we gathered again. I felt guilty, because in a way I'd looked forward to the weekend, to taking the plunge, having somewhere to go and people to see, but now I was in it, I felt overwhelmed, caught in a slipstream.

'Are you in A&E? You poor thing.'

'Nope, I'm watching *Ozark*.'

'I'll come straight away.'

So I drove home, filled with remorse and a tinge of self-loathing, after all those hugs and vague promises to meet up again. All the way to Harrogate, my hands gripped the steering wheel, my gaze fixed on that horizon, on what lay ahead, my mission should I choose to accept it. The faded sepia flushed into full colour, a clearer picture I could focus on, contemplate from every angle. I knew what those fifteen years had done to me. What had they done to her? She was out there, somewhere . . .

When I got back, dumping my suitcase in the hall, I anticipated a mess to clear up, but Sam had clearly not come out of his room so far that weekend, Fred's face was inches from his screen and Angus was on the golf course with Mabel. I made spaghetti and left it in the oven for everyone to help themselves, stabbing and twirling at a bowl while I checked my emails. There was a message from Min.

Hope you're OK, and Angus's toe survived. Lovely to see
you again. X

Min. She'd nobly eaten a whole slice of Erica's cake,
chewing heroically, smiling her thanks when I'd offered
her a glass of fizz to wash it down. My hands stilled on
the keyboard before I typed my reply.

So great to catch up! Angus is hobbling round like an old
man, the stupid bugger. Let's do it again soon.

I felt bad for the lie, but *really*? It was just too much,
trying to reconnect like that. Getting the band back
together, cast reunion, friends reunited . . . That was for
Richard Curtis movies, not real life. What on earth was I
thinking? Over my dead body. They'd have to contact me
via the planchette.

Deep down in my smouldering core, though, I knew
what I'd been thinking.

I was thinking that I didn't have much else to do.

I was thinking that I really should get out more.

I was thinking that Isabella might be there.

Not thinking. *Hoping*.

2

The next morning, I lay in bed staring at the ceiling, still feeling guilty about bailing on my old schoolfriends. But I didn't really know them any more, and felt too old to be hanging about doing things my heart wasn't in. To be honest, my heart wasn't in that much nowadays. The passionate friendships and romances of my twenties had burnt out, in my thirties I was too busy trying to cobble together a career and get pregnant, but the mum-friends I wearily fostered when I had children had fizzled when the kids became old enough to look after themselves. What was wrong with me?

Beside me, my husband snored loudly, and woke himself up.

'Wazzat?' he mumbled, before rolling over and falling asleep again. I still hadn't forgiven him for his lacklustre intercession, for not appreciating how difficult my weekend would be, for failing to be my knight in shining armour. Shite in a stained rugby shirt, more like. Mabel lay curled in the crook of his knee, also snoring. There wasn't room for her in the bed, but I feared in the pecking order it would be me who had to vacate it before she did. There were three people in this marriage, and one of them was a dog.

A thud on the landing told me that Fred was up and heading for the bathroom. He'd shifted from evening baths to morning showers since he'd started secondary school the previous September, a development that made my chest feel tight, caused me to stay up at night looking at old photos of him on my phone. My baby; that chubby, adorable toddler who'd morphed into a pre-teen overnight. Now that Liam was at university, and Sam kept himself to himself, Freddie was my last child to cling to, though I knew better than to reveal that mortifying maternal longing. Fred was self-conscious, tipping into awkwardness, Sam was generally appalled by me, and Liam was entranced by his brave new world. I knew Angus felt it too, which was why he had Mabel. Where was *my* Mabel?

The Labrador stretched, pushing her hind legs hard against me. I sighed and rolled out of bed, shuffling towards the landing to pick up Fred's discarded wet towel. In the cottage in Ambleside, the Harpur Harlots would be emerging from their rooms, hungover to the teeth but determined to enjoy their 'me-time'. For a second I felt a sharp stab of envy. I should have stayed. In the early years of motherhood, I craved those indulgent moments, the luxury of a break from the relentless treadmill of childcare. But lately, me-time involved hanging out with someone who was pretty boring. Given a spare afternoon,

I frittered it away doing pointless errands, like I was doing now. While my tea brewed in the morning, I'd taken to applying a layer of fresh grouting to the tiles above the countertop. They didn't really need it, but I had the apparatus, and the time, so . . . I put down my groat float, feeling guilty again. Giving up a weekend with friends to revamp some kitchen tiles. I really needed to get out more. Preferably somewhere I actually wanted to go.

'Hi, Mum.' Fred busied himself with the complex chemistry of his breakfast – Cheerios with Blueberry Wheats and a hefty sprinkling of granola, topped with too much milk.

'Hi, love. What are you up to today?'

'Football. Fortnite. Max.' He mumbled through his cereal, milk dribbling down his chin.

One of the delights of living in a friendly, bustling town like Harrogate was that our boys could have a degree of independence, coming and going as they pleased, getting themselves where they needed to be. As an only child raised in the countryside and faithfully chauffeured by my obliging father, I didn't want my own children to grow up coddled and reliant, but increasingly felt all Angus and I had achieved was to cut ourselves off from our kids' activities. We'd made ourselves redundant. The other day I'd offered to walk with Fred to his friend Max's house, and been met with an amazed stare.

'Lovely. You have a nice time, then.' They were so inadequate, these interactions. When what I wanted to say was: *Maybe think of me when you're away. Do you want to hang out later? Don't grow up too fast. Don't leave me. I love you. Do you love me? Where did my little boy go?*

I drank my tea, and did another couple of tiles. Outside it was a glorious sunny day; we were having a sodden spring, so I should take advantage of it. In the garden, I checked my pots, topped up my bird feeder, rounded up Fred's footballs and dumped them in the bench box. At the end of the lawn stood Angus's 'studio', the shed where he did his recordings, earned the money that paid the mortgage on our five-bedroom Victorian semi on the edge of the Stray, Harrogate's central park. I should be thankful for that shed, for those recordings, but whenever I looked at that scruffy wooden shack, I just felt a vague resentment, similar to when I got shoved by Mabel. How come Angus had fallen on his feet, while I was still hobbling round with a bad case of gout?

In 2022, the cost of living crisis hit us hard. Both made redundant within months of each other, we'd spent weeks staring at bank statements, gibbering with fear. We should never have converted the loft; we were still paying for it. But Angus had a buoyancy and verve that stood him in good stead (even if both those qualities were sometimes irritating). Previously a radio comedy producer, he started a podcast called *Elephants' Graveyard*, which he described as '*Gardeners' Question Time* for gadgets.' In less than two years it was a sensation, one of the biggest retail shows, his recordings now filmed and broadcast to more than a million subscribers on YouTube. He was raking in thousands a month – a bigger salary than he'd ever made in radio. What's more, he loved it and it was piss-easy. He just shambled along to his garden office with one of his dad-mates, or a comedian he'd lured away from Harrogate Theatre, and spent an hour in there gassing about battery life and storage space. There were always coiled wires littering our dining table. They drove me mad.

Meanwhile, I'd set up a mosaic business on Etsy and was making around £300 a month after expenses, barely enough to keep me in takeaway coffee – certainly not enough to pay for weekends in the Lake District. When I was working full-time as a copywriter (officially four days a week, but don't make me laugh), I always moaned I hadn't a spare minute, but it turned out that, when I did have it, I didn't know what to do with it. Sometimes I'd be tinkering with my plant pots, listening to Angus guffaw in his outhouse, and feel like going in there and laying into him with my trowel. It was ridiculous to be envious of your husband for finding a productive, lucrative career in his fifties and saving your financial bacon, and yet here we were. Me, digging viciously into the soil, then packaging up a set of tiled coasters to send to someone in Swansea. I tried to get back into advertising, but no one wanted me, and I didn't really want them either. I was ready for a new thing, but didn't know what it was right now.

You silly old trout.

Izzy in my head, laying into me with a verbal trowel.

Bloody well pull yourself together and find something useful to do.

I could always rely on her for bracing advice.

Stop being such a crosspatch and pour us both a drink.

She was a good influence, and a bad one.

Let's go to the pub.

How many Sunday lunchtimes had we taken ourselves for a leisurely roast that got out of hand? Staggering out into an evening well-advanced, arguing about where to go next, falling asleep on each other on the bus, realizing we'd left our coats behind, heading back to fetch them, agreeing to have one for the road before we left again. But drinking wasn't all we did. There was so much more to it than that. Hanging out, talking, laughing. So much laughing.

Maybe I should insist we have a family roast together today. But Angus was editing, Fred was off meeting Max, and Sam was almost as AWOL as Isabella. At fifteen, he'd retreated into some sort of teenage shell and, short of hammering on it with my spade, it was impossible to get through to him. So instead, I spent the day pottering, messing about. When the evening approached, I'd done a few more tiles, bought a pepper, replanted an Acer, made a banana loaf. Just after six o'clock, the phone rang, and I sprinted towards it, nearly spilling my wine in my haste.

'Hello?' I tried not to sound too eager.

'Hi.' Liam's dutiful Sunday-evening phone call. Sometimes he forgot, and I never pushed it. The fact that he'd remembered this week, and was nearly on time, made tears prick at my eyelids. *You silly old trout.*

'Hi, dar . . . How are you?'

'OK.'

'It's so nice to hear your . . . what have you been up to?'

'This and that. Played rugby this afternoon.'

Oh God, that meant head injuries, early onset dementia. 'Wow, sounds brilliant. How's the studying going?'

'All right. Where's Dad?'

'In the shed. I'll get him in a minute.'

I poked him for information, he grudgingly gave it, which was how these conversations went. There was probably some girl waiting for him, pouting in the doorway, ready to drag him out on the town.

'Get your father,' I said to Fred, eventually, because Angus would never forgive me otherwise.

'I went to the Lake District with some friends this weekend,' I said, neglecting to mention I cut it short. 'We swam in Lake Windermere.' Liam's mum, gadding about with the girls, carousing, cold-water swimming like a legend. I should have thrown myself into it, dammit. What was wrong with me?

'Cool.'

There was a silence while I tried to think of something else to say about my jaunt apart from 'In the end, I couldn't be bothered.' As I dithered, he must have been keen to break it too, because he said, 'Which friends?'

'Just some old schoolfriends.'

'Oh right.'

'Do you remember Isabella Harris?'

I don't know why I asked that. Just wanted to say her name, for some reason, to see how it made me feel. He did meet her on several occasions, years ago.

'No.'

'She used to babysit you sometimes. When you were little. She always brought ice cream.' *Auntie Izz-Bizz*, he used to call her. It seemed impossible to imagine, now.

'No, I don't remember. Was she there then?'

'Um, no.' *Bloody well pull yourself together.*

Then Angus marched up, snatching the phone and muscling me aside. 'Mate! How's it hanging?'

Soon they were talking about overlaps and ankle taps, and Angus was roaring with laughter and giving me Vs as I tried to wrestle the handset back. This phone call would make his evening, whereas I wasn't sure what it did to mine. I put a load of sausages in the oven, and left them there for everyone to help themselves. After aimlessly wandering round the house, I rooted out some old photo albums and spent an hour staring at them. A group of us celebrating in the pub after A levels, the table littered with nuts and cigarette packets. Me and Izzy on holiday in Portugal, lying on the beach in sarongs. My wedding photos, Angus grinning in his kilt as I lifted my dress to do the cancan, Izzy just about in shot, her own legs flailing, laughing hysterically. Baby photos, our boy-bundles held by wan, exhausted, ecstatic parents; proud grandparents;

again, Izzy there, her face alight with wonder. The passage of time was so relentless, no time to slow down and take stock, wonder where you went wrong. You just got on with it.

Later on, in bed, I stared at the ceiling again as Angus read *All Hell Let Loose* by Max Hastings, occasionally murmuring 'Shiiiit'.

'Isabella wasn't there.'

'Who?' Still deep in the Second World War, he turned to me, his eyes glazed.

'Isabella Harris. At the Ambleside cottage. She didn't come.'

'Where?'

'The cottage. This weekend. She didn't come.'

He blinked, dopily. 'Who?'

'My friend from school.'

'Who?' he said again.

'Never mind.'

When I finally slept, my dreams were full of cackling laughter, and an uneasy sense that I'd somehow missed the joke.

3

On Monday, after a standard night of regularly awaking with heart palpitations, drenched in sweat, I went to the office to do some work. Or to put it another way, I wandered across the park to my shared studio, a converted disused garage, to make a mosaic coffee table that I'd later struggle to offload on Etsy, while making intermittent conversation with my 'colleagues' – a lunatic artist called Serendipity Holt, and a carpenter called Jacob Levy. What a way to make a living. Not that I actually did.

The nature of my work, if it could be called that, was haphazard. Mostly, I reclaimed items of furniture I bought in car boot sales and second-hand shops, upcycling them in a way that usually involved attaching smashed bits of porcelain. I'd started off buying real mosaic tiles, but the cost of production became prohibitive – by the time I'd actually finished an item, I'd need to sell it for about £400 to make ends meet. So instead, I sourced old crockery, flower pots, bathroom tiles – and broke them up. Then I applied them to whatever bit of furniture or accessory I'd found. The results were erratic – sometimes I'd produce a quirky and attractive piece; other times I'd turn a heap of junk into a different heap of junk. When you mention mosaic, most people think of gorgeous Roman floors with epic and exquisite designs, but my pieces had neither the scale nor the intricacy. Just a helter-skelter assembly of colourful bits embedded in whatever mortar I could get hold of cheaply. I made mosaic coasters, trivets, trays, occasional tables – the odd vase if I was feeling ambitious (curves were tricky), selling them online and at local markets.

I'd like to say it was rewarding, but it wasn't – financially or creatively. It was just something to do, that got me out the house. My share of the rent on our workshop came to £150 a month, which ate into my meagre income, but I was able to refer to myself as an 'eco-entrepreneur' rather than 'currently unemployed', and thus cling to a china-fine sliver of self-esteem.

When Izzy and I first met at school, she wanted to be a travel journalist, and I wanted to be a magazine editor, so we decided that when I was in charge of my own publication, I would commission her to see the world and occasionally join her at internationally renowned hotels, where we'd sip champagne in rooftop bars and fend off the advances of billionaires. It didn't quite work out that way – after university (her Edinburgh, me Newcastle), we moved to Manchester, where Izzy wrote restaurant reviews and I went into advertising, eventually working as a copywriter, like Peggy in *Mad Men* but without the flair or sass. Although a compromise on both counts, we did OK, and sometimes I got to be her plus-one at a launch or opening, get a taste of the high life. It was at one of those events that I fended off the advances of, not a billionaire, but a comedy promoter called Angus Stewart, so in effect, Izzy introduced us. I wondered what she'd make of my new enterprise, Mortimosaic. No, I didn't need to wonder. She'd hoot with laughter: 'Mortimo-*what*?' She always called me by my surname – never Gwen, but 'Mortimer', like we were old army muckers in one of Angus's war tomes. Sometimes, she even greeted me with a salute: 'Wotcha, Mortimer.'

With this bric-a-brac of memories and musings, I went into my workshop humming the tune to *The Great Escape*, which made Serendipity, or Dippy, as she was known, gaze at me with vague disdain. She was twenty-seven, and thought I should probably be in sheltered accommodation, playing bridge and drinking tea through a straw. Spectacularly beautiful and enviably firm, Dippy wore dungarees with nothing underneath – as a result, Angus didn't visit me there any more because he just didn't know what to do with his eyes. Her dirty-blonde dreadlocked hair wound in a bun on top of her head, she had numerous piercings and a tattoo along the inside of one arm: 'No More Walls', which was apparently Anaïs Nin. Dippy loved talking explicitly about all the sex she had; one of the many reasons conversations with her were excruciating.

'Someone got laid this weekend.'

I assumed she meant herself, which wasn't news, but as she looked me up and down, smirking, I realized she was referring to me.

'What, because I'm *humming*?'

'Ya hum, ya got sum.' This was drawled in an American accent, and wasn't worth a reply, so I busied myself getting my sanding equipment out and checking the state of my table, which I'd picked up at the side of the road the previous week. It was low and square beech, battered and stained, but about to become a swan of small furnishings.

The nature of Dippy's work, if it could be called that, was contemporary art. She'd take a large canvas, and paint an idyllic scene in little dots – a technique called pointillism. Then she'd scrawl a phrase, word or quote in huge letters across it, effectively ruining it. So you might get a depiction of an old Yorkshire mill in the snow, quite pretty, with 'BONE-CLINIC WHITENESS' steaming across like demented graffiti. Dippy badly wanted an exhibition, but was unable to find a gallery run by anyone as crazy as she was. I was fairly sure she earned even less than me, but since she looked and sounded like Cara Delevingne, I also assumed she would be fine falling back on the family trust fund or securing a rich boyfriend. At the moment, she was working on a view of Hebden Bridge – I anticipated her daubing 'THE SKY IS EMPTY' across it at a later date.

Our garage, despite being fairly shoddily converted, had a large skylight that made it a suitable artists' space, though it sometimes leaked during rainstorms and we had to put out buckets to catch the drips. But today was fine, and Dippy positioned her canvas directly under the aperture to get the best light. For a while, we worked in not-very-companiable silence, occasionally glancing across at the results of each other's labour with scorn. Having sanded down the table, I put a base coat on the legs and sorted through my mosaic fragments while it dried. I'd picked up a mismatched box of old plates from a junk shop and smashed them, so had a pleasing array of colourful china shards to choose from. If I isolated all the green bits then I could create some kind of plant that could stretch its tendrils across the tabletop . . .

'Hello, my dearies.' Jacob wandered in, carrying a floorboard.

The third in our creative triumvirate, Jacob was so much older that Dippy couldn't compute it. I guessed he must have been in his mid-sixties, a cheerful, gentle soul who irked me almost as much as she did. He lived alone in a small flat in the Duchy, went on frequent trips to Greece, and was relentlessly upbeat. I was suspicious of anyone who seemed as contented as he did, though it was clear he was the most talented and successful of us. Jacob made exquisite little cabinets out of whatever wood he found lying about, sold them for a fortune, and regularly appeared in interiors magazines that raved about his craftsmanship and vision.

'Now, what have you girls been up to?' he said, putting down his board.

Dippy immediately started telling him about her latest sexual conquest, a sordid tale that he listened to with amiable interest. After she'd exhausted herself describing her exhausting night, Jacob turned his attention to me. I picked through my shards, selecting and arranging.

'I went to the Lake District with some old schoolfriends.'

'How charming. Did you get up to all manner of naughtiness like Serendipity here?' He always called us by our full names, though anyone calling me Gwendolyn made me feel like I was about to get detention.

'Not really. I had a hash brownie?'

'How decadent.'

'We consulted a Ouija board.'

'Intriguing. Did it tell you anything?'

It told me that my long-lost friend was dead. Best not get into that. 'I don't know, I wasn't really listening.'

'Why not?'

'I was disappointed my friend wasn't there.' Oh, so we were getting into that after all, my tongue as rogue as the Ouija planchette.

Both of them looked up, Jacob attentive, Dippy alert to the prospect of gossip, even if it concerned an old lady she didn't care about.

'Who wasn't there?'

'Isabella.' I winced. Didn't know why I said it, when it was the last thing I wanted to say.

'Was she your girlfriend?' breathed Dippy. 'Before that other bloke?'

30

'Do you mean my *husband*? No. She was my friend. My . . . er, best friend.' It always felt childish, that phrase. Best Friends Forever! Bezzies. Kindred spirits. Whatever.

'Well, where was she? What happened to her?'

'I don't know. She just . . . went.'

'Went where?'

'I don't know.'

'What the actual eff? Is she even alive?'

'Yes! Of course, she's alive. But we don't really speak any more. I haven't seen her in fifteen years.'

'Crappity bappity.' That was over half Dippy's lifetime. 'She probably *is* dead then.'

'Dippy, when will you understand that fifty-three isn't that old?'

'When hell freezes over. Which it already has for you.'

'Why are you thinking of her now? Because you didn't see her at the weekend?' Jacob's voice was soft, probing, deadly.

God, it was like being on *The Drew Barrymore Show*. I didn't know why I was suddenly opening up, to these two people I wasn't that bothered about. Suddenly, I just wanted to talk about it, to tell this slightly damp garage about my failed friendship. If they were there too, so be it. Keeping my eyes on my arrangement, I assembled my plant, adding flowers in jewel-coloured shards.

'I don't know why, but I thought she might be there. The others . . . they didn't matter as much. But she was different.'

'How come?'

'Dunno. Just . . . Since the first time I met her, I really, really liked her.'

In an instant, a shutter snap, as if I was in one of those old photos. Frozen in time, that moment in school when she strolled into the classroom, long dark plait swinging. The cool boy, couldn't remember his name now, sidled up, and she just held up a palm; *talk to it*. And then she shot me a sidelong glance, and walked over to me, grinning, and I knew. Click.

'We were friends for years, saw each other all the time, talked every day.'

On the phone, later on email (which was new then; we discovered it), sometimes writing letters, because that was still a thing. Postcards, with messages indecipherable to anyone but us. And whenever we met, talking, talking, talking – so fast, gabbling in our eagerness to get it all out, exchange that essential information. When Angus first met her, he said we spoke our own language, one that he couldn't understand. He called it Gwizzle, a mash-up of our names.

'And then she just . . . disappeared.' My voice went off a cliff; I gulped, concentrating on picking out green pieces, to distract myself from the sense of my own inadequacy. Had she 'just' disappeared – pouf, gone, in a puff of smoke? There were signs, maybe. But I was distracted. Other things going on.

'So you haven't spoken to her? In all that time?' Jacob sounded so sad for me, I felt sad for myself all over again.

'No. I tried, to call and text and email. But she never replied.'

'Hang on.' Dippy's voice was sharp, pointed as her little painting dots. 'So, one day, she just . . . *went*?'

'We might have had a bit of a . . .'

'Fight?'

'No. I don't know. I can't remember. Maybe a . . . disagreement.'

I really couldn't remember. It was all blurry and indistinct, like a bad dream. What had we talked about, that last night? Drinking was involved, and I was so tired. Two kids. Going back to work. It was all broken up like the china shards in my box. Jagged edges, a picture I couldn't put back together.

'Well, you should just go and apologize.'

I choked out a laugh. 'After fifteen years? And also, why are you assuming it's my fault?'

'Because you're a bit of a B.I.T.C.H.?'

Jacob said gently 'It's never too late.'

I reached out to touch the legs of my table. They were dry. Time to put on a top coat. 'It doesn't matter,' I said. 'It was a long time ago.'

'It's obviously bothering you,' Jacob observed, turning his floorboard this way and that. 'Turn that bad wood into something good.'

I hummed noncommittally and set about repainting the legs in a tasteful sage, with a performative air of purpose. Dippy was working at the bottom right-hand section of her canvas, on what looked like a barge. Jacob started cutting his board into sections. It was all very peaceful, but I felt unnerved, shaken. The plant image hadn't worked – there wasn't enough green there. Showering my shards back onto the tabletop, I began to rearrange them, like a jigsaw. What design would emerge? It could just be random, or I could try to make something of it. She was in my head, the whole time, urging me on: *You silly old trout. Find something useful to do. Stop being such a crosspatch.*

I thought about that night, the last night I saw her. Made myself try to remember it. We met at a restaurant on the outskirts of Manchester, but not one she was reviewing for work. I was still breastfeeding Sam, worried about leaking everywhere. We had some wine, and then some more. I remembered the conversation turning tetchy . . . why? On the one hand, it seemed ridiculous that I couldn't remember this super-charged moment, the last time I saw my best friend, but on the other, how was I to know it was significant at the time? It was just another dinner. Afterwards, I texted her, some vague drunken apology, but she didn't reply. And then didn't answer my calls. I went round to her flat and there was no one there. I thought: *Fine, I'll give her some space.* But then I was so busy, and so tired, and the few weeks turned into months, and . . . what had I been doing? Why did I let it slide?

'I'm going to do it,' I murmured, positioning the final piece. There was more brown than green, so I'd made a tree with a few emerald fronds emerging – either the first buds of spring, or the last foliage clinging on for dear life as winter took hold. 'I'm going to find her.' Get in touch with my roots! Branch out! Nurture the green shoots of friendship! I felt high on the buzz of decision-making and creative endeavour.

'Who?' Dippy looked up from her painting, glassy-eyed.

'Isabella.'

'Who?'

'My friend.' My best friend. Still. We were perennial.

Dippy frowned, puzzled. 'I thought you said she was dead?'

4

I hadn't kept a diary since I was a teenager, so there was really nothing to go on. If I had, I could have looked back, to that night in June 2009 or whenever, and maybe I'd have written something useful, something revealing – *I said, she said,* etc. Anything that could shed light on what the hell happened, why she stormed off and why I never saw her again. Before that, too – was there anything she mentioned or did in those last months that might give me a clue? Some passing remark, new boyfriend or holiday plans. But I didn't have a handy journal to harvest, so that night, in bed, with Mabel's back legs pressing into my ribs, I channelled the unremitting force of her hindquarters, and googled. I googled, *hard.*

I mean, you did this for an ex, right? Even if you didn't really care about them, weren't that cut up about it. Still, you found out what they were doing, vaguely hoped it was unsatisfying, that they were living in misery and penury without you. One of my former boyfriends got a CBE for services to charity, and I was *so* annoyed. But he had a receding hairline, which soothed me a little. You looked them up, kept tabs, just to check. Idle curiosity, schadenfreude, whatever. Yet I never did that with Isabella. Maybe sexual resentment worked in a different way to platonic pique. I didn't want *her* to fail, be unhappy, unfulfilled, so I never looked her up to find evidence of it. I hoped she'd made a good life for herself, without me, but the trouble was, I couldn't find any evidence of that either, because I couldn't find her at all.

Which was weird. *Everyone* was on the internet. Even if you didn't actively engage in social media, were a bit of a Luddite, you left some sort of digital footprint. Either something to do with work, or a mention in a local newspaper, or a Strava profile or *something*. I found hundreds of Isabella Harrises, but none of them was mine. There was an interior designer Isabella Harris and someone called Isabel Harris who'd been arrested for being drunk and disorderly in Alfreton, and an Isabella R. Harris (my Izzy's middle name was Raizel) on LinkedIn who definitely wasn't her, and a Dr Isabella Harris who worked at a university and looked nothing like the real thing. There were dozens of Isabella Harrises on Facebook and I went through all of them without a hit. So, I started searching 'Isabella Harris restaurant reviews' and again there was nothing, or at least, nothing after she disappeared. It was like she'd ceased to exist.

Maybe she'd got married and taken someone else's name? In which case, without knowing her new surname, it was impossible. I went through my email archives to see if I could find one from her – I'd had the same email account for decades, but my files didn't go back that far. After endless digital exchanges, I could just about remember her old email address – izzy_harris – but even if it still worked, what would I say, after all this time? 'Hey Izzy, just catching up, how's it going?' Come on, Gwen. How to broach the yawning gap in our friendship, reforge that bond, pick up where we left off. I would have to do better than that.

After mulling on it for half an hour, I wrote: 'Hey Izzy, just catching up, how's it going?' and pressed 'Send' before I could think about it, my legs numb with mortification. When the immediate bounceback arrived – 'Undeliverable – a communication failure occurred' – I felt weak with relief. I was going to have to track her down in person. An analogue pursuit.

Browsing my inbox, I saw a new message sent by another restless middle-aged woman:

Hi,

That was completely exhausting, don't think my liver will ever recover. Hey, you live in Harrogate, don't you? I'm in York, just down the road – let me know if you fancy a catch-up!

Min x

She was the best of the bunch, Min. The most likeable, easiest to be around. We'd been good friends at school but then she went abroad for a gap year, and although we kept in touch, we weren't close. But then I remembered she and Izzy used to meet occasionally, because Min worked for some sort of online magazine and Izzy used to do reviews for them. This was just before Izzy cut herself off – initially, I'd assumed she was just pissed off with me, but gradually learned she'd pulled away from everyone. Holly had tried to invite her to her fortieth birthday party and got nowhere, and at Bhavini's wedding, I remember standing shivering on the steps of Manchester Town Hall being pestered with queries about Izzy's whereabouts. We all missed her. At the time, I didn't know if that made it better or worse – it suggested it wasn't personal, but on the other hand maybe it indicated some sort of major crisis. One that I'd somehow ignored.

Again, I wondered why I hadn't pushed harder, enquired further. A few months after that last dinner, I sent her a postcard – a photo of a donkey in a hat I picked up in Cornwall – with the message: *Why the long face? Because I haven't heard from you.* Again, nothing. I was a bit peeved after that – it wasn't like I didn't have my own problems to deal with – so stopped bothering. Let her fester. I assumed she'd resurface eventually. People do, don't they? Then I got pregnant again, and had Fred, and he had colic, and then I had to go back to work, which was awful, and by the time I came to, five years had passed and it felt like a different lifetime. Five years, in the blink of an eye. And then it felt like too long ago that I'd let go of the rope. Too late to grasp for it.

Anyway, Min was nice, and maybe she could be useful, too. I tapped out a reply:

York's next door! I go there a lot for auctions and emporiums. Let's do lunch sometime?

After that, I spent some time looking up basic signs in BSL – going to school with Min, we'd all learned a bit but I couldn't remember much of it. Lip-reading got tiring for her eventually, and if she was going to help me, I needed her to understand why it was important. Why it mattered.

Then it was 2 a.m. and my eyeballs were fried so I went to sleep and dreamed of donkeys in hats, a baby who cried forever, plates piled up and up, a man signing the word 'Missing' – pulling his fingers apart like he was opening an invisible newspaper. And a girl leaning against a hockey stick, laughing.

I needed Min to understand why it was important. Why it mattered.

Even if I didn't quite understand why myself.

5

'Maybe she's a spy.'

Although I wasn't familiar with it, the sign for the word was obvious, hooking your finger like a spyglass and pulling it away from your eye. Min tended to sign as she talked, even though her speaking voice was fairly clear. She went deaf at around eight years old after getting meningitis, and since we were silly schoolgirls who didn't know any better, we always thought that sounded really romantic, like a Louisa May Alcott novel. Because Min was pretty – petite, stylish – and outgoing, she was popular at school. As a deaf student, she had her very own teaching assistant to help her in lessons – Carla was a Leeds University graduate with several tattoos and piercings, worshipped by us all. We used to beg her to take us to the pub after school, and she always refused, but she did teach us quite a bit of British Sign Language, which came in very useful. For a while, our group's collective obsession with signing meant we basically conversed that way – apart from Erica, who never seemed to get the hang of it. It was our own secret code; we could be rude, subversive or outrageous without being found out. As we talked, I found it coming back to me, along with the mental image of sitting in the sixth-form common room mocking Mr Sullivan's shiny bald head, while he watched us, confused and suspicious.

I laughed along with Min. 'I think that's unlikely.' It was true Isabella was a keen traveller, fluent in French and Italian, but spies didn't really exist, did they? Not like James Bond. It was more of a dull desk job, monitoring the dark web, or something.

'The internet thing is weird though.'

'Yes.' It was definitely mysterious. But, in a way, that made my quest all the more intriguing. If I'd googled her and she'd appeared instantly then it would all have been too easy, boringly straightforward. It was better this way. Tricky, carefully handled. On some level, I felt she was watching me, challenging me. *Come on, find me. If you can. If you dare.*

It was the following Friday, and Min and I were in a quiet, cosy tapas restaurant in York, having our 'catch-up'. After bitching about the Lake District weekend, which Min had also found rather trying, I'd casually introduced the subject of Isabella, and she'd embraced the discussion, offering various theories. Danielle Seitzman, New York-based, swore blind she'd seen Isabella jogging in Central Park, Rachel once saw her at a party in Ibiza, Amanda said she'd moved abroad, Erica had heard Izzy had married a Scottish laird and relocated to Inverness, Chloe thought she'd gone into rehab. With speculation coming thick and fast, it was hard to work out which options were feasible. But it was fun, to sit there scoffing and gossiping, when ordinarily I'd have been hauling my sorry arse to my garage, or re-potting a japonica.

'What do you think?' I asked Min, though a mouthful of patatas bravas. A question which, of course, she couldn't hear *or* see.

'What? You? Think?' I signed stiltedly, still chewing. 'Where is she?'

Min sighed. 'I don't know,' she said. 'We saw each other quite a bit, but there was sometimes a part of her . . .'

'What?'

She frowned, remembering. 'There was a part of her that was . . . elsewhere. Like she had a secret life.'

This stopped me in my tracks. Because my initial instinct was to deny it – ridiculous! Isabella was entirely present, had no secrets, was completely open and honest. We communicated in some form pretty much every day, and there was nothing I didn't know about her. But . . . was that really true? Towards the end of that time, I'd been distracted, exhausted. She'd also been busy with work or something . . . I cast my mind back. Now I thought about it, in those last few months she was slightly withdrawn, evasive. I remembered asking her if she was dating anyone, in a jokey way, and she'd answered defensively, as if the question was insulting. I thought she was just feeling sensitive, approaching forty, being quizzed by a smug-married, and dropped the subject. I tried to dredge up more examples of her mood or behaviour, but like many of my reminiscences, everything I looked back on felt fuzzy and indistinct, as if it happened to someone else, or I couldn't trust whatever conclusion I might draw.

'When did you last see her?' I asked Min. The sign for 'When' was a recollection in itself, drumming your fingers on your cheek meditatively.

Min wrinkled her nose as she thought back. 'Someone at the magazine had birthday drinks,' she said, finally. 'Izzy came, but left early.'

'How come?'

'She was upset. She left in a hurry. Said something about seeing someone she knew.'

'She left *because* she'd seen someone? Or left because she was *going* to see someone?'

'I'm not sure.'

'And then you didn't see her again?'

Min took a sip of water. 'The next time we asked her to do a review for us, she said she wasn't available – and wouldn't be any more. I texted her to find out why but she didn't answer. And then . . . my boyfriend and I were splitting up, and I found out I was pregnant. I was a bit of a mess.'

'I'm sorry.' Although we hadn't seen each other very often back then, I remembered contributing to the whip-round Holly had organized when Min's daughter was born, and sending her a card in which I'd scribbled something like 'Hope she's a sleeper!' But it hadn't really registered that she was doing it all on her own. I felt a pang for that version of Min, the struggling single mum, and that made me feel even more guilty about my lack of effort. I hadn't bothered with her *or* Isabella. Too busy floundering in my own mire.

'It turned out all right. But it wasn't easy. And it meant I wasn't exactly in the mood to go locating missing magazine contributors.'

I rubbed my heart with my fist, and she smiled. 'It's OK, it was a long time ago. That's the problem; I can't really remember that much.'

It was strange how great swathes of our lives seemed to be . . . missing, like Isabella. Gone, only half-remembered, hidden behind a veil, out of reach. You were going full pelt, trying to hold it all together, make ends meet, and the pay-off seemed to be that it all became a blur. Or a blank, even. Sometimes Angus would ask me about a night out we'd had, or someone we knew, or a place we'd been, and I'd have no recollection whatsoever. Just a gap where the memory should be. Perhaps because it wasn't that important, and I was clinging to the moments that mattered. Or else I really was going senile. I'd pretty much forgotten an entire holiday in France that Angus and I went on before we got married – sometimes I got out the photos to mull over the brown, replete woman lounging on a deckchair, or the one laughing as she ate a ripe slice of melon, or the one waving out of the bougainvillea-framed window of a gîte. They were all me, but seemed like a

Gwen from a parallel universe – a Gwen who knew how to relax and enjoy herself. I had to find her again, and bring her out into the sun.

I was glad Min seemed to have trouble remembering too – it meant I wasn't a dotty old bat, or at least not the only one. And maybe Isabella *was* a spy. Somehow it felt easier to imagine she worked for MI5 than admit she just walked away because she didn't like us – *me* – any more. In fact, the more I thought about it, the more likely it seemed. She was glamorous, well-connected, well-travelled, multilingual. She was single, childless. She was increasingly evasive, mysterious. She went abseiling that time, off Millers Dale Viaduct! She said it was a charity thing, but maybe it was *training*.

'OH MY GOD, WHAT IF SHE'S A SPY.'

I said it as a joke, much as Min had, and we both giggled, enjoying the absurdity of it. In a way though, it was no more nonsensical than Erica's theory of the Scottish laird. Izzy hated midges, thought they were out to get her. She'd make a much better spy than a . . . What was a female laird? A lairdy? Not Izzy's scene at all.

'No, hang on. What if she *is* . . . a spy?'

Still sniggering, Min caught my expression and checked herself. 'What . . . really?'

'People can be spies.'

She looked thoughtful. 'Bhavini said she saw her going into Thames House once.'

'*Did* she?'

'Well, she couldn't be sure, but said it looked like her.'

'What if it's that, then.' It was official. My friend was not a ghost, but a spook. Crappity bappity, as Dippy would say.

'Although,' Min continued, tucking into our Spanish omelette, 'Holly heard she was working as a dog walker in Edgbaston.'

'Bullshit,' I replied. 'She's allergic. No, it's definitely espionage. The internet thing confirms it. You don't get taken off the web without a seriously good reason.'

'Well,' Min said, 'she's going to be even more difficult to track down now.'

But that made it even more interesting.

Come on, find me.

If you can.

If you dare.

6

'Of course she's not a fucking spy,' he said.

That evening, over a takeaway, Angus brought me back down to earth.

'What do you know?' I snorted. 'Have you got a direct line to the Foreign Office or something?'

'It's just bollocks,' he insisted. 'Izzy ghosted you. What's the more likely scenario: that she thought you were a shit friend and fucked off accordingly, or that she was gearing up to go on a secret mission to Monte Carlo?'

'That's very reductive.'

'Ballsacks.'

Angus always got loud and sweary after a few beers. Or maybe he was loud and sweary to begin with. A lot of the reviews of his podcast said things like 'Too many F-words' and 'Why does he need to curse so often when he talks about noise-cancelling headphones?' Ironically, those reviews provoked a lot of expletives. But his certainty was making my own wane.

'Maybe she *was* a spy, and now she's in witness protection, with a new identity.'

'She's definitely not on the internet,' said Sam, tapping away on his laptop as he crunched poppadoms.

'Oooh, are you looking her up?!' I was ecstatic that he was showing an interest in my life.

He shrugged. 'I wasn't sure you knew how.'

Jesus Christ, my children had a low opinion of me. As did my husband, and dog. Mabel was lying across Angus's knees on the sofa, gazing up at him adoringly and grumbling if anyone approached. Occasionally he would feed her a piece of naan bread, and her tail would thump in gratitude. Later they'd probably have a hot tub together or something.

'Can't you just ask her parents?'

It was a mundane suggestion from my husband, but admittedly a sensible one, assuming they were still alive. Obviously, I knew them, or did at one time. A charming couple who lived in an old rectory in Hathersage, surrounded by newspapers. I always liked staying there, because she had a handsome brother, a friendly cat, and they were free-and-easy with the sherry decanter. But I felt shamed by the idea of contacting them: *Sorry to bother you – your daughter hasn't talked to me in fifteen years – could you possibly tell me where she is, and maybe arrange a reintroduction?* I would look exactly like what Angus said I was – a shit friend. Increasingly, that's what I felt I might have been. It felt easier to infiltrate Thames House than approach her perplexed family with my begging bowl.

However, I had to stop whingeing and speculating, and do something. 'OK. I'll drive down, see if they're still there.'

'You've got L rizz,' observed Fred, who was hoovering up chicken korma. Translation: you're a loser.

'Thanks, I'll put a sign on the car saying I'm your mother,' I assured him, pouring myself some more wine.

'Erm, what the sigma?'

'LANGUAGE,' boomed Angus, making Mabel jump. He had no understanding of Gen Alpha slang and always assumed it was profane – the pot calling the kettle black. Or, as Fred might say, Ohio calling the roadmen sus. But in the same way I liked learning BSL, I enjoyed keeping up to date with Fred's idioms, and embarrassing him by using them myself.

'Anyway, I'm telling you, she's a spy.'

Angus took a massive glug of his Hells Lager. 'I've got a mate.' He hesitated, like he was about to break the Official Secrets Act. 'Does a podcast called *Spooky-Doos*. Like *Serial*, but with spies.'

'What does that even mean?'

'I don't know, I've never listened to it – don't tell him. But he knows people. I could get him to look into it.'

'All right.' I figured the more people were on to this, the better. The Harpur Harlots, the podcast community, my workshop contingent. Like a search party. Usually, I hated parties – unwilling outings where I either drank and got sleepy, or didn't drink and got bored. But this one sounded good. I thought of the parties Isabella and I had been to

50

over the years. Sixth-form shindigs with sticky floors and over-enthusiastic tongues. Each other's university grinds, which constituted several gaps in my memory. Significant birthdays of various mutual friends, dancing to Beyoncé and working out how much they'd put behind the bar. Ditto weddings. There was one wedding in particular; it might have been Amanda's. A big barn just outside Bakewell, at least £30K, her father a bit too weepy for comfort. Isabella snogged one of the band members; I instigated a limbo contest. We decided to call it a night and phoned a cab, but couldn't get out. As in, we couldn't get out of the venue. We were in the garden, but there was no gate, or so it seemed. The tequilas might possibly have impacted on potential exits. We could see the taxi, but couldn't get to it; ended up climbing over a wall, posh skirts bunched around our waists, wheezing hysterically, tumbling to the ground on the other side and lying on our backs looking at the stars and groaning. It was my favourite bit of the evening, nothing else as memorable as that. In fact, maybe it was Chloe's wedding, who knows.

A search party. It sounded like fun, and Lord knows I needed some.

7

Izzy was maid of honour at our wedding, although she refused to call it that, arguing that it made her sound like a stuck-up virgin. Instead, she dubbed herself 'Mistress of Revelries', assuming responsibility for a huge dance-off between the bridesmaids and groomsmen. She choreographed the whole thing with Amanda, who'd taken dance lessons for her own nuptials. This was before wedding dance-offs were a thing, so no one filmed it to put it on YouTube. In fact, I think Angus's cousin may have filmed it on a camcorder, but he was so pissed it came out all blurry and he fell over halfway through so we had to ditch the footage. That's how I felt about most of my past – like it was filmed by Angus's drunk cousin and therefore fuzzy and useless. But my memory of that dance-off was as crystal clear as if it happened yesterday – six of my best friends, including Izzy, doing the moves to Madonna's 'Vogue' with entirely straight faces, interspersed with the boys offering up 'Boom! Shake the Room', Angus weeping with laughter, my mother with her head in her hands. If I listened hard enough, I could still hear the echo of it, like the Big Bang reverberating through space.

On Saturday, although I still had indigestion from too much rich food the day before, and felt queasy anyway at the prospect of rooting out Isabella's elderly parents, I got in the car and drove all the way to Hathersage. It was time to get this search party started.

The journey was straightforward, less than two hours down the M1, and I used the time to listen to Angus's mate's spy podcast, *Spooky-Doos*. In each thirty-minute episode, Jackson DeLantro (clearly a made-up name) and his team of 'agents' discussed an espionage case plundered from the national archives, with an *X-Files*-style soundtrack rumbling along underneath it all. I don't know why I was supposed to feel 'spooked' by cases that were done and dusted more than sixty years ago, but nevertheless I found myself pulled in by the story of Carl Hans Lody, a German spy in the First World War who became the first person to be executed in the Tower of London in 150 years. And then by Eddie Chapman, a thief-turned-German-agent-turned-double-agent who changed sides so many times it made me dizzy, and I couldn't remember who he was working for at all.

One thing that seemed to unite these spooks was sloppiness. They never really believed anyone was watching them, and always ended up getting careless, forgetting to encrypt their messages or whatnot. I felt that I, with my heightened sense of paranoia, would have made a much better spy. Which made me sure that Isabella *was* one. She and I were united in our wariness. We always used to walk down streets convinced someone was following us, or be in her flat, drinking, and hear suspicious noises like an intruder was trying to break in. Once, in her Chorlton flat, she was sure someone was lurking in the back garden, and made me go out there armed with a floor mop. It turned out to be a big black bin bag that had blown onto the rotary dryer. Sometimes when I was with her, I felt like I was on my guard, and in hindsight that was a sign that you didn't need an Enigma machine to decode. She was a spy all along. I was sure of it. That was why she peeled off from us all: to protect us. Or so that we didn't get too close to the truth, whatever.

But, assuming she *was* still a spy and an active agent, she could just give me the wink and I would keep it to myself. I wouldn't interfere with her operations, and we could be friends again – I could even be a good cover for her. Because I was a really unlikely person for a spy to be friends with. An almost-stay-at-home mum who made mosaics, and was so dull even the dog ignored me – it wasn't like I was going to be passing on secrets to the Soviets. Oh, it wasn't the Soviets any more, was it? Or maybe it was again. See, I was no kind of threat at all.

Would her parents even know though? Presumably she would have to keep them in the dark, too. I'd better not barge in with the spy theory, then. Keep it low-key. My hands felt slightly clammy on the steering wheel as I drove alongside the winding River Derwent – if this was how I approached an unannounced visit to my friend's parents, then God knows how Isabella coped on missions. She must be a lot steelier than I remembered. This was the woman who absolutely lost her shit and phoned the fire brigade when an owl accidentally flew into her bedroom one night. When I arrived to help, I found her sobbing and wielding a broom: 'HIS HEAD GOES ROUND LIKE LINDA BLAIR'S.'

Hathersage is a very pretty village in the Peak District, our stomping ground, though my parents now lived on the other side, in Buxton. It was the kind of place that attracted hikers and café dwellers – old folk who wandered into tearooms, their heads rotating like owls. When Angus and I decided to move out of Manchester, we considered the area but decided that Harrogate was a happy medium – not as full-on as the UK's second biggest city, but not as sleepy as the proper countryside. However, as I pulled up outside the Harris family home, I wondered if we'd made a mistake. It was ravishing, like something out of an Agatha Christie drama. A wisteria-clad Georgian former rectory, window boxes loaded with Michaelmas daisies, all nestled in a shingle driveway. When I was a teenager, dashing in and out, I never noticed – never bothered with any of the beauty on my doorstep. Why was it that when you were in it, you didn't see; didn't appreciate? I paused for a while, relishing the sound of birdsong, the gentle breeze lifting the foliage that wreathed the house. Then I took a quiet moment just to panic about exactly what I was doing.

What if they weren't in? But they must be in their eighties now; where would they go? Maybe they didn't live here any more. Maybe they'd emigrated. Maybe they were in an old people's home. Maybe, unlike Isabella, they *were* dead. What on earth was I doing here? I pushed the doorbell, humming the theme to Miss Marple under my breath.

When Izzy's mother opened the door, I gasped, firstly because I didn't really expect it to be so easy, and secondly, she looked *exactly* the way I remembered. It must have been at least . . . *thirty* years since I'd seen her? No – I was at their ruby wedding anniversary dinner, which was when we were in our mid-thirties, so it was around twenty years. Almost a quarter of a century, though, and she looked just the same. She'd always been a good-looking woman, but this was incredible levels of anti-ageing. Not a grey hair I could see, and she wasn't even that wrinkly. Good bone structure, but I also wondered if she'd had work done. Honestly, she could have been on the cover of *Tatler* or something, it was unbelievable. Maybe it was her Italian heritage; although Constanza had been brought up in London, her own mother – Izzy's Nonna – had been a native Florentine who made her own tortellini. Italians were famously long-lived and this must be why Constanza looked entirely unchanged – all that olive oil.

Rather unflatteringly, the feeling wasn't mutual. Constanza Harris stared at me blankly, and I was forced to reintroduce myself to my best friend's mother, who'd known me since I was a teenager.

'Um, hello. It's Gwen. Gwen Mortimer? I'm so sorry to bother you.'

Her fingers on the doorframe tightened, but her face – that amazing, youthful face – cleared immediately.

'Gwen! Is it really you? How lovely to see you! Come in, come in!'

She pulled the door open, revealing their elegant hallway, and I followed her through to the sitting room. I peeked in the kitchen on my way – as always, there was a cat curled on the Aga, presumably a different one to the one I used to fuss in my teens, but really, who knew? Perhaps there was a rip in the space/time continuum in this part of Hathersage.

'After all these years!' Mrs Harris was saying, as she moved newspapers off sofas so we could sit down. 'What brings you here, my dear?'

'It's just as I remember.' I was playing for time, because I hadn't thought any of this through properly, and now I was here, looking her in the face – that *amazing* face! – I honestly didn't know what to say. *Is your daughter a spy? She won't talk to me. Make her talk to me! Where is she? What cream do you use?*

'Oh, we keep meaning to do things, but we never get around to it.' Their sitting room – not a lounge, of course – was classic and classy in a way that would never really need tweaking. I was always redecorating because I was never sure of my taste, and kept changing my mind about what sort of image I wanted to project. 'Let me get Julian. Julian!'

Isabella's father wandered in, carrying a copy of *The Times*. He looked reassuringly older, frailer.

'Ah, hello, Gwen,' he said, like it was 1987. 'Would you like a sherry?'

Constanza clicked her tongue in irritation. 'It's far too early,' she said. 'We're not animals. Perhaps a cup of tea?'

'That would be lovely,' I said, figuring I'd have time to get my shit together while she made it. She went off the kitchen while Julian chatted to me as if I was still at Harpur High.

'Are your parents well?' he asked, as he always did.

'Yes, they're good,' I replied, which was true if you didn't count various ailments and anxieties particular to their generation.

'Jolly fine weather today,' he observed. 'Makes a change from all this dratted rain.'

'Wonderful.'

'I don't care what Coco says, I *am* going to have a sherry,' he announced. 'It's six o'clock somewhere!' And he poured himself a glass from the little decanter, which was what he always did, and where it always was, and I mimed a toast as I always did, and he had a little sip and gave me a wicked smile. And I felt my eyes fill with tears because he made me feel like I was sixteen again, and in a way, I wanted to be, with Izzy upstairs putting her shoes on before we went out to The Crown with our fake ID.

'Here we go!' Constanza re-entered the room, carrying a tray. She was astonishingly spritely. After busying herself pouring and stirring, she sat back. 'Now, what good fortune brings us this visit?'

It was the polite elegance of that phrase that told me she'd used the tea-making time as much as I had. Now, I wanted her secrets almost as much as I wanted Isabella's. I fervently hoped I was as beautiful and alert at eighty-odd. Or even at my age. Because she was so disarming, I took a deep breath and decided to be (partly) truthful.

'I've come to ask you about Isabella.'

Constanza raised her eyebrows, looked enquiringly at her husband, then back to me. 'What about her?'

'Is she OK?'

'She's perfectly fine, as far as I'm aware.'

'Right.' I pondered. It was weird to think of Isabella being 'fine' and yet also completely MIA. 'It's just that . . . we had a bit of a falling out and . . . haven't spoken in a while . . .' The understatement of the century. 'So, I . . . just wanted to check.'

'I'm so sorry. You were always such good friends.' Isabella's mother looked genuinely concerned, but there was something else there, something I couldn't put my finger on.

'Yes. Yes, we were.' Poleaxed by Julian, I now felt thoroughly sorry for myself, ready to start weeping and waiting for them to fix it all. They could restore Isabella to her rightful position as my friend, and sort out a viable career for me while they were at it. If Constanza could also give me the name of her beautician then we'd be fine and dandy.

They were both looking at me expectantly, like the next move was mine, and I wanted to say: *No, you tell me what to do.* Seeing them made me realize I was sick of being a grown-up, with weighty responsibilities and wise responses. I wanted to be childish, and selfish, and stupid, and have someone else deal with the mess. At fifty-three, I'd done my fair share of adulting and would like to regress, thank you very much. Maybe if I went home now – home-home, not Harrogate-home – my mum would pack my PE kit, give me my lunch money for Monday, and I could just go back to Harpur High, in my peacock-blue-edged blazer. There was something comforting about the idea. While I'd forgotten much about my past, I was sure I could remember how to conjugate French verbs and solve quadratic equations, and I certainly wouldn't angst about boys this time round. I'd be a much better student.

'Do you know where she is?' I croaked.

'Who?' asked Constanza, which was definitely disingenuous, rather than a senior moment.

'Isabella.'

Julian leaned forwards. 'Don't you?'

There was a split-second when I considered lying, before I realized how ridiculous it all was.

'No,' I said, forlornly. And then abandoned any attempts at dignity. 'Will you tell me where she is?'

Julian went back to the decanter and poured another sherry, which he handed to me.

'There you go, poppet.'

I sipped, dejectedly.

'I think,' Constanza began, delicately, 'that whatever has gone on between you and Isabella, you should probably sort out for yourselves. Perhaps Julian and I shouldn't be involved.'

'Oh,' I said, miserably. 'No, of course.'

'Not that we don't want to help, of course, but Isabella values her privacy.'

'Yes,' I agreed, disconsolately.

'After everything that's happened.' Constanza went to the decanter and poured herself a glass.

I nodded, like I knew, but at the same time my mind raced. *After everything that's happened? What's happened?* Now I understood what I hadn't been able to put my finger on – it was their lack of surprise at it all. That we'd fallen out, that I hadn't seen her, that I didn't even know where my supposed best friend lived. They weren't surprised! There was something they knew, and they either assumed I knew it too, or if I didn't, they weren't going to tell me.

Was it that she was a spy?

Or was it something else entirely?

We finished our sherry and I failed to extract a single iota of further information about Isabella. Then I went into the kitchen to pat the cat just in case it was the one I'd known when I was a teenager, offering hearty and profound goodbyes even though the trip had been a waste of time. When I finally got in the car and looked at my phone, it was 2.57 p.m., and there were four missed calls from Angus. I set a destination on the satnav and started the engine.

No, it hadn't been a waste of time. I now knew that something was definitely afoot. Isabella's parents might not want to tell me, but I would find out, by hook or by crook – my money was on Jackson DeLantro coming up with the goods, confirming Izzy's spook status as soon as Angus contacted him. We'd go from there.

In the meantime, I was going home. Home-home, not Harrogate-home.

8

On my way to my mum and dad's, I called Angus back.

'Izzy wasn't a spy,' he said as soon as he answered.

'Stop talking about her in the past tense,' I muttered irritably, my eyes on the road.

'All right, Izzy *isn't* a spy.'

'How do you know?'

'My mate Dave says so.'

'Who's Dave, and who made him head of the Secret Service?'

'He's the podcast guy, *Spooky-Doos*.'

'Hang on, Dave is Jackson DeLantro?' I chortled. 'I knew it was a made-up name.'

'Actually, due to the nature of his work he prefers to operate under a pseudonym.'

'He's definitely a pseud.'

'Well, he put some feelers out and it's come back a no.'

'Maybe she has a higher level of clearance than he does.'

'Come on, Gwen, don't be a dick.'

'I just spent an afternoon with her parents and got serious spy vibes.'

'Maybe *they're* spies then. But Izzy wasn't. Isn't.'

I sighed, my gaze roaming across the rolling green hills that flanked each side of the road. It was so pretty here, where the Harpur Harlots had grown up, had our first adventures. Was it really so implausible that while most of us went into regular professions like advertising and retail, one of us had gone into espionage?

'OK, I didn't find her anyway.'

'Maybe best to leave it then.'

'No.' There was no way I was going to fall at the first hurdle. Isabella had to be found. At least I knew she definitely wasn't dead now. 'I'm not a quitter.'

'What's got into you? Why have you waited fifteen years to get worked up about this?'

It would be easier to locate Isabella via the Ouija board than answer that question. I just felt, profoundly, that it was time.

'I was worked up before,' I said slowly. 'I just didn't do anything about it.' I'd spent most of my adult life ignoring my impulses, dismissing them as indulgent – when you're two years old, you can throw food on the floor and scream and stamp, but grown-ups (women) have to just get on. Curb our instincts, keep the peace. But I couldn't explain why *this* impulse was the one I was indulging, above all others. I mean, I'd also always wanted to go kayaking around a European island, and often had the urge to track down a particularly unpleasant account executive I used to work with in order to tell him what a prick he was. I'd never scratched those itches – when would I ever have the time or the balls? – yet I intended to scrape this one to the bone. Given that Angus didn't seem too keen, it seemed better to keep my compulsion to myself for now.

'Anyway,' I continued, noting with interest that I was currently driving through a quaint village called Hope, 'I was calling to say that since I'm in the area I'm going to stop at Mum and Dad's. Might stay the night.'

'You know they'll get into a tizz.'

'Yeah.' My parents enjoyed fretting themselves into a frenzy about minor stuff, so they could ignore what they were really scared of: the badger that visited their garden digging a network of tunnels that one day their house would fall into. Successful distractions included my dad owning more unread books than he could possibly read and resenting the wasted shelf space, my mum worrying that one day she would start liking sensible shoes, and both of them obsessing over whether the lemon drizzle cake at their local farm shop was deteriorating in quality. Me turning up unannounced on their doorstep was DEFCON 1, akin to the badger popping his head up through the living room floorboards. But if I didn't drop in, they would somehow find out about it. The Peak District was a small place, gossip-wise – more like Peek District; someone always spotting you and reporting back. It was best to get on with it. And, after seeing Coco and Julian, my nostalgia atoms had been awakened and were bumping up against each other, demanding more.

* * *

'Gwennie! What are you doing here?' My father was in the front garden holding shears. Half of the ivy that covered the front of the house was pulled off, but a great swathe clung stubbornly to the wall. 'Nesta! Nesta! Nesta! Nesta! Nesta!'

My mother came stumbling down the path at the side of the house. 'What it is?'

'It's Gwennie. She's here.'

'Oh, Gwennie! Is that it? I thought it was Brock.'

'It wouldn't be him, would it. He only comes at night.' My father put down his shears, giving the remaining ivy a disapproving glance. 'Now, Gwennie, what's going on? Have you had a row with Angus?'

If I had, they'd take his side. My mother thought the sun shone out of Angus's arse. 'No, I was just in the area so thought I'd drop in.'

'Just in the area! Well, you can come in and have a biscuit.'

'Thought I might stay the night, actually.'

'Stay the night! That would be nice. Bill, you'd better change the sheets; next door's cat got on the spare bed last week.'

My mother and father had retired to a semi-detached house on a stoically suburban avenue in the genteel spa town of Buxton. Everything about their property and existence was modest, restrained, and faintly apologetic. 'We don't want to be a bother,' was their motto, and it applied whether they were refusing to return a cold cup of coffee in a café, or waiting for vital test results in A&E. They might be in a tizz, but they would never want to inflict that tizz on anyone outside the confines of their household. Although by no means rich, my father could have afforded to pay someone to take the ivy off the wall, but would have decided that the job was beneath the contempt of any professional landscaper, and that it was much better he tackle it himself. If he did his back in as a result, well, he'd pop a couple of pills and soldier on. No; no need for a doctor's visit, they had more important things to deal with. The pain would wear off eventually.

When we were finally settled in the kitchen with a packet of Hobnobs, and my mother had told me about all the old folk in the vicinity who'd recently died, my father turned his attention to the elephant in the room.

'So, why were you in the area, Gwennie?'

I wasn't keen on telling them the reason, which I knew they would worry at like a dog with a rope. But I couldn't think of another motive for coming down, and any hastily devised excuse might open an even bigger can of worms. The most obvious one would be to say I was down for an auction or house clearance, but my parents thought my new enterprise was utterly ridiculous, and any mention of it caused them to assume pained expressions and say who did I think I was, Kirstie Allsopp? On balance, it was better to come right out with it.

'I went to see Julian and Constanza Harris.'

My mother and father looked blank.

'Isabella's parents.'

Immediate, extreme consternation. 'Oh no! Has something happened to her? That poor girl.'

'No. I just . . . You know we lost touch? I thought I'd look her up again.'

They exchanged a bemused glance. 'Why would you do that?'

'Why not?'

My mother picked up a Hobnob. 'I mean, why now? Hasn't it been a while?'

In for a penny. 'Fifteen years.'

My father set down his coffee cup. 'Fifteen years! Well, bless me. Doesn't time fly.'

'When you're having no fun. Yes, it's been fifteen years and I thought I'd see what she's up to.'

'And then what?'

I frowned. 'And then . . . what?'

Mum fixed me with a beady eye. 'Once you've looked her up, then what?'

This felt like an unnecessarily aggressive unpicking of my plans. 'Then I'll see if she wants any mosaic coasters. I don't know, we might hang out again or something. Catch up.'

She sniffed. 'Feels like there's a lot of water under that bridge.'

I didn't come here to be interrogated. Well, I did, but in a different way. They should be asking me about the boys, and how much money Angus was making, and if we'd get Mabel spayed because we didn't want to be lumbered with a litter of puppies.

'Lovely-looking girl, Isabella,' observed my mother, taking her biscuit to look out the kitchen window at the back garden.

'Yes,' I agreed. She had been extremely striking, and if Constanza was anything to go by, she still was.

'Good cheekbones,' said Mum, turning and eyeing my own inferior ones. I rubbed my face defensively.

'Don't upset yourself.' My dad patted my arm, consolingly.

'I'm not upset about Isabella having better bone structure than me.'

'I didn't mean that. I meant, don't wade into that water.'

I frowned at him, puzzled.

'The water under the bridge,' my mum explained.

'There could be unexpected currents,' he said, flogging the metaphor to death.

'It's all drama nowadays,' observed my mother. 'People getting all het up on Facebook and Twitter with their . . . hot takes. Trolling. Catfishing.'

It was evident that my dear mama was now very much out of her depth, experimenting with social media lingo in much the same way I attempted Fred's Gen Alpha slang.

'Swipe left,' she concluded, triumphantly. 'Sometimes it's best to leave well alone.'

My parents never liked me to 'interfere' with anything. *Leave well alone* was one of their mottos, marching hand in hand with *Don't be a bother.*

'I'm not trying to meet a new man on Tinder,' I said. 'Just looking up an old friend.'

'Well, be careful,' said my dad. 'Stirring things up.'

'I can look after myself,' I said grumpily, forgetting my back-to-school scheme. 'I'm fifty-three.'

'To think I have a fifty-three-year-old daughter,' my mother wittered. 'And me still in heels!' She maintained the theory that flat shoes were only for women who'd given up.

Starting my speech about my age not being aged, her screech stopped me short. 'WAIT! Bill, that damned cat's back.'

Standing to look out the window, I saw a handsome grey cat winding his way down the garden path. Both my parents sprang into action, as quickly as eighty-somethings could spring. My father grabbed his cornet, which was sitting on the counter. He played occasionally with a local brass band, though moaned that no one paid any attention to the conductor, and the post-rehearsal custard creams were stale and in short supply. My mother rushed to the back door, pausing to snatch up an enormous— not water pistol; more of an aqua-AK-47. They both erupted into the garden, Mum firing on all cylinders while my father played some sort of march, behind her. The cat yowled and scarpered, causing a flock of birds to take flight noisily from the birch tree at the edge of the lawn. Having successfully evicted the feline with maximum force, my parents returned, breathless and triumphant.

I felt very tired. 'Shall we get a takeaway? I'll pay.'

My father shook his head, panting. 'No need for that. I'll make a risotto.'

Mum bustled around, still wielding her weapon. 'Did you do the fresh linen, Bill? I'll do it, shall I?'

'No, I'll do it.'

'You can't be doing the linen *and* the rice.'

'You do the chopping, I'll do the changing, and then I'll root out the arborio.'

In a way, this part of the trip was a great success, because it put to bed any silly ideas I had about wanting to move back home and be babied. There was no way I could witness their ongoing war with Macavity, help my dad rip out a load of ivy, listen to my mum talk about dead people, and wait for a badger to invade. However little I was doing with my life, at least I was nominally in charge, free to plunge into deep waters if I felt like it.

After dinner, leaving them sitting in the dark kitchen with the night-vision goggles, I put myself to bed with a hot-water bottle – the house was freezing, as they didn't like to bother the radiators. My mother's shoe collection had seriously impinged on space in the spare room, and the duvet cover on the bed featured an enormous sloth hanging on a branch, a design that reeked of random bargain aisle purchase. Even so, I enjoyed having a bed to myself without Angus reading brutal war biographies next to me. It was a bit of peace. Weird, slothful peace, and yet I couldn't wait to get home. Harrogate-home.

But when they saw me off the next morning, my mother gave me a cheese sandwich wrapped in cling film for the journey, and I cried all the way back up the M1.

9

By Monday, I had decided to get in touch with Dave/ Jackson DeLantro myself. After brooding on it for the rest of Sunday, without even a phone call from Liam to distract me, I surmised that Angus, in typical blasé fashion, wouldn't have bothered imparting key details about Isabella's situation, and that as a result Dave's conclusion was inaccurate. Maybe Isabella wasn't a spy, but she wasn't not a spy on the basis of two feckless podcasters devoting five minutes to the discussion over a few Doom Bars. Dave needed to apply himself properly to this question, with all the facts at his fingertips. Provided by me, rather than my useless spouse.

I didn't tell Angus any of this, because he disapproved of the whole enterprise, thought I should *leave well alone* like my parents, which made me think he'd never liked Isabella in the first place. Maybe he was jealous – when we first got together, he occasionally complained, in a jokey way, about how often Izzy and I saw each other; that our Gwizzle was gibberish; that I was never available for dates because I was with my friend, going for dinner or hanging out at her flat, or accompanying her on one of her spontaneous activities. Izzy liked signing up for new things, impulsively, seeing how it played out. We went bouldering on the moors, did life drawing classes, line dancing, volunteered on hospital radio, went on a sunrise walk to listen to the sound of a nightingale. Many of these were never to be repeated, but even when the jaunt turned out to be a disaster, there would be something in it for us. A shared pant at the bottom of Cratcliffe Tor, having climbed precisely four feet up it. A smothered laugh over a very visible penis, that Isabella had drawn as a sausage dog. The way Izzy's hand found mine when we finally heard that bird. I drew the line at abseiling off Millers Dale Viaduct though, and Angus probably benefitted from that decision. In fact, I vaguely remembered that we went to the pub instead, and when she called, euphoric, I couldn't hear her over the noise of the bar. Or was that another night?

Anyway, Angus was unsettled and possibly green-eyed at the idea of me rediscovering a friendship that once took up so much of my time. So, I contacted Dave without letting him know, figuring since men never tell each other anything anyway, he was unlikely to ever find out about my discreet indiscretion. I emailed Dave through his website, which was murky in every sense, with a black background and titles that shimmered and vanished. Why did he bother with it, when all the information on it was so vague and esoteric? And yet at the bottom, there it was: JDLantro@spy.com – embarrassingly on-the-nose.

Hi Dave,

I'm Angus Stewart's wife. I think you've already spoken but I have a couple of follow-up questions if that's OK? I wondered if I could give you a call?

All the best,
Gwen Mortimer

Within minutes I got a reply.

Gwen,

Sure thing. If you don't mind, I'll call you in a couple of hours? Number withheld and all that.

JD

Enigma-wanker. I sent him my number and sat back, tutting my derision. These people. Thinking they were important, that their dumb little dealings had some impact. Like anyone cared whether Dave busted the story of a spook who bungled his operation fifty years ago. He was the botched mosaic table of the espionage world, and I was sure he wouldn't have any useful information for me, but I wanted his input nonetheless, if only to disregard it.

I spent the afternoon in my workshop, irritably moving bits of broken china around, trying to turn scarlet shards into a butterfly for one of my trivets, while Dippy painted a canal and nattered about cunnilingus.

'He's just got a good technique, you know? Some guys, it's like a great big fish flopping about, but he's got real delicacy . . . Talking of delicate, that's a neat bird.'

'It's supposed to be a butterfly.'

'Is it? Oh yeah, a Red Admiral. Did you know, females will only mate with males that hold territory? They're basically gold diggers, innit.'

Jacob's new cabinet was taking shape, and was a thing of great beauty – a phoenix emerging from the ashes of Dippy's verbal garbage. Jacob was always incredibly zen, which was irksome since I always wasn't. He'd just spent half an hour contemplating a spirit level, while I ferreted about for teabags, knocked over my tea, and cut my finger on a rogue ceramic shard cleaning up the spillage. Was there an activity that might help me achieve that level of abstract pleasure? I worried that it was being halfway down my second glass of wine. There was that kayaking holiday in Menorca that I kept looking at online, but I'd never actually been in a kayak and might not take to it. Maybe when I finally tracked down Isabella, she would go with me and we could watch Spanish sunrises and find our spirit level together. I sucked my sore finger, watching Jacob resentfully.

'Did you manage to contact your friend?' He didn't look at me, focusing on his gentle polishing.

'What friend?' Dippy reared up from her canal.

'The one who went off,' I said, abandoning the trivet and going back to my table arrangement. I'd prepared my tree design and was about to apply adhesive.

'Oh, the dead one.'

I sighed. 'Yes, the dead one.' And then, as I started slapping on a layer of glue, 'I think she might be a spy.'

Dippy dropped her brush. 'REALLY?'

'Um, maybe.'

'What, like Jodie Comer?'

'Who's Jodie Comer?'

'A spy. She's more of an assassin, though.' Dippy picked up her brush, mulling. 'But it's the same thing, isn't it? Spies are just contract killers. Like, legal murderers.'

This conversation, more than anything, made me question my theory. The idea that Izzy, rather than being a local restaurant reviewer, was actually an international hitwoman, seemed somewhat far-fetched.

'I don't think everyone who works for those agencies is an assassin,' observed Jacob, stirring his wood glue. 'What makes you think your friend is one of them, though?'

'She's not on the internet,' I said, selecting a piece and setting it in the gunk. 'It's like she doesn't exist.'

'I've got a friend like that,' said Dippy. 'She says 5G is a conspiracy, that the towers infect us. So she, like, got herself taken off the web.'

I was instantly intrigued. 'How did she do that?'

Dippy shrugged. 'Her ex is really good with computers. She got him to delete everything. He, like, deactivated her email accounts, shut down her Facebook page, that sort of stuff.'

'He could do that?' This was actually useful information. Sod Dave DeLantro, I'd get Dippy's nutty friend's ex on the case.

'Yeah. She kept her Insta up and running, though, as she needed to update her followers.'

'Right.'

'She makes, like, really nice tinfoil hats, and sells them.'

' . . . Are you taking the piss?'

Dippy dropped her brush again, she was laughing so hard. 'Sexy . . . hazmat suits . . . you should get one!'

'Fuck off.'

'Seriously though. A *spy*?'

'For your information—' But then my mobile rang, and it was a withheld number, which meant it was my source, Dave Jackson DeLantro, calling with a vital update. I snatched up the phone and flounced off to stand on the dusty track outside, resting my back against the wooden frontage.

'Hello?'

'Is that Gwen? It's JD.' JD? *JD?* Give me strength. 'How are you doing? Sorry it took a while, got tied up in a bit of . . . business.'

Looking up false shadows on the moon landings, no doubt. I cleared my throat. 'That's OK. Thanks for calling. I just wanted to follow up on Angus's question about my friend.'

'What question?'

God, he was being deliberately obtuse. 'The one about my friend.'

'What friend?'

'The dead one. *No*, sorry, my friend who disappeared. Isabella.'

'I'm afraid I don't know what you're talking about.'

'But didn't Angus speak to you?'

'I haven't seen Angus since that convention . . . when was it? Sometime last year. Give him my regards.'

The lying, two-faced git. Internally spitting curses at my good-for-nothing husband, I pulled myself together. 'Sorry, I think there have been some crossed wires somewhere along the line. But . . . I need some information about someone who I think might be working for the government, and Angus thought you might be able to shed light on it.'

There was a brief pause. 'Someone who might be working for the government? Our government?'

I hadn't really given that much thought. *Our* government, surely? Though now I came to think of it, Izzy had Italian blood. So maybe she was working for . . . Berlusconi? Mussolini? I couldn't remember who was in charge of Italy, but felt instinctively that they were bad; worse even than whoever was in charge of us.

'Maybe an . . . organization of some kind? An agency?'

'And what do you want me to do?'

'Er . . . find out if she actually is?' I felt, suddenly, unutterably stupid, as stupid as it was possible for a fifty-three-year-old woman, who'd done many stupid things, to feel.

'And how did you think I was going to do that?'

'I don't know . . . We thought you might have . . . contacts.'

'And do you think if I had those contacts, they would just give out information like that?'

I was wrong. It was definitely possible to feel more stupid. I said nothing, to try to keep the stupidity spirit level on an even keel.

He carried on. 'So, I just call my contacts at MI5 and say: "Hi guys – there's this woman here who thinks her friend is a spy – can you confirm?" And they'll say "Hang on, just logging on to our spook database. Yep, here she is – do you want her current operation details?"'

Silence was still the best and only option at this point.

'Her undercover name is Minky McCha-Cha,' he continued, obviously a graduate of the same School of Sarcasm as Angus. Maybe that was where they met.

'There's no need to be rude.'

He began to laugh. 'I'm sorry, but what are you on?'

HRT, antihistamines, evening primrose oil, caffeine, paracetamol, magnesium, CBD gummies and whatever lingering alcohol was left in my system from last night. I was also on the edge.

'I just need to know where she is.' The tears in my voice were evident. I pinched the bridge of my nose, slumping back against the peeling wood of the garage door. Why hadn't I done this earlier, before time made it an impossible task? The web I couldn't find her in was between us, layers and layers of gossamer fibres that had become thick and impenetrable over the years. I missed her and wanted her back, but had left it too late.

There was another silence, this time from him, while I snivelled, wallowing in my own idiocy.

When he spoke again, he sounded kinder. 'What's her name?'

Through snot, I mumbled thickly. 'Isabella Harris.'

'Middle name?'

I stood up straighter, wiping my nose. 'Raizel.'

'Unusual. Good. Age?'

'Fifty-three. No, fifty-four.' Izzy's birthday was in September, before mine. She was a Libran – balanced, sociable, with an eye for detail. That was what she always said, and then she'd add, with a snort of laughter: 'And they don't believe in all that bollocks!'

'All right. Write down everything you know about her, and send it to me in an email. I'll see what I can do.'

I caught my breath. 'Do you think you can find her?'

'Maybe. But . . .' He paused again. 'What if she doesn't want to be found?'

I frowned, turning round and scratching at the peeling paint with my fingernail. 'I'll cross that bridge when I come to it.' That bridge, with a lot of water under it. Why would she not want to be found? Or, to be more specific, why would she not want to be found, *by me*? 'How will you find her?'

'I won't. I don't think I could. But I know someone . . .'

'Don't tell me. He has a podcast.'

'How did you guess? *Where Were They Then?* It's about historical missing people cases. I'll put you in touch.'

'Thanks. And Dave . . . I mean, Jacks— er, JD?'

'Yeah?'

'Can you not tell Angus we spoke? He wouldn't understand.' If Angus wanted to nip this search party in the bud, then I would keep him out of the loop.

'Sure thing, kiddo.' It sounded like something Indiana Jones would say. Jackson DeLantro/Dave/JD really was a knob. But he was a knob who might help me find my friend.

'Thanks.' I hung up, and went back into the workshop, where I found the adhesive had dried out, so I had to strip it all off and start again. As I scraped away, Dippy alternated between sex stories and jokes about electromagnetic fields. By the time I had a clean slate, Jacob had carved an exquisite leaf design into one of the doors of his cabinet, and Dippy's canal was nearly complete. They were always more productive than me.

Back where I'd started. But in other ways, things were moving along nicely.

10

Isabella introduced herself to me, aged thirteen, by holding out her hand and saying 'Braithwaite. Pandora Braithwaite. And you are?' She was very pretty with long brown hair and a kind of no-nonsense air, so it made sense.

'I think I might be Adrian Mole,' I apologized, taking her hand. In those days, I wore round glasses as an affectation and kept a diary where I wrote things like 'I AM ON THE BRINK' and 'Went shopping, bought a nice hat. Mum took it off me, said it was a yarmulke. How was I to know?'

She laughed, the dirty cackle I would grow to love. 'That's perfect! We're a match, then.'

And we were.

Izzy moved to the area from Oxford, because her father took a job at Sheffield University. In those days, Sheffield was . . . well, let's just say it was a world away from dreaming spires. They lived in Ecclesall for a while, and she started school near there, but their house got burgled twice in six months, so they upped sticks to Hathersage because it was where Charlotte Brontë stayed when she was writing *Jane Eyre* – Constanza, Izzy's mother, had a thing for her. They actually ending up buying the vicarage Charlotte stayed in, and Izzy told me that before meals, instead of grace, Coco would bend her head and quote Jane – *I must keep in good health and not die* – and then they would eat.

As a consequence, Izzy felt she grew up in the shadow of Charlotte, and was torn between wanting to follow in her footsteps, and being determined to do something different. Her father was an English professor, which made it worse. In school, she was a charming rebel, excelling at art and languages, careless of the rest, frustrating the teachers who saw her potential. She was a strange mix of elegant and coarse – she moved gracefully, lightly, like a dancer, but could belch like a drunken sailor. All the boys worshipped her, of course, and her pickiness added to her allure. In her time at Harpur High, she only ever went out with one of them: Richard Spencer, whose parents owned an antiques shop in Bakewell. They split up just before university and he spent the last few weeks of that summer term looking like a ghost. Poor Dickie.

Harpur High was (and still is) a progressive state school in a fairly affluent area – the kind of place that well-to-do socialists could send their kids without having to compromise their principles or worry that their darling children would fall in with a 'rough crowd'. Aspiring to the status of the surrounding private schools, Harpur was hockey-mad and, from the age of fourteen, students played competitive matches against the poshos. One of the first things Izzy and I did together was try out for the third-year team, rejoicing when we made it, along with a bunch of noisy, riotous girls who were all vicious with a stick. From then on, we were a gang, but Izzy and I were the Kray twins at the heart of it.

In the same year, Izzy signed us both up for the Duke of Edinburgh Bronze Award, because for some reason she thought that our certificates would be handed over by the Duchess of Devonshire, who lived in the nearby Chatsworth House. Izzy idolized Deborah Mitford, the duchess, and was desperate to meet her, eager to do anything that might result in an encounter. I have no idea why she thought doing DofE would be our way in – personally I thought she had more chance of marrying the Earl of Burlington.

Anyway, having signed up we had to bloody well do it, which involved all sorts of hard work and awful camping trips. One of the tasks was to do a stint community volunteering, and we faffed ourselves into a flap trying to find something cool and enjoyable before plumping for whatever was available. I ended up working at a local vet, chatting to old ladies and their budgies, sweeping dog hair and ripping up the registration cards every time a pet was put down.

Meanwhile, on the outskirts of Sheffield, Izzy was volunteering at the Bluebird, a café for people with special needs. Appalled by the basic catering, she was soon making her mother's delicious *carbonara* and *ciambella* for them all, doing a roaring trade. She had the time of her life doing that job, and it was the spark of her future career – that initial judgement of the establishment. She had not just an eye, but a tongue, and years later, after university, when her attempts at breaking into travel journalism had come to nothing, she bumped into the old manager of the Bluebird who told her the *Derbyshire Times* were looking for reviewers. So, although she never got to meet the Duchess of Devonshire, she told everyone that the Duke of Edinburgh gave her her first proper job. And she felt that Charlotte Brontë would have approved.

What else? We sang in the school choir, because I fancied a boy who was also in it. Never spoke to him, not once in three years of rehearsals and concerts. At every one of those performances, Izzy's father Julian would sit in the audience with the scores open on his lap, following it all, and her older brother Luca would sit with a copy of *The Count of Monte Cristo*, only he'd coloured in the 'O' of 'Count'. This never failed to make me laugh, and never failed to infuriate Izzy, who considered it an act of unforgivable impudence. Luca went to a different school, and his remoteness made him glamorous. I was very disappointed when he left home to study for a degree in Rome.

When Izzy and I went to university, we arranged it so that we weren't too far apart. She went to Edinburgh to study Italian, and I went to Newcastle to read English. That would have been disastrous if we'd been a couple – the reason she split up with Richard was because she knew it wouldn't work – but for friends it was fine. We were near enough to provide support and the occasional weekend's entertainment, but we didn't have a romance to nurture. In the holidays, we travelled as far as our student budgets would stretch – cheap flights or trains to various locations in Europe, where we stayed in dubious hostels and consumed dubious substances. We touched what was left of the Berlin Wall, visited Napoleon's tomb, threw coins into the Trevi Fountain, ate roasted pig at the world's oldest restaurant, sang 'I Have Confidence' outside Villa Von Trapp.

The early years post-uni were a comedown, but we got each other through it. Both moved to Manchester, partied as hard as our salaries would allow. We did a succession of random jobs, trying to break into fields we were really interested in. When we finally got somewhere, Izzy would sneak me into restaurant openings and I'd smuggle her into my ad agency's events – they were always wooing someone with wine. Izzy had another boyfriend by then – Lixin Lee, who ran a Chinese restaurant in Altrincham. In the same way she called me 'Mortimer', she always called him 'Lee'. I slightly resented it, feeling the surname was *my* thing. He was OK, but quite driven; one of those people who has a five-year plan. She split up with him because he asked her to marry him. 'I'm twenty-five!' she said. He was ten years older, and when he produced a ring, she did the maths. Must have been really awkward, as he did it in the restaurant, with a fortune cookie. Poor Lee.

Izzy didn't actually write the restaurant reviews at first – she didn't instantly become A.A. Gill. She would go and make notes, and the real reviewer – a man – would write it up. Her boyfriend after Lixin was the reviewer – Arnold Schmidt. I feel like that relationship was more about her mining him for information, because thanks to him she got a new job where she still didn't get to write the reviews, but got sent to better restaurants. And then we went to Paris – a hardcore weekend at a hotel in Le Marais – and she met this famous reviewer, Jean-Luc Riche, and he got her an amazing job in London. Just put in a call. I was devastated, but obviously hid it. It was a fantastic opportunity. Arnold Schmidt didn't last long after that. Poor Arnie.

Izzy spent a couple of years in London, going to all the best places, building up quite a reputation for herself. She worked for a supplement called *Milieu*, which was very cool and cutting edge. Sometimes I would go down, sometimes she would come up, and I thanked my lucky stars that Manchester had a happening restaurant scene. And then, one day, she came back for good. Very abruptly, just turned up on my doorstep with a bag, saying she'd decided to come home. She stayed for a few days, and then found herself a flat to rent. Obviously, I asked her why she was here, so suddenly, but all she would say was that she was tired of London. NO, now I remember another thing: I recognized the Samuel Johnson quote and I said, 'Are you tired of life, too?' as a joke. And she said, 'When a man is tired of London, he is tired of life. When a woman is tired of London, it's something else.' And I wanted to ask her what the something else was, but she changed the subject, and I forgot.

So, she was back in Manchester, working for a food magazine called *Scoop*, and it was all great – we slid into our old ways, hanging out or talking every day. By then I'd met my husband and had to really make an effort to make sure things didn't change – that I didn't become one of those friends who found a man and disappeared. But when I had a baby, I couldn't help it. Liam just took up so much of my time, and when we met up, I couldn't help talking about him – moaning, probably – and it was maybe then I sensed we were moving apart. And then I had another baby, and Izzy had bought a flat in Chorlton and was working really hard to pay for it and . . . there would be weeks between us contacting each other. But now I think that came mainly from her, rather than me. She was disengaging, somehow.

The last night I saw her, we went out for a meal. It took ages to arrange it, finding a date, and she postponed a couple of times, making me worry she didn't really want to meet up. I have to work really hard to remember this, because at that point I had two young kids and was just back at work and hating it; everything was a fog of childcare and trying not to disappoint my boss. I drank too much, asked her something about boyfriends, and she mentioned someone, I can't remember who he was, and I said something jokey and she seemed to take offence. And she said she was thinking of moving back to

London, that she hadn't sold her flat there, just rented it out. That upset me, the idea of her going again, but I was also a bit envious because Angus and I were saving to buy a house and she was casually mentioning she owned two flats; I think her parents helped with the deposit for the first. So I was feeling resentful because my parents couldn't afford to give me thruppence, even though I'm an only child, and there she was with her property empire . . . Anyway, she walked out, I think, and I drank the rest of the wine on my own.

She never contacted me again, though of course I tried. I rang her mobile, but she didn't pick up; sent letters to her flat in Manchester, and the one in London, and they all got sent back – return to sender, or whatever. I spoke to the new tenant of her Manchester flat and he said he'd rented it through a company and didn't know her at all. I don't know if she owns either of them any more – maybe I should look into that.

One last thing, and I don't know if it's significant. When I had my third son, Fred, I got a card in the post, but there was no signature. I didn't really recognize the writing, could have been a random relative, but I always wondered if it was from her. It was postmarked Oxford, which was where she lived as a child. Maybe she went back there, to the dreaming spires.

I don't want you to think I was a bad friend. I did try. It's always on my mind – did she walk away because of me, because of what I said or did, or was it something else?

* * *

Thanks so much, JD – is that enough to go on? Sorry if I got a bit carried away there. It's just I know her so well.

I thought I'd forgotten everything, but it turned out there was still plenty I could remember. Though which of those details would be the thing that might track her down . . . who knew? It was a needle in a haystack. A coin in the fountain.

Best to get it all down, just in case.

11

There was an auction at Jumble's of Fulford, one of my favourite houses near York, and I met Min for lunch beforehand, because she was good company, and an excellent sounding board, happy to discuss where Izzy might be hiding. We met in a new place Min suggested, a Japanese restaurant where you had to perch on stools to eat inventive tempura. It was hard to eat and talk clearly, but it made me up my game, signing-wise. I'd taken to looking up a few new words and phrases before bed every night, and felt I was coming on quite well.

'So, how's it going with Jane Bond?' Min sipped her green tea while we waited for the food to arrive.

I sighed. 'Not so good.' It would have been cool to have a best friend who busted trafficking rings and rumbled terrorist plots, but this theory was starting to feel like a red herring. There was a mystery here, but not *that* kind of mystery. I was sad about it, because in the film of my life I'd have found Izzy and immediately been pulled into one of her undercover operations, ending up at a masked ball in Monte Carlo, slipping poison into an evil oligarch's glass, which beat grouting kitchen tiles hands down. But, according to Jackson DeLantro, if she was a spy, we'd never know about it, and if she was *that* kind of spy we'd never find her, which didn't suit my narrative at all. I wanted to know everything – where she went, why she went, what she'd been doing in the interim. We needed a new exciting theory; maybe Min could help me devise it.

'Last time we met, you said everyone had opinions on where she was, but I can't remember them.'

Min nodded, her mouth full of wasabi peas. 'When Holly and Erica were trying to track her down for the Harlots weekend, they asked everyone – were you not on the email chain?'

I thought back, the messages flying back and forth as we'd geared up for our big reunion. I'd mostly ignored them, because they'd included a lot of 'bantz' and mundane details, and I'd felt apprehensive about the meet-up generally. 'Didn't Holly organize it all?'

'She took over, but it was Erica's idea, I think. Because it was coming up to forty years since we got into the team. She said it was our ruby anniversary, remember?'

'No, I definitely didn't see that. Ruby? Bloody hell. Why didn't I get the emails?'

'Give me your phone.' Min held out her hand and I unlocked it and passed it to her.

Forty years. I didn't want to think about that. Min's fingers jabbed at my screen as I remembered those first training sessions – the endless drills, the back aches, the bruises, the viscous mud on a damp autumn day, the hot showers after. And I pictured the Harlots on the pitch – the intense concentration on Rachel's face as she whipped the ball out of reach, long legs pumping, Chloe's sly grin after a feint, Bhavini storming up the wing bellowing 'Set the press!' Why could I recall stupid details like that, yet forget the really important things?

'Yes, I thought so.' Min looked up, her eyebrows raised in amusement. 'All the emails were in your junk mail. I'm moving them to your inbox.'

My husband the technophile despaired of my hopelessness with gadgets, but I was resigned to my own ineptitude. 'Remind me, what were the various theories about Izzy?'

The waiter brought our food while Min looked at emails on my phone. 'Erica said she'd heard Izzy had married a Scottish laird and moved to Inverness, and did anyone know anything about it? No one did. Danielle said she'd seen her jogging in Central Park . . . Rachel saw her at a party in Ibiza, Amanda said she'd gone abroad . . . Chloe thought she'd gone into rehab – the Priory, she said, but Chloe really makes stuff up. Bhavini said the thing about seeing her going into Thames House, Holly said dog walker in Edgbaston.'

'It's all bollocks, isn't it.'

Min grinned, handing me my mobile. 'Yes, just hysterical gossip. Since we talked about it, I've decided the most likely thing is she got married, has a different name, and just isn't

94

that bothered about seeing anyone. What's that saying doctors use? If you hear hooves, don't assume zebras.'

'What?' The noise levels had increased, as a large group had arrived, and I couldn't understand her gestures.

'IF YOU HEAR HOOVES, IT'S NOT ZEBRAS!' Min shouted. 'IT'S HORSES.' The sign for 'horse' was just as you'd imagine, rolling your fists like they were holding reins, and for some reason it struck me as funny.

'Izzy's a horse,' I signed, sniggering. 'A big, knackered horse.'

Min laughed. 'A Harpur Harlot Horse.'

Suddenly, I felt quite fondly towards the Harlots, bunch of old nags that we were. Since the Lake District weekend, a few of them had been in touch. Rachel had texted a photo she took of me, fag in one hand, hash brownie in the other, with the caption 'NAUGHTY GIRL!!!' Bhavini had invited me up to her place in Hebden Bridge, Holly had sent details of some sort of protein powder she was promoting, and Erica had passed on the recipe for her carrot cake. I had no intention of making it, but figured it was nice of her all the same.

'Are we meeting up again, then?' I found myself asking, and then just as quickly started concocting excuses. Mad busy, Mortimosaic was really taking off, Fred was going through a rough patch at school, Angus had left me and was setting up home with Mabel, etc . . .

'Funny you should ask that, Holly texted me the other day asking the same question. Everyone said they had fun and that we should do it again. There are vague plans to have dinner in Manchester, since it's sort of in the middle of everyone.'

Manchester. Where Izzy and I used to live. 'Let's do it,' I said, snatching up a battered prawn. 'I'll even find a venue.' There was a restaurant Izzy loved in the Northern Quarter; she used to hang out there all the time. Maybe it was still open.

Min beamed. 'Excellent! I'll set up a WhatsApp group and we'll fix a date.'

* * *

As I drove to Fulford, I felt daunted by all the things I had to do: book a table, finish making a table, find Izzy . . . Actually, it was just those three things, but I was discovering, forty years after I made the school hockey team, that throwing any minor task in my logistical path gave me a feeling of chronic incapability. I didn't have much to do, but anything I *did* have to do made me mildly panicky and inept. Sometimes I could spend a whole day fretting about picking up a joint from the butchers and posting a parcel on the way. When I looked back at the periods when I was *really* busy – working full-time, looking after three young kids, or further back, at school, juggling training and matches and homework and exams and teenage romantic intrigue – how on earth did I cope? And why couldn't I cope now?

At Jumble's, I wandered around, feeling hectic. The room was too crowded and hot, and none of the lots were right. Looming wardrobes and heavy chests, huge mirrors and squatting Eames chairs. A big jumble. Overwhelming. I fanned myself with my brochure, dizziness taking hold. Once, at school in assembly, on a particularly warm day, I remembered the same feeling – maybe pollen asthma, or the beginnings of an actual panic attack, while we sang 'He's Got the Whole World in His Hands'. The *whole world?* In His *hands?* It was too much. I'd started to breathe erratically, desperate little gasps, grasping for Izzy who was standing next to me, warbling away. Instantly her arm was around me. 'Are you OK?' she whispered, quietly, discreetly, because she knew part of my panic would be the exposure. And then she murmured 'The wind and the rain? He's holding them? What the fuck is that about?' As my breathing eased into laughter, the panic receded.

People started taking their seats and the auctioneer stepped up. Sitting there, crammed in, waiting to bid on a load of Wedgwood Jasperware that was bound to go over my budget, I couldn't take it any more. Whispering apologies, I edged along the row and escaped, my heart hammering like the gavel, the beginnings of a hot flush taking hold.

After leaning against the wall outside to calm myself down, I went to Jumble's regular shop next door, browsing the humbler offerings as my heartbeat returned to normal. The little things – clocks and antique jewellery, delicate spectacles, pocket watches, and . . . crockery. A rickety pile of Spode plates beckoned, and I began to sort through them, searching for bargains to break. Although my current job gave very little satisfaction, there was one part of it that provided a small primal pleasure – smashing things to smithereens. I was already looking forward to splintering the cheapest dish in this mix, shattering it into a million pieces and then putting those pieces back together. While I did that, I could ignore everything else.

But then, there it was, right there, on a plate. A painted rendering of Charlotte Brontë, her hair severely parted, her gaze tranquil yet piercing. Even better, the words inscribed underneath her name: *I must keep in good health.* The grace Izzy's mother used to say at the table before dinner! Izzy's hero. Izzy's bête noire. Izzy's maxim. Here, on a plate!

It was kind of awful. Hideous. But surely – *surely* – it was a sign.

Reader, I bought it.

And then drove home, my breathing calm and even.

Izzy was a horse. Not a zebra; not an outlandish wild beast. Just a bog-standard, plodding pony. I could find her. I could do this. It would be OK; we could put the pieces back together.

12

Another thing that occurred to me. That Duke of Edinburgh Award we did – the camping bit. I hated it. Someone brought a fruit cake, and gave me a slice, and I was about to eat it only Mr Grainger's spaniel, lugged with him on the expedition, dashed into our tent and ran off with it. After a miserable, cold, uncomfortable night, when I really wanted to go home, have a hot bath and watch episodes of *The Comic Strip* on VHS, it was the last straw. I cried and ate one of Izzy's Lion Bars, the chocolate crumbs dropping all over my sleeping bag, while Mr Grainger chased his spaniel round the field screaming that dogs can't eat raisins.

But Izzy *loved* it. She was a mass of contradictions – usually very well groomed, she didn't mind being unwashed, or roughing it. She was a finicky eater, a gourmet – unless she was round a campfire. She wasn't outdoorsy – unless she was outdoors.

Is. I'm sure she's still all those things. I hope so.

She never lost her taste for camping. After university, when we were living in Manchester, she used to go off all the time, armed with her sleeping bag and portable stove. I found it inexplicable, that this woman, who got spooked walking home from the bus stop in West Didsbury on a sunny Tuesday, would happily embark on solo expeditions to the Brecon Beacons or wherever. It was one of her 'things'. In general, I wasn't interested in accompanying her as it definitely wasn't *my* thing – in fact, I think sometimes she used to go with one of the Harlots, maybe our hard-partying friend Rachel, who did Combined Cadet Force and was always covered in camo paint. But Izzy and I had an agreement: once a year, we would spend the weekend together, and one night we'd do whatever she wanted, and the other night I would choose. Cliché that I am, I always booked a spa – if I could, I would be massaged twenty-four hours a day, by a whole team of people, and only break off to eat. Izzy always chose camping, upgrading the experience to make it Gwen-friendly – yurts, tree-houses, bell-tents, gypsy caravans, little pods tucked away in woods. For that one night, I would indulge her, and for that one night I would enjoy it, looking forward to my deep-tissue full-body pummelling the following day. Once, over a late-night hot chocolate she'd gleefully boiled up on her little gas stove, I asked her why she liked it so much.

'It makes everything simple,' she said. 'When I'm in the real world, my head is full, but here . . . it's empty. It's just the essentials, and I like everything reduced to that.'

It was easy to understand what she meant, but equally, I felt camping just made the essentials much, much tougher, so my head was even fuller, because it was going to take me an hour to make a cup of tea, and another to pluck up the courage to use the compost toilet. Camping toppled my already-towering mental load.

But, for years, that's what we did – our push-me-pull-you girls' weekend of spa and spartan. Until the last time we went, a couple of years after Liam was born: when we were planning it, she said she wasn't keen on camping, and suggested two nights in the hotel I'd chosen. I was astounded, and weirdly disappointed – ready for the pill before my jam – but she said she was 'over that shit'. That was so not what the 'old' (former, not aged) Izzy would say that I felt something was wrong, but when I tried to bring it up during the weekend, she fobbed me off.

Now I think about it, she stopped signing up for things, as well, in those last months. Izzy always used to talk about stuff she was doing – classes she'd enrolled in, adventures she'd booked, random hobbies she'd taken up. Inevitably I'd get roped in to some of them, would laughingly complain and end up having a great time – I relied on her to drag me into activities, force me out of my comfort zone. But she stopped. Looking back, she was retreating into *her* comfort zone, but I don't know why. Maybe she was depressed, maybe she was ill, maybe it was something else.

I wish she'd told me. I wish I'd made her tell me.

Isabella's Not Dead

* * *

Hi, JD, just thought I'd add that into the mix. Let me know if your friend needs anything else, or has any leads. ATB,

Gwen

13

'I heard you're organizing this Harlots get-together, then.'

It was Holly, Queen of Gatherings, calling out of the blue the following week. Holly had always insisted on presiding over any social organization, with accompanying spreadsheets and passive-aggressive financial tot-ups.

'Not really,' I hummed. 'I just said I'd maybe find us a venue.'

'We'll need an area for drinks beforehand, then a table for dinner. With good veggie options for Erica. Preferably a place with rooms if people want to stay over.' It was said as a challenge, the implication being this would defeat me.

'Sure thing,' I said, pretending the blurred reflection in my kitchen window was Holly, and giving her the finger.

Despite my chronic incapability, booking somewhere a group of women could get comfortably legless and maybe kip after shouldn't be a huge stretch. Moreover, I intended to fold in another function to the evening – continuing my search party. But Holly didn't need to know that.

'I also hear you're trying to track down Izzy Harris.'

For Christ's sake, Min was such a gossip. 'Not really. I just thought I'd see if she was around and could join us.'

'So, she is alive then?'

'Of course she's alive!'

'And in Manchester?'

'Well . . . maybe.'

'Hmmm. I thought Birmingham.'

'Ah yes, your dog walker theory. Despite the fact that she's allergic.'

'Didn't she used to have cats?'

'Cats aren't dogs.'

Holly sniffed. 'My friend Alison said there's a woman called Izzy Harris who walks dogs in Harborne, where she lives.'

'Maybe there is. There are lots of Izzy Harrises, it turns out.'

'So, you know where she is?'

She was really getting on my nerves. 'Not exactly. But I'm following up some leads.'

'I'll put a few feelers out again. Erica can help, they used to get on well.'

They didn't get on well; Izzy thought Erica was earnest and overbearing and Erica mostly ignored Izzy, probably because she didn't understand Izzy's jokes. But I figured the more eyes peeled, the better. 'OK. Let me know if you hear anything.'

'Will do. Let me know where you're thinking of booking.'

So that she could pooh-pooh it. 'Will do.'

Killing the call, I reflected that there was now an added urgency to my search. I had to find Izzy before anyone else in the Harpur Harlots did. I had to get to her first to prove that I was the best friend. Nonetheless, I wanted their help because they might hear things through our wider circle of acquaintances – classmates, former boyfriends, whatever. I went online and looked up the Northern Quarter restaurant Izzy used to love. It was called Lever-something. The Lever Club! There it was, still going, part of a hotel; perfect. Maybe there would be someone working there who remembered her. She used to know the owners, and they even named a cocktail after her – a rose martini called The Raizel: 'Packs a punch, just like me!'

Min had set up a WhatsApp group called Mancunian Reunion, and we'd all agreed on a date in May – this time, Gracie Wagstaff, who hadn't been able to make the original Lake District weekend, had said she'd managed to get childcare. There was an online system on the restaurant's website, so I booked a table for nine people, congratulating myself on being extremely efficient and productive. Fired up by my success, I sent a message to everyone:

Hi guys! I've booked the Lever Club, very swish, for Friday, 24th May. Drinks in the bar at 6.30, dinner at 8. Rooms are available in the hotel for anyone who wants to stay overnight.

Then I messaged each Harlot individually:

On a related note, I thought I'd see if Izzy can join us
this time – let me know if you've heard from her or have
any ideas about her whereabouts.

It was a long-winded way of going about it, but it meant
only *I* would see each reply, and thus any accompanying
theories/hearsay. I didn't want Holly or Erica muscling
in on my investigation. This time, I would be doing the
spreadsheet; it would contain all known or surmised
locations of Isabella Harris, however tenuous, and I'd
unpick every last one.

14

'What are you up to?' Angus bounded in from the garden, the dog at his heels.

'Updating my Etsy shop.' My husband was hugely supportive of my creative endeavours, which irritated me beyond belief, because I knew they didn't deserve his encouragement, and I couldn't bring myself to reciprocate, because his did.

'Nice one. Do you want to come to the pub with me and Mabs?'

Mabel's tale wagged, but it wasn't an invitation. She went by many names: Mabs, Queen Mab, The Mabster, Mabelly-Wabelly. Sometimes Angus called her 'Norm' – she was named after a silent comedy actress called Mabel Normand, who was in films with Charlie Chaplin. 'She was funny, even without saying anything,' Angus would say, fondly scratching his hound's backside. If I went with them, she'd sit rammed next to him on a bench; he would occasionally feed her a crisp, and they'd nuzzle like two loved-up teenagers.

'I've got a lot on.' Someone in Hartlepool had bought one of my mosaic trivets – a hummingbird design suggested by Dippy. That was £26 in the bank, once the transaction fee and postage was taken into account.

'Aw, come on.'

'We can't leave Fred on his own.'

'Sam's upstairs, he'll be fine.'

So the three of us went to the pub, a traditional boozer called The Stray Dog, on the edge of the park I walked across on my way to 'work' most days. It was our local, so that's where we went, even though the manager Selwyn was a bloke who liked a spot of banter, but confused it with insults. You'd say he was a bit of a character, if you were being kind, but I wasn't inclined to be, since I once tried to flog him some mini-parquet-wood-tiled coasters, very classy, and he said they looked like mouldy pieces of toast.

'Whassup, you pair of twats,' he said as we entered.

'Good evening to you, too,' returned Angus amiably, as we settled at the bar. 'I'll have a pint of IPA. And a white wine for the lady, please.'

'Don't see no ladies round here, heh-heh!'

'Very funny, are you here all week?'

'White wine for the dog then, but what'll the wife have?'

I pointed to Mabel. 'I'll have what she's having.'

'She looks like she's had a bit too much, truth be told.'

The best way to deal with Selwyn was to ignore him as he drained his pool of piss-poor takedowns and eventually subsided into comparative silence. But Angus was offended by Selwyn suggesting his dog was fat, because 'truth be told', she *was* on the chubby side. Muttering to himself, he swept our drinks off to the furthest table, The Mabster waddling after him.

'Bloody cheek,' he grumbled, as I ripped open the bag of crisps I'd bought and dumped it on the table. 'You've got a lovely figure,' he assured Mabel, as she craned her neck to snuffle at the salt & vinegar. 'So, what were you really doing, hunched over your laptop looking all furtive?'

I started guiltily, a crisp between my finger and thumb. 'Nothing. Well, I'm supposed to be organizing another get-together for the Harlots.' His eyes widened. 'My school hockey team? The weekend in Windermere?'

'But you hated that. You made me call you to get out of it.'

'I know, but . . . I guess it was good to see them again. Min is nice; I've actually seen her a couple of times since.' There was no way I was mentioning Izzy. Angus thought the whole thing was mad and was obviously dead against my search, since he scuppered the whole Jackson DeLantro lead. So he'd just have to believe I'd found a sudden enthusiasm for socializing with my teammates, however unlikely that seemed.

'Who's Min?'

'You remember her, she was at our wedding. She signed alongside Izzy's speech.' Dammit, I'd mentioned her. I couldn't help it; it was a compulsion.

'Oh yeah, the girl with the fringe. She taught me some rude words.'

I grinned. 'That's Min.' She was an expressive curser, but also inventive. Some BSL swearing was pretty obvious, observable by teachers, so Min got sneaky, teaching us all to use appalling (sign) language without getting caught. She would also make the gestures with a completely straight face, so Mr Sullivan would never suspect what he was being called, or told to do. Recalling one of her choice phrases, I signed in Selwyn's direction, smiling affably, as Angus sniggered. But then, as my gaze wandered, it snagged on a man turning from the bar with a pint in his hand. Something about him, glasses slipping down his nose, the hunch of his shoulders, bony knuckles clutching the glass, something familiar; where had I seen him before . . .?

'Richard Spencer!'

'Who?'

Leaving my husband and his first love at their table, I rushed over to Izzy's first love, my hands outstretched, causing him to back away, alarmed by my eagerness. In his and my haste, his pint sloshed over the side of the glass and onto his shirt – I tried to grab it to steady it but accidentally upended it all over him, so we spent the first few minutes of our reunion exclaiming and apologizing, grabbing napkins and dabbing. Unlike her mother, Izzy's school boyfriend looked older than his years, a little battered and bruised, though maybe he'd just been collared by Selwyn – everyone came out of those encounters slightly harried. He had a shambling professor air, like Giles in *Buffy the Vampire Slayer*, only weedier.

'Hi, I don't know if you remember me? Gwen? Gwen Mortimer. We were at Harpur High together. I was . . . friends with Izzy.'

Richard Spencer looked at me strangely, still mopping his shirt. 'Yes, I remember you,' he said eventually.

'Long time no see.' I was manic, breathless, far too keen, but it felt like providence. I wanted to find Izzy, and here was her ex – another sign, like the plate in Jumble's. It was meant to be.

'Well, actually no.'

'What?' Wrapped up in my own enthusiasm, I waved to Selwyn, preparing to buy Richard another drink, and use the opportunity to ply him with questions. Maybe he knew something, maybe she'd been in touch, maybe they'd reconnected, for old times' sake. Like the cigarettes Rachel bought to the Lake District cottage – I didn't ever smoke, but had a puff out of fondness. Maybe Richard was Izzy's Marlboro.

'It isn't long time no see.'

Completely distracted, I stared at him blankly. 'Sorry, what do you mean?'

'We saw each other quite recently.'

'What?'

Richard put down the damp napkin, still regarding me with an odd light in his eye. 'In Waitrose, earlier this year. You were pushing a trolley, but the wheels veered and bashed into me.'

'What?'

'Don't you remember?'

A Waitrose regular, I went either to stock up on food or just to browse posh condiments, idly fingering various harissa pastes, or drooling over fig jam. A trolley would suggest I was actually doing some shopping, which meant I would have been somewhere between mildly irritated and mad with rage. Definitely not relaxed and ready to chat. And then I *did* remember . . . a rogue wheel, pushed too quickly, crashing into a random man, him apologizing, though it was my fault, and then him saying something like 'Oh, it's you! Hello.' He obviously felt he knew me, and although I didn't recognize him at the time, of course I pretended I did for the sake of politeness. In fact, now I vaguely recalled saying 'Fancy seeing you here!' which felt innocuous enough to be safe. It was Richard Spencer all along. Maybe I knew it, on some level. Or maybe the realization had been dripping in, bit by bit, ever since, like the beer seeping down his trousers.

'Of course! I'm so sorry, I hope I didn't cause any lasting damage.' I found myself surveying his legs, as if he'd be in a cast or a splint or something, thanks to my cack-handedness. But instead, thanks to my cack-handedness, he looked like he'd wet himself. Selwyn was right; I *was* a twat.

'What'll you two wankers be having then?'

The publican's genial tone cut through our awkward silence. I gestured to Richard's soaking clothes. 'Can I buy you a drink? Please?'

Selwyn laughed heartily. 'You know we've got urinals through there?'

Richard looked down at himself, wincing. 'I'd better go home.'

'No! No, please, stay. I feel so bad. Let me buy you a beer.' I hadn't had a chance to ask him about Izzy.

Seeing my pleading expression, he relented, pointing to one of the handpull signs, and after tolerating another of Selwyn's laboured putdowns, I delivered a fresh glass, managing not to spill it. Pulling up a stool, I sat next to Richard Spencer. Dickie. Spenbo. Try-Hard. Rich-Richie. Just some of the many nicknames he endured in school. Some of the boys called him Ant because his parents sold antiques. Kids could be cruel, but they could also be astonishingly basic. I tried to remember what Izzy had seen in him. She said he was clever and . . . what was the phrase she used? *Hidden depths.* 'He gets it,' she'd said. He wasn't as basic as his nicknames. And Izzy was anything but basic. She needed layers.

'So, how've you been?'

Richard raised his eyebrows. 'Since Waitrose? Or since school?'

'Er, both, I guess.'

He sighed, like he was indulging me. 'Fine? In the last few months, I've bought a new house, which I can almost afford if the interest rates don't go any higher. In the last few decades, I got married, divorced, went teetotal, started drinking again, got a cat, and changed careers. How about you?'

'Oh, you know, this and that.' I couldn't be bothered any more. 'Do you ever see Izzy?'

He gave me a wry smile, pushing his glasses up his nose. 'Do you?'

Cards on the table. 'No, not really. I was wondering how she was.'

'Dump you too, did she?'

I sat up, affronted. 'It wasn't like that. We just drifted apart.'

'What makes you think *I* would know how she is?'

I shrugged. 'It just seemed like fate. That I was thinking about her and . . . there you were.'

Richard sipped his pint. 'So, you think, having distanced herself from all her friends, Izzy would single me out for special attention? A boy she went out with at school? I don't flatter myself that I'm that significant a figure in her life.'

'Oh, well, I'm sure she . . . er, she . . . liked you very— Hang on – "distanced herself from all her friends"? Why do you say that?'

He raised his eyebrows. 'I was under the impression there were quite a few of you in the Ghosted Club?'

'How do you know?'

'Because in the last few months I've had several approaches from people asking if I know where she is.'

Holly, arranging the reunion weekend. But who else? '*Several* approaches?'

'Members of the hockey team? I can't remember their names.'

Everyone having a go. I slumped at the table. 'No one knows where she is.'

'She always was a dark horse.'

'*Was* she?'

Richard cupped his glass meditatively. 'In a couple, one person is always keener than the other. That was me, of course. So, she would always have seemed more remote, I suppose. But she was very . . . self-contained.'

'She's not dead.'

'I apologize. I'm sure she's still very self-contained.'

'Yes, she's contained herself so well that none of us can find her.'

'Best of luck in your quest, then. Maybe one day you'll run into her with your shopping trolley.'

'I'm really sorry about that.'

'Don't worry about it.'

'Are you still in the antiques business? Your parents' place in Bakewell?'

He shook his head. 'These days I'm a cloud architect.'

'Wow.' I had no idea what that was, but if he couldn't sell me some old crockery then it didn't seem that crucial to find out. 'Well, it was nice to see you again.'

'Likewise.'

I shambled back to Angus, who was still necking with Mabel. 'Get a room, for God's sake.'

He looked up, his cheek glossy with doggy saliva. 'What was I supposed to do, with you over there chatting up that bloke? Who is he?'

'Richard Spencer.'

'Who?'

'Schoolfriend.'

115

'Should I be worried that you're going to start up an affair with an old flame?'

'He's not my old flame, he's Izzy's.' There I went again, saying her name.

'Oh, aye?' Angus glanced at Richard appraisingly. 'Bit spoddy for her, isn't he?'

'They went out nearly forty years ago, so I don't think it's relevant.'

'And yet there you were pumping him for info like Selwyn at the handpulls.'

'I *wasn't.*'

'Were.'

'I was just catching up with an old friend.' My face was hot like an old flame, the desperation to not look desperate consuming me. When Angus and I met, I downplayed my relationship with him to Izzy, not wanting her to feel like a third wheel. And I sometimes used to soft-pedal my friendship with her to Angus, not wanting him to feel left out either. I would put my feelings for one on mute when I was with the other. Why did I do that? Because I wanted them each to feel they were the special one.

If Angus realized how set I was on this search, then maybe he would feel that we had fizzled out. And it wasn't that at all.

Angus tenderly pulled one of Mabel's ears. 'I know Izzy's not dead,' he said. 'But maybe it would be better if you pretended she was.'

'That's a horrible thing to say.' I glared at him. 'And why would I want to do that, anyway?'

Mabel's eyes were closed as she enjoyed the caress, and Angus focused on her, not looking at me. 'Because it might be easier.'

'Easier than what?'

His gaze slid to mine, and I immediately started scrutinizing my empty glass. 'Easier than knowing why she went,' he said gently.

Like Dippy, he seemed to assume that it was somehow my fault. And perhaps he was right. I knocked back the last of my wine. It was time to go home. 'Come on, the boys will want their dinner.'

We trooped out, heads down to avoid attracting Selwyn's attention. But at the door, I felt a hand on my shoulder. Angus carried on, pulled by the dog.

'There is something.' Richard was standing there, still drenched. 'It was a long time ago.'

I faced him. 'I haven't seen Izzy in fifteen years. That's a long time.'

He hesitated. 'Yes. That long.'

'What?'

Richard took a deep breath. 'I saw Izzy, about fifteen years ago. She came to visit me. I was living in Derby then. She somehow got hold of my email address, and asked if we could meet.'

'What, just out of the blue?'

'Yes. It was weird, because I assumed she must have something important to say to me, and of course got stupidly excited, thinking she wanted to get back together.

Mad, because I was engaged at the time, but, you know, the male ego. But then we met in a café for a cup of tea, and just . . . chatted. Small talk, nothing much. It was pretty strange. Then she finished her tea, got up and left.'

I screwed up my face. 'That was it?'

He shook his head. 'Not quite. She was standing there, about to go, and she looked at me, hard, and said "It's not you, then."'

'What?'

'That's what she said.'

'"*It's not you, then.*" What does that mean?'

'I have no idea. Probably nothing. I don't really know why I'm mentioning it. I haven't told anyone else.'

'Why'd you tell me?'

He looked at me sideways, doing the glasses-up-the-nose thing. 'Because you seem desperate. And I . . . am familiar with that feeling.'

'Right.' The only person he'd told. Because I was desperate. A winner and a loser, at the same time.

'It's probably nothing.'

'No, it's interesting.' Interesting, and total baffling. But at the same time, it stirred a memory in me – *Dickie! Why didn't you say so?* – the faintest echo, a recollection so vague and ephemeral that it vanished before I could grasp it.

'See what I mean?' said Richard. 'Dark horse.'

Yes, maybe she was, I thought, turning to join Angus on the street outside. But at least she was still a horse, for now.

15

Just when I was starting to think Dave/JD/Jackson had let me down, I got a reply from him:

Stop emailing me fucking theses about your friend. I just need bullet points. No, in fact, I'll give <u>you</u> bullet points:

- Find the exes
- Contact former colleagues – Derbyshire Times, Milieu, etc. You need co-workers – companies won't give out info
- Go back to the hockey team – one of them knows something, even if they don't know they know
- Edinburgh? Rome?

What's her date of birth? I'll get Garth to do some additional digging. Do you have a recent photo?

Stay safe, JD

Stay safe? Who did he think I was, Litvinenko? His tone was extremely abrasive. Also, *Rome*? Like I was just going to get on a plane and start wandering round Piazza

Navona holding a mugshot of Izzy? Who was this Garth? Probably lived in a bunker with his mummified mother. These podcast people were weird, and I included my own husband in that assessment.

Looking at JD's list again, I decided there were a few things on it I'd either already done or intended to do. I'd found one of her exes, and planned on looking for the others. I was going to revisit Izzy's old haunts in Manchester when I met up with the Harlots for dinner. Contacting her former colleagues was a good idea, if only I could remember any of them.

Racking my brains, I tried to think if she'd ever mentioned friends at *Milieu*, or *Scoop*, the magazine she'd worked for when she moved back up north. The only person I could recall was a nosy editor she'd moaned about – what was she called? Something weird and American . . . . Dammit, I couldn't remember. Maybe I had a copy of the magazine somewhere? I raced up to our old study, which, since Angus had moved to his garden studio, had become a – well, 'bin' would be the best way to put it. Liam's stuff in boxes, random gadgets Angus got sent by companies hoping for a mention on his show, stacks of crockery I might one day get round to smashing, plus various odds and ends I'd dumped there whenever I was 'tidying' the rest of the house. It was a disaster zone, frankly, but it was also very useful, because since Angus and I were both lazy hoarders, there was loads of shit in there that anyone more scrupulous would have thrown away. Which meant it was likely there would be some old copies of Izzy's magazine that I'd treasured like a proud loyal friend.

After an hour of searching, the room looked even worse and I hadn't found a single copy of *Scoop*. I was sweaty, sweary, and had done my back in moving one of Angus's bastard monitors. Moreover, I'd accidentally set off a robot hoover and couldn't get it to stop, so it was bashing round knocking things over and making a right racket. I decided that once I'd found Izzy, I was going to tackle this room once and for all, turning it into . . . I didn't know what, but it would be something stripped back and exclusively feminine. All this goddamn clutter was driving me demented – I longed for an entirely empty space, clean and fragrant, devoid of junk.

Years ago, Angus and I went to New York for a few days, and stayed in a hotel so trendy that our room had nothing in it. At least, it looked that way because everything was hidden, tucked behind screens and in secret cabinets, to give the illusion of minimalism. Even the bed had to be pulled out of the wall. In fact, it was all hidden away so effectively that it took us over an hour to find the minibar. In our shit-littered bin room, I sank onto an old armchair covered in folded duvet covers to enjoy the fond memory. That was a great trip. We had drinks in a rooftop bar on Times Square, and went to a posh restaurant Izzy recommended – again, I couldn't remember what it was called – it was possibly just a number – but it was on Madison Avenue and was *so* glamoro—

MADISON. That was the name of the editor! Madison James. I'd even met her, at one of Izzy's work parties in Chinatown – the sharpest blonde bob, the longest legs, the reddest lipstick on her teeth. I dug into a box of Liam's old school shirts to dig out my phone and google her. She came up immediately, now working on the editorial team at the *Manchester Evening News*. There was a picture of her, still with that razored crop and hard stare. She was like a Mancunian Anna Wintour.

Her email address was right there on the paper's website, so I sent her a message straight away:

Hi,

Sorry to bother you – I'm an old friend of Isabella Harris, who I think you used to work with? I'm trying to get in touch with her about a story, and wondered if you had any contact details?

Best wishes,
Gwen Mortimer

Feeling sated and zen, I kicked the still-zooming hoover and left the mess behind to go downstairs and make myself a well-deserved cup of tea. As the kettle boiled, I did a few more tiles – the wall was coming along nicely, as neat as Madison's bob. When it was finished, I might prise them all off and start again. I took my cuppa into the living room and sank onto a blissfully empty sofa. Maybe I'd have a relaxing read. Jacob had given me an interiors magazine his woodwork had been featured in – perhaps I could find a chic new kitchen design, give everything a bit of a spruce-up, once the wall was finished.

It was right there in the magazine rack, because the rack was a mini version of the bin room: full of random ancient newspapers, supplements, periodicals, leaflets, and even the odd receipt. This tatty old wicker basket had survived two house moves with us, untouched. And inside, hidden between *Good Housekeeping* and *Classic Military Vehicle* magazine, reposed a grubby, battered copy of *Scoop*.

It was the first edition Izzy appeared in, as their new columnist. On page 56, there was her photo – she had had it taken specially, by a professional photographer; a proper headshot. We spent ages poring over the thumbnails, working out which was the best one, also working our way down a bottle of rosé. By the time we'd finished I was wheezing with laughter, Izzy squinting terribly as she did impressions of herself posing. 'They're all gross!' she'd shrieked, her wine sloshing around in her glass as she despaired. 'I am the Elephant Woman!' Which, of course, was so far from the truth that it made me laugh even harder. She looked beautiful in all the photos, but especially the one she eventually chose, dark hair brushed to the side, tumbling over one shoulder, a mischievous side-eye to camera. Her cheekbones were better than mine. Her legs were almost as long as Madison's.

Legs! Eleven! *That* was the name of the restaurant in New York Izzy had recommended.

After snapping the photo on my phone, I forwarded it to JD, then sipped my tea contentedly. I was ON FIRE.

16

The Chop House That's a Cut Above

Scoop*'s new columnist Isabella Harris is
overwhelmed by Altrincham's latest meaterie*

22 October 2004

I had the beginnings of a migraine when I arrived at
Brisket, a tingling at my left temple that heralded
a bad night. Usually these develop into full-blown
attacks within hours, leaving me clammy and
comatose in a darkened room. But, almost as soon as I
entered Brisket's rustic, yet elegant dining room, and
was presented with a glass of plummy Malbec, my
headache began to recede. There's something about a
fine slab of meat that really hits the spot, and I'd go
so far as to say that this superior steak house brings
medicinal qualities to its menu.

My date for the evening was my *buona amica*
Ms Mortimer, who often accompanies me on these
culinary outings, because I appreciate her waspish

take on the food and surroundings. Ms Mortimer isn't easily impressed, but even she had to admit that Brisket's blend of homely charm and outer-city style is a winning combination.

We began with Brisket's take on small plates – a shared platter of mini crab cakes drenched in a piquant red pepper aioli, paired with 'cocktail chops', which my companion observed were more akin to lamb lollies. Well, they were certainly melt-in-the-mouth. Our second glass of red went down as easily as the first, and by the time the main course arrived we were meat-giddy and ready to tuck into something juicy.

I went for the famous rib-eye, served with parsley butter, balsamic beef tomato and Brisket's signature 'onion hoagie', the sweetest, crunchiest wedge of caramelized onions. The steak was tender and flushed pink – the lingering prickles of my migraine stood no chance against the injection of succulent protein.

Contrarian that she is, Ms Mortimer plumped for the grilled European sea bass, saying that since I was doing the turf, she would surf. Her dish was equally well-presented, the beautifully moist and flaky branzino nestling on a fluffy bed of pea puree dotted with chargrilled Mediterranean vegetables. She deigned to deem it 'a decent fish dinner,' which was high praise indeed. Both meals were washed down with another glass of the really excellent fruity red – was it the

Malbec we started with, or something else? My notes became intermittent at this point . . .

Desserts finished us off entirely. My unashamedly retro banoffee pie came laden with 'burnt' banana crisps, drizzled with a punchily salty toffee sauce and scattered with chocolate curls – possibly overkill, but I was overcome, and couldn't manage anything more than a moan of greed. My companion's velvety dulce de leche cheesecake left her winded and unable to speak. After reviving herself with another glass of the Malbec/Merlot/Whatever, she managed to suggest that this particular pudding should be outlawed. We were going to try the cheese course but thought it might precipitate a trip to A&E, so instead we both had a glass of ripe, full-bodied house port, then asked our very helpful waiter to roll us into a taxi.

If I were to offer a tiny criticism, I would note that the headache I suffered the following morning surely eclipsed the migraine that was brewing the night before, and can only attribute it to the . . . er, richness of the food. Ms Mortimer also suffered from an unfortunate bout of dyspepsia. Maybe an excess of amino acid? Who knows? Perhaps I should go back. After all, like I said, Brisket's menu has medicinal qualities . . .

Brisket, Market Street, Altrincham
£££

From: Gwendolyn Mortimer <GMortimer@haremail.com>
Sent: 2 May 2024 19.17
To: JDLantro@spy.com
Subject: Re: my friend

JD,

DOB 24/09/69

GM

PS – You might find the article attached useful. Not MY thesis – Isabella's.

From: Madison James <Mad_James@man-news.co.uk>
Sent: 2 May 2024 22.31
To: Gwendolyn Mortimer <GMortimer@haremail.com>
Subject: Re: Isabella Harris

Gwen,

We should probably meet. Can you come to the offices? Or better still, lunch?

Madison

17

On Sunday evening, when Liam phoned, I was making stew and stewing. Why would Madison James want to meet me? If she knew where Izzy was, why couldn't she just tell me? If she didn't know, why couldn't she just say so? What was with this peremptory summons?

'We lost this morning. Suraj broke his arm.'

'That's great.'

'He's in a cast.'

'Cool.'

'Well, it's not. He's out for the season.'

'Do you want to talk to your father?' I beckoned Angus over and he took the phone off me, pointing to the oven. Shit. Dumping the scorched remains on the counter, I decided we could have fish & chips instead. In fact, Fred could make himself useful and get them, while I retreated to the sofa to scroll the Harpur Harlots' WhatsApp messages that were coming through, with their various half-arsed, far-fetched theories on Izzy's whereabouts.

No replies from Holly or Gracie, but Danielle had resurfaced from New York, with her jogging-in-Central-Park theory – however, she'd only seen her from a distance, 'five or six years ago'. Ditto Rachel, who swore she'd spotted Izzy dancing on a beach at a party in Portinatx, but didn't actually approach her or contact her in any way because 'I was off my tits at the time.' Again, years ago. Erica said she'd heard Izzy had moved to Brighton, but couldn't provide any further information or sources. Hadn't she said Inverness before? Useless! Bhavini said she'd seen someone who looked like Izzy outside Thames House but she was wearing a scarf and sunglasses and 'maybe it wasn't her, after all'. Amanda said she'd emigrated blah blah, Chloe said her sister's friend bumped into her in a rehab clinic in Somerset and that Izzy said she had an addiction to painkillers caused by a rotator cuff injury which she got playing tennis with Tim Henman. Chloe hadn't changed at all since school, when she used to claim she was an extra in the film *Labyrinth* and had snogged David Bowie.

I hadn't bothered messaging Min because we'd already talked about it. Her suggestion, that Isabella had simply changed her name and wasn't interested in seeing anyone, was probably the most likely scenario. The most disappointing, as well. I wanted to believe our friendship meant more than that – that it was worth more than one half walking away indifferently, for no particular reason. Although I was partly to blame for letting things slide, I remembered the sense of loss that lingered for months after she disappeared. Her silence was loud, faintly accusing.

I felt it, even though I had no idea why she'd gone. Had *she* missed *me*, during that time? Had she yearned for idle phone chats, gossipy brunches, boozy evenings where the laughter echoed long after? Did she have a new companion for her impulsive sign-up activities? Who was her plus-one at restaurant openings now? Did she regret casting me off? Or did she think she was well rid?

I imagined finding her, confronting her – maybe we'd have a big row, get it all out. Who knew what the argument would be about; the prospect was strangely energizing. There would be revelations galore, but it would all end in happy tears, and a trip to the pub to reminisce. We'd never really argued in all the time we'd known each other. Well, maybe once. When she was approaching thirty, a few of us got together to organize a surprise birthday party for her – in fact, it was a Harlots thing, probably initiated by Holly, in one of her bullish social bouts. Izzy somehow got wind of it and had a go at me even though I had very little involvement. It wasn't a row as such – more of a *tense conversation*. She said 'I don't appreciate you going behind my back like that; I would have liked some control over the guest list', which was pretty unreasonable given that everyone meant well – it was just a party; who cared who came? Anyway, the plans were shelved and afterwards she apologized, saying she'd overreacted: 'I just don't like the idea of being the centre of attention.' Which was ironic, because Izzy tended to be the centre of attention wherever she was – she was just compelling that way. Even in that old hockey team photo of us all, your eyes were drawn to her, and it wasn't just about being beautiful or tall, though that helped. It was *je ne sais quoi*. Which was an aptly oblique phrase for Izzy – you could never pin her down. *Like she had a secret life*, Min said. *A dark horse*, Richard said. *Isabella values her privacy*, her parents said.

What was she hiding, back then? And where was she hiding, now?

'Are you coming?'

I blinked up at Angus, who was looming over me with a tea towel over his shoulder, looking cross.

'Fred's back. Get a move on, or it'll get cold.'

We ate straight from the paper at the kitchen table, Mabel sitting with her chin on Angus's lap, waiting for morsels of batter to come her way. Fred was badgering his father for V-Bucks – Angus often complained that instead of giving him pocket money he should just set up a standing order to *Fortnite*. Sam was reading a copy of *Empire*, turning the pages with greasy fingers. He'd taught himself Final Cut Pro, fancied himself as a budding Christopher Nolan, which I figured was better than watching porn, though he probably did that too. Given his predilection for art-house cinema, perhaps he watched classy erotica, with nice lighting and an elegant narrative? *Subtitled* porn? It was the best I could hope for. Dippy watched a lot of ethical porn and was always banging on about it. Maybe I should recommend it to Sam. No, that wouldn't work.

Maybe I should get Dippy to – *no*. It was another thing I would have talked to Izzy about. She would have hooted with laughter, then made a sensible suggestion. Probably something like 'I think it's best if you stay out of anything involving your son and porn.'

'Not great news about Suraj.'

'Hmmm?' I sucked vinegar off my thumb, as Mabel drooled.

'His arm.'

'What?'

Angus shook his head disapprovingly. 'Liam *knew* you weren't listening. What's up with you?'

I couldn't say, because it would mean mentioning porn, or Izzy, and both were undesirable subjects at the dinner table. 'I was thinking of booking a trip to Edinburgh.'

'For the festival? Great idea. I might do a live recording of *Graveyard*. Get some Pleasance guys in.'

And be surrounded by comics and nerdy technophiles, eager to talk about Oculus Quest? No thanks. 'It's so busy then. I thought earlier. Maybe next week.'

'That's a bit sudden.'

'I'm trying to inject some spontaneity into my life. Anyway, it's Edinburgh, not Ulaanbaatar.'

'But there'll be no shows on.'

'Plenty of other stuff to do. And you don't have to come. You can't leave Mabel, anyway.'

Angus stared at me, his eyes narrowing. 'Why are you so eager to go to Edinburgh on your own?'

Because your podcast friend, who you lied about, suggested it. 'Just fancied a trip. You're always saying I should get out more.'

For years I was tied to the house, looking after three children. Sometimes it felt like a prison, and I yearned to escape, to go anywhere, do anything. In those days, just nipping to the chemist felt like a break. Going to the dentist, lying down in a chair, was a treat. My ambitions were tame, restrained, curtailed. Either by my leaking boobs, a suddenly sick child, or my inability to stay up beyond 9 p.m. When the kids got older and my time became, if not my own, then at least loaned back briefly, I found I'd lost the ability to stray. Angus went off on golf weekends, work trips. When he decided he wanted a dog, he went on a series of recces to various rescue centres around the country, to find 'The One'. Those trips stretched my patience, particularly an extended Scottish stay that felt unnecessarily leisurely, leaving me to hold the fort. He encouraged me to go off and do *my* thing, but I didn't know what my thing was any more. The most I managed was the occasional trip to an auction house or car boot sale. Even after I was made redundant, an afternoon spent browsing bric-a-brac in a market hall in Leeds was the sum total of my 'getting out more' ambition. Perhaps I should take a leaf out of Izzy's book and sign up for something. That kayaking holiday, maybe. But who was I kidding? I'd probably hate it and want to come home. It was like those people who got abducted and ended up falling for their kidnapper – I'd got attached to my jail-base and didn't want to leave.

Although I'd said it on the spur of the moment, to get Angus off my back, maybe a short sojourn to Edinburgh was just what I needed. It was a lovely city, only a train ride away. I could stay in a nice hotel, see the sights, the sea, go up Arthur's Seat. And, while I was there, casually find out if my old friend was back in her university town. Tick off another thing on JD's list.

'If you're in Edinburgh, you'll have to go and see my mother,' said Angus.

Bugger. I'd almost rather Isabella *was* dead than do that.

18

Angus's mother was, to put it mildly, extremely challenging. Or to put it less mildly, a gold-plated, X-rated, permanently aerated March Hare. The first time I met her, Angus tricked me into it. He booked a friend's holiday cottage in Berwick-upon-Tweed for a weekend minibreak, and as I was on the threshold, going in, excited about our getaway, he said, 'By the way, my mother's here.' Like it was an accident, like he hadn't deliberately booked a two-bedroom cottage and invited her. It was unforgivable, particularly given her . . . *eccentricities*, but he said later, when I drunkenly berated him: 'Best to get it done. Because if we're going to stay together, you have to get over it. And so does she.'

Morag Stewart's brand of bananas was to take *all* brands of bananas – a whole bunch – and wield them in rotation, or simultaneously. Sometimes she was jealously maternal, and accused me of stealing Angus, encouraging him to neglect his poor mother, whereas other times she became overly familiar, like we were sisters, and would start asking me about our sex life. Sometimes nothing was good enough – our house was a wreck, the dinner I'd made inedible, the kids feral, the dog disgusting. But then she went too far the other way, and praised everything so profusely that it was embarrassing and overwhelming. 'Such beauty!' she'd shrieked, when I'd once dressed up for a birthday dinner. 'I feel like a HAG compared to you, you gorgeous creature!' You never knew where you were with her. Well, you did – on a knife edge. She could go from one state to another in a day, a minute, or a second. It made for relaxing, super-fun Christmases.

Angus said she'd been unhinged by his father's death, which happened when Angus was at university. Doug had a heart attack moving sacks of potatoes in their barn, and Morag had found him, 'dead among the tatties', which sounded like a warped P.G. Wodehouse novel. But rather than call the police or whatever, she sat with the body for three days. *Seriously* fucked up. She claimed she was traumatized, and that she thought he might rise again, like Jesus, but another of her strange traits was her . . . salacious morbidity. All old people loved talking about death – my mother pretty much kept a shopping list of people in the vicinity with terminal illnesses – but with Morag you got the sense that it was a faint turn-on. She would describe friends' cancer symptoms lasciviously, recount the frisson she got as an acquaintance's coffin disappeared behind the curtain. Sometimes she talked about stroking Doug's dead body, and it was almost like she got off on it. What else did she do to it during those three days in the barn?

It was a wonder Angus had turned out so well-adjusted, but he always said he learned early on to ignore the bad stuff. It was a sign of great fortitude, I supposed, even though in everyday life it irritated the hell out of me, him being so buoyant. There I was, with two loving, supportive (though batty in their own way) parents, and I turned out a sour-faced cow, whereas Angus was relentlessly upbeat and positive. His niceness was unfair. In retrospect, though, he was right to get that initial weekend over with – he said if I hadn't been able to get through it, if I'd left (the cottage, his mother, him), then he'd have been gutted, but it was better to know straight away, before we got too serious. I once asked him: if I'd said 'It's her or me', what would he have done? He said anyone who asked that should get a disappointing answer – and that applied to her as well, were she to ask the same question. She obviously never had – maybe she wasn't *that* mad.

Also, Morag had one redeeming feature. She was really rich. And she was very generous with her money, intermittently. She contributed to the deposit for our first house (eventually), bailed us out when we were both made redundant, sent the boys bulging envelopes stuffed with inappropriate amounts of cash. It wasn't that I was waiting for her to die or anything though – she regularly told us she'd left all her money to the Scottish Widows, so she was worth more alive than dead. I originally assumed she meant some sort of charity for bereaved women in Scotland, being one of them herself, but it turned out she actually did mean the bank. Only Morag Stewart would bequeath her worldly riches to a financial institution.

Anyway, it wasn't just the money that made me want her alive, on balance – it was the fact that, despite her being nutty as a fruitcake, Angus was very fond of her. He saw her flaws – he wasn't blind to them – but he overlooked them, just batted them away. Over the years, I'd learned to do the same, by consuming a couple of stiff gin and tonics before I saw her, enough for everything to be reduced to a happy fug. Morag now lived in a huge flat in Stockbridge, from which she would sally forth to Harvey Nichols on St Andrew Square, to browse the handbags and drink cocktails in the Forth Floor Bar. I knew this, because I'd once or twice been forced to do it with her, cringing as she flirted with the waiters. No doubt, if I went to Edinburgh, that was the price I would have to pay for being there. Was it worth it, to find Izzy? If only Constanza Harris had been my mother-in-law – I would have loved to go to Harvey Nichols with *her*. Coco's flirtation with the waiters would have been the classy erotica to Morag's brash porn.

To hell with it. I booked a hotel just off Princes Street for two nights the following week, and resigned myself to my fate.

19

From: Gwendolyn Mortimer <GMortimer@haremail.com>
Sent: 6 May 2024 09:53
To: Madison James <Mad_James@man-news.co.uk>
Subject: Re: Isabella Harris

Dear Ms James,

It's good of you to get in touch. I'm very happy to meet – I'm actually in Manchester towards the end of the month for an event. But is it necessary? I don't want to take up your valuable time – perhaps we should arrange a phone call instead?

With best wishes,
Gwen

From: Madison James <Mad_James@man-news.co.uk>
Sent: 6 May 2024 11.02
To: Gwendolyn Mortimer <GMortimer@haremail.com>
Subject: Re: Isabella Harris

Gwen,

No, I think it's best if we talk in person. The situation is delicate, and besides, I'm very interested in your story.

Madison

From: Gwendolyn Mortimer <GMortimer@haremail.com>
Sent: 6 May 2024 12.14
To: Madison James <Mad_James@man-news.co.uk>
Subject: Re: Isabella Harris

Madison,

To be honest, I don't have a story. I just want to find Isabella. I'm sorry if I've messed you about.

Gwen

From: Madison James <Mad_James@man-news.co.uk>
Sent: 6 May 2024 14.37
To: Gwendolyn Mortimer <GMortimer@haremail.com>
Subject: Re: Isabella Harris

Gwen,

I don't mean a news story. I mean your story. Of what happened with Isabella. Because I have one too.

M

From: Gwendolyn Mortimer <GMortimer@haremail.com>
Sent: 6 May 2024 14.39

Isabella's Not Dead

To: Madison James <Mad_James@man-news.co.uk>
Subject: Re: Isabella Harris

Friday 24th? Lunch?

Gwen

From: Madison James <Mad_James@man-news.co.uk>
Sent: 6 May 2024 16.57
To: Gwendolyn Mortimer <GMortimer@haremail.com>
Subject: Re: Isabella Harris

1pm, Le Capri, Clarence Street

M

20

The first thing I did when I arrived in Edinburgh the following week was buy a coat. I always forgot how cold it was – how you could gaily board the train in Yorkshire in a light cardie but as soon as you got off at Waverley station you'd be shivering like a whippet. So I took myself to St James Quarter and wandered in and out of shops until I found a decent anorak to ward off the Scottish chill. The city was looking pretty, sunshine brightening the dour-brown brick of the buildings, illuminating the imposing hulk of the castle squatting on its rough-hewn volcanic plug. Even without the festival, there was a buzz about the place. Having visited Izzy regularly, not to mention spending several inebriated weeks here during various Augusts, I knew Auld Reekie fairly well and was happy to while away an hour strolling and admiring. Then I checked into my hotel and was allocated a small but perfectly comfortable room where I spent the evening ordering room service and devising a plan of attack. By breakfast the following morning, I was ready.

There were two principal destinations I needed to check out, and two individuals I needed to see. Firstly, the flat Izzy rented in Marchmont for the second and third years of her degree. Izzy loved that flat and always said she wanted to retire there. She was also good friends with her landlady, who lived in the apartment above – I wanted to see if she was still there, and if Izzy had ever been back. I couldn't remember the landlady's name, or the exact address, so couldn't look her up or contact her in advance, but I was prepared to wing it. Secondly, Izzy's favourite tutor at the university, now semi-retired – Dr Irving. He was pretty ancient, at least ninety, but was still listed on their website as a teaching fellow. I'd emailed him saying I had a question about a student he'd taught, and he'd agreed to meet me at a café near the Italian Cultural Institute that afternoon.

Finally, there was a restaurant called Cosa Bolle where Izzy used to work during term time. It was owned by a garrulous Italian family who'd taken her to their collective bosom. When she made it as a restaurant reviewer, she took great pleasure in giving them a glowing write-up, and said the cutting hung proudly in the entrance. Cosa Bolle was still in business, and I had a table booked for 8 p.m. Unfortunately, I had to meet my mother-in-law for drinks at Harvey Nicks beforehand, but figured I'd load up on gin and tonics to dull the pain. When I called her to say I was coming, the conversation was predictably erratic:

'Well, you're not staying with me! There's no room.'

Morag's flat had four bedrooms. 'Don't worry, I'm staying in a hotel.'

'How can you just land this on me with no warning?'

144

'You don't have to see me at all if you don't want to.'

'Of course I want to see you! My darling daughter-in-law, light of my life. What else has a lonely old woman like me got to do all day? I long for you all to come and stay. Why isn't Angus coming? Is something wrong? Has he left you? I did wonder.'

'No, he's just staying home to look after the boys.'

'In my day, it was the women who stayed at home. The men went to work. Your relationship is unnatural, I must say. Does he still have the hell hound?'

'Mabel? Yes, they're very much in love.'

'Filthy! You should wait until he's out and take her to the vets, have her put down. Then he will love you again.'

'I'll bear that in mind.'

So. Marchmont landlady first, then Dr Irving at the café on Nicolson Street, then Mad Morag in Harvey Nicks, then dinner at Cosa Bolle. Bed by 10, massive fry-up the following morning and back on the train by 11 a.m. Done.

It didn't work out that way.

Firstly, I couldn't find the bloody Marchmont flat. Although I didn't remember the exact address, I'd been there so many times, I thought I'd just let my feet walk me there, and muscle memory would take over. That was true to a certain extent, but once I got in the general vicinity my muscles got confused and let me down. Was it Chalmers Crescent, Mansionhouse Road, or Hatton Place? Maybe Lauder Road? They all looked the same. Surely I'd recognize it when I saw it? I'd once slept in the bath there, when all the beds were taken after a party. I remembered the crick in my neck like it was yesterday, but the exact location was a blank. Luckily, one street on, I hit the jackpot. Cumin Place; of course! Obviously, I used to pronounce it phonetically, snorting at the hilarity, whereas Izzy always insisted on pronouncing it like the spice, making me snigger even more and call her Hyacinth Bucket.

Now I was here, I found the flat easily, in a grand, double-fronted house with huge windows and a willow tree in the garden. Immediately, a memory-rush overcame me – sitting in that left-hand bay, drinking coffee, hungover to the teeth while Izzy tried to make bacon sandwiches by putting raw rashers in the toaster. Clumsily climbing this willow tree at 3 a.m., breaking a branch and clinging on for dear life, until Izzy pointed out I was about two feet off the ground. Going upstairs to ask Mrs . . . what *was* her name? . . . for flour because we'd decided to make bread, then having to go back for yeast. The bread turned out like volcanic rock but we ate it anyway because Izzy didn't have anything else other than cat food – she was feeding two wild moggies who lived in the back garden. I remembered *their* names – she called them Orion and Carina – what was the point of that? Why did my useless brain treasure that information but ruthlessly delete the useful stuff?

At the front door, I studied the various doorbells. Izzy's old flat was A, so Mrs Landlady must be B – I pressed it firmly, then immediately experienced the same worries and doubts that assuaged me when I visited Coco and

Julian. Why would she still live there, why would she even be alive, why would she be in, what was I doing here, etc.

'Hello?'

The voice on the intercom sounded too young. Not Mrs Landlady.

'Hello. My name is Gwen, and I was looking for Mrs . . . sorry, I don't know her name but she owned flat A, where my friend lived.'

'Hang on, hen, I'll buzz you up.'

Ascending the communal stairs, I was struck by the same old smells – woodfire smoke and toffee – and again wondered why my olfactory senses should be so efficient when none of the others were. At the top, on the landing, a younger woman greeted me, her hand held out. Solid-looking, hair like a bike helmet, set hard, lace-up shoes.

'Yous looking for Mam?'

'I don't know, are you . . .?'

'Susan Lavery.'

'Mrs Lavery! That's it. I'm so sorry, I couldn't remember.'

'Jane. My mother. But she's dead, I'm afraid, these fourteen years.'

'Oh, I'm sorry, I didn't know.' That was another doorway bricked up then.

'Yous knew her way back? Come in, hen!'

Given that Mrs Lavery was dead, there didn't seem to be much point in prolonging the conversation, but it would have looked rude to turn about, so I followed Susan into a flat that looked very similar to how I remembered Izzy's. Same layout, and same neutral decor, just no carousing students – only Susan, in her sensible flat shoes. My mother, with her reverence for heels, would have been appalled. I cleared my throat and prepared for pleasantries.

'Yes, but not well, I'm afraid. My friend Izzy used to live below, and I used to visit her.'

'Izzy? Not Isabella Harris?' Susan's face lifted.

I jumped. 'Yes. But . . . how do you . . .?'

Susan grabbed my arm, quite animated. Her hair remained still. 'Auntie Izzle! She used to babysit me! When I was a wee girl!'

'No!' I was astounded. This dead end had suddenly opened up. 'Really? Izzy?' She used to babysit Liam, early on, always turning up with ice cream and a book she'd got from the library. Once I left them together, reading *Phoebe and the Hot Water Bottles*, Liam's eyes round with wonder. Afterwards, he told me it was about a man who left his daughter at home alone and she nearly died in a fire. Said it was the best story he'd ever heard.

'I'm looking for Izzy,' I said to Susan. 'Trying to find out where she might be.'

Susan handed me a cup of tea. 'You lost touch, then? That's a shame.'

'Yes.' I wasn't inclined to elaborate, given that it looked like Susan hadn't encountered Izzy since she was in nappies.

'Well, I havenae seen her since I was a girl. Mind you, you're not the first to come looking for her.'

Those Harlots again, sniffing round, Holly busting a gut to get everyone together. 'Oh, did Holly Griffiths get in touch? We were trying to organize a reunion.'

Susan shook her helmet-head. 'No, I can't remember her name, but it wasn't that. This was years ago.'

'What? How many years?'

'Well, it was just before Mam died, so maybe about fifteen years?'

Fifteen years ago. When Izzy disappeared. Someone went to Mrs Lavery's house to see if she was there? That was odd.

'A woman? But you can't remember her name?'

Susan screwed up her face, trying to recall. 'Too long ago. Clara? Clover? No, it's gone. She was very nice, said she was trying to look up an old friend. Brought shortbread.'

'What did she look like? How old?' Who was this mystery friend? A woman who cared so much about Izzy's whereabouts that she'd rooted out her university landlady? A better friend than me, certainly. I'd taken fifteen years to do it, whereas she'd done it straight away.

'Again, I couldn't say. Just ordinary-looking. Nice.'

'Would you recognize her if you saw her again?'

'I don't know. Maybe.'

'Hmmm.' I gulped my tea, thinking feverishly. Who could it be? Maybe Izzy's mother, but no one would describe her as ordinary. Besides, Susan said this woman was looking for a friend. Who was she? One of the Harlots?

'Was it one of these women?' I pulled up the old photo of the hockey team on my phone and showed her the screen.

Susan squinted. 'Is that Auntie Izzle? Ach, she looks so bright!'

'Yes, that's her.'

'And yous next to her?'

'Yep. Anyone else you recognize?'

'Maybe . . . one of them?'

'Which one?' I tried not to sound impatient.

Her finger hovered over the screen. 'No . . . sorry. It could have been any of them, but I couldnae say which.'

Another dead end. Though given that this happened fifteen years ago, it scarcely mattered, in that it shed no light on where Izzy was *now*.

'Well, thank you very much for the tea.' I drained the cup, eager to get on.

'I'll give your best to Mam.'

Picking up my bag, I paused. 'I thought you said she was . . .?'

'Aye,' Susan nodded vigorously, her hair not shifting an inch. 'But I get out the cards most nights and we have a wee chat.' She pointed at the deck on the table, the sun symbol beaming out at me.

'Right. I didn't know you could use tarot that way.' Susan might look sensible but she was as loop-de-loo as my mother-in-law.

'The arcana move in mysterious ways. I could do yous a reading if you'd like?'

'Nope, thanks, I'm good. I must be off.' What a dingbat. But as I opened the door and saw her there at the table, dealing out the cards, something made me stop. 'Susan?'

She looked up, her eyes already glassy with concentration. 'Yes, hen?'

I didn't know why she called me that, when she was so much younger than me. She seemed an old soul, though, I thought, scribbling my number on a piece of paper I'd dug out of my bag.

'If Mrs Lavery . . . your mum . . . says anything about Izzy . . . you know, through the cards. Will you let me know?' I placed the paper on the table, next to the Magician, feeling like the Fool. Why was I doing this? Not sure. Maybe just to cover all bases. If there was a netherworld, and Mrs Lavery was in it, and knew where Izzy was, then I wanted to know. Even though I definitely didn't believe in all that rubbish. Tarot, Ouija; what a load of hokum.

'Aye, Gwendolyn Mortimer. You can be sure of that.'

Gwendolyn Mortimer. How did she know my full name? *Shiiiiiiit.* Properly freaked out, I rushed out the door, breathing hard, stumbling down the stairs in my haste. How did she know, how did she know, how did she know?

On the front garden path, I came to in the shade of the willow tree, still panting and shaking.

I'd written my name on the frigging piece of paper I gave her.

Seriously, Gwen, get a grip. Izzy's ghostly laughter followed me all the way out of Marchmont.

21

There were no photos of Dr Irving online so I didn't know what to expect, but there couldn't be many nonagenarian gentlemen sitting in the Busy Bean on Nicolson Street. Sure enough, I saw him as soon as I arrived, tucked in the corner reading a book that looked as old as he was. When he saw me coming towards him, he tried to rise in his seat, but it was clearly beyond him and he sank back, his hands shaking with the effort.

'No, please don't get up. I'm Gwen. Thank you so much for meeting me, Dr Irving.'

He looked far too old to be teaching. Too old to be venturing out at all, really. He was thin and frail, with a full head of very white hair and little rimless glasses perched on his nose. But the blue eyes behind them were bright and sharp.

'Not at all, I'm delighted. It's not very often that lovely young ladies ask to meet me. Call me Alaric.' The blue eyes narrowed provocatively and he gave me a cheeky little grin, revealing teeth so white and even that they must have been false. He patted the seat next to him invitingly.

Jesus, Alaric was an old rogue. Izzy never mentioned that. I sat down, putting my handbag on my lap. 'Can I get you a drink? A coffee?'

'Thank you, my dear, but no. I had a pot of tea last Tuesday and if I have anything else, I'll be pointing Percy at the porcelain for the rest of the day.'

'Ooooookay. I'll just grab something and then we can chat.'

'Grab away, dear girl.'

Queueing up for my coffee, I decided to overlook his doddery innuendo in much the same way I ignored pub landlord Selwyn's shiticisms. They did it to get a rise, but I had to rise above it. Back at the table, we appraised each other. Now I was here, it seemed highly unlikely that Izzy would have had recent dealings with such a long-in-the-tooth Lothario. Still, it was always worth following up a lead, even a frayed, lewd one.

'You're just as she described,' Dr Irving observed, tucking a leather bookmark into his tome.

'What?' I was surprised, and flattered, and disturbed. 'Izzy described me?'

'She talked about you a great deal.'

It was intoxicating. 'What did she say?'

Alaric Irving took off his glasses to polish them, scrutinizing me with those vivid blue eyes. 'She said that you were the yin to her yang.'

'Oh. That's good, right? Except . . .' I pondered.

'Yes?' He paused his polishing, looking amused.

'Yin's the black half?'

Dr Irving nodded, putting his glasses back in their case, tucking the cleaning cloth around them in a finicky way. 'Yes, the yin is the shade to the yang's light. The cloud to the sun.'

I clattered my coffee cup into its saucer. 'That's a bit unfair.' Izzy had sometimes accused me of being a Negative Nancy, mostly in a jokey way, but it still stung.

He chuckled. 'I'm sure she didn't mean it like that. More that you were opposite but interconnected forces.'

Time to get to the point. 'Well, we're not interconnected any more. That's why I wanted to meet you. We sort of fell out. I haven't seen her in a long time, and don't know where she is. So I'm trying to track down other old friends to see if anyone's had any contact, or heard anything.'

'And you came to little old *me*?' Dr Irving's wrinkled face lit up with glee. 'I had no idea I was so important. How gratifying.'

'Izzy spoke of you very fondly.' It was worth massaging the old reprobate's ego, though that was as far as I would go in massage terms.

'Ah, she was a dear girl.'

'She's not dead!' Why did everyone talk about her like she'd carked it?

Alaric sat up, affronted. 'Of course. I only used the past tense in terms of my dealings with her. I taught her more than three decades ago, and I haven't heard from her in a couple of years.'

154

'A *couple* of years? You mean, you've heard from her that recently?' I was outraged and elated. Izzy clearly preferred this liver-spotted scoundrel to me, but here was a revelation in terms of my investigation. Someone who'd had contact! I felt like Jodie Foster hearing the first alien radio signal. This was immense.

'She sent a card when my wife died. And maybe another when I moved house.'

'Do you . . . do you still have that card? Oh, I'm so sorry about your wife, but . . . did you keep the card?'

'I keep all my correspondence. I have an impeccable filing system. Would you like to see my binders?' He gave me a naughty little wink.

'Yes,' I said boldly. I wasn't sure why, but it seemed important to see the card; to see evidence of Izzy's continued existence, even if it meant I had to fend off the advances of this old roué.

Gingerly, Alaric pushed himself to his feet. 'My lodgings are just around the corner and I would be delighted to escort you.' He held out a trembling arm and, picking up my bag, I tucked my hand under his elbow.

As promised, Alaric lived a short walk along Nicolson Street, in St Patrick Square, but at his pace it took us a good fifteen minutes to get there. It was an exercise in patience for me, and just exercise for him – by the time we arrived outside the neat Georgian townhouse, he was breathless, tutting and fumbling for his keys, leaning on the iron railings of the basement for support.

I'd steeled myself for the digs of an old don, stuffed with mahogany and velvet, books piled high, grime everywhere, but his ground-floor flat was modern and minimal. Pale oak floorboards, clean lines, entirely spick and span.

Seeing my eyes wandering, he grunted. 'I moved here after Estelle died. Did a bit of a death-clean. Besides' – he couldn't resist adding – 'it's good to have somewhere elegant to, er, entertain.'

'It's a regular shag pad.'

'There's no need to be vulgar. Now, come through to my little play-den.'

He led me through to what was obviously a study, or office, though again everything seemed new and carefully organized – the desk in the corner bare except for an iMac, the same blue IKEA armchair we had at home, rows of shelves with books arranged . . . by *colour*? Highly irregular for an old-school academic. Alaric shuffled over to a white filing cabinet, and started rifling through it, propping himself up on the open drawer. By the time he'd finished, he was breathless again, but he handed me the card triumphantly.

My first piece of evidence. I received it reverently, turning it over to study the picture. It was a simple painting of a wildflower field, and inside Izzy had written:

Dear Alaric,

I am so very sorry for your loss. We are thinking of you.

Ti voglio bene,

Bell X

I looked up. 'Why Bell?'

Dr Irving tapped the card affectionately. 'It's a nickname I've had for her since university. Short for Isabella, but also Currer Bell.' He raised his bushy eyebrows as I showed him a mystified face. 'One of Charlotte Brontë's pseudonyms? Dearie me, Ms Mortimer.'

Not for the first time, I felt like a Philistine, and thought of Angus's friend Dave, calling himself Jackson DeLantro. Pseudonyms were for pseuds. I turned back to the message.

'Who is "we"?'

Alaric Irving gazed at me pityingly. 'Her husband, of course. Who else would it be?'

'Her husband?' I nearly dropped the card. 'She's married?'

Izzy's beloved tutor shook his head, sadly. 'You really *did* lose touch, didn't you?'

I turned away, thinking of that Bakewell wedding, Amanda or Chloe's, where we climbed over the wall. And mine, where Izzy made that speech – that hilarious, heartfelt, speech, signed by Min. And then the dance-off, vogueing, her face impassive as she flawlessly executed the moves. Or Holly's incredibly stylish wedding in the Cotswolds, where we were each other's plus-ones, where Izzy went to stroke a donkey in the field next to the church, and it tried to eat her hat, and later we led everyone in a conga around a field, with Bhavini playing the fiddle. Whatever happened at Izzy's wedding, I wasn't there to see it, and that made me unutterably sad. I wasn't there to make a speech, or lead a dance, or get drunk, or have my hat eaten, or do anything fun or meaningful. I'd missed her *wedding*. I'd missed so much.

I was determined not to miss any more. I wheeled back to Alaric, my expression hardening.

'How many more cards have you got?' I asked, holding out my hand.

22

Alaric had had several cards and letters from Izzy over the years, it turned out, and he reluctantly handed them over on the proviso that after I'd read them, I would send them back to him. He fussed a bit about the invasion of her privacy, but I'd developed a steely thread by that point, and persuaded him that this evidence was essential for my investigation. To be quite honest, I took advantage of a frail old man, but felt the end justified the means. He said he had no idea where Izzy lived, that she'd never told him, though he got the impression she moved around a lot. Did he think she could possibly be a spy, I asked, and he laughed so hard his false teeth nearly fell out.

'Do you think you're in a John le Carré novel?' he whimpered, wiping his eyes. 'Of course, I worked at Bletchley, during the war.'

I was briefly distracted. 'Really? On that Enigma thingy?'

He gave me a withering glance. '*No*, Ms Mortimer – I was four years old when the Second World War started. Goodness, you do have a tendency towards melodrama, don't you. I'm sure whatever is going on with Isabella, she's not a modern-day Mata Hari. Do rein in your conspiracy theories.'

I left St Patrick Square with a bundle of correspondence stuffed in my bag, feeling jubilant and only a tiny bit guilty, because Alaric Irving was a Don Juan don, and sarky bastard. My package felt like it was burning a hole in my bag – I couldn't wait to get it all out and devour it. I decided to head to the Harvey Nicks Bar early, get stuck into the letters, and my pre-mother-in-law dose of gin & tonic. Walking down the bustling Nicolson Street towards St Andrew Square, I felt very satisfied with my trip thus far. Things were progressing nicely.

Alas, when I arrived at the Forth Floor, Morag was already ensconced, perched at the bar wagging her finger roguishly at the guy behind it, who looked appalled.

'Gwennie!' she shrieked when she saw me. 'Over here!'

I really didn't like her calling me that. She'd done it ever since she'd heard my parents do it, but it was an intimacy reserved for those who'd wiped my arse as a child, and she wasn't part of that exclusive club. Still, it was better than Gwyneth, which was what she called me whenever I was out of favour. 'Forgetting' my name in order to convey her contempt was pretty effective – she'd been known to call Angus 'Hamish' on occasion, to achieve the same aim. Mabel was consistently referred to as the hell hound, or 'Martha', and the boys got random gospel names, birthday cards addressed to 'Matthew', 'Mark', 'Luke' or 'John'.

Angus's mother was tall, like him, and bony, with grey hair dyed an irregular but vibrant red, which she wore in a twenties-style bushy bob. She was always caked in make-up, applied in a slapdash manner, and dressed in lots of chiffony layers, with the overall effect presenting as a kind of chaotically messy Clara Bow. In fact, I once read one of Bow's film characters described as a 'naughty inebriated flapper', and that summed up Morag Stewart pretty well.

'Hi, Morag.' Resigned to deferring the letter-reading, I dumped my bag under the stool and sat alongside her, nodding sympathetically to the barman, who looked pale and distressed.

She pouted coquettishly. 'You know I always have to tell you to call me Mother.'

Christ alive. 'Well, I actually *have* a mother already, but thank you.'

'Ah yes, how is Birdie doing?'

'Nesta. She's fine thanks.'

'And Bruce?'

'Bill's good. Into gardening at the moment.'

'What a terrible cliché. I must say, your people are desperately middle class. Thank goodness Angus came along! You might have been stuck with some dull solicitor, or worse, a binman.'

'Thank goodness.'

'Would you like a little drinkie? I'm having a Porn Star Martini, because that's what Duncan here recommended, bad boy!' She rapped him on the knuckles with her sunglasses.

The wan Duncan stammered something along the lines of he'd done no such thing, and I ordered my G&T, giving him a consoling pat on the arm.

'What on earth are you wearing? You look dreadful.'

I fingered my newly purchased light anorak, an attractive shade of beige. 'It was cold when I arrived.'

'Warmth is not worth it for that. Burn it.'

'I will do later.'

Ordering my second G&T as soon as the first arrived, I settled in for a hellish evening. Morag was in full flow, excited to have company, roused by recent injustices. Her doctor refused to prescribe her the new weight-loss drug she'd read about because he said she didn't need to lose weight, but it wasn't *his* place to say, and it was her mental health at stake. She'd just failed her driving test for the sixth time, and when she asked what she'd done wrong, the examiner said 'Not responding appropriately to traffic lights,' but she felt traffic lights were more of a guide than a rule, and her instructor – a charming young man who obviously worked out – had never told her otherwise. I couldn't help but be impressed by this – learning to drive at the grand old age of eighty-two seemed a remarkable feat. That was the wrong thing to say, it turned out, but I'd knocked back my first gin and wasn't thinking straight. Morag hated anyone mentioning her age and thereafter I ceased to be Gwennie for the next three anecdotes.

'You're looking raggedy, Gwyneth,' she interrupted her own story to tell me, just to add salt to the name-wound.

'Why don't you get Botox? Or better still, a facelift? Angus can afford it. You could get a new bosom at the same time.'

'Maybe I will.' I was shorter than Morag but built along the same scrawny lines, like an older, uglier Anna Kendrick. It was true that in my fifties I'd started looking worn and drawn. I didn't fancy a big operation, but maybe a bit of tweaking was a good idea, like revamping the kitchen tiles. The previous summer, a wasp had stung me under one eye, and the resulting swelling had actually been quite becoming, making me wonder if I should go out and find an obliging insect to do the other side.

Morag clapped her hands. 'I can give you the name of a marvellous consultant. *I'll* pay!'

'No hurry. I've got a lot on at the moment.'

She huffed. 'That mosaic nonsense? I had a look at your Etsy site the other day, and frankly, I wouldn't have any of that stuff if *you* paid *me*.'

Frankly, that wasn't far off my business model. 'I'm actually busy trying to track down an old friend.' Duncan had passed me my second drink by that point, and the Forth Floor Bar had become deliciously fuzzy.

Morag was instantly agog. 'Who? I didn't know you had any friends.'

'An old schoolfriend called Isabella Harris.'

'The beautiful girl at your wedding?' With the true cunning of the madwoman, she was able to retain devastating details and use them as weapons. 'Why would you want to stay in touch with her? She'd put you in the shade, I'm afraid, Gwennie.'

'Because I liked her and I want to see her again.' Two drinks in, everything had become very simple. I would find Izzy. I would get Botox.

'Well, it's nice to have a project.' Morag sipped her cocktail, pensively. 'When I was but a gel, there was a young man who pestered me for a date and then dropped me when he'd had his wicked way. Years later, I was still upset about it so I tracked him down and made him pay.'

Now *I* was agog. 'What did you do?'

Morag looked coy. 'I . . . made him pay.'

'Yes, but what?'

She frowned, puzzled by the question. 'I made him pay. I made him write me out a cheque for services rendered. He'd got very rich, you see. As a film producer.'

'As a . . . who was it? Would I have heard of him?'

She looked coy again. 'I couldn't possibly say. But have you heard of . . . *Chariots of Fire*?'

'You shagged and blackmailed the producer of *Chariots of Fire*?'

'Gwyneth! Those are ugly words to use. He was more of a financial backer, and I merely suggested a judicious recompense.'

'But . . . where did you meet him?'

Morag sighed, misty-eyed. 'At Eton.'

I gaped, began to form another question, then shook my head. Morag talked such bollocks she made Chloe Coulson seem like a truth-teller, but it was nearly 8 p.m. and I had my dinner reservation. At least *my* project was benign and pure.

'I've got to go, I've got an appointment.'

Instant outrage. 'Where?'

'Cosa Bolle, on Nelson Street.'

She sniffed. 'Vile place, so loud and foreign. Why are you going there?'

'I told you, I'm trying to track down my friend. She worked there.' I slid off the bar stool, unsteadily, and picked up my bag.

'Why can't I come? Are you just leaving me alone here, at the mercy of Duncan?' Along the bar, I could see him cringing as he wiped down the counter.

'You said you had a prior engagement.'

'That was when I thought it would be boring to spend the evening with you. Now I know you're spying on your friend, I'm interested.'

'I'm not spying. In fact, if anything, *she's* the spy.'

'You see, this is far more intriguing than I thought it would be. I will come as well.' She got to her feet, beckoning Duncan imperiously. When he came over, unwillingly, she leaned over the bar and tucked a roll of notes into the waistband of his trousers. He flinched away, stammering incoherently, and she tittered, knocking back the last of her Porn Star Martini.

'There you go, you naughty man. *Hasta la vista*, baby boy!'

With that, she took my arm and together we sailed out of Harvey Nicks in search of a cab.

23

Morag and Izzy met a few times – not just at my wedding, but once when Morag was staying at our old place just outside Manchester. It was a poky three-bedroom terrace in Didsbury: we had baby Liam in the back bedroom, us in the front and a boxroom in the middle. Morag turned up unannounced one night when we were giving Liam his bath, just let herself in shouting, 'It's only me!', poured herself a glass of wine and then lounged in the doorway to the bathroom commenting on her grandchild's penis.

'It's very small,' she complained, pointing. 'I'm sure yours was never that tiny, Hamish.' Angus was out of favour for some reason, I think because he'd called her 'Mum' on the phone when she preferred 'Mummy'.

'He's a baby,' replied my husband, hauling Liam's gleaming little body out as I hovered with a towel.

'Nevertheless,' she sniffed, 'it might hold him back.'

She continued to refer to Liam's 'tiny little todger' for years after, and it might have given him a complex but he appeared to have inherited Angus's Teflon quality and always seemed remarkably sanguine about it.

Later that evening, Izzy came to pick me up as we were going out for dinner. I really didn't want to cancel as I was excited about my night out, had expressed some milk and was ready to let my hair down, new-mum-style – that is, go to Pizza Express, have a large glass of pinot grigio and moan about how Hamish slept through the night-feeds like a useless bastard. He was out of favour with me too – for the first eighteen months of Liam's life, I bitterly resented my husband for not having efficient mammary glands. By association, I was even less keen on my mother-in-law and her withered old dugs, so figured if she didn't like the idea of me going out then she could go fuck herself.

Izzy turned up at eight, by which time Liam was tucked up in his cot, and Angus was attempting to make pasta for himself and his mother. Morag was thoroughly aroused by her own disapproval, making disparaging comments about the state of the house, my skills as a homemaker, my instincts as a mother, my baby belly. I was mostly ignoring her because I was used to it and knew that, in less than half an hour, I would be sinking my white wine and enjoying a glorious bitch. But Izzy had other ideas, having observed all this for a few minutes while she waited for me to get my things together.

'You are so incredibly rude,' she said to Morag, with friendly curiosity. 'Why on earth?'

Morag was briefly silenced by Isabella's audacity. Then intrigued, because she also enjoyed novelty. 'I don't know,' she mused, one finger on her chin as she pondered. 'I suppose because it enlivens things, don't you think?'

'Sours things,' proposed Izzy.

'They know I don't mean it,' offered Morag.

'Do they, though? You say it all with such conviction.'

'What's the point in saying things with no conviction?'

'Oh, I find saying things lightly can often be more effective.'

'That's never worked for me,' said Morag firmly. But when we left, she waved cheerily, and called Isabella Isabella.

Afterwards, in Pizza Express, Isabella asked me why I never confronted Morag, why I didn't fight back, and I swilled my lovely white wine around my glass as I considered the question.

'Partly because it would upset Angus . . .' I said slowly.

'Partly . . .?'

'Also . . . I can't confront like you do.' She looked quizzical. 'Lightly. Elegantly. I'd just go all in, like a bull in a china shop. I'm afraid of overdoing it, so I . . . underdo it.'

'Ah.' Izzy sipped her wine delicately. I gulped mine. 'So you're keeping a lid on it. To prevent a huge eruption.'

'That's it.'

'But it's got to come out somewhere.'

'I'll probably take it out on Angus at some point.'

'Hamish, you mean?' Izzy grinned.

'You managed her perfectly. Maybe she'll adopt you as her daughter-in-law.'

'Oh, I actually rather liked her. It's much easier when it's all out in the open. When the lid is off.'

'What do you mean?'

Izzy looked thoughtful. Or maybe troubled. I was halfway down my wine by then and everything was already a bit blurry. 'She says it all but she doesn't really mean it. Sometimes people don't say it but you know it's there, under the surface. That's much worse.'

I still didn't know what she meant, or who. Did she mean me? Bottling it and bottling it up? It didn't feel that way though – it felt like she was thinking about something else. Some*one* else. But then our pizza arrived and I needed to soak up the booze, so the moment passed.

The deeper I got into this search, the more I was remembering, like sobering up after a big night out. What else would filter through as I got nearer the mark? Part of me wasn't sure I wanted to know. But the other part pushed on regardless.

* * *

In the cab to Cosa Bolle, Morag got out a red lipstick and haphazardly applied it. 'What do you hope to achieve from this evening?'

I gazed at the vibrant, bustling throng outside. People getting together, chatting, laughing, drinking, sharing, doing. Maybe one day Izzy and I would be amongst them again.

'A clue,' I said, thinking of the letters, still unread in my bag. Another shard, to add to the existing fragments, and assemble into a picture that would tell me where she was.

'Like Poirot.' Morag got out a compact and regarded herself with satisfaction.

'It's not a murder case.'

'Oh, but it is.' Morag put her mirror away. 'It's the death of a friendship. We're investigating who killed it. You, or her.'

I was silent, because I couldn't decide if it was the most profound thing she'd ever said, or the most ludicrous.

'My money's on you,' said Morag.

'Well, it's *my* investigation,' I said. 'You're just along for the ride.'

24

Cosa Bolle was a restaurant in the mould of Coco Harris's living room. Established in the sixties, they clearly felt they'd got everything right first time, and if it wasn't broke, there was no point fixing it. So there was a step-back-in-time quality to the place: the green-and-white striped canopy that fringed the exterior, the tile-effect linoleum floors, battered Bentwood chairs and tables covered with red paper cloths. The walls were dark panelled oak, hung with photos of famous people who'd dined there: Sean Connery, Andy Murray, Billy Connolly, Robbie Coltrane, Nicola Sturgeon, Tilda Swinton, Emma Thompson, Mhairi Black. And then, as I moved along the display, there she was. A shot of Isabella Harris, leaning against the bar, holding a glass aloft and smiling at someone off camera. Next to it was a framed copy of her review, the review that called Cosa Bolle 'the best restaurant in Edinburgh by a Royal Mile'.

The photo gave me a shock, because I hadn't seen it before, and when I looked more closely, I couldn't be sure if in fact it had been taken after she'd 'disappeared'. Her hair looked different; lighter, shorter. And . . . yes, there was a ring on her engagement finger! That *bitch*, swanning off to get married without me. When I finally caught up with her, I'd give her a piece of my mind.

Next to me, Morag surveyed the space with unbridled disdain. Speakers were blaring out 'That's Amore', and the atmosphere was frenetic, staff bustling round, diners gabbling and gesticulating. We needed a drink, pronto.

I waved to a waitress, who came hurrying over, tucking a notepad into her apron. '*Buona sera*, you have a booking?'

'Yes, Gwen Mortimer.' I'd reserved a table for one, but assumed an extra setting wouldn't be a problem. Sure enough, the waitress gave Morag only a passing glance before leading us to a booth in the corner. She handed us laminated menus and dashed off to attend to a rowdy party nearby. Morag held the plastic-covered card between finger and thumb, heavily powdered nose wrinkling.

'It's all so basic,' she complained. 'They'll bring bread in a basket and individually wrapped butter.'

'What's wrong with that?' After those G&Ts, my head was swimming and my tummy rumbling. A basic injection of carbs was just what I needed. The waitress came back and I ordered a carafe of red, ignoring Morag's grumbling.

'There's an Ivy in the New Town, we could have got a table. I saw David Tennant there the other day; he's terribly dishy.'

'No shortage of celebs who come here, according to those walls.'

'But the Ivy's menu is more extensive than . . . this.' She shook the card, shuddering.

'We're here for research, it doesn't matter what we eat. Anyway, I think it looks very nice.'

There were only three options on the main course menu: meat, fish, vegetarian. Literally that – no dishes specified. Then there was a pasta menu that was exactly the same: meat, fish, vegetarian. And a pizza menu that copied the format. I liked its simplicity, limiting my choice so that I wasn't spoiled for it. The waitress brought our drinks, and took our food order briskly. I went for main meat, and Morag, looking pained, plumped for pasta fish.

The wine was good, rich and fruity, though Izzy would probably have had better adjectives. As a student, when she waitressed here, she used to take home the dregs at the end of her shift. I remember drinking from three separate bottles in her overgrown back garden, while the cats, Orion and Carina, wove around our legs, miaowing. It was an extraordinarily vivid memory – I could actually hear the cats' cries in my ears, a feline tinnitus that pierced through the babble of the other diners. Taking a hefty belt of the (full-bodied? Aromatic?) wine, I told myself to get a grip, to focus. A waiter passed, dropping a basket of bread on the table, plus butter pats, as predicted by Morag, and she shook her head sorrowfully. However, a handsome man then began to wander around playing the guitar, and that cheered her up no end. She started chewing seductively and fluttering her eyelashes at him. Unlike Duncan the barman, he fluttered right back.

With Morag occupied, I was free to make my plans. Ripping up chunks of bread and slathering them in butter, I knocked back my red and scoured the room looking for a manager. I needed someone who'd been around forever, who was likely to remember Izzy, the photo and the circumstances of its taking. But the waiting staff all looked really young – they were probably doing what Izzy did, supporting their studies.

'Signora. *Pollo in potacchio.*' A waiter appeared, carefully lowering a steaming loaded plate. 'And signora. *Pasta alla chitarra* with fresh mackerel ragù.'

It smelled delicious. Even Morag was diverted from eye-shagging the guitarist. I found myself trying to describe the food as Izzy would have done – luscious tender morsels of chicken drenched in tomato, with hints of rosemary and garlic. Crisp roast potatoes snowflaked with sea salt. Washed down with that unctuous red wine. Was 'unctuous' a word? What did it mean? Maybe not what I thought it meant. Anyway, it was great – in fact, we'd finished the carafe and urgently needed another. I picked up the empty vessel and waggled it at that sweet, hard-working waitress, who nodded at me and marched off.

Morag was doing one of her monologues again. Hamish never called her; he was an ungrateful swine. The flat needed redecorating and she couldn't find any workmen who weren't crooks, eager to take advantage of a poor defenceless woman. Her friend Fiona had recently had a novel published – Morag had read the first thirty pages and was forced to throw it out the window. She, Morag, could write a much better book and would do so when a publisher was obliging enough to get in touch and offer her a contract. But they were all charlatans, just like the builders. Her friend Sophia's husband Otto was dying in a hospice and had banned her, Morag, from visiting, even though she knew she would be a great comfort to him. It was so selfish of her, and Morag was thinking of sneaking in during visiting hours when she knew Sophia would be at her Pilates class. She planned on wearing a blonde wig so the nurses would think she was Otto's wife. She longed to stroke his hand as he died.

It was remarkable that, despite her constant harping, Morag was still able to hoover up all that pasta, and help me polish off our second carafe.

'Anyway,' she said, when she'd finished her dish and exhausted her litany of complaints and morbid sexual fantasies. 'I thought you were here to investigate? You haven't done anything.'

This was not quite true. I'd eaten my own delicious meal, and downed all the red, during which time I'd spotted the man I needed to talk to. He was an older gentleman, and he was visiting each of the tables in turn, chatting genially to the customers, occasionally directing a waiter to replenish water, or bring another bread basket. It was slow going, because Cosa Bolle was a big place, and busy, but he'd get to us eventually. I just had to distract myself with this yummy (mouth-watering? Exquisite?) food and wine while I waited.

We ordered another carafe while we perused the dessert menu, a smaller laminated card that said 'Chocolate, Fruit, Cheese'. I was really on board for this lack of complication. Keep it simple, straightforward: Food. Wine. Man. Then later: Bed. Letters. Sleep. Tomorrow: Bath. Breakfast. Train. Everything reduced to the basics, like Izzy's camping trips. The room was swirling around me, but I could focus on those stark, fundamental things. Bullet points. Exes. Flats. Co-workers. Jackson DeLantro was right not to dress it up. Richard. Lixin. Arnold. Tick them off, one by one.

By the time the manager reached our table, there were two of him. I didn't know how I'd got so drunk. Well, I suppose I did: Gin. Wine. Limoncello. The shots had come along with our puddings – mine a sumptuous, unctuous, slobbery-making chocolate . . . thing. A mousse? A soufflé? Something gooey and evil. Morag had some sort of tart – apt – made of pears. The guitarist plucked a rose out of the vase on our table and gave it to her, which sent her into transports of delight, as I gorged on my gorgeousness, delectable trickles dribbling down my chin.

'Ladies, I hope you enjoyed tonight's meal?' The manager's voice was soothing, assured; he knew we had. Everyone here had. The best restaurant in Edinburgh by a Royal Mile. I blinked at him woozily.

'So nice,' I said dreamily. 'Bread. Meat. Chocolate.'

He bowed appreciatively. I had him where I wanted him. He was eating out of my hand, just as I'd eaten out of his.

'Do you know Izzy?'

'Izzy?' He frowned, concerned, as if I'd suggested the chicken was tough. But it wasn't. It was unctuous.

I tried to pull myself together. 'Isabella Harris. She used to work here.'

His face cleared. 'Bella? Yes, of course. She is a very valued customer and dear friend. You know her?'

Is. Is. Is.

Finally, here was someone who understood that she wasn't dead.

'She is also my . . . valued friend.' My tongue felt thick and flaccid in my mouth.

'You should have said! Allow me to introduce myself. I am Matteo, at your service.' He snapped his fingers at a passing waiter. 'More Limoncello, *per favore.*'

Oh dear. Well, it wasn't my fault now. 'Have you seen her recently?'

'Bella? No, not since . . . her birthday. She always comes here on her birthday.'

I sat up, as straight as my inebriation would allow. 'Her birthday? Her *last* birthday? So . . . *September?*' That was . . . I couldn't do the maths in my state. But it was less than a year. She'd been right here, less than a year ago. I was closing in!

'Yes, September. We had a little dinner. Carbonara and ciambella.'

177

The dishes her mother used to make. Like her wedding, it cut me to the quick. 'How lovely. Who was there? Lots of friends?' If it had been a big do without me, I would throw my empty plate at that wall.

Thankfully, he shook his head. 'An intimate occasion. Her husband, close family.'

The 'husband' again. I smiled and sipped my shot. 'How delightful.'

Morag, who'd been watching this exchange through narrowed eyes, decided now was the time to play Captain Hastings to my Hercule.

'She lives here in Edinburgh then? How odd, I've never bumped into her, and I see everyone!'

I felt passionately grateful to my crazy, abusive mother-in-law, using her wicked wits for my benefit.

Matteo shook his head. 'No. Not Edinburgh.' He didn't elaborate.

Where, goddammit. I tried to think of how to press him without coming across as creepy, but my own wits were sadly blunted.

'She must have moved back to Manchester, then,' mused Morag, the wonder woman.

'No, but . . .' Matteo stopped, and seemed to collect himself. 'I'm not sure,' he said smoothly. What was he hiding? *Why* was he hiding?

'You must get in touch with her again, it's been ages,' continued my magnificent mother-in-law, prodding me with the stem of her rose. 'Such a shame you lost her number.'

'I must,' I agreed, gazing at Matteo hopefully. Would he bite?

He didn't. He merely bowed, said he was glad we enjoyed our meal and hoped we would visit again. I thought that was fairly likely – if I didn't find Izzy beforehand, I'd be back in September to gatecrash her annual birthday dinner.

'You're quite useless,' Morag observed, as I signalled for the bill.

'You're quite useful, for a basket case,' I mumbled; I really must get back to my hotel before I passed out.

'You should have forced him to give you her number.'

But I wasn't sure he had it. He definitely knew more than he was letting on, but I felt instinctively that, despite Izzy visiting occasionally, she was still holding back. Alaric didn't know where she lived; it was likely Matteo didn't either. God, I was tired. Or was I just drunk? No, I was tired, and drunk, and emotional, and homesick, and pissed off, and sad, and what was Morag doing? Please no. *No.* The guitarist was playing 'Time to Say Goodbye', which was surely our cue to do it, but there she was, up and out of her seat, heading towards the strumming man, ready to join the chorus.

'*Time tooooooooo say gooooooodbyyyyyyyyyeeeeee,*' Morag warbled, like a raddled, off-her-face Sarah Brightman. Despite my drunkenness, I cringed so hard I nearly jarred my neck, but the guitarist swung round, delighted, as my mother-in-law sashayed towards him, waving her arms, her eyes closed in ecstasy. She was turned on by death, but also, it seemed, by inappropriate musical displays. Ironically, at that particular moment I was also turned on by death, which seemed the easiest way out of this situation. Maybe I could grab someone's steak knife and end it all.

But the other diners felt differently. An uninhibited, Limoncello-fuelled crowd, many of whom were European, they were lapping it up, cheering and joining in. The thing that was actually impressive was that Morag knew the Italian bits as well. Or did she? I didn't speak Italian – maybe she was just making it up. Her audience didn't seem to mind – she couldn't sing for toffee, but made up for it with full-throated brass neck. As the song went on, I found myself bellowing along with everyone, making vaguely Italianish noises and thinking that Izzy was quite right – this *was* the best restaurant in Edinburgh by a Royal Mile. Proper vibes. Making Britain great again, by making it less like Britain. I realized, dimly, that I was actually enjoying myself, for the first time in ages. It was stupid, and embarrassing, and awful, and so not how I envisaged the evening playing out, watching my insane mother-in-law croon a choon in my ex-best friend's former workplace, but hey-ho, you don't get to pick and choose these moments. They just happen.

'*EEEEE OOOOOHHHH SOOOOOOOO!*'

Ending on a triumphant high note, Morag flung her arms wide, knocking a tray of plates straight out of a waiter's hands. The subsequent smashing and shouting provided quite the climax to what was undoubtedly a towering performance. Maybe she'd get her photo put up on that wall. I found myself vaguely wondering if I should harvest the broken crockery for one of my projects, but then rejected the idea as over-ambitious. I could barely stand, for one thing.

Never apologize, never explain. Morag simply shrugged at the mess and began a tour of the tables, accepting compliments and congratulations, while the waiters cleared up and the handsome musician put his guitar away.

After that it was a bit of a blur. I paid, I think, offering garbled apologies to the poor staff sweeping up splintered dishes. Matteo was very polite, but ushered us out and swiftly procured us a taxi, anxious to get rid of Morag before she did any more damage. We tumbled into the cab, both whooping as we realized how utterly wasted we were.

'That was fun. Let's break back in tonight and look through their files.' Morag started reapplying her lipstick, like she wanted to look good for the reconnaissance job.

I squinted at her in the darkness. 'It's a restaurant, not Whitehall.'

'You said she was a spy.'

'That was just a stupid theory.' Now, in my dumb drunkenness, I could see just how stupid it was.

'You're too tepid. If you're doing this, you have to go all in.' Morag glared at me, her eyes glittering. 'You have to find her, make her pay.'

'What?'

181

'For dumping you. Make her pay. That's what I would do.' She tossed her head, bright bushy curls bouncing.

Take the top off the volcano, Gwen. Let it all out. I shook my head, or tried to. 'You don't understand. I'm not tracking her down to punish her. I just . . . want to be her friend again.'

Morag's vivid red lip curled. 'That's pathetic.'

It probably was, even by my standards. And yet I wanted it, more than a kayaking holiday, or my version of Mabel, or a proper job. The cab stopped outside Morag's flat, at least I assumed it was, and she staggered out, losing a shoe in the process. As we drove away, she scooped it up and jabbed the heel at me like she was giving me the finger. She was all right, Morag. I'd underestimated her. Well, no, that wasn't the right word. I'd judged her, harshly, without appreciating her better qualities. Her deviousness, ruthlessness, lack of scruples – all excellent attributes. Maybe I'd start calling her Mother.

Back in my hotel room, I tumbled into bed in my clothes, the room spinning. Finally, the letters! But when I pulled them out of my bag, I couldn't read them. None of the words made sense, all swarming around and blinking at me, like Jackson DeLantro's website. I couldn't make anything out.

Sta-tue . . . Extra . . . Extri . . . Extricated . . . Anon . . . Anon . . . Anonymity . . .

Hiccupping, I pushed everything to the floor and got out my phone to text Angus. There was a message I hadn't noticed, from an unrecognized number. Maybe Matteo had alerted Izzy, and she'd texted me! I opened it, and by closing one eye, just about managed to read it.

Mam wanted you to know. The Hermit. Coming up over and over again. Sue

What the fuck did that mean? With a groan, I threw the phone on the floor and crashed out, the room still revolving, the cats miaowing in my head.

Pseudonym. Pseud. Sue.

Isabella. Bella. Bell . . .

25

Oh God. Oh God. Oh God.

I didn't want to wake up, desperate to defer the moment when I realized just how ill I was. How very, very ill. But my heart was insistent, pounding away like the worst alarm in the world. Then an answering thump in my temples, a lump in my throat building, threatening. My mouth, dry as Jacob Levy's wood shavings, croaked for liquid, any liquid. I'd drink the dregs of a toothbrush holder just to rehydrate. Oh God, but I felt sick. Everything I'd drunk was pooling in my oesophagus, bubbling like a cauldron, ready to shoot right back up. I couldn't move, because if I did, my head would explode. So I just had to lie there, enduring the godawful pain and nausea and guilt and boredom and hunger and thirst and the smell of rancid, 100 percent proof sweat.

I lay like that for an hour, panting and groaning. Then I decided to try and move, which turned out to be a bad idea. That lurking bile made good on its threat, surging up my throat; up, up, up. It was coming too quickly to get to the bathroom, and, hamstrung by hangover, I couldn't move that swiftly or dextrously anyway. But I mustn't puke in this bed; this pristine, white hotel bed. Unthinkable. So, in a sick-split-second decision, I lay flat on my back, facing the ceiling, turning my mouth into a little vomit-volcano. No keeping a lid on this one. It erupted and trailed over my face and neck, and I used my hands to catch the dribbles of barf-lava so they didn't fall on the precious thread count. Then I had to lie like that, cupping my own sick to my face, until the surface tension developed enough to hold. As life-experiences went, it was a low point.

Half an hour later, I managed to make it to the bathroom to wash it all off, moaning as the headache continued to make its presence felt. I lay in a hot bath for another hour, hoping the heat would disperse the crapulence. Oh God, oh God, oh God, please make me feel better. Please make it improve enough that mere existence didn't feel like torture. I knew it was my own fault, but it wasn't my fault – it was Morag's, and Matteo's, and really, it was Izzy's. She should be here with me, holding my hair back and soothing as only a best friend could. She'd done that, once, in the Marchmont flat – as I chundered into the bath I'd once slept in, she'd offered me toilet paper and wise words. 'Get it all out, that's the ticket.' Then we had leftover kebabs and I was right as rain and ready to drink again by lunchtime. Oh God, I missed being young. It was so difficult to accept that, at my age, my limit was two spritzers. Any more and I spewed like Regan in *The Exorcist*. I flapped about in the bath, miserably. I had to get out or I'd miss my train. Could I manage some food? Could I keep it down? Poor me.

After chugging paracetamol, ibuprofen, and a dusty Berocca I found at the bottom of my bag, I gingerly made my way downstairs to the breakfast room and ventured towards the buffet. I was concerned about the delicate balance of my stomach, but this monster demanded appeasement; vital sustenance. So, I loaded up with bacon, hash browns, beans, a fried egg, toast and marmalade, muesli and yoghurt, fruit, and a bonus mini-croissant. It was just going to have to be an eating day. An eating day, and a bleating day – every now and then an involuntary whimper would escape my lips. My fellow hotel guests shot me uneasy glances, but I was too unwell to care.

The pain was indescribable, but I ate through it, consuming everything on the table like a trooper, brave and stoic. I imagined Izzy beside me, patting my shoulder, offering encouragement. 'Replenish and restore, Mortimer! Replenish and restore.' The painkillers hadn't really worked, so I popped a few more, washed down with fresh orange juice. By the time I'd finished, although I still felt horrific, at least I could breathe in and out without thinking I might die.

After managing to settle up without keeling over, I fell into a taxi outside and gunned for the station, stifling eggy burps, any one of which threatened to follow through. Morag had sent a breezy text, making no mention of mortal illness. She'd drunk just as much as me – what was she made of? Was intolerance just a phase of your fifties –

did you come out the other side with the cast-iron liver of a twenty-something? That was a life-stage to look forward to. Or was it just that my mother-in-law was one of the Devil's handmaidens, immune to the effects of His liquor?

Angus had also sent a message: Had a few sherbets, did you?

How could he possibly know? Then I saw my last text sent to him the night before, just before I passed out: Morag porn star bitch but OK. Mother mummy ha ha Hamish. Unctuous meaning? Hmmm.

I replied, It was a lovely evening. Nice to catch up with your mother, to remind him that he was a bad son who didn't call, and I was a dutiful daughter-in-law who visited. I couldn't mention Izzy, and certainly couldn't mention my current state, because he would enjoy it too much, crowing and holding it over me. We both gloated over each other's overindulgences, because it made the better half feel virtuous, responsible, grown-up. And it was just fun to laugh at someone else's self-inflicted agony. Oh God, I wished my head would stop throbbing. To distract myself, I read that mystifying anonymous text again: Mam wanted you to know. The Hermit. Coming up over and over again. Sue

Mam. Hermit. Sue.

I mused, slowly and painfully.

Mrs Lavery. Tarot. Susan.

The dead landlady had made contact! Despite the fact that it was bollocks, I was thrilled. As moderately thrilled as my tender head would allow. This had all started with a

Ouija board, why not throw open the search party to the spirit world? Now to unpick the meaning . . .

I googled 'the Hermit' on my phone. There was a picture of a grizzled man who looked like Gandalf, standing at the top of a mountain, holding a lantern and some sort of staff. What was that about? 'A withdrawal from events and relationships to introspect and gather strength.' 'A stop sign.' 'Seclusion.' 'Reclusive.' But the Hermit Reversed could indicate that reconnection was required. Was Sue's Hermit up or down? I texted her to ask, and then sat back, my head pounding. Must remember that any activity had to be done tentatively, carefully, like an old bloke standing on a summit.

At the train station, I bought a flapjack and a coffee, then went to find my platform. Thank the Lord, the train was already waiting. Tentatively, carefully, I collapsed in my seat, waiting for the surging head-pound to recede. I had to change at York but maybe I'd have staged a partial recovery by then. Staying alive already felt marginally easier. I leaned back in my seat, closing my eyes. Withdrawal. Seclusion. Reclusive. The question was *why*? Why had Isabella backed out of life like that? Why were her activities so circumscribed; cautious, careful? No internet presence, low-key birthday dinners, not telling anyone where she lived, little to no contact with old friends. She was keeping her cards close to her chest. I wanted to lay them out, and read them; root out all the secret messages. Withdrawal, seclusion, reclusive, withdrawal, seclusion, reclusive . . . As the train pulled out of Waverley station, my eyelids drooped, lulled by the rhythmic pulse of the train.

At York, I was rudely awakened by someone's bag bashing me as they lumbered down the aisle, and roused myself to find drool on my cheek and my hangover still hanging round like Mabel at the dinner table. Exiting the train, I slumped on a bench and waited for my connection. Oh God, I wanted this journey to be over. I wanted this day to be over. I wanted to skip to the point where I felt normal again, skip to the point where I'd found Izzy and we were friends again, fast-forward to a successful, contented, teetotal new me.

By the time we pulled into Harrogate, I was done. The hangover hadn't abated. It had baited, and now it was just taking the piss. My head was still pounding, my stomach churning. I'd eaten three packets of crisps between York and Knaresborough. What had I actually achieved from this Edinburgh jaunt, apart from ravaged innards? Izzy's old landlady was dead and communicating vague messages through playing cards. Her former tutor was the world's slowest skirt-chaser. Her workplace had yielded little except a possible birthday rendezvous. She might not even go back this year. This whole trip was a busted flush. I'd been sick on my own face. Sue texted back: It's coming up every which way. Didn't I know it.

I staggered out of Harrogate station, lugging my suitcase, feeling profoundly depressed, sorry for myself, annoyed at myself, tired, ratty, hungry. And still very, very hungover.

Waiting in the car park was Angus, leaning against the car, Mabel chewing a stick at his feet.

'Thought you might like a lift back,' he said.

189

I'd never been happier to see him, not even on my wedding day.

'I'm not hungover,' I said. 'I feel fine.'

'Sure you do,' he replied, taking my case. 'You look great. Really healthy and energetic.'

'I might go on a run when we get back.'

'Great idea.'

Back home, he brought me a cup of tea and a biscuit, and for a second I caught his hand as he put it all on the bedside table. Reclining against a mass of pillows, in fresh pyjamas, having ingested another hefty dose of painkillers, I felt almost human.

'I'm not so keen on your mother,' I said. 'But you're all right. I can see why the dog likes you.'

He squeezed my hand. 'Did you have a good time? Apart from the terrible infection you picked up?'

'Yes,' I said. 'It was very beneficial. Invigorating Scottish air. A tonic.' And then I winced, remembering the gins that went with it.

Angus went down to watch *Ozark*, and I drifted off, dreaming of tarot cards spreading out in front of me, telling me all their secrets. When I woke again, it was the middle of the night and, in a rush, I remembered that the trip hadn't been a disaster at all. It had been a triumph. Because I had Izzy's cards and letters to Alaric, all waiting to be read, all waiting to be laid out, and unpicked, and deciphered.

Who knew what secrets were within?

26

Modigliani postcard from the Estorick Collection of Modern Italian Art, smudged postmark

Dear Alaric,

Have you been here? It's a lovely place with a little café, you'd adore it. Anyway, I just wanted to say happy birthday, and hope you're settling in at the new place.

Ti abbraccio forte,
Bell

Letter, no date

Dear Alaric,

Thank you so much for your email. The wedding was beautiful, a tiny church near Positano, just us and our families, with dinner after at a wonderful fish restaurant, on a terrace overlooking the sea. We couldn't have hoped for a more perfect day. Well, I suppose we could, in some ways, but to misquote Charlotte, we must be satisfied with tranquillity!

A presto,
Bell

V&A William Morris notecard

Kensington, London W8

Just a short note to say the move south went well and I am loving my new job! Jean-Luc really did come through for me – thank you so much for introducing us. It's busy busy busy but there are so many opportunities here. It was awful leaving Manchester – I miss everyone, especially Gwen – but I feel like a whole new world has opened up to me.

However, the flat is <u>small</u>.
Bell

Postcard of Trevi Fountain, postmark June 2010

Dear Alaric,

Greetings from your favourite city. I've thrown so many coins here I'm due dozens of visits back. Luca is well, sends his love, and says he will bring you a cornetto when he is next in Edinburgh!

Saluti,
Bell

Letter, no date

Beth Morrey

Dear Alaric,

This is just to apologize for how I was when I saw you. I must have made no sense at all, and was no fun either. I'm sorry. It's been quite a time, but I'm hoping to put it behind me and move on. Once I've extricated myself, I'll be in touch, but in the meantime, thank you for being a shoulder to cry on and perdonami.

Bell

Letter, no date

Dear Alaric,

Thank you for your email, it was lovely to hear from you though I am so sorry that Estelle is ill. I hope the operation goes well and she has a swift recovery – you'll be back in your olive grove in no time!

My news is that, at last, I've been able to move back to Manchester. It was a struggle to put everything in place but I think it'll be OK. London was exciting but never really felt like home – despite everything, my northern roots were tugging at me! I've got a new job and a new place, I get to hang out with Gwen again and be nearer my parents. They're still in Hathersage, still drowning in every edition of The Times ever published. Luca is still living it up in Trastevere, though he's met a girl and I think she might tame him.

193

Anyway, I'll be up at Cosa Bolle for my birthday so maybe I'll drop by to see you and Estelle then.

A presto,
Bell

Manchester Art Gallery greetings card, Portrait of an Unknown Model, *Modigliani*

Dear Alaric,

Her eyes are terrifying, aren't they? I mean, there are no eyes, which makes her inhuman. I find her anonymity terrifying as well.

I'm going away for a while, I wanted to let you know. Please don't worry, I know what I'm doing – a mali estremi, estremi rimedi.

Addio,
Bell

Postcard of Christ Church, Oxford

The most wonderful gallery here. Michelangelo, Raphael, Veronese, Mantegna.

Was it Michelangelo who said the thing about every block of stone having a statue inside it. Sometimes I feel like the statue inside the block of stone.

Scappo x

194

* * *

Alaric may well have had an impeccable filing system, but everything got jumbled up in my bag and it was all in the wrong order. The lack of dates didn't help, but people only really wrote dates on letters if they were in an E.M. Forster novel. Would rearranging them make anything clearer? I translated the Italian, which thickened the plot further: '*A mali estremi, estremi rimedi*' meant 'Desperate times call for desperate measures'. Why was she desperate? What was happening? Why did she tell Alaric she was going and not me? What did I do wrong? Where did she go?

And '*scappo*'. The meaning differed depending on which translation I read. Sometimes 'gotta go' or 'I'm off', but also 'I run' or 'I escape'.

What was she running from? Was she still running, or had she stopped? And if so, where did she end up?

All this had just muddied the waters and not moved things along at all. I was stuck, like the statue in the stone.

I needed a breakthrough.

27

On Friday, 24th May, I arrived late at Le Capri because my train to Manchester was delayed, and I hadn't been able to find a cab outside the station. It was raining hard, I'd forgotten my umbrella and by the time I'd actually managed to hail a taxi, I was drenched. The restaurant was one of those smart, soulless places, full of suits having business lunches, talking earnestly about revenue forecasts. I sidled in, hoping to sneak to the toilets first, to do something with my straggly hair and streaked make-up, but it was impossible to sidle with a suitcase – I was all packed ready for my night out with the Harlots, and had a hotel room booked for afterwards. Once I was through with this lunch, I intended to check in and make myself look presentable so that Holly or Rachel or whoever wouldn't sneer at me like I'd let myself go. But first I had to meet Izzy's former colleague, Madison James.

I still didn't understand why she'd insisted on meeting in person. According to Madison, the situation was 'delicate', and she was interested in 'my story' because she had one too. I supposed it was just a journalist's hankering for sensationalism, but couldn't help feel a prickle of excitement and intrigue. OK, maybe Izzy wasn't a spy but . . . perhaps she'd become embroiled in a controversial news story, and now gangs or politicians were after her blood. I didn't see how a food critic could get pulled into that sort of thing, but you never knew. Shady folk like *Sopranos* mobsters met in restaurants; maybe she'd overheard something and had to go to ground. Wiping rainwater off my forehead, I lugged my case in between tables, looking for the sign for the Ladies.

'Ms Mortimer?'

Shit. There was Madison James, looking fearsomely immaculate. Razor-sharp blonde bob, fire-engine lipstick, sheath dress that spoke of dedicated hours in the gym. I took her hand, realizing mine was wet with rain and sweat.

'Call me Gwen.' I said it like an apology, not deserving of titles in my current state.

She inclined her head, and led me to our table, right in the middle of the restaurant, with no room for my case. Sliding into a seat, I tucked the offending luggage in tight next to me and tried to look businesslike.

'Thank you so much for meeting me, Gwen,' said Madison, smoothing her hair behind her ears and flicking a napkin onto her lap. 'I felt it was better if we talked in person.'

'Sure, no problem.' I looked around for a menu, realizing I was incredibly hungry. There hadn't been time for breakfast that morning; getting everyone else fed and out of the house had taken precedence, and now I was ravenous, happy to hoover up whatever bland small plate Le Capri wanted to offer me. A waiter arrived, and I beamed at him, but my companion got in first.

'The usual Chablis, thank you. Gwen, what would you like to drink?'

'Just a sparkling water, please.' There was no way I was having a repeat of Cosa Bolle's bolloxed. I needed my wits about me. 'And . . .' But my request for the menu was lost to the genteel hubbub as the waiter whisked himself away. My stomach growled in protest. My damp head itched.

'So, Gwen,' Madison began, leaning forward and clasping her hands together. She had extremely well-manicured nails. Everything about her was well-manicured, highlighting my own bedragglement. 'When did you last see Isabella?'

I jumped, nudging my case to one side. Talk about getting to the point. 'Oh! Well, I . . . let's see . . . it's been . . . erm . . .' Not for the first time, I felt embarrassed by how long it had been. How much did Madison know about me and Isabella? I was her plus-one at so many events, accompanied her on review trips, featured in the subsequent write-ups; maybe she'd talked about me in the office, referred to me as her best friend . . .? 'Around fifteen years ago.'

Madison leaned back, nodding. 'Yes, that was what I thought. Same here. You see, I've been waiting for someone else to get in touch about her. I didn't expect it to take so long.'

'What do you mean?' I sat up, inadvertently knocking my case to the ground, nearly tripping up the waiter who was coming back with our drinks. While I righted it, he set a bucket on the table, with a bottle of white wine nestling in ice, put a glass in front of her, filled it, and presented me with my water.

Madison paused, her wine glass at her lips. 'Fifteen years ago, Isabella came to the office. After hours. Said she needed to speak to me, urgently.'

'What did she say? How did she look?' There were a million questions jostling for position, but for some reason those were the most pressing.

Madison frowned. 'Not much, and . . . different.' She hesitated. 'She said she was taking a sabbatical. You have to understand, Isabella was one of our most popular reviewers, a valued member of the team. Our readers loved her, she used to get fan mail. And then she announced she was taking off, leaving us high and dry. I was furious. But, when I saw her that night, she was strange, rattled. She'd emailed out of the blue, and came to the office the following evening. Most people had gone home. But . . .' She rotated the (probably Tiffany) ring on her finger. 'She was wearing a scarf on her head, sunglasses, a trench coat. Like . . .'

'Like a spy?'

She raised her eyebrows, looking amused. 'Well, yes. It was kind of silly. But she was obviously het up.'

'About what? What did she say?' The waiter walked past again but I was far too engrossed to get his attention. My empty belly would have to wait.

'She said she was going away for a while, and that if anyone contacted the office asking about her, that we should let her know. She left me a private email address.'

'What was it?'

She picked up her phone and scrolled. 'CurrerB@pronto. com. She said not to use it unless someone had come forward. Obviously, I ignored that, and sent a couple of messages asking when she was coming back. She never replied.'

The Charlotte Brontë pseudonym again. I resolved to send a message to that address as soon as I was out of this restaurant. And had dried my hair. 'Who did she think was going to ask about her?'

'No idea.' Madison poured herself another glass and continued. 'As time went on, and she didn't turn up at a rival publication, and didn't reply to my messages, I began to worry. I realized that during those last few months, she'd been distracted, not herself. But by then I had no idea where she was, and couldn't find anyone else who knew either. So, I just chalked it up as one of those things, a mystery.'

'*Did* anyone ask about her?'

'Yes,' she replied. 'I had an email. A strange one.'

'Who from?'

Madison shrugged, irritably. 'It was anonymous. From an account that didn't look real. A random mix of letters and numbers.'

'What did it say?'

'It was pretty similar to yours, actually. Maybe a bit chattier. Said they were looking for Isabella because they had a story she might be interested in. But when I dug down, asked for more info, the replies were cagey. And when I suggested a meet-up, there was no reply at all. Which was why I was keen to meet *you*, see if you were willing to show your face.'

'Why didn't the person want to meet you?'

'I don't know. I passed the message on to Isabella, but she didn't get back to me. By that point it felt like I was just wasting my time, so I let it slide. But I always wondered what was going on. And now, you've come along.'

'Yes . . .' My tummy rumbled and I ignored it. 'Now I've come along, asking about her. Aren't you supposed to let Izzy know?'

'All in good time. First, I'd like to do some more digging, this time in your direction.'

I spread my palms. 'There's nothing to dig up here.'

Madison James winked at me over the rim of her glass. 'I'm a journalist, Gwen. There's always something.'

Feeling uncomfortable, I sipped my water. This was wrong, somehow.

'So, Gwen,' Madison continued, topping up her glass yet again. 'What do *you* know?'

The case had moved under the table, rolling between us. I clutched the handle defensively. 'Nothing. That's the problem. I don't know where she is, or where she's been.' It was mostly true, but also, I felt instinctively that I shouldn't tell this woman, who I didn't really know, who drank nearly a whole bottle of wine on her own at lunchtime, who gave out Izzy's private email address, what I knew about my friend's whereabouts. Izzy's voice was in my head again, telling me not to: *Trap shut, Mortimer. Keep schtum.*

'But why are you suddenly interested, after fifteen years?' Despite the wine, Madison's eyes were sharp and probing. She could clearly hold her drink better than me, but maybe she'd had more practice, mining all those sources.

I shrugged. 'There was a school reunion. She didn't come. I wondered where she was.'

'But you didn't wonder before now?' Something in the twist of her scarlet lip made me feel that sense of shame again, and I pulled the case towards me under the table.

'I've always wondered.' I thought of Sue Lavery's Hermit, coming up every which way – initially it had seemed like the Hermit was Isabella, retreating from society, pulling up the drawbridge. But maybe the Hermit was *me*, oblivious to what was going on, cutting myself off. It was time to reconnect, but not with Madison James. Suddenly, I remembered Izzy moaning about her: 'She's so nosy, but everything she smells is off.' That light in her eye – the gleam of the grape, and muckrake. Madison wanted my dirt, so she could add it to her own. I needed to clean up my act.

Downing the rest of my water, I set the empty glass between us. 'I guess it'll just have to stay a mystery.' Getting to my feet, I dragged my suitcase out from under the table.

'Here's my card,' Madison pushed it across to me, tapping the telephone number with a glossy nail. 'Get in touch if you hear anything.'

'Will do.' Would I buggery. There was clearly no lunch to be had at Le Capri, only leeching. 'Will you tell Izzy that you saw me?'

'Yes.' Madison stood gracefully, holding out those beautifully buffed fingers. I had to hand it to her, she'd be able to drink me under the table. An unprincipled, boozy hack; what a cliché. 'But I have a feeling that after fifteen years, she's not going to be very interested.'

I couldn't help being hurt by that. How would Izzy react when she got Madison James's email? *Your old friend Gwen was sniffing around.* Would she be pleased, annoyed, worried? Indifferent? Maybe she'd get in touch herself.

But she'd get an email from *me* before any of that could happen.

28

~~Where the hell are you? Where the hell have you been?~~

~~Hi, long time no see! I bumped into Richard Spencer the other day – remember him?!~~

~~I hope you don't mind my emailing like this – I got your address from~~

~~I can't believe you got married without telling me~~

From: Gwendolyn Mortimer <GMortimer@haremail.com>
Sent: 24 May 2024 17.27
To: CurrerB@pronto.com
Subject: Hello

Not sure how to start this. Or if this is you. Or if I should be sending it. Anyway, here goes.

Hello. How are you? It's been a really long time. I hope you are OK. I am fine. Three kids now. And a dog, Mabel, who doesn't like me much. We live in Harrogate. I don't work in advertising any more – I'm an eco-entrepre-neur now, working with a group of local artists. Liam's at university, doing really well, playing a lot of rugby. Sam wants to be a film director. Fred's my youngest, he's into fossils and shooting things online. Angus rarely leaves his shed.

Anyway, just wanted to catch up and find out how you are. It would be really good to see you if you're ever in the area. There are some great restaurants here!

Right, I'd better go – I'm off out with the Harpur Harlots to-night – remember them?! We're hitting Manchester – maybe I'll look up some of our old haunts!

Anyway, it would be great to hear from you.

All the best,
Gwen x

The email took me an hour and a half to write, during which time I polished off a packet of nuts and a tub of Pringles from the minibar to placate my grumbling tummy. As soon as I sent it, I worried about mentioning the Harlots – did that just make me look lame, hanging out with people from school? And too many exclamation marks, trying far too hard. She probably didn't give a shit what my kids were up to. 'All the best'? *All the best??* Jesus, Gwen, you fossilized loser. I plucked a miniature bottle of gin from the fridge and necked it angrily.

Then I had a shower and got ready to go on my lame night out with old schoolfriends.

29

Thank God I was meeting Min beforehand for a pre-dinner bitch and catch-up. I went round to her hotel room, still anxious about the email. After knocking and waiting in the corridor, I berated myself for being an idiot, and texted her: 'I'm here!'

Min opened the door waving a mini bottle of champagne. 'Oh, you look excellent.'

I did a twirl. 'So do you.'

She was wearing a vivid red jumpsuit, her long black hair left down to hide her hearing aids. She said they didn't actually make her hear properly, but helped with lip-reading, allowed her to perceive dull sounds and reverberations which helped her orient herself, and be more aware of what was going on. 'I'd know if a bomb exploded,' was how she put it. But she also said that sometimes she switched them off entirely, to get some peace, like discarding your bra at the end of the day.

I was wearing a dress I'd bought for an advertising do, before I got made redundant – a kind of leopard-print flowing thing. Dresses weren't usually for me – for the last

Harpur Harlots get-together, since we weren't actually going out, I'd worn trackie bottoms and a black sweatshirt that said 'NON'. It didn't seem worth tarting myself up to sit in the front room of an Airbnb, particularly when we'd started communing with the dead. But for the Lever Club, one of Izzy's old haunts, it felt appropriate to make an effort. After bemoaning my straggly locks in Le Capri, I'd given myself a proper blow-dry so my auburn-brown hair was swishing along with my frock. For once, I felt well put together, and briefly wished I could see Madison James again to show her I could hold my own in the style stakes.

'Have a glass,' said Min. We clinked them and I inspected her room to make sure it wasn't better than mine. The Lever was a boutique hotel, or 'restaurant with rooms', and because those rooms weren't that numerous, some of the Harlots had booked into other places nearby. We'd pretty much colonized the Northern Quarter for the night, and I felt a frisson of excitement as I strolled around Min's accommodation with my glass of fizz. So what if it was lame to socialize with some old hockey teammates? At least I was out, in a nice dress. AND I was on a mission. Someone at the restaurant might remember Izzy and give me another clue. But I definitely wouldn't get as drunk this time.

'What's your daughter up to?' I asked Min, who was strapping herself into a pair of towering heels. She had a fourteen-year-old called Li-Mei who she described as terrifyingly independent and generally terrifying. The sign for 'daughter' was to make the letter D with two fingers. I was always sad I never had a girl – I imagined they just sat quietly, colouring in, whereas when my three had rampaged around the house, I'd longed for some hearing aids to switch off.

'Oh, she's off at some sleepover. Oli's at home with the cats.' Min's boyfriend Oliver, not Li-Mei's father but nonetheless a long-term fixture, was an art dealer, who I suspected was incredibly rich. I was keen to find out *how* rich, but felt that Min and I weren't yet on the kind of footing where I could say, 'Exactly how much money does he make?' There would have been no such qualms with Izzy – when she split up with Lixin, the one who asked her to marry him, she briefly worried she'd made the wrong decision. To cheer her up, I asked what was the most disappointing thing he did in bed, and laughed myself sick as she described how he used to arrange his clothes in a neat little pile before they had sex. Once he had to stall foreplay in order to go back and pair his socks. Telling the story made her feel much better.

'How are your three?'

The sign for 'child' was to tap an imaginary little head; for a teen you just tapped a head higher up. Two of my children were now taller than me, so it wasn't a very accurate gesture, but I appreciated her question all the same. To be honest, I hadn't paid that much attention to my boys' activities recently, and was glad to dwell on what they were up to, even if I felt a tad detached from it.

'Liam's got a girlfriend.' Angus told me Liam had mentioned her; a girl from Bristol who was studying economics. He hadn't said much more, but Angus got the impression it was serious, and the knowledge made my heart ache a little. 'Sam came out of his room the other day to ask for a new laptop.' Apparently the one he had wasn't powerful enough to edit on, which made me worry about porn again. 'And Fred finally bullied us into getting him a phone.'

Min made a face. 'Li's got one, I hate it. Girls are so vicious on WhatsApp.'

I felt passionately grateful to have grown up long before social media existed. Maybe Izzy was right to have no online presence – it certainly stopped people from pestering you and telling you to kill yourself because you had bad skin. Liam was so laid-back I'd never really worried about him, and Sam was extremely tech-savvy, but Fred was a more sensitive soul under the insouciant exterior. Or was it just because he was my youngest? The sign for 'baby' was, of course, to rock an imaginary infant in your arms. Sometimes I wished he was back there, that warm weight nestling in my elbow. Looking after a newborn was a bit like Izzy's camping trips, everything reduced to the basics – that is, keeping them alive. It gave you focus, purpose. Now those tiny bundles were off romancing at university in Nottingham, editing films (please not porn) and rocketing round Harrogate with a mobile phone, they had their own sense of purpose, whereas mine was AWOL, like Isabella.

'Anyway, who's coming tonight?' Min straightened up to check herself out in the mirror, keeping an eye on my reflection.

'Everyone,' I replied, trying to help myself to another glass of champagne but finding the mini bottle empty. Good; I didn't want to get drunk, just less uptight about my email. 'Well, everyone who came to Windermere, plus Gracie. Not Izzy, obviously.'

'Are you any closer to finding out where she is?'

What was great about Min was that she was genuinely interested in my investigation and sympathetic to my loss. She also had sensible suggestions, and didn't tell me to rein myself in or get a grip, like Angus did. I didn't feel like getting a grip; more like letting rip, and reckoned Min would probably encourage me in that. She was nosy, but not in a nasty way like Madison James. Everything she smelled was sweeter.

'I just sent her an email.' I grimaced, remembering the exclamation marks.

'You found out her email address? That's huge!'

'Well, *an* email address. I don't know if she uses it any more.' I was checking my phone constantly, flicking between inbox and junk. I went to sent and showed the screen to Min. 'What do you think?' I felt embarrassed asking her to read what I'd written, but needed someone to tell me I wasn't a total idiot. But maybe asking her to approve proved I absolutely was.

'It's fine,' she said, scanning my inadequate prose. 'I mean, what are you supposed to say, after all this time?'

211

'Something wittier and more profound?'

But Min was oblivious, still reading.

'So she hasn't replied yet?'

'No.'

'Well, the night is young!' Min picked up her handbag. 'Shall we?'

We made our way downstairs to the bar, where several of the group had already gathered. Seeing us arrive, Rachel whooped.

'Harlots in da house!'

That was what we used to shout to each other in the sixth form. Min laughed but I cringed, because it was a bit much, really, making me want to crawl back into my shell. This wasn't a girls' night out – we were in our fifties, for fuck's sake. But then I caught Min's eye and she signed something, grinning. At first, I couldn't work it out, but then remembered the same gesture delivered to Mr Sullivan with a straight face – crossed arms, with the top hand's index and little fingers out like horns, and the bottom hand's fingers fluttering: 'Bullshit'. I signed back, mimicking the gesture then making my hand into a fist and nodding it back and forth: 'Bullshit. Yes.' Min shrugged and gave me a thumbs-up. It was all bullshit, but we may as well enjoy it. I was the Hermit, who needed to reconnect. Putting my arm around her shoulders, I pushed her towards the girls, ready to get stuck in.

30

'So you see,' slurred Amanda, 'I was right to leave him! It all makes sense now.'

Not very much was making sense.

'I don't get it,' said Holly, sloshing red wine into her glass. 'Since when did you leave him?'

'Well, I've been planning it since the weekend in Windermere.'

'Right, but I saw you both at Dan and Tonia's barbecue last Sunday.'

Amanda sniffed. 'We had to put on a united front.'

'So when did you actually do it?'

'Today!' Amanda punched the air. 'It's done!'

Rachel leaned forwards, elbows on the table. 'What, you told him you wanted a divorce?'

'No.' Her eyes glittered triumphantly. 'I just left. Packed a bag and went! Just like that!'

'Does he know you're coming here tonight?'

'Well, he knows I'm meeting you lot, yes.'

'Then as far as he's concerned, you haven't left him, you've just gone out for the night?'

'That's not the point,' Amanda insisted. '*I* know.'

'Where will you go tomorrow?'

'Oh, I have to get back, Hugo's tutor is coming over and Lila's got a horse-riding class.'

Rachel set her drink down very carefully. 'So, you've left him, but just for the evening?'

'It's the principle of the thing.' Amanda scanned the table defiantly. 'I feel like a new woman! To me!'

We all raised our glasses half-heartedly, Rachel rolling her eyes and Holly muttering that Amanda put the 'div' in 'divorcee'. Further down the table, Bhavini and Erica were arguing about HRT – Erica favoured a natural approach, naturally, whereas Bhavini claimed to bathe in oestrogen gel. Honestly, I was surprised Erica hadn't turned up at the restaurant in wellies with a chicken under one arm. I was starting to appreciate the group as a whole – our shared history made conversation easy, and individually they were pretty funny. Holly and Rachel were raucous and filthy, full of gossip, Amanda was crazy but unintentionally amusing, Bhavini was forthright and extremely well informed, and when she wasn't making up stories, Chloe could be very entertaining. Min was cool. But I failed to see the appeal of the homespun Erica, who always wanted to explain how you were doing something wrong, and how you could do it better, like her. 'I bake all my bread from scratch – it's easy if you're prepared to put in the effort.' 'Contact lenses are so unecological – I wear spectacles made from plastic waste harvested on beaches.' 'We have no screens in our house – we prefer to make our own entertainment!' Smug cow.

I turned my attention to the new addition to our party, Gracie Wagstaff, who'd managed to get childcare this time, and had turned up looking dazed and scruffy, her hair straggling from its topknot. Gracie was a yoga instructor, with biceps to die for, but she was also tremendously scatty and kept losing her train of thought whenever she spoke. She'd had her twins via IVF in her early forties, said it had totally wiped her out. I figured since they were still fairly young and demanding – double trouble – her brain had basically put itself on pause for the duration. Sometimes when you buried yourself in something, it was hard to resurface.

'Great that you could come tonight.'

Gracie blinked vaguely, like she was trying to place me. 'I know! I was so disappointed to miss out on . . . where was it?'

'Windermere.'

'That's right. But it's so . . . And I can't . . . yet, because my husband works weekends, usually. What is it that you do now?'

'I make stuff with mosaic, not very well.' I didn't particularly care what Gracie thought of me, so there was no reason to dress it up.

Her eyes widened. 'Mosaic! Gosh. That sounds . . . pretty?'

215

I shrugged a shoulder, dismissing it. 'Keeps me out of mischief. You do yoga still? Didn't Izzy and I once come to one of your classes? In a wood?' I remembered Izzy signing us up for a session in a forest near Alderley Edge – she loved it, but I kept worrying about ticks.

'Oh, my forest-bathing classes! I just do stuff inside now, it's easier. It's a shame Izzy couldn't make it tonight.'

'Yes, no one has seen her in ages.'

'Well, I suppose it's a bit difficult for her to travel that far.'

Stirring my cocktail with one finger, I paused, frowning. 'What do you mean?'

She fluttered a hand. 'All that way. From . . . you know . . .'

I sucked my finger, staring at her. 'No. I don't know. From where?'

Gracie looked surprised. 'Oh, I just assumed . . . isn't she in Italy?'

'What makes you think that?' Someone else had said she was somewhere in Europe, but for some reason, I'd discounted it. The Harlots' sightings and theories were always so random and ill-sourced. Or entirely made-up, like Chloe's.

'I know her brother's wife, Portia. They're based in Rome, I think. But I'm sure she said Izzy was there as well.'

All roads lead to Rome. And here was a big new lead. But not one I welcomed. If Izzy lived in Italy, then I couldn't really see us picking up where we left off, unless I made some major life changes. Could Angus present his show from the Eternal City? Could Sam and Fred change schools? Could I prowl the piazzas looking for Italian ceramics to smash? It was quite the thought experiment.

'Or maybe she said she was there on holiday?'

I sighed. The trail always went lukewarm. And it wasn't like I was going to get on a plane to Rome on the say-so of a hazy Gracie.

I picked up my empty glass. 'Do you want another?'

'Oh yes, please! A . . . what was it? The pink thing? A Neapolitan?'

'Cosmopolitan. Coming right up.'

Leaving her to drift, I headed back to the bar. Earlier on, I'd asked various Gen Z staff if they remembered an Isabella Harris and they'd all looked at me like I was a mad old bat. But I'd consumed a couple more units since then and was ready to give it another go.

'A cosmopolitan and a Raizel, please.' The cocktail the Lever had named after Izzy was just a martini with added rose liqueur, but its elegant simplicity was apt and I'd been delighted to find it still on the menu. The one I'd just drunk had gone down a treat. The bartender nodded and started mixing.

'Do you know who owns this place now?' In Izzy's day, it had been a prominent Yorkshire family who intended to franchise their business. That didn't seem to have happened, but the Lever appeared to be doing well nonetheless.

The bartender shook his head, his eyes on his shaker. 'I've only just started here. You could ask the manager? He's just come in.'

'Oh right, where is he?'

He pointed along the bar. 'Over there.'

I looked, and over there, looking a lot older and wiser, was Lixin Lee, Izzy's nearly-ex-fiancé.

BINGO.

31

Annoyingly, Lixin didn't recognize me. This was galling because when he was going out with Izzy, we'd spent a fair amount of time together, and at one point he'd wanted to marry her, so it was a bit rude of him to forget his would-be wife's best mate.

'Gwen? Gwen Mortimer. Izzy's friend. Isabella Harris?'

Maybe he didn't want to remember. The proposal must be a fairly bad memory. Izzy had to say yes, because he asked in front of onlookers, but said no in private almost immediately after, plus her public yes had been so muted and unenthusiastic that people had already started to talk.

His puzzled frown cleared. 'Ah, yes. Shortimer.'

'What?'

Lixin looked grimly amused. 'Izzy used to call you Mortimer. I called you Shortimer.'

'Why?'

'Because you were short with me.'

I was affronted. 'I'm sure I wasn't. And also, that's a rubbish nickname. I used to call you Poor Lee.'

Now it was his turn to be piqued. 'Why?'

'Because I felt sorry for you. After the fortune cookie thing.'

'That's also rubbish.'

'Have you seen her?'

'Who?'

'Izzy!'

'Why would I have?'

The whole time we were talking he didn't stop what he was doing, which was folding napkins with alarming rapidity. I would have thought that was a job for a lowlier member of staff, but Lixin always did like to keep himself busy. I pictured him pairing socks during sex and tried not to smirk.

'I'm looking for her.'

'Haven't seen her in years.'

He wasn't looking at me as he tucked and pressed his linen, and I didn't know if I believed him or not. 'She's never been back here then?'

He shook his head, still folding. 'The Chetwynds don't own this place any more. They moved down south.'

'How come you're working here?'

'I knew the family through Izzy. When they sold up, they sold to me.'

'You own the Lever? All of it? Including the hotel?'

He smiled, finally meeting my eyes, as smug as Erica praising her own home-made bread. 'Maybe Izzy should have said yes to the fortune cookie.'

But I couldn't imagine Izzy married to this brisk, sardonic hotelier even if he was a *rich* brisk, sardonic hotelier. Lixin had soured with age, the tart gimlet to Izzy's Raizel.

'Can I have a discount on my room then?'

'I'll tell housekeeping to leave a chocolate melting on your pillow.'

He wouldn't have suited Izzy as husband material, but I liked him all the same.

'Nice seeing you again, Poor Lee.'

'Same, Shortimer.'

I left him with his pile of napkins and went back to join my friends. Amanda was still toasting herself, and Erica was now droning on about kefir to Min, who winked as I arrived with the drinks, and tapped her ears. She'd switched off her hearing aids. I giggled and deposited the cosmo with Gracie.

'Cheers!'

'Who was that man you were talking to?' Amanda nodded, faintly disapprovingly, in the direction of Lixin.

I shrugged. 'Some bloke I used to know, back in the day.' For some reason I didn't want to mention Izzy, brandish her romantic past. For her sake, but also for Lixin's. If they'd got married, maybe Izzy and I would still be friends. I turned away from Amanda to quiz Bhavini about her oestrogen gel, and put him out of my mind.

Poor Lee may have been a poor lead, but it was a good night anyway, because, having organized it, I felt duty-bound to make sure everyone enjoyed themselves, including me. I did the rounds, talking to everyone, asking them about themselves, what they were up to, how things were going. And, mostly, I was interested in the replies. Holly was trying to start her own PR consultancy, working herself to the bone and neglecting everything else; Rachel's mum was having treatment for cancer but doing very well; Bhavini was thinking of taking a sabbatical to study for a master's and wasn't sure what to do about money. Erica, planning a trip to Croatia over the summer, was working out how to get there without flying, which made Chloe recount a disastrous date she once had with a pilot, which in turn caused Amanda to briefly lose control of her pelvic floor. A famous actress had come to one of Gracie's yoga classes but she couldn't remember who she was, and the photo surreptitiously taken on her phone was too blurry for identification. Claire Foy? Emilia Clarke? We all squinted over it, but by that point, *everything* was a bit blurry. In a good way.

Back in Windermere, I couldn't be bothered with all this, but now, like Erica baking from scratch, I was prepared to put in the effort. So it was fun, chatting about kids, and work, and marriage, and single life, and good telly you'd seen, and books you'd read, and diets you'd abandoned, and boys or girls you'd snogged at school, and suddenly you were wheezing with laughter, squeezing each other's arms, and then it was midnight, and you were all hugging, being gently encouraged to leave by the Zoomer staff, who were eager to get on with their own nights out and leave you fifty-somethings to your face cream regimes in your various hotel rooms around Manchester. I fell into bed shortly before 1 a.m., not too pissed, not too sober; just right – the Goldilocks zone of drunkenness.

The night was no longer young – it was well into middle age – but there was still no reply from Izzy.

32

Of course, I was drunker than I thought, and subsequently iller than predicted. I had to keep reminding myself that my ancient enzymes were incapable of breaking down alcohol efficiently, and that although I felt pleasantly fuzzy and fine when I drifted off, sometime during the night the hangover gremlins had gleefully drained me of all life fluid. When I awoke, it wasn't as bad as that morning in Edinburgh, but I definitely felt like Gwyneth Paltrow's noxious alter ego. My phone had died in the night since I forgot to charge it, so I plugged it in and in the meantime got busy with painkillers, vitamin supplements, and a hot shower. Then I went down for an almighty breakfast with some very green-about-the-gills Harlots. Afterwards, with my mobile out of action and desperate to see if Izzy had emailed back, I logged on to a communal iPad in the Lever Club lobby, scrolling through spam from various womenswear brands in search of a reply.

Nothing. Was the account no longer active, was she ignoring me, or did she just not check it very often? There were people like that, who didn't bother; who abstained from the malignant cesspit of social media, who didn't obsessively watch reels of tradwives weaving willow baskets on Insta, who didn't gawp at clips of the latest Omaze house on Facebook. I wasn't one of them, feeling much the same about a digital detox as I did about an actual one – it was for other people. I was more than happy to tox myself up.

'Have you finished?'

I jumped, guiltily, to find Rachel, Amanda, Min and Erica in a huddle behind me. Rachel was sporting leisurewear and looked like she'd just been on a run, but at least Min had bloodshot eyes and Amanda was still in her pyjamas. Earlier, Erica had eaten muesli and blueberries for breakfast and had patronized every paracetamol-popper at our table. Clove oil was a natural painkiller, apparently.

Amanda gestured to the iPad. 'Finished?'

'Sure, be my guest.' I logged off, and picked up my bag.

'Has she replied?' murmured Min, gesturing to the iPad.

I could see Amanda browsing the John Lewis sale online. Maybe looking for new bedsheets for her spinster pad.

'Nope.' I decided to go back to my room and lie down. There were several painful realities, physical and emotional, to digest.

'Has who replied?' Rachel took a swig from her water bottle. She was wearing leggings with a camouflage print and I pictured her going off on her CCF weekends as a teenager. We always used to take the piss, shouting 'AttennnnnSHUN!', saluting her or pretending we couldn't see her whenever she stood near undergrowth. She still gave off army major vibes, and I found myself stammering in response to her question.

'Um. No one. Just a . . . a job offer I was hoping to get.'

Min regarded me quizzically as Rachel stepped forward, intrigued. 'Oh, you didn't mention you were on the lookout?'

'Not . . . seriously, you know, but I can't make mosaics forever. Got to look at the bigger picture!' I laughed like a loon, then took a deep breath to stop myself gabbling. *Come on, Mortimer, pull yourself together.*

'What's the job?' Erica was appraising me with faint contempt.

'Erm . . .' I cast wildly about the lobby for inspiration. 'Hotel manager.'

She smirked. 'Where?'

Fucking hell. 'The . . . er, Ritz.'

'The *Ritz*? As in, the Ritz, London?' Amanda had abandoned John Lewis, gearing up alongside Rachel for an epic piss-take, just for old times' sake.

'No, obviously not that one. There's another one, in Harrogate. The Harrogate Ritz. Very nice. Has a spa.'

Min shook her head, sorrowfully, as Amanda sniggered, her hangover dissipating now she had someone to rag. 'You'll have to book us all in. A Harlots' outing; maybe you can get us a staff discount.'

I hugged my bag to my chest. 'Haven't got the job yet. Probably won't get it, to be honest.' I edged past them. 'Anyway, I've got to go and . . . pack.'

'You should hang around here a bit. Do some research.' Rachel grinned. 'Maybe they'll let you clean the rooms.'

'Oh, fuck off.' My patience, always threadbare, failed to resist the tensile stress.

'*There* it is. The Gwen we know and love.' Rachel and Amanda high-fived each other, united in mockery as I turned and trudged irritably towards the lift.

'Dearie me,' said Min, catching up. 'What was that all about?'

I covered my face with my hands, massaging my forehead for comfort, wishing there was clove oil on my fingers. The area between your eyebrows is called the glabella – I knew this because Fred told me when he started studying biology at school. He told me the term also refers to the underlying bone that is slightly depressed. Glabella, Bella, Isabella. It all came back to her.

'I don't know. I just . . . Emailing Izzy, her not replying, all of it . . . I couldn't face the questions, the speculation. I felt like . . . a loser.' I couldn't remember the sign for it, so made an L-shape with my thumb and forefinger, then dipped the thumb towards the floor.

'Hmmm.' Min gazed at me speculatively. 'So instead . . . you're a budding Basil Fawlty.'

'Oh, fuck off.'

'The Gwen we know and love.' She grinned, and I gave her a different finger, feeling slightly less depressed. My BSL was really coming on.

By 10 a.m. I'd checked out. But, still below par, I found myself not heading for the station as planned, instead strolling idly through the city, wandering around Piccadilly Gardens, an open space that had been redeveloped several times by Manchester councils with varying degrees of success.

Izzy had told me there was a Lowry painting of the square as it was in the 1950s, with the original sunken gardens and fountain in the middle. Izzy liked Lowry, and art generally, and often went to the city gallery on Mosley Street, which was just around the corner. Before I knew it, I was there too, outside the huge Athenaeum, designed in the Italian Palazzo style. Italy . . .

I went in, through the bright entrance atrium to the galleries, and ambled round admiring Pre-Raphaelite paintings, women with manly faces playing lutes, nymphs with small pointed breasts, flowers and fruit, stormy seas, until I came to the Lowry room and found the painting of the gardens. I stared at it for a while, trying to work out why Izzy liked it so much.

It was like every Lowry I'd ever seen – wartime colours, lanky figures, bustling yet remote, childlike yet wise. The gardens were dwarfed by the urban buildings that surrounded them, looming ominously, crowding the sky. If Dippy Holt painted the same scene, what words would steam across it? GREEN VERSUS GREY, maybe, though in Lowry's hands, everything had a grey overlay. Staring at it, I realized that for a long time my life had been that same dull shade. Cloudy and remote. One of the reasons I kept circling that kayaking holiday online was because the photos of it looked so vibrant – the sky so blue, the sea so crystal clear, the buildings so white and immediate, everything clean and crisp, like just-grouted tiles. I'd felt that need to get away, be somewhere else, new and fresh, but now I wondered if what I really needed was to get away from myself, from what I'd become. I was Lowry-sepia, and yearned to be more vivid.

How had it come to this? When I had children, a great smog descended, and in concentrating on them everything else disappeared. Gracie Wagstaff was there right now, lost in the motherhood mist, unable to focus elsewhere. And the money-earning mist on top of that – that frantic, hamster-wheel need to pay the bills every month, keep on top of mortgage payments, pay for this and that and that and that and that, knowing that if you ever stopped then it would all fall apart. I was so busy, so harassed, so distracted, that I forgot to pay attention, just whirled, feverishly, oblivious.

Then Angus got his big break, which became *my* break, and suddenly I could take my foot off the gas and look around. But when the murk cleared, my life was still grey and drab and depressing and I had nowhere to go. Izzy always booked our holidays, our travelling adventures – without her I was static, aimless. Amidst the bustle of the

Lowry painting was the figure of a woman standing still. Technically, she could go anywhere – sit on the benches, head to the fountain, go to the shops, and yet she just stood, immobile. That was me, unsure, unwilling to make my next move.

I dragged my gaze from the painting and trudged on, vaguely heading for the exit. As I made my haphazard way through the rooms, another picture caught my eye. A woman with hair similar to my own, something familiar about her. Like Lowry's figures, she was elongated, with fine arched eyebrows and a sulky crimson pout. But it was her eyes that made you pause, stopped you in your tracks. They were just blank holes – nothing there. Leaning forward, I read the sign next to her – Modigliani, *Portrait of an Unknown Model* – and realized why I'd had that sense of déjà vu. It was the image on that strange postcard Izzy had sent to Alaric. What had she said? *I find her anonymity terrifying.* It didn't seem that scary to me – more like the portrait was unfinished, waiting for the Italian painter to come and fill in the gaps, give her life, make her real. Like the stock-still woman in the Lowry painting, she was biding her time.

All this art was making my head hurt. Instead of leaving, I went to the café, and appeased my lingering hangover with tea and cake. As I guzzled, I googled, on my fully charged phone. I googled the kayaking holiday again, relishing those glorious turquoise hues. I googled Izzy, to check she hadn't reappeared digitally – there was still no reply to my email, but no bounceback either. I googled Arnold Schmidt, Izzy's boyfriend after Lixin, and discovered that he'd tragically died in a boating accident on Lake Como. Italy again. It happened five years ago – I wondered how Izzy felt when she heard the news. Again, it seemed wrong that she should go through that – a former boyfriend dying, in such terrible circumstances – without me. Getting married, confronting mortality, doing big life things, things that you would want to talk through and process. Maybe she processed them with someone else – a newer, nicer friend who wasn't caught in her own stultifying web. On some primal level I was starting to remember what we'd argued about before she left, what she'd said, and what I'd said – or rather, what I *hadn't* said. I'd been so distracted, stuck in my own hole. Wrapped up, oblivious, selfish. I hadn't listened.

There in the café, I googled, and jabbed, and selected, and made my move. By the time I left, finally heading for the station, I'd booked a flight to Rome for the following week.

A mali estremi, estremi rimedi. Desperate times . . .

33

Back home, I spent the weekend subtly packing, unsure how to break the news to Angus. I was like Amanda Simmons, leaving her husband without telling him. Maybe I could just go to Rome and he wouldn't notice? It was only a couple of days – he'd be in his shed, or walking his beloved Mabel, or in the pub being abused by Selwyn, or on the golf course scoring bogeys or whatever. Angus could spend *hours* there, whole days lost to his obsession with getting a little ball in a hole in a really boring, long-winded way. I didn't have a hobby, unless you counted Rightmoving market towns, or occasionally going to the Turkish Baths on Parliament Street so I could have a massage and look at the tiles. Perhaps when I found Izzy, we could go together. She might be based in Rome, but she could manage the occasional visit, to take the waters in a historic spa.

Which brought me back to the pressing issue: how to fly to Italy without Angus realizing and kicking up a fuss. If I told him where I was going, and why, he'd think I was mad. He might laugh at me and take the piss. Or worse, he might see how serious I was. I didn't think I could bear that; he would perceive it as a kind of marital transgression, like he wasn't enough for me. Because the truth was, he wasn't – Isabella gave me something he couldn't. Not just friendship, support, female perspective and shared history. With her, I was a different person. Wittier, more daring, more fun, more sophisticated and open to new experiences. Take this trip, for example – I was not the kind of person who flew to Rome on a whim; not someone who booked things spontaneously, nonchalantly; not someone who did something crazy, hoping against the odds that it would turn out OK.

As well as Izzy, I wanted to find *that* person again.

And so, I sneaked around the house, tucking clean underwear in my suitcase, rooting out my passport, looking up useful Italian phrases like 'I am English, can you help me?' 'Where are the toilets?' and 'I'm looking for my long-lost friend, have you seen her?' Fred came home from Max's, ravenous, and I irritably made him fish fingers and chips, all the while looking around the kitchen for a European plug adapter for my phone charger. Sam came out of his room, made a fish finger sandwich and disappeared again, off to edit his great oeuvre on the new laptop that his father scored him as a freebie by plugging it on his show. When he'd gone, I rushed up to our bedroom to dig out an old sundress that might be appropriate for a roam round Rome. Angus came in and asked me what I was up to and I had to pretend I was doing a clothes sort for the charity shop.

On Sunday, Liam phoned while I was folding washing that included clothes I wanted to take on my trip. There was a secret pile inserted into the family stacks: Angus, Sam, Fred, Me and Roman Me. With the phone tucked between ear and shoulder, I chatted to him while I shook out a flimsy white shirt that might look stylish on the piazzas.

'I'm going to Bristol next weekend.'

'That sounds nice.' Did I own a sunhat?

'To meet Anna's parents.'

'Lovely.' Rome was bound to be warmer than Harrogate, could I risk just taking sandals?

'They've booked dinner at a restaurant, I think it's somewhere posh. What should I wear?'

'Sounds great.' I'd better pack some trainers just in case.

'Can you put Dad on?'

When I handed the phone to Angus, he looked at me through narrowed eyes and I flushed guiltily, as if he'd seen my Skyscanner account. I'd booked the tickets with my own money – Angus and I had a joint account for household stuff but we both had personal funds for recreation. I didn't want to pay for Angus's Titleist golf purchases and also didn't want him to know how much I spent on visits to my hairdresser. The flights plus a central Airbnb had definitely been a personal expenditure, and a hefty one at that – I was going to have to sell a lot of mosaic creations to pay for it. Whisking myself back up to our room with the washing, I furtively shovelled items into the suitcase under our bed.

Later, Angus and I ate dinner in front of the TV, watching old episodes of *Buffy the Vampire Slayer* because he fancied Sarah Michelle Gellar and I fancied the vampires. I thought of my half-filled case upstairs and wondered if I should just come clean about Italy, about the whole search. But it was like being a Slayer – the more people you told, the messier it got. I was in so deep now – best to just get it done quickly and move on. As Buffy said, 'Seize the moment, cause tomorrow you might be dead.' So I ate my plate of reheated pasta in silence, and thought about the googling I'd done in the Manchester Art Gallery.

Izzy might not have an online presence, but her brother Luca Harris did. I couldn't fathom why I'd never searched for him before, because he came up straight away. He worked at an Italian publishing house, was on LinkedIn, and even had a Facebook page, though he didn't post very often. His profile photo was of him with his arms around a very attractive blonde woman who must be his wife, Portia, and he lived in an area called Monti, which sounded trendy. It wasn't a huge stretch to imagine that his sister, with her love of good food and art and culture, had visited them there and liked it enough to stay. I pictured turning up to a vociferous Italian welcome. 'You loon, Mortimer,' Izzy would chortle, over focaccia and taleggio. And I would remind her that last time we were in Rome together, I threw a coin in the Trevi Fountain, so I *had* to come back. It was my destiny, inescapable.

I felt fatalistic about the whole thing, like it was all inevitable. I had to find her, whatever it took. And Angus wouldn't understand, so it was better not to tell him.

Buffy staked a vampire and he disappeared in a puff of smoke. Pouf, gone. Simple as that.

34

On Monday, I headed for my 'studio' with the intention of making something I could sell to pay for my impending trip.

The coffee tree-table had turned out well, and I'd shifted it for £100, but packaging and posting ate into my profit – I needed a good number of portable, easy-to-dispatch items. Up in the bin room, I'd unearthed a box of broken tiles I'd found outside a hardware store – there was a load of plywood already in the workshop; that was a dozen trivets right there. On top of the tiles, wrapped in a towel, was the Charlotte Brontë plate I'd bought at Jumble's. I got it out and examined it. White china, with a blue lustre rim, around ten inches in diameter, it was a hand-painted depiction of the writer, looking pensive and slightly nervy. The likeness was pretty good, and the quote 'Keep in good health' was perfect; twee but sweet. Hopefully, Izzy would appreciate it one day – I wondered about taking it to Rome with me but decided transporting crockery abroad was too onerous, so I put it away again and loaded the tiles in my rucksack. If they disintegrated en route, then that was one less job to do.

Dippy was already in situ, still working on her Hebden Bridge painting. Now the main image was complete, she was busy ruining it, scrawling a phrase across the deep green backdrop: 'SHUT-IN SODDEN DREARINESS'.

'What's that?' I pointed.

'Rochdale Canal,' she replied, without looking up.

'No, the quote.'

'Ted Hughes.'

'I thought you hated him.' Dippy was firmly on Team Sylvia.

She turned. There were flecks of paint on her eyelids, like badly applied make-up. 'I do. The point is he was wrong, and the painting shows it.' She gestured at the image. 'It's vivid and lush and beautiful.'

'Hmmm.' As usual, Dippy was . . . dippy. I unloaded my box and started sorting through my tiles. 'Where's Jacob?'

'Gone to Greece.'

Jacob enjoyed several jaunts every year to his favourite destination. I thought of crystal-clear waters, blue sky and whitewashed houses and felt briefly envious, but I was off on my own adventure, my suitcase packed and ready under the bed. As I worked, I felt a tingle of excitement, of possibility. After years of shut-in sodden dreariness, my world was finally opening up to something vivid and lush and beautiful.

Since the birth of Mortimosaic, I'd got used to feeling that the pieces I created were always on the cusp of crap, but that day the fire of creativity was in my fingers, ceramic shards coming together in delicate, striking arrangements. The tiles I'd found were a gorgeous mix of jewel colours, and I'd treated myself to a bag of golden dust grout in an online sale. As I rubbed away the excess mortar, thin gilded rivers were revealed, snaking around the bright fragments – I'd grouped the colours in a spiral pattern, so each one looked like a rich, multihued ammonite. For once I felt satisfied with my endeavours, proud of what I'd achieved.

'Gwen?'

'Hmmmm?' Absorbed in my work, I turned around vaguely.

'Would you do me a favour?' To my surprise, Dippy's expression was friendly, hopeful. And a bit nervous.

'Sure, what is it?'

She gestured to her painting. 'Would you make me a frame?'

For a while I didn't say anything, partly because I didn't quite understand what she meant, and partly because I did.

'A frame?'

Dippy nodded. Her dreadlocks were swept into a topknot, held in place with a paintbrush. She took it out of her hair, and used it to point at the canvas. 'There's something missing. And I thought . . . what about a mosaic frame, made from Yorkshire pottery?'

I felt another frisson, this time for a different reason. I could go up to Hebden Bridge, source something from the . . . well, source. I could contribute to this artwork, do something different, be part of something. It was an intriguing prospect.

But . . . I had my quest. Izzy took precedence. I shook my head. 'Sorry, it's a nice idea but I'm really busy at the moment.' Couldn't resist the boast. 'I'm going to Rome tomorrow.'

Dippy twisted the paintbrush back into her hair, looking disappointed. 'Oh, right. Rome?'

'To find my friend.'

She wrinkled her nose. 'The dead one? She's in Rome?'

'Maybe. I'll find out.'

'Maybe?' Dippy stared at me. 'A long way to go, on the off chance.'

'It's worth a try.'

'Hmmm.' She turned back to her canvas and began to paint again, adding a question mark after the word 'dreariness' – I was pretty sure the punctuation was hers rather than Ted Hughes'. Overall, I had to admit the painting was kind of stunning. Weird, but stunning, a bit like Dippy herself.

I went back to my own business and by the end of the day had produced twelve very fine trivets, each one its own artwork. Arranging them on the workbench, I took photos for my Etsy page. They looked distinctive, quirkily pretty. If they sold at the usual price of £30 each then that should make a dent in my Italy debt, pay for the flights at least. It was all coming together, and I felt happy and positive about my choices, my plans – the culmination of my investigation, leads followed up, loose ends tied, back by Thursday evening for dinner. Angus would barely notice I was gone.

'Think about it, yeah?'

'What?'

'The frame.'

'Oh, right. Maybe when I'm back.' I shouldered my empty rucksack. 'Anyway, gotta go.' *Scappo*. 'Got a flight to catch.'

'OK. Good luck. Say hello to your dead friend for me.'

'Sure thing.'

No question marks at all.

35

And so, on Tuesday, I flew to Italy. It wasn't quite as simple as I'd imagined it would be. Firstly, I had to get up early, well before Angus, taking advantage of his semicomatose state to mutter something in his ear about an auction in York, thus giving myself an alibi. Then I retrieved my suitcase from the bin room where I'd hidden it the previous evening, and lugged it quietly downstairs. In the kitchen, Mabel regarded me balefully from her bed – usually she slept with us, but this morning she preferred to be at a vantage point where she could stare at me like she knew exactly what I was doing and thoroughly disapproved. To placate her, I offered an air-dried sausage from the treat tin, cursing as she turned her head away and refused to acknowledge me. Bastard dog. Grabbing my case, I closed the front door softly and hustled away from the house, feeling elated and terrified.

Getting to Manchester Airport required two different trains; I had to change at Leeds, where I bought a bacon sandwich and a copy of *Vogue*. Although I had no interest whatsoever in *Vogue*, I thought it would look cool to carry a copy of it around Trastevere. Unfortunately, due to a platform mix-up, I ended up leaving the uneaten bacon sandwich on a bench, a feast for the pigeons.

At the airport, I browsed duty-free, and failed to find a Toblerone with my name on it. On the plane, I bought a tiny pack of pretzels for £400 and resisted the urge to order a gin & tonic, since it was only 11 a.m. and it cost more than a flat in Chelsea. I wished I wasn't wearing the sun hat – there was no room in my suitcase, so the only option was to wear it, but now I felt like an idiot sitting there with this big floppy straw thing perched on my head. Wrenching it off, I rolled it up and put it under my seat.

The two-hour flight passed pleasantly enough, getting idle glamspiration from *Vogue*, looking at a map of Rome and learning basic Italian phrases. Sign language was much easier than a foreign one. BSL was instinctive, intuitive, made sense. Italian was sexy, but also confusing and had too many syllables. However, by the time we began our descent, I'd learned 'I am sorry', 'Please speak more slowly' and 'Can you offer a better discount?' I knew 'wine' was *vino* because Izzy always called it that, in an exaggerated northern accent. She also used to say *Andiamo!* before we went anywhere, and I never asked what it meant, just accepted it as a regular continental noise she made. Now I saw it was 'Let's go'. With this selection of choice phrases, I figured I was pretty much fluent and could sally forth with confidence.

This theory was tested when I emerged from Ciampino Airport and headed for the taxi rank. It was hot, much hotter than England – that vivid blue sky I'd craved was dazzling, everything louder, more intense, pulsing with unfamiliarity. I'd been to Rome before, but nearly three decades ago, and I remembered nothing useful about it, like how to get around, how far the airport was from the city centre, or what the hell I was doing here.

Standing there with my suitcase and bags, the stupid floppy hat obscuring my view, the southern European sun burning down, Italian chatter all around me, beautiful Voguey people striding around like they knew where they were going, everything so strange and alien . . . I wished I'd taken Dippy up on her offer and gone to Hebden Bridge to source local pottery. That would have been easy and safe and sensible, whereas this was . . . mad.

I took a deep breath, fighting the rising panic. I was a fifty-three-year-old mother of three, with a successful career (behind me) and plenty of useful skills, although it wasn't immediately apparent what the ability to grout neatly would bring to this current situation. 'Stay cool, Mortimer,' Izzy murmured in my head, and I steadied, catching the eye of a taxi driver leaning against his cab.

'*Via Gregoriana, per favore*,' I said, giving the address of my Airbnb. I had no idea what 'how much will it cost?' was in Italian so I just made it up: '*Quanta costa?*'

The taxi driver gesticulated and said something rapid and indecipherable.

'I'm sorry?' I said, in my fluent Italian. I hadn't previously considered that although I was now a master of the tongue, I wouldn't actually understand anything anyone was saying to me. My mouth was wildly impressive, but my ears were a massive letdown.

He said the same thing again, with the same result.

'Can you offer a better discount?' I suggested, fluently.

'*No*,' he said, which I did understand.

'*Per favore?*'

He gesticulated again and said something even more rapid and indecipherable.

'Please speak more slowly,' I said, in his language, although given that I didn't understand anything he was saying in it, slowing down wouldn't make any difference. But I was enjoying my own expertise; this cosmopolitan exchange with a native. It was a beautiful moment; Izzy would have been proud of me.

'I can drive you to Via Gregoriana for forty euros. It is a fixed rate, non-negotiable,' said the taxi driver in perfect English, which was the real-life equivalent of one of Dippy's scrawled phrases across a canvas – ruining everything. Sulkily, I nodded and loaded my bags into his boot.

'*Andiamo*,' I said. '*Vino*.'

Driving through Rome, I thought some of the sights looked familiar but couldn't decide if that was because I'd been there before or just seen lots of pictures. The Colosseum, for example – had we actually visited it, or did I just get a postcard from Izzy? Or maybe we simply drove past, and I counted that as a tour? Everything looked very glamorous, very Roman and very busy. Where would I even begin?

'I'm English, can you help me?' I asked my taxi driver, recalling the useful Italian phrases learnt on the sly while I was doing the washing at home. He shrugged, his eyes on the road.

'I'm looking for my long-lost friend, have you seen her?' Leaning forwards in my seat, I showed him Izzy's *Scoop* profile picture on my phone. *Amica perduta.* The BSL sign for 'lost' was to push your hands apart like you were scattering marbles. Izzy was a marble lost in Rome, a needle in a haystack.

The taxi driver glanced at the phone dismissively. 'You are crazy,' he said. His English was annoyingly good, even better than my Italian.

'*Grazie prego*,' I replied, feeling that at least I'd made a start.

* * *

Via Gregoriana was extremely central, a crucial consideration when I booked my accommodation. The apartment was small and basic but clean, the key accessed via a lockbox on the street. After dumping my bags, I surveyed my domain, home for the next two nights. A kitchenette with a sofa opposite, plus an extremely compact bedroom with very little manoeuvring space around the bed. Plain, anodyne. Still, it was better than the place Izzy and I stayed in our twenties; a roach-infested hostel near the Termini station, boasting a broken lift with a sign that read *Trappola mortale*, along with a rudimentary drawing of a skull and crossbones. Our room had bunk beds that creaked, but not as much as the room next door, where the bed squeaked loudly and rhythmically all night, forcing Izzy to sleep with a stained pillow over her face. On reflection, it might have been a brothel. I couldn't remember if we visited the Colosseum, but I recalled those details very clearly. This neat little apartment would do nicely, a handy HQ for my search.

I put on my sundress and shades, pulled my silly hat firmly on my head, and set off on my expedition: Luca Harris's place of work, which just happened to be right around the corner.

Andiamo!

36

'Where the fuck are you?' said Angus.

He'd called when I was on the end of Via Gregoriana, looking at Google Maps on my phone. Teobaldo Verratti, the publishing house where Luca worked, was located only a few streets away, and as long as I didn't get mown down by a moped, it looked like a fairly straightforward route. When I saw the call, I thought about ignoring it but decided on balance that it would be better to answer straight away, and keep up the pretence.

'York. I told you. There's an auction.' Not too many details – this was where less accomplished liars fell down, embellishing their stories. Keep it simple. My palms felt clammy; Rome was very hot. My hands were also shaking, and I had the beginnings of a headache – I hoped I hadn't caught Covid on the plane.

'York. York as in . . . York?'

It was handy that Angus never listened to me when I told him anything. 'Yes. York as in York.'

'Are you sure?'

I gripped the phone with my sweaty, quivering fingers. 'Yes. I'm sure it's York.' Behind me, I could hear an impassioned argument between two people that sounded cartoonishly Italian. They only needed to break into opera to completely ruin my story.

'Hmmm. Anyway, Liam called.'

'On a *Tuesday*?'

'Yeah. I think something might be up with this Anna.'

'Who?'

'Come on, Gwen. Anna. The girlfriend.'

'Oh, right. What did he say?'

'Not much, you know Liam. But . . . I don't know. He sounded rattled.'

'I'm sure he'll be OK.' It was nearly four o'clock and I wasn't sure how long publishing houses stayed open. I wanted to get there before Luca went home to his gorgeous wife.

'Yeah, maybe I'm worrying unnecessarily. Oh, and your mother called as well.'

'*Mum?*' She never phoned; calling was a huge bother to the recipient, so it just wasn't done. Once my father slipped a disc and had to be taken to A&E but she didn't tell me until afterwards and then only a text: 'Not to worry, all done and dusted!'

'Something about a badger?'

'Oh God.' Maybe Brock had finally attacked via his network of tunnels. The rise of the roaming empire. Why did everything have to kick off at once? I couldn't deal with this now – not when my investigation had reached its apex.

'I'm sure it's nothing serious. Anyway, just to let you know, I'm meeting Min later, might stay at hers tonight. Can you hold the fort for now?' Clever Gwen, sow the seed. I would actually be away for two nights, but I'd worry about that tomorrow.

'Who?'

For God's sake. 'Min. Rude Min.'

'Oh yeah.' He paused. 'Min. Right then, have fun in . . . York.'

'Will do.' I killed the call and went back to Google Maps, trying to memorize the route. Right, left, left. *Andiamo.*

It was only five minutes away, but it was an intense experience, walking there. I seemed to be in everyone's way, lumbering around like Marcus Brody in an Indiana Jones film. It was as if everyone else was operating in a different dimension, one where they had the reaction speeds of bluebottles. I kept bumping into people and apologizing – across three streets, I said '*Mi dispiace*' over a dozen times. I said it so much that I had to stop and look up a different apology on my phone, just to ring the changes. On the next road, I said '*Mi scusi*', over and over, constantly stumbling on the cobbles, distracted by the grand old buildings, limewashed orange, burnished grout-gold in the sun. Everything was so big and bold and luminous – I felt like the *Portrait of an Unknown Model* with her eyes filled in, able to see for the first time. In my twenties, I was oblivious to all this beauty and bustle, only cared where the next cocktail was coming from. But now I drank it in – the elegance and the history and the teeming *life*. If Izzy lived here – and I felt that if she didn't, she should – then I would happily become a regular visitor.

Teobaldo Verratti was on the fourth floor of a handsome ochre building on the corner of Via dei Due Macelli. There was a smiley young lady in reception who nodded when I said 'Luca Harris, *per favore?*', picked up the phone, rattled off something I didn't understand and then pointed at the lift saying '*Quarto*'. I got in and pressed '4', trying to ignore the sudden weakness in my legs. It was one thing to doorstep Izzy's parents in Hathersage, quite another to bulldoze her brother at his office in Rome. Some might say it was extreme. But I was here now and there was nothing else for it.

Up on the fourth floor there was another, less smiley, young woman who looked me up and down, reminding me that my sundress was H&M circa 2019. I wrenched my hat off again and held it behind my back.

'Luca Harris, *per favore?*'

She stared at me steadily, still unsmiling, and then said something that my ears stubbornly refused to make sense of.

'*Mi dispiace?*'

More gobbledegook.

'*Mi scusi?*'

The word she said sounded like 'prance'. Did she want me to do a twirl for her? To complete my humiliation? In my confusion, I resorted to sign language: '*I'm searching for my lost friend.*' The sign for search was to pull your fingers away from your eyes, turn them into little hooks like binoculars, and circle them. Then the scattering marbles sign for 'lost', and then the sign for 'friend' – clasping one hand over the other. I used one hand to stop the other shaking – I was starting to feel quite light-headed; the heat of the city, versus the receptionist's cool gaze.

'Il signor Harris is at lunch,' she said, finally, taking pity on my desperate capering. 'You will have to wait.'

I glanced at the clock above her. It was nearly four thirty. Wow, some lunch. Turning back to the receptionist, I resorted to my last remaining phrase, the only one I hadn't used since I'd arrived:

'Dov'è il bagno?'

She pointed, I saw the toilet sign and escaped with a sigh of relief. At least I had time to wipe off the sweat, calm myself down, smarten myself up. Staring at my face in the mirror, I thought how manic I looked, the whites of my eyes visible, trembling hands, hectic flush. Mind you, I was pretty sure that was how I looked on my last visit to Rome, having imbibed several dubious substances at a party in Borgo. Not to worry, as my mother would say.

Back in reception, I sat down and waited. And waited. The little hand on the clock kept going round, and still Luca Harris did not come back from lunch. What if lunch bled into dinner? Would he ever come back? I fanned myself with my copy of *Vogue*, which I'd brought along to add an air of sophistication. To think I could be in Hebden Bridge right now, glorying in the sodden dreariness.

Finally, at six o'clock, there was a kerfuffle in the lift, it opened, and a group tumbled out, chattering and laughing. They looked like they'd had a very good lunch indeed. I stood up, gingerly, waiting for my moment. Any second now, he'd notice me. The receptionist was all smiles, welcoming them back, even though they were a bunch of slackers who'd clearly boozed the day away. I couldn't make Luca out in the crowd, but saw the receptionist beckon someone and point in my direction, whispering. He had his back to me, but when he turned enquiringly, I saw it was him, my best friend's brother, who used to read his defaced *Count of Monte Cristo* instead of watching us sing in the school choir, smirking when Izzy berated him afterwards. He looked older, silvery and slightly heavier, but still had that air of glamour, now seasoned by years in the most glamorous of cities. As he came towards me, I felt very strange, like the years were rolling back, back, back, damp Lowry-grey mixing with blazing Modigliani-yellow and swirling, swirling, swirling in front of my eyes.

'*Non ci credo*,' he said, a puzzled smile on his face. 'Gwendolyn Mortimer.'

'*Andiamo*,' I whispered, woozily. *Vogue* fell from my grasp and I followed it to the floor, hard and fast as a bluebottle.

37

There's the gentle sound of waves lapping at the shoreline. I'm lying flat on my back, unable to move, unable to open my eyes – the baking sun has me prone and sizzling, a pig on a spit. There's an ache in my temples, from the caipirinhas last night, but it will be gone by the time we go back to the bar – those blazing rays will fry it away, or if not, a quick dip in the ocean will do the job. With a gargantuan effort, I roll myself sideways – Izzy is lying next to me, a copy of *The Secret History* splayed open on her face. Pages flicker with each outward breath.

'What shall we do?' I mumble, barely able to move my cracked lips.

'We're doing it,' she grunts back, scratching a mosquito bite on her arm.

'No, I mean. What shall we DO. With our LIVES.'

The pages of the book flutter as she laughs. She pulls it off her face and turns to look at me. My skin is brick-burnt but hers is a subtle olive-brown.

'What do you *want* to do?'

'I don't know, that's the problem.'

'Then don't do anything till you know.' She rolls over and pulls the book back.

I scratch and fret in the sand. We're too old to be indecisive; we have to get going, before the world leaves us behind.

'Should I take that job? The one at OBD Murphy?' It's only a research position, lowly, badly paid, but a good agency, with prospects. Not what I had in mind, though. Not the cool job at the magazine. But the magazine didn't want me.

'Do you want to?' Her voice is muffled by the book.

'I don't know, that's the problem. You have to decide for me.'

'Why me?'

'Because.' I grab a handful of sand and watch it sift through my fingers. 'I trust you.'

Her hand gropes about, finding my gritty one. She holds it firmly. 'Trust your gut,' she says.

'My guts are not to be trusted,' I reply. 'Not after last night.'

'Neither are mine.' Or does she say 'Neither am I'? I can't hear her through the book. The sun is so hot, heavy on my lids.

'I'm going to cool off.' Hefting myself up, I tramp in burning sand towards the shoreline. Ahead of me, the vast North Atlantic Ocean beckons, nothing between me and America. I wade in, flip to float on my back, letting the currents tug me this way and that. It's easier to let another force decide where I go.

'Gwen!' When she calls, I roll over in the swell, and realize I'm much further out than I thought. Kicking hard, I start to swim back to shore, but the tide is going out and keeps pulling me back. Isabella is charging towards the sea, waving and calling. The water, which looked so blue and inviting, is now a churning mass of grey. I flail about, panic-stricken. Izzy is calling something but I can't hear her.

'Gwen! Gwen! Gwen!' I think it's my name, then realize it isn't. She's shouting something else. What is it?

'Mortimer! STAND!' She bellows. Thrashing down frantically, I immediately find my footing. Rearing up, dripping and panting, I look down at myself. I'm standing on my own two feet, thigh-deep. Glancing back at Izzy, I can see she's clutching herself, rocking with laughter.

'Mortimer!' she hoots. 'When will you *listen?*'

* * *

Stand. Stand. Stand.

'Gwen! Gwen! Gwen!'

My shoulders were being shaken gently. Everything was dark, like Modigliani had painted over my eyeballs again.

'Gwen! Can you stand up?'

Moaning, I allowed myself to be hauled to a standing position. Various hands supported me as I tried to make sense of it all. We appeared to be in some sort of reception, a group of very stylish people talking a language I didn't recognize – or did I?

'*Può farmi uno sconto?*' I murmured.

'*Che?*'

'*Sconto. . .*' I repeated.

'Gwendolyn.' A familiar face appeared in front of me, its expression amused. 'A discount for what?'

'Oh,' I frowned, pondering. 'Luca. The Cunt of Monte Cristo.'

Someone gave a scandalized laugh. Luca smiled. 'I think she's fine, guys. *Andiamo!*' He hooked his arm across my shoulder and led me towards the lift. 'Come! I'm taking you home.'

'I live in Harrogate,' I told him. 'Near the Stray – 12 Cavendish Drive.'

'Not your home, mine. Don't worry, it's not far. Can you manage, do you think?'

The next few minutes were a blur as I tried to work out what had happened to me, while Luca explained what had happened to me.

'You fainted. Everyone was very worried. You still look a little pale, are you OK?'

'I think I'm just . . .' Today. This long day. The drama. The heat. The abandoned bacon sandwich. The tiny bag of pretzels. 'Hungry.'

'Ah! That's something we can remedy. Now. Hold on.'

And suddenly we were zooming down cobbled streets on his moped, which was undoubtedly a '*trappola mortale*', but a very cool one, and I felt that although I'd left my sunhat and *Vogue* behind in reception, I'd never looked more sophisticated than I did now, hanging on to

Luca Harris as he drove me through Rome, zigzagging between cars and pedestrians, occasionally shouting '*Basta!*' at people who dawdled. If only Angus could see me. Well, he'd do his nut, seeing me driving off with another man in Italy, when he thought I was at a house clearance auction in York. If only *Izzy* could see me. 'Mortimer,' she'd say. 'You effing legend.' But maybe she would see me soon; perhaps she was close by, and her brother would bring us together.

Luca lived in another elegant terracotta block a five-minute drive away. There was no lift in this building though, and by the time we reached the fifth floor I was puffing and in danger of passing out again.

'*Tesoro, a casa!*' He flung his keys on a console in the spacious hallway and I followed him, suddenly wondering if Izzy was actually staying there – maybe I was about to encounter her for the first time in fifteen years, right now. The idea was terrifying; what would I say, how would I act, and how on earth would I account for being here? 'Just happened to be passing!' There was a breeze blowing through the apartment; ahead, I caught a glimpse of a living room with long windows and fluttering curtains, but Luca turned right along a corridor and led me into a large bright modern kitchen where a blonde woman was standing against a peninsula, chopping onions. She looked up as we entered, encountering me and glancing anxiously at Luca. Recognizing her from the photos, I jumped forward, holding out my hand.

'You must be Portia.' I was so relieved she wasn't Izzy, that I didn't have to deal with that fraught first encounter, that I may have been a little over-enthusiastic. 'Gwen.'

Portia smiled, still eyeing her husband. 'Nice to meet you, sorry about my smelly fingers.'

She was one of those sweet, posh, pretty women. Lovely at dinner parties, ideal arm candy at soirées, would never say the wrong thing or make anyone uncomfortable. I was disappointed, somehow. Thought Luca would want someone a little spicier, who might occasionally shout and throw things.

'This is *Gwen*-Gwen,' said Luca, plucking a hunk of bread from a bowl on the counter and handing it to me.

Portia raised her eyebrows, but I was too busy scoffing to follow it up. 'Are you hungry?' she asked, pushing forward a dish of olive oil and vinegar.

'Yesh,' I mumbled, still cramming carbs in my mouth.

'She fainted at the office just now,' explained Luca. 'We think her blood sugar may be a little low.'

'Are you diabetic?' asked Portia, alarmed.

'No,' I muttered, 'Just weak.' But the bread was restoring me; now, I wanted to look around their flat, and ask many, many questions.

'Sit down,' said Luca, leading me to a dining table at the far end of the room. It was set for two. Portia hastily came over with extra cutlery and a wine glass.

'I'm so sorry to barge in.' I swallowed the last of the slice and gestured at the fork and spoon she'd put down.

'There's really no need, I feel much better, I'll leave you to your dinner.' Getting invited over was exactly what I had planned, but now I was here it was mortifying, and I longed for my tiny Airbnb with its inadequate kitchenette.

'Not at all,' said Portia, politely. 'There's plenty.'

'I insist,' said Luca. 'It's been so long, we must catch up.' He went over to a cupboard, fetched a bottle of red wine and plonked it on the table. For a man who'd enjoyed a very long lunch, it was an impressive reset. Maybe that was why he lived in Italy.

Portia served salad, and a very simple pasta dish that just seemed to be tomato sauce and olives, with nuggets of mozzarella, but was delicious in a way that conjured images of her wandering round a market, selecting the ripest, freshest, most succulent produce. The wine was excellent, just as restorative as the bread, and soon I was gassing away, reminiscing with Luca about school, and the Peak District, and our parents. He was as dry and suave as I remembered, so charming that I could see why Portia's politeness was slightly brittle. You'd have to watch a man like that; he was just too appealing. Izzy's *je ne sais quoi* obviously ran in the family.

She relaxed a little though as we made our way down the wine and I talked at length about Angus, the boys, and the dog, about making mosaics and hooking up with the Harlots.

'Those hockey matches,' mused Luca, using bread to mop his plate. 'My mother made me go to one, to be supportive. You were brutal.'

To Portia's dismay, I lifted up the skirt of my sundress to show them my leg. 'Look!' I pointed to an old lumpy scar on my knee. 'Hockey ball. Rival team from Bakewell. Alex Charnley. I got in her way. She called me a fucking loin.' I sighed fondly at the memory.

'Izzy has one on her elbow from getting whacked with a stick,' Luca observed, as he returned from the kitchen with a plate of something chocolatey. He put it down on the table next to me. 'Panforte,' he said. 'Help yourself.'

I helped myself heartily. It tasted like rocky road, chewy and sticky and nom-nom-nom, and for a while I forgot that Luca had given me a way in. All evening, I'd been wary of mentioning Izzy, of pointing at the elephant in the room, or rather, the elephant who *wasn't* in the room. It felt like circling an abyss; once I leapt, I'd be dragging us all in and we wouldn't be able to go back. It might be awkward or upsetting or even ruin the evening completely, and I was having such a nice time eating good food in Rome with this handsome man from my past, even if his wife was watching. But what was I here for, otherwise? It had to be done.

Swallowing a last morsel of gooey nutty yumminess, I sucked my fingers and took the plunge. 'So, how *is* Izzy?'

Luca smiled, sliding the panforte towards his wife. 'I was wondering when you'd get around to that.'

'Is that why you came?' Portia asked. 'To see Isabella?' Her relief was palpable. Poor woman, imagining that I'd 'dropped by' her husband's office to see him. I felt flattered that she thought I might be a threat. She was a lot prettier than me, not to mention at least ten years younger.

'Yes,' I said baldly. Previously, I'd imagined I'd be more enigmatic and inventive, throw in a bit of coincidence, circumstance, serendipity. But I'd waited and fainted in Luca's office; it was pointless to try to maintain any degree of dignity. 'I want to know where she is.'

Luca swirled the wine in his glass. 'Why?'

It was an interesting question. 'Because it's been too long,' I said. 'And none of us is getting any younger. Apart from your mother.'

He grinned. 'I heard you paid them a visit.'

'Coco's incredible.'

'It's all Botox.'

'NO!'

'NO!' This was from Portia, who sounded personally wounded.

Luca put a reassuring hand on her arm. 'Of course not. It's a picture in the attic.'

I laughed, but Portia looked confused. My imaginary version of Luca's wife would have got that joke.

'They didn't tell me anything.' It was tactically unwise, to reveal this, but I felt I owed it to Luca to let him know his parents were the soul of discretion.

'Of course.' He was unperturbed.

262

'Will *you?*' I met his eyes.

He turned away, and for a long time gazed into space, running his forefinger up and down the stem of his glass.

'I won't tell you where she is,' he said at last. 'But I will tell you one thing.'

'What?' I leaned forwards, entranced. The person closest to Izzy – apart from her husband, whoever he was – could be about to give me my biggest clue yet.

'I didn't agree with her decision,' he said, flatly. 'I thought she was wrong.'

'What?'

'Her decision to . . . go. I felt it was a mistake.'

There was a silence as I absorbed that information. 'Will you tell me *why* she went?'

He stared at me, hard. 'Don't you know?'

And as I looked back at him, I felt like maybe I did, always had, but the knowledge was buried so deep that I couldn't access it, or didn't want to yet. I'd remember properly when *she* told me. I concentrated on tracing a finger across my plate, picking up rogue crumbs of panforte, to avoid his penetrating gaze. 'Is Izzy in Italy?' I asked, shuffling the conversation along.

'No.'

I paused, my chocolatey finger halfway to my mouth. Having come to Rome on very slim odds – 'a long way to go, on the off chance,' as Dippy had said – nevertheless I felt bitterly disappointed to have met yet another dead end. Luca got up, walked over to a very fancy coffee machine and began fiddling with it. Portia started clearing plates, and I could feel myself being dismissed, but wasn't quite ready to go. Having come all this way, on a wing and a prayer, I wanted to get my money's worth. Sipping from the potent cup he handed me as he sat back down, I gave it one last shot.

'Why did you say "*Gwen*-Gwen" earlier?'

Luca and his wife exchanged glances. 'Because your name comes up occasionally,' Luca said eventually.

'In what context? A good way or a bad way?'

'Good, but . . .' He paused, considering. 'A bit like you'd talk, fondly, of someone who'd died.'

So Isabella wasn't dead, but I was. 'That's a bit harsh.'

'Well, you were on the scene, and then you weren't.'

'Not my fault.'

'Wasn't it?' The hard stare again, making me squirm uncomfortably.

'Is Izzy in Manchester? London? Oxford?' Go on, throw me a bone.

But Luca shook his head. 'It's not for me to tell you her business.'

It was irresistible. 'Is she . . . a spy?'

Portia choked on her coffee. Luca looked incredulous. 'A spy? Of course not!'

'Well, you would say that.'

He chuckled. 'Maybe. Maybe I'm a spy too, a brother-and-sister team.'

'That would actually make sense.'

'We're too old to be spies.' Luca got to his feet, collecting the cups.

'Espion-aged,' I deadpanned. He grinned, and Mrs Harris looked unhappy. Poor woman. I decided it was time for my exit.

'Thank you so much for dinner,' I said. 'I'd better be going.'

Portia perked up. 'Where are you staying? We'll get you a taxi.'

'Via Gregoriana, but I'm sure it'll be fine. It's not far.'

'Don't worry, I'll order on the company account,' said Luca. 'We had a business meeting in my office, after all.'

He walked me downstairs again, which I thought was very gentlemanly, given that he would have to climb all those flights back up. His wife would be on tenterhooks, waiting.

'You came all this way, to find Izzy?' He regarded me curiously, the same way I looked at the Lowry painting.

'Not just that.' As soon as I said it, I realized it was true. 'I wanted to escape for a bit, and couldn't think of a reason.'

'She gave you a reason,' he said slowly.

'Izzy used to push me to do things,' I mused. 'She's still doing it, even in her absence.'

Luca nodded. 'That's Izzy,' he said. 'She always was a bossy cow.'

'I've got one more question,' I said, seeing the cab was waiting outside.

'Shoot.'

'What does *basta* mean?'

He laughed. 'It means "That's enough!" Or "That'll do!" I probably over-use it, particularly on my *motorino*.'

'Useful.' I added it to my Italian lexicon.

Luca gave me his hand, a twinkle in his eye. '*Arrivederci*, Gwen. Enjoy your escape.' He kissed me on both cheeks and I smelled his aftershave. Mmmm. Portia was right to worry. Izzy was a dark horse, and her brother was an Italian Stallion.

'I will,' I replied, climbing into my chariot, and waving goodbye.

Andiamo. My search continued.

38

The next morning, I awoke in my small double bed, in my dinky bedroom, in my compact apartment in Rome, and decided to pretend I lived there. Izzy had pushed me to escape, and now I was free. A single woman, at liberty to do as she liked – what would that woman do with a day to herself in Italy's capital city?

First, she would go to the nearest bakery and buy one of those custard pastry things. Memories of my last trip here were erratic, but I did recall consuming this Italian speciality in excess: a luscious buttery crescent filled with some sort of vanilla cream. Research was needed to establish if they were as delicious as I remembered.

My discreetly packed suitcase yielded black culottes and a flowing white shirt. The sunhat was in Luca's office, so I wrapped my hair in a green scarf and put on some red lipstick for drama. With yesterday's sandals, this constituted a decent outfit for a single, footloose and fancy-free woman to waft about town in. Donning my sunglasses, I set off, trying to channel Luca-on-a-moped vibes. '*Andiamo*,' I murmured to myself. There was a little bakery around the corner, and there I found *cornetti alla crema*, my creamy, dreamy delicacy. I breakfasted on three of them, along with a frothy cappuccino, and then wandered off with no real destination in mind.

It struck me that I'd always holidayed with other people. As an only child, trips with my parents were an intense experience, cowed by their anxious desire to show me a good time. In my twenties, I went away with Izzy, who had strong views about the things we should do or see – though I was mostly happy to go along with her choices. Angus came along, and I holidayed with him, then him and the children – more recently, Angus, the children and the dog, since my husband insisted on bringing her with us. Holidays were busy, noisy, and not particularly restful or indulgent. Yet now, here I was, sashaying without a care in the world; no one to tell me where to go or what to do, no one to complain that they were bored, no one to cater for but myself, no one to clear up after. It was a heady feeling, and I intended to make the most of it. This was my Roman holiday, not thinking about the people I'd left behind – not even thinking about Izzy, since she wasn't here. I took the day off, followed my feet, trusted my gut.

Five minutes of leisurely strolling brought me to the Spanish Steps, the famous sweeping ascension on the Piazza di Spagna. The widest and longest staircase in Europe, so Izzy told me, 135 clean white travertine steps stretched up, leading to the dazzling alabaster edifice at the top – the Trinità dei Monti church, chock-full of exquisite frescos, lofty monuments and sculptures carved by masters of the craft. A must-see destination.

Not must-see for me – instead, I went and goggled at the frontage of Valentino, on the piazza, then walked along Via Borgognona, a gorgeous cobblestone street, browsing chic little boutiques. I bought a slice of pizza and scoffed it while staring at the shoes in the window of Gucci. Then I popped into Zara, the classiest branch I'd ever seen, and bought some gold hooped earrings, which I put straight on. If someone back home asked me, I'd say 'Oh these? Just picked them up at a little place in Rome.' You could probably get them in England too, but that wasn't the point. I had an ice cream on Via del Corso, didn't bother trying to understand the flavours, just pointed at something pink and fluffy. Slurping it, I walked past a McDonald's, which managed to look exactly like every other McDonald's I'd ever seen, but also uniquely Roman. And then I found myself back at the Trevi Fountain, where I knew I'd end up, because I threw the coin in with Izzy all those years ago.

Like the Spanish Steps, the fountain was one of the most spectacular examples of its kind, thirty metres high against the backdrop of the dazzling Palazzo Poli facade. In the centre stood a statue of nautical Neptune, being driven towards the water on his chariot pulled by two winged horses; one calm and docile, the other rearing up – opposing but interconnected forces. The pool sparkled invitingly – *Come, give me your gold and your dreams will come true . . .*

It was Izzy who explained to me how the coin toss worked. Most people knew that you threw a coin in the fountain to guarantee that one day you would come back. You had to do it properly though – your right hand throwing over your left shoulder. A lesser-known tradition was that you could throw a second coin to find romance in the city, and a third to marry there. We argued about how many coins to throw. Izzy thought it would be romantic to find romance in Rome, whereas I thought it would be a logistical pain, given that we were only there for four days. I also had no desire to get married there because of the cost implications of flying my family and friends over for the wedding. I threw one coin; Izzy threw three, calling me a Penny Pessimist. Her postcard to Alaric said that she'd got married in Positano – not quite Rome, but at least Italy, so maybe there was something in it.

Right then and there, I decided to create a new tradition, and threw FOUR pennies in the fountain, one after the other. Four coins for friendship. I would find Izzy and we would be friends again – maybe we'd even come back here together one day. Then I thought, sod it, and threw a fifth coin in, which represented my wish for a viable career. Then I thought I'd better go before the Trevi Fountain overflowed with my small change.

I carried on wandering, down wide boulevards and cobbled side streets, around breathtaking piazzas, through elegant formal gardens with more modest fountains and lush palm trees. When it got too hot, I tiptoed in to a Baroque church gaudily festooned with paintings of wrestling gods and sculptures of angels. It was cool and peaceful after the bustle of the city streets, and I sat there for a while enjoying the silence, feeling pure and holy. Then I decided I was ready for a little drink, so found a bar not far from my apartment, ordered a glass of chilled rosé – '*Vino, prego*' – and drank it perched on a stool in the window, just watching passers-by and living in the moment.

I did all this, and found the colour and vibrancy and dynamism and excitement my life had been lacking of late. I let it infuse and charge my soul as I put the me in Rome.

I did all this, and ignored four calls from Angus. I ignored calls from my mother. Ignored a call from Morag. Ignored a call from Dippy. I had no idea why all these people were calling me, but it felt irrelevant. Whatever the problem was, there was nothing I could do about it, because I was in Rome, having the time of my life. *La dolce vita!*

When I finally sank into my little bed in *casa mia*, I was aching and exhausted but euphoric, drunk on the buzz and beauty of the Eternal City, intoxicated by my own stupendous self-gratification. What it was to please oneself so spectacularly! To indulge one's whims! I should do this more often!

But another part of me thought: *Basta*.

39

Getting home to Blighty was a real ball-ache. My taxi to the airport was late, and the driver insisted on practising his English on me by asking if I'd ever met someone called Jorginho. I gathered he was a footballer and explained my lack of interest, but he gave me a blow-by-blow account of his latest season anyway. I wished Fred was here; he would know how to have this discussion. In fact, I missed my whole family, even Mabel, but was also not looking forward to seeing them at all, because it would mean facing the music. Why did people say 'face the music'? Music was nice. Confronting Angus would be more like facing a rabid snarling beast. First thing in the morning, I'd sent him a text with as little detail as possible: Sorry, got caught up, back soon! There had been no reply.

On the flight back to the UK, I got stuck next to a woman who kept asking me if I'd seen certain films, and then when I said I hadn't, explaining the plots to me. In *forensic* detail. I thought I was going to die from fake-smiling and pretending to care, and in the end, I stopped pretending, but she didn't stop detailing the narrative of *Eternal Sunshine of the Spotless Mind*, telling me I really should see it, even though I didn't need to now because I knew everything that happened in it, down to the outfit Clementine was wearing when she went for the date with Joel on the frozen river.

By the time we landed in Manchester, my me-day in Rome seemed like a distant memory, as far removed as my trip there with Izzy. It felt like a dream. Had I even been there? Could I persuade myself that I'd never really gone, so that when I faced the rabid snarling beast, I could say with conviction that it never happened? It was a strategy to consider, and I mulled on the possibility of extreme denial as I waited in the queue at passport control. There were no phone messages to ignore; my family appeared to have given up on me, and I began to feel hopeful that they'd all been distracted by their own business, and I'd get back to find an empty house. Maybe it would just be Mabel, whose disapproval was at least unspoken.

The airport looked like a Lowry painting, dull and grey, full of depressed-looking travellers who lacked Italian style. Now I was back, I started to see that in many ways my trip had been a failure, in that I was no closer to finding Izzy. All the trails had gone cold. I was out of ideas. Where was Jackson DeLantro when you needed him?

At that precise moment, my phone buzzed. I was going to ignore the call like all the others but saw it was an unrecognized number. Incredulous, I snatched it up.

'Hello?' I whispered. Everyone around me was silent, staring into space.

'Hi, is that Gwen? It's JD.'

'Hi, JD.' Did he have something for me?

'I've got something for you.'

'Really?'

'Why are you whispering?'

'I'm in an airport.'

'Careful what you say,' he said, like some sort of MI5 handler.

I snorted. 'What have you got?'

'Your friend is a difficult woman to find.'

'But have you found her?'

'Yes and no.'

'What does that mean?' My whisper became a rasp. Reception was patchy and people were giving me looks.

'We have reason to believe she may be in Manchester.'

So close! 'We? Is this you and your bunker friend?'

'He's— Garth doesn't live in a bunker.'

'Oh sorry, my mistake. Carry on. Why do you think she's there?'

'There is no record of your Isabella Harris living or working anywhere in the country. But there is a freelance restaurant reviewer called Charles Wellesley based in or around Manchester.'

'What's he got to do with Isabella?' Perhaps Charles was her husband?

'We think Charles Wellesley *is* Isabella.'

There was a silence as I considered the implications of that statement. 'Why would Isabella be Charles Wellesley?'

'Charles Wellesley is an early pseudonym of Charlotte Brontë.'

'CHARLOTTE BRONTË?' Various people around me craned and stared, but I was too flabbergasted to care.

Well, well, Wellesley. Jackson DeLantro and Garth Bunker had seriously come up with the goods. I pondered this radical new information as JD continued: 'Despite the different names, the writing styles are very similar. Wellesley is quite a renowned figure in the hospitality industry because a mystery surrounds his true identity. Several restaurant critics operate in this way, and in this business, it would make sense for a woman to pretend to be a man to maintain greater anonymity. If we're correct in this assumption, if you find Charles Wellesley then you'll find Isabella Harris.'

'What publication does she . . . he work for?'

'He's written for national newspapers, magazines, and websites, but many of the establishments he's reviewed are in and around Manchester. A few in London, occasionally elsewhere around the country, but there's a concentration in the north-west. Crucially, he writes a regular food diary column for a magazine called *Mancunium*, and according to that, he seems to be based in . . . Chorlton.'

'Wow.'

Where Izzy's old flat used to be. Was she back there? After all this time? Could it really be true? Had Izzy changed identity simply to build a profile as an incognito food critic? Surely not; there had to be something else behind it.

'I'll email you an article and you can see for yourself.'

'Thanks JD, you're a star.' I had to hand it to him and his bunker friend. Sometimes, you just needed a nerdy podcaster to get things done. Two were even better. 'I really appreciate it. Please pass on my thanks to . . . er . . .' It was no good, I couldn't remember his name, just kept thinking of Norman Bates.

'Garth. No problem, give Angus my best.'

'Will do.' Not likely. I wouldn't be able to give Angus anything, he'd be too busy giving it to me, both barrels.

Heady with this new information, and wanting to put off the inevitable encounter with my husband, instead of taking my first connecting train to Leeds, I took a cab to Chorlton. It was time to face, not the music, nor the monster, but the mysterious Charles Wellesley.

40

Summertime, and The Living Is Easy

Our resident food guru Charles Wellesley gives us an insight into his seasonal snooze-fest

The Latin word for summer is 'Aestas', from which we get the word 'aestivate', meaning 'to spend a hot or dry period in a state of torpor or dormancy'. In our increasingly sultry summers, I often find myself winding down, too bothered to bother with finicky preparation and certainly not inclined to slave over a scorching oven. Luckily, during this season, we have a glut of rich and ripe produce which really needs no adornment or fuss. The order of the day is for simple, light and excellent ingredients, thrown together casually, languidly, served with a glass of something chilled and refreshing. Herewith my recommendations to sate your Aestas appetite . . .

In the morning, my spouse and I might break our fast with granola – oats roasted (on a previous colder day) in agave syrup and olive oil, served with whatever fruit happens to be around, a handful of nuts, seeds and a luscious dollop of yoghurt. Now, I know that all sounds suspiciously wholesome, so let's ruin it with a naughty *cornetto*, the Italian croissant; sweeter and denser, filled with *crema pasticcera*, which is a very dramatic way of saying custard. There's a darling delicatessen on Manchester Road called Da Mario – Mario is quite a character – and their bakery sells *cornetti* which would not taste out of place in the heart of Testaccio. *Bravo*, Mario!

For lunch, we might make a hearty salad with halloumi – the vegetarian's rump steak – and pea shoots, which are so easy to grow in pots, indoors or out. Add some almonds for extra crunch, and fresh peaches for sweetness. Serve with my home-made rose lemonade and you have a delightful and deeply colourful *pranzo*. Or, you know, you could just head to newly opened Ryebank, which offers a cunningly curated midday menu, and lovely views of the Fields.

As the midsummer heat dissipates later in the day, my better half and I will venture towards the oven, briefly, to drop in a garlic bulb drizzled in olive oil. While this dissolves into gooey sweetness, I'll throw together a simple pasta dish with the finest ingredients I can find. Plump, juicy tomatoes, carefully cured black olives, homegrown fresh basil, maybe a few fat lardons and a shaving of Mario's Parmesan – *perfetto*!

Fresh bread, slathered in butter and the roasted garlic, completes the meal. Wash it all down with my version of the Hugo cocktail – this summer's tipple of choice. Prosecco, elderflower cordial, a dash of soda water, mint. My twist? A piquant summer toast, from *Jane Eyre*: 'I must keep in good health, and not die.'

Cin-cin!

41

So Isabella was dead, but Charles Wellesley was alive and well, and all over the internet. As JD said, he'd written for numerous publications but reviews seemed to veer towards Manchester and the north-west. The piece JD sent me, written that month, was firmly Chorlton-fixated, and I felt sure it meant Izzy had returned to her old stomping ground. I was closing in . . .

My taxi headed for Claude Road, where Izzy used to have a flat. Maybe she never sold it; maybe she was back there. It was a great place – a maisonette with one bedroom and a boxroom – occasionally, I'd ended up in the 'cubbyhole', as she called it, when an evening had stretched into the early hours. The kitchen had French doors that opened onto a tiny courtyard strung with fairy lights. We'd always joked that it was where Carrie Bradshaw would have lived if she'd been British, and much less successful. *Sex and the Shitty*, Izzy used to say.

The road was pretty much as I remembered, and I instructed the taxi driver to stop right outside the old property – a large converted red-brick Victorian house, with faux-Tudor timber eaves. I gazed up at it, wondering if I'd see Izzy in one of the windows. The building looked smarter now, and as I ventured into the front garden, it was clear that it was no longer divided up, but had been turned back into one house. Maybe Izzy bought the attic flat, and knocked through? Tiptoeing up to the front bay, I peered in – to my alarm, a child playing in the living room looked up, saw me, and burst into tears. She ran away, screaming, and I jumped back in horror. Was that Izzy's daughter? Seconds later, the front door opened.

'Can I help you?'

The woman on the front step, with the child on her hip, was not Izzy. Much younger, and much frostier, though that was fair enough given that I'd been nosing round her property and freaking out her offspring.

'I'm so sorry. My friend used to live here, and I wondered if she still did.'

The woman looked me up and down, and I was suddenly aware that I must present an odd appearance, travel-bedraggled, standing there with all my luggage. I clutched my case defensively.

'Isabella Harris?' I squeaked.

She sniffed. 'You're the second person to come round asking for her. I don't know her.'

'Who was the first?' There were several occasions when I'd been pipped to the post by a fellow seeker, and

I didn't know if that was significant, or just a random coincidence.

'No idea. It was earlier this year. Brought cookies, said she was a neighbour.'

'Maybe she was?'

'Doubt it, I never saw her before. Anyway, I don't know who this Isabella Harris is, I'm afraid.'

The dismissal was implicit. Wheeling my case around, I trudged back to the street, lugging my case, feeling defeated. Dead ends everywhere. Dismally, I headed for the high street, berating myself. Whatever else it was, Rome had been a fun jaunt. But going to Chorlton felt . . . desperate. What was I doing here? I needed to go home, right now. And yet . . . I found myself wondering about the delicatessen Izzy mentioned in her column. Da Mario's, only a little way up the road. There were various voices in my head – maybe even Izzy's – telling me to stop, to knock this on the head, come to my senses, *basta!* And yet . . . I marched on, until I reached a large double-fronted shop with a crimson awning, tiny metal tables outside, customers leaving with bulging bags. Little Italy. I went inside.

Here was my taste of Rome again, in Chorlton-cum-Hardy. A counter stocked with cheese and meat. Baskets overflowing with loaves of every kind. Shelves loaded with different varieties of pasta. Fresh vegetables, olives, hummus, arancini, macarons. The array was dizzying. And right there, amongst a selection of pastries, the *cornetti*.

I bought one, and took it outside, to savour it, to try to recreate the moment in Italy, and the moment before that, with Izzy, when we stood laughing on a piazza together with custard running down our chins. *Cin-cin!*

I bit, and chewed, and tried, but it was no good. This was Manchester Road, in the drizzle, and I felt like an idiot. It didn't taste the same here – I couldn't savour the sunshine or the excitement or the Roman flavour. The *cornetto* was sticky, sickly sweet, wrong. The holiday was over, and it was time to go home. To go home and face the music, the monster, whatever.

The train from Manchester to Leeds was dirty, and late. The train from Leeds to Harrogate was dirty, and late. There was no one waiting for me at the station, no one to give me a lift home, no one to say are you OK. I was dirty and late, and exhausted and also another thing which I did not want to name. It was nearly dark, and I'd been AWOL for well over forty-eight hours, with nothing to show for it. There were no taxis to be had, so I had to walk home, dragging my stupid suitcase. It wasn't that far, but I was so tired it felt like my legs might fall off.

As I neared our house, I could see the lights on and felt a little spark of happiness that soon I would be inside it, finding out what Fred and Sam had been up to, grouting my kitchen tiles, being ignored by the dog. A nice, peaceful, normal evening at home. But as I went up the steps, I heard a shout: 'She's here!'

The front door was wrenched open, and Angus charged out, followed by my father, *and* my mother *and* my mad mother-in-law. *All* of them looked mad, mad as fire, and I quaked in my falling-apart sandals, my suitcase toppling back down to street level.

'Where the fuck,' thundered Angus, 'do you think you've been?'

42

'Language, Hamish,' drawled Morag, who was holding an empty cocktail glass. 'Gwyneth, you're looking dreadful,' she added, using the receptacle to gesture down my broken body. 'Dragged through a hedge backwards. Where have you been? And where did you get those earrings, they look so cheap.'

'You know where she's been!' exploded Angus.

'York!' I said, my voice high and unnatural. I wanted whatever Morag had been drinking. Dutch courage was definitely needed to maintain my extreme denial.

'Bollocks!' bawled Angus. 'You've been in Rome!'

My resolution crumbled instantly. 'How did you know?'

'Because you're a bloody idiot!' he replied. 'Don't you realize that when you phone someone who's abroad, you can hear it in the ringtone? I knew as soon as I called you yesterday.'

'Oh.' I pondered this new piece of information. 'But how did you know I was specifically in Rome?'

'I didn't know exactly where you'd gone. I asked everyone but no one knew. So I . . .' He hesitated. 'I went to your workshop and spoke to . . . that girl.' He winced.

'Oh.' For the first time, I felt bad for what Angus had been through. He hated seeing Dippy in her gaping dungarees, it made him completely overwrought. 'I'm so sorry.'

'It was fucking awful,' he moaned. 'I didn't know where to look or what to say. She asked me if I had a speech impediment.'

'I think you might have Tourette's,' said Morag. 'Let's go inside. I need another one of these.' She wiggled her glass.

'We're here too,' said my mother, helpfully. My father nodded to indicate his presence. His hand was bandaged.

'Yes, why is that?' My parents didn't like going further than the end of their drive.

'Brock,' said my father. 'He finally attacked.'

'My God.' I pointed at his hand. 'Was that him?'

'What?' My father looked down at his bandage. 'No, I got this de-stoning an avocado.'

'So what did Brock do?'

My mother sighed deeply. 'We knew it would happen eventually. He just wouldn't stop digging.'

'What happened?'

'The rockery fell in. Our garden's ruined, and apparently it's undermined the foundations of the kitchen.'

'Wow. One little badger.'

'Brock's not little,' pronounced my father. 'And there's not one of him. There's at least two, according to the night-vision camera.'

'So you're here because your house is unsafe?'

'Yes, and because you are too. Abandoning your husband and children.' My mother folded her arms, glaring at me. 'That poor man.' She glanced at Angus, her face softening.

'Shall we get that drink?' I said to Morag.

Inside, it looked like the foundations of *our* kitchen had been undermined, rubbish everywhere, takeaway cartons littering the table, wet washing draped on the backs of chairs. It always amazed me how chaotic males left alone could be. Truly astonishing levels of disarray. I bent to scratch an indifferent Mabel, while Morag messed about with the cocktail shaker and my parents sat primly at the dining table. With a grim face, Angus handed me a lukewarm plate of curry and rice and I fell on it enthusiastically, joining my parents at the table.

'So, do you want to tell us exactly why you pissed off to Rome without telling anyone?'

Gesturing with my fork, I used eating as a delaying tactic. When I'd envisioned confessing, my parents and mother-in-law had not been involved. Now they were here, it made everything more complicated, and I didn't know where to begin.

Mad Morag turned, wielding her mixer like maracas. 'She was looking for her more beautiful friend, of course.' Whipping out a glass, she poured the contents of the shaker into it and pushed the result towards me. The liquid was rich and dark, like blood. Knowing Morag, maybe that's what it was.

'Thank you, Mother,' I said.

'Isabella?' asked Angus. 'That wild goose chase? I thought you'd given up on it.'

'I got a lead,' I said, through a mouthful of rice. 'All leads goad to Rome.'

'This is bullshit,' spluttered Angus. 'You went all the way to Rome to look for Izzy? What were you thinking?'

'Did you find her?' asked Morag eagerly.

'No,' I said, reaching for some leftover naan bread. 'But I had a nice time.' Fortified by several sips of Morag's fearsomely potent concoction, I now felt quite bolshie about the whole thing.

'But why didn't you *tell* me?' asked Angus. 'Why didn't you just say, "By the way, I'm going to Rome"?'

'Because you would have tried to stop me.'

He was silent, digesting the undeniable truth of this.

My mother, however, was not so easily put off. 'So selfish and irresponsible. What if one of the children had needed you?'

'They had their father.' I gestured towards dumb Angus. 'Not a babysitter. An actual parent.'

'But it was dangerous, going off like that,' said my father, with his bandaged paw. Jeopardy was everywhere, even in an avocado.

'What? It's Rome, not Acapulco.'

'This has all got out of hand.' Angus finally found his voice. 'This . . . pursuit. It's ridiculous. You're a grown woman.'

I took another gulp of Morag's cocktail and slammed the glass down on the table. 'What is this, an intervention?'

They exchanged glances. 'Well, yes,' confessed my father. 'To save you from mortal peril.'

'Yes,' asserted my mother. 'To save your poor husband.'

'Yes,' breathed Morag. 'To save your pathetic, ravaged soul.'

'Yes,' snapped my husband. 'To save you making a massive fool of yourself.'

Mabel panted approvingly.

It was time for some home truths, fuelled by Morag's firewater.

'So,' I said, putting my knife and fork down neatly, deliberately. 'Where was the intervention, Dad, when you went on that silent retreat when I was fourteen? It was supposed to last three days, but you were gone a week, and when you came back you only communicated via Post-its.'

My father waved his trussed-up fingers. 'I'd just been made redundant, was having a bad time. The silence was . . . golden.'

I turned to my sanctimonious mother. 'And where was the big family heart-to-heart when you went to stay with your sister in Penrith for "a few days"' – I did the bunny ears – 'and didn't come back for a fortnight? I was doing my A levels. I thought you were having a breakdown.'

My mother's arms fell to her side. 'I was going through the Change. Everything was all over the place.'

'Well, *you* were. All over Cumbria.' My laser-gaze focused on Angus. 'And *you*. When you lost your job. You wanted a dog, went on all those "little research trips".

Except the Scotland one – that wasn't "little", was it? You were gone two weeks. Two weeks, to visit a dog breeder? Who happened to live next to a golf course? Did you need to help the foetus gestate on the ninth hole?'

Angus looked down at the table, red-faced. 'It took longer than I thought it would.'

'But who was looking after the kids, and the house, while you were gone? Who womanned the decks?'

'I seem to remember you weren't too happy when I came back,' Angus muttered.

'Two weeks, versus three days. Do the maths.' I took a great, triumphant glug of my gory nectar.

'Now do me!' said Morag, encouragingly.

I was only too ready to oblige. 'You're off your rocker, the whole time. A hardcore nutjob, away with the fairies, out of your tree.'

Morag cackled ecstatically.

'The point is,' I concluded, 'we all go off the rails sometimes. My rails took me to Rome for a couple of days. It's not a big deal. I'm back now. No harm done.'

At that point, three things happened.

One: The door slammed, and Fred charged in, his hair on end, dragging his backpack along the floor behind him.

His haunted eyes razed around the room before coming to rest on me. 'Max doesn't want to be friends with me any more,' he wailed. 'His dad just dropped me off and Max said I wasn't to go round again. He's friends with Zach and Oscar nowwwwwwwwww.' He dissolved into tears.

Two: There was a thud on the stairs and Sam erupted into the room waving his laptop and looking stormy.

'It's CRASHED,' he bellowed. 'It's all GONE. Everything I've worked on, GONE.' He threw the device on the table, and it slid across, coming to a halt by my empty plate.

Three: The door banged again, which confused us all, because everyone who could possibly be here was here. Except Liam, who now staggered in, with red eyes, and a rucksack on his back, carrying a huge plastic bag of washing. Morag and my parents flocked to him, hugging him, fussing him. Liam fended them off, then pinched the bridge of his nose with his finger and thumb. Angus put a hand on his shoulder and squeezed.

'What are you doing here, mate?' he said. 'Term's not finished yet.'

Liam raised his head, trying to smile and failing. 'Anna and I . . . We split up . . . I was supposed to be in Bristol. Didn't know where . . .' He dropped his bag and, horrifyingly, began to cry.

My giant baby boy. Laid-back Liam, who always took everything in his stride, was sobbing, surrounded by his ineffectual grandparents. He needed his mum. Yet when I tried to get up, my legs didn't work. The combination of traipsing across town, suburb and city, and consuming Morag's lethal cocktail, had rendered them useless, dead. But he needed me. They all did. I gazed up at my eldest son, at his dear crumpled face, and held out my arms.

'Sweetheart,' I breathed. 'Come here.'

43

The first thing I did was pack them all off to bed. Which was difficult, because there were so many of them, and not enough beds. Morag was in Liam's room, so we made up the sofa for him in Angus's garden studio. He was better off in his own space, out of the madhouse. My mother and father wittered their way to the spare room, fretting about youngsters today, and the two younger boys sloped off to their own bedrooms looking anguished. By the time we got to our own bed, Mabel was already there, sprawled across our pillows in the running position, snoring loudly.

Angus clucked affectionately. 'Look at her. Tired after all the drama.'

I resisted pointing out that during all the drama Mabel had been flat out under the kitchen table. Huffing, I shoved her over to his side and got in, my legs still weak from Morag's devil juice. She claimed it was an Aunt Roberta cocktail, which sounded quite staid, but obviously the name belied the contents, which Liam said included absinthe. At one point it seemed unlikely I'd ever walk again. I had boys to soothe, domestic harmony to restore and parents to dispatch. If I could just get a good night's sleep, then I'd regain my strength and be ready to tackle my to-do list tomorrow.

Angus unearthed his latest war biography from a pile of washing and got in next to me, kissing Mabel on the snout.

'So, have you got it out of your system?' He turned on his reading light.

I considered. My investigation hadn't been a success, in that I hadn't found Izzy. But on the other hand, it had got me out of the house and given me a sense of . . . *purpose*. It felt like a long time since there was something I *had* to do, and my search party had afforded me that compunction; that get up and go. OK, so I still didn't have my friend, but I liked myself a bit more, even if I'd been an idiot. At least I was a proactive idiot, rather than a passive one.

'No,' I said, because I didn't want to make it easy for him.

He sighed and opened his book. He was reading an account of the Normandy landings called *D-DAY*, which I remembered because he'd told me the D stood for 'Day', which meant that D-Day was short for Day-Day. I'd laughed like a drain and he was very offended because military history was important. I didn't understand his predilection for war tomes, or golf, or the technology behind noise-cancelling headphones, and he didn't understand why I wanted to find Izzy. We had to agree to disagree, consent to dissent, concur to demur. Opposing but interconnected forces. That was marriage.

'One day though,' I added, 'I'll take you to Rome and show you round. I speak really good Italian.'

He grinned at me sideways. 'So do I. *Cronometrara l'oscillazione è fondamentale.*'

I was impressed. 'That's very good. What does it mean? Of course, I know, but I want to check that you do.'

'It means "Timing of the swing is extremely critical."' He laughed at my confusion. 'I've got a golf buddy who's from Naples.'

'I don't think it's the most useful phrase.'

'You never know,' he replied. 'There's a course near Rome. Olgiata. *Molto bello.*'

'*Ti amo,*' I said. 'Even though you're annoying.'

'Right back atcha. But next time you go off on an expedition, leave me a Post-it note.'

*   *   *

The next morning, I got up early, grouted a few tiles and tidied up the mess from the night before. Then I found some bacon in the fridge and made a sandwich with lashings of brown sauce, plus two steaming cups of tea. Loading it all on a tray, I took it out to Liam. He was awake when I went in, staring blankly at the ceiling. I put my offerings on the little table next to the sofa and squeezed in near his massive feet.

'How are you feeling?'

He frowned. 'Bad.'

Picking up my own mug of tea, I cradled it. 'This is a rite of passage,' I said. 'We've all been there.'

He gave me a dismissive glance.

'I got dumped in my first year. Guy called Camberwell Michaels.'

'You're kidding me,' said Liam. '*Camberwell?*'

'Yeah, he was a poet. Did readings and everything. Wore a thin scarf. I thought he was so cool. Anyway, one night he met me in the pub and said that he needed to be challenged in a relationship to help his art. Basically he was saying I was too nice – too accommodating. So we split up and he started going out with a girl called Renata who kept a collection of knives. I was devastated. But you know what?'

'What?' Liam's lip was curling a little, partly mocking, partly amused.

'I looked him up on Facebook and he's a *banker* now! A corporate shill!'

'I'm not sure what your point is,' said Liam.

I wasn't sure either. 'My point,' I said slowly, 'is that you never know how things are going to pan out. You're right in it now, and it's hard and painful and upsetting. But five years from now – even five months – who knows where you'll be. You might be back together; you might be going out with Zendaya.'

'Anna might be a poet,' murmured Liam.

'Think how boring *that* would be,' I said, and he laughed, finally.

'It's nice to be back home,' he said. 'Just for a bit. Particularly if you make me bacon sandwiches.'

'Stay as long as you like,' I assured him. 'But just to warn you, if you hang round here, you'll be roped into one of your father's *Graveyard* episodes.'

'Or you'll stick tiles on me.'

'I love you.' I leaned forward to hug him. 'And any girl would be lucky to have you. Even Zendaya.'

* * *

Back inside, I encountered a wan Freddie assembling his cereal library. Sitting next to him, I pulled the jar of granola towards me.

'So why did you and Max fall out? Was it an argument?'

Fred shook his head, his mouth full. I waited.

'He's been playing online with Zachary. Says Zach can do a 360 noscope, and that I'm a noob.'

'Right.' I digested that information, along with roasted oats. 'Do you really want a friend who makes judgements like that?'

Fred gaped at me. 'Of course I do!'

'OK.' Obviously, a different tactic was required. 'But in the last few weeks, you've only seen Max, no one else. Haven't you got any other friends?'

He pondered, his spoon hovering. 'I like Jonny. But he's not as into Fortnite.'

That made me like Jonny too. 'You can't base a friendship on Fortnite.'

'You can.'

God, twelve-year-olds were infuriating. 'What I mean is, don't put all your eggs in one basket. It's nice to have a best friend, but sometimes it's better to have lots of good friends. Maybe you should widen your circle a bit.'

Fred scooped up a Blueberry Wheat. 'Like you?'

'What do you mean?'

He chewed and swallowed. 'Those hockey people.'

'Well, yes, I . . . I suppose so.'

'Hmmm. Maybe I can text Jonny. And Amos. He's OK. At least he can crank 90s.'

'Splendid. Invite Jonny and Amos round and you can be noobs together.'

'Mum, don't say stuff like that, it's just embarrassing.'

'That's what I'm here for. To be an immense embarrassment.'

'You're Level 400 embarrassment.'

'Finish your cereal, and put the bowl in the dishwasher when you're done.'

While he did that, I found a Post-it in a drawer and wrote a note for Angus: *I'M GOING OUT. SORT SAM'S COMPUTER.*

I'd fixed two out of the three. He was better qualified to deal with the remaining one.

* * *

Dippy was in our workshop, putting the finishing touches to her Hebden Bridge painting.

'It's looking good.' It really was. The colours were deep and vibrant, the stark black of the canal locks against the soft grey of the mill and the lush green of the backdrop. The quote scrawled across it was incongruous, jarring; an aspersion. The whole thing was a challenge, which I guess was what my old boyfriend Camberwell had been looking for.

'Thanks.' Dippy raised her head briefly, before returning to her work. She continued without looking at me. 'Sorry if I shat the bed telling your bloke where you were. He seemed agitated.'

'Don't worry, he'll recover.' He might recover from my Rome trip but he'd never get over seeing Dippy's nipples. 'Anyway, I came to say I'll make you your frame.'

'You what?'

'Your mosaic frame. I'll do it. If you still want me to?'

Dippy stood up, putting her paintbrush on the stand. 'Yeah. I still want it. Will you really?'

'Yes. I'm sorry I said no before, I was being an arsehole.'

'Not an arsehole. Maybe a bit of a knob.'

'Well, I've stopped that now. I'll go up to Hebden Bridge next week, source some local pottery. Is that OK?'

'Hippity-hoppity.' Dippy smiled, a megawatt beam, and I was glad Angus wasn't around to see it. 'So, how did it go in Rome? Is your friend dead after all?'

'Yes,' I said. 'I think she might be. To me, at least.'

* * *

298

The rest of the day was spent catering for my family, eating with my family, tidying up after my family, and arguing with my family. Thanks to a handy podcasting associate, Angus had fixed Sam's computer and given it back to him, telling him he was a drama queen. Sam cried with relief, and after he'd gone up to his room, I asked Angus if he'd checked for any dubious material.

'Dubious?' he asked.

'Porn!' I squeaked.

'Oh, no!' he assured me. 'Not the dubious stuff, anyway. Only the classy kind.'

My dad and I cooked a risotto, and we all ate together, crammed around our dining table which was only supposed to seat six. I asked Morag why she was here, and she said she'd met a man on the internet who turned out to be a con artist, and that she'd come down so that Angus could help her find his IP address so she could have him killed.

'Couldn't you have done that remotely?' I asked.

'I think killing is always best done in person,' she replied.

By the end of the dinner, I felt almost fondly towards all of them, apart from Mabel, who ate a whole garlic bread off the table and then farted continually under it. But to get out of clearing up, I offered to take her on the evening walk, and before anyone could object, I grabbed her lead and headed for the door, thinking what a nice day it had been. Just hanging out, doing jobs, talking, messing about, being together. From now on, I would relish these moments, focus on them, find my purpose in them. I'd widen my circle of friends, like Fred. I'd put the last few weeks behind me, and move on.

Dragging an unwilling Mabel, I let myself out, checking my pockets for poo bags, calling goodbye to everyone indoors, standing on the steps appreciating the lovely summer evening, sunshine streaming across the Stray, illuminating everything in its path. Including the woman opposite, a stationary figure on the pavement across the road. I stopped in my tracks, stock-still, staring, unable to believe my eyes. After all that effort, after all this time . . .

Right there, opposite my house, very much alive and well, was Isabella Harris.

PART TWO

44

'Stay right there!' I yelled, and dashed back into the house.

Dragging a protesting Mabel, I threw her lead to the floor in the hallway, stormed up the stairs, two at a time, barged into the bin room and started rooting round in a frenzy. It was there, I'd just seen it, where was it? Why did nothing in this room stay in one place? It was like the opposite of Harry Potter's Room of Requirement – whenever you needed something, it disappeared. Finally, I found what I was looking for, wrapped in its tea towel on top of one of Angus's robot hoovers. Grabbing it, I charged downstairs, scooped up Mabel's lead, wrenched open the door and bounded down the front steps, anxiously scanning the pavement opposite.

She wasn't there.

'Dammit!' Did I dream it? Was she a figment of my imagination? Had I got so caught up in the search that I was now delusional? Maybe I just saw someone who *looked* like Isabella . . . but no – *there* she was, in the park across the road, walking rapidly away, glancing over her shoulder. Definitely her.

'Hey!' I shrieked. 'Wait!'

Catching sight of me, she broke into a trot. My best friend was actually running away from me. Why was she here in the first place if she was just going to turn tail? What the hell was going on? It was utterly baffling and bizarre. But one thing was for sure; she wasn't going to get away with it. Not after all this time.

The chase was ON.

Winding Mabel's lead round my hand, I set off after her.

Now, running was never my forte. And at fifty-three, when the most exercise I did was the occasional half-arsed swim in the local municipal pool, or a Pilates class because the centre was near a nice wine bar and the session finished at 6 p.m., fitness in general was also not my forte. My legs were still aching from the last few days, plus I was accompanied by the dog, and my towel-wrapped package. But I was fuelled by desperation, and anger, and sadness, and confusion – emotions that had been simmering for more than a decade and had just reached boiling point. There was no way I wasn't getting answers, face to face, right now. Or at least, as soon as I caught up with her.

'Stop! Come back!'

Unfortunately, it seemed Izzy had used our years apart to get super-fit. I could tell by the way she was running, her leanness, the smoothness of her motion – that bitch worked out. Furious envy propelled me – I gathered speed, dragging the poor dog, who also didn't count fitness as a forte. Luckily for me, Isabella glanced around to check our progress and stumbled on uneven ground. I took advantage of her brief loss of pace to increase mine, and as she started up again, I found myself taking a flying leap – Ethan Hunt taking down a suspect, *Mission Impossible*-style – arms stretched out, my body an imperfect arc. Together, Mabel and I brought her crashing to the ground, all of us slamming into the damp evening grass of the Stray in a chaotic and painful tumble.

For a while, we lay there panting and groaning, working out how badly injured we were. There was a throbbing in my right knee that would probably plague me until the end of my days. The dog looked seriously pissed off, having been forced into strenuous exercise rather than indulged in her usual gentle perambulation around the park. Miraculously, my package had survived intact, cushioned by its tea towel.

'So,' said Isabella, breathlessly. 'This is Mabel.'

She manoeuvred herself into a half-sitting position and held out her hand. My bastard dog licked it, tail wagging, the suck-up mutt.

While we both recovered, catching our breath, I checked her out. She definitely had Sarah-Connor-in-*Terminator* vibes; strong shoulders and well-defined biceps, flat stomach revealed by her rucked-up T-shirt. But she also looked older, lines around her eyes and mouth, and there were streaks of grey in her hair, which was scraped back against her head. She was stretched tight, like one of Dippy's canvases.

'I got you a present,' I said, sitting up and holding out the bundled towel.

'Right,' said Isabella, receiving the package gingerly and allowing the fabric to fall off, revealing the Charlotte Brontë plate. 'Cool. I mean . . . weird, but cool.'

'Why did you run away?'

She gazed at me steadily for a second. 'Now, or then?'

'Both.'

'Now . . . because I suddenly lost my nerve. And then . . . well, that's a long story.'

'I've got time.'

She looked down at the grass we were sitting on. 'I don't think I can,' she said. 'Not now.'

'Then why are you here? And how did you know where I live?'

She gave me a faint smile. 'You're an easy woman to find. Particularly since you told my brother your address.'

'And you're a difficult one, since you won't tell anyone yours. Why are you here?'

'To tell you to back off.'

That hurt. 'You could have emailed.'

'I thought it might be more effective in person.'

'Well, you got that right. This . . .' I gestured to us both, still in a heap on the ground. 'This is pretty effective.'

'It was a mistake. I have to go. But please, just . . . leave me alone.'

'Why? No. I can't.'

'You managed it for fifteen years.' She sounded bitter, which hurt even more, because it was true, but also it wasn't – fair, but unfair.

'I didn't want to. But you made it pretty difficult to stay in touch.'

She pressed a hand to her throat. 'I know. I'm sorry . . . I really am. But it's all so complicated, and difficult to explain and . . . I just can't. I'm sorry. I'm sorry.' Her voice broke, and she raised her palm to her forehead.

'Please. You're here now. Just . . . stay, for a bit. Let's talk. And then, if you still want to go, fine. But don't go without saying *anything*.'

She shrugged helplessly, dropping her hand, fingers plucking at blades of grass. 'There isn't anything to say.'

'Let me be the judge of that. I have many questions.'

Isabella lifted her head, her eyes burning. 'But will you hear the answers?'

I swallowed. Face to face, that last evening we spent together was coming back to me, the shards assembling to create an image that was fractured around the edges but clear enough – disturbing enough – to make me want to look away. I didn't want to see it, didn't want to fix it all in place because then I'd have to acknowledge my part in it all, how I failed my friend.

'Yes,' I said. 'This time, I'll listen.'

45

We went to The Stray Dog, which wasn't ideal, but it was the nearest place, and I felt like Izzy might bolt again if I dithered. Selwyn took one look at us both and started up with the banter.

'Ay, ay, ay, Paula Radcliffe, you just done a sub-two hours?' He chortled, clocking my red, sweating face. 'The toilets are that way.'

'Cut it out, Selwyn.' I was far too tired for any of his shit. 'What do you want to drink?' Turning to Isabella, I pulled a tenner from my pocket.

'Just a Coke, please.'

'Two Cokes. And some water for the dog.'

'I'll throw in a free electrolyte.'

'For Christ's sake, Selwyn, shut up.'

Isabella carried our drinks to a table in the corner, and I followed, bearing Mabel's water. For the first few seconds we sat in silence, as the dog slurped noisily.

'Interesting landlord,' she observed, finally, indicating Selwyn, who was now targeting an old man who'd come in for a quiet pint.

'He's an institution,' I replied, because Izzy shouldn't be allowed to criticize my local, having never graced it.

She pulled out the re-wrapped plate and examined it, tracing the *I must keep in good health* quote with her finger. 'Where did you find this?'

'At a shop in York. It made me think of your mother.'

Izzy smiled. 'It's missing the *and not die* bit,' she pointed out.

'I think that's implicit in a toast to good health, personally.'

'You're right.' She took a sip of her Coke. 'Charlotte overdid it.'

'She was a crap writer.'

'Very poor sentence construction.'

'So, how've you been?'

Izzy put down her glass, with a thoughtful expression. 'Not bad. Can't complain. You?'

'Same.'

That was the last fifteen years dealt with. 'Why'd you fuck off like that?'

She shook her head. 'So you're just cutting to the chase? I don't even get some small talk?'

'What, you want to be eased in gently? Hi, Izzy, you're looking well, I hear you got married, Positano must have been beautiful, Richard Spencer sends his regards, as does Lixin Lee, and Susan Lavery who you used to babysit, and Matteo from Cosa Bolle, and Alaric Irving, and all the Harpur Harlots, *none* of whom know where you are. So, why'd you fuck off like that?'

Izzy raised her eyebrows. 'You *have* been busy.'

'Like I said, I've got time. So let's do this. Out with it.'

'What?' She rubbed Mabel's head distractedly, and I realized my dog was now resting her chin on Izzy's knee, taking sides, the faithless hound.

'Say whatever you need to say. Get it off your chest, lay it all out. I'm ready.'

Her eyes flashed – anger or tears, I couldn't tell which. Maybe both. 'I told you – I've got nothing to say.'

I tried a change of tack. 'Your brother said he thought you made a mistake.'

'Luca said that?' She chewed her lip.

'He said he didn't agree with your decision.'

'No, he always made that clear. But he respected it, nonetheless. Unlike you.'

'I respected it for fifteen years. Not any more.'

Izzy drained her glass. 'Why now?'

Scanning the bar, I saw the old man, finally left alone to enjoy his pint. Except he didn't look like he was enjoying it. He looked like, having got rid of Selwyn, he wanted him back.

'Because,' I said slowly, 'I realized that it's the third act of my life. And I'm starting to look a bit lonely onstage. It's a bare set, no audience, and I have no lines.'

'You have a tiny violin,' snapped Izzy. 'And what, I'm supposed to be your director?'

310

'That's what I thought at first,' I said. 'But now I think you need to be in the company.'

'What about Angus?'

'He's backstage. Dressed in black, everyone ignores him.'

She smothered a laugh. 'What about your kids?'

My smile back was twisted. 'They're in another play now.'

Izzy sighed. 'Listen, I get it. But it's not my responsibility.'

'No, but . . . how's your play going?'

She shrugged. 'I won't deny it's not Broadway. More . . . Edinburgh Fringe one-woman show. But you can't have everything.'

'Who's your backstage man in black?'

'My husband, you mean?' Her expression softened. 'Miles. Miles Braithwaite.'

'*BRAITHWAITE?!*' I pictured her, the very first time we met, introducing herself as Adrian Mole's girlfriend.

She laughed, properly. 'I know. I'm Mrs Braithwaite.'

'Wow. It really was your destiny. Did you meet in Rome?'

'No; Croydon.'

'Shame. The coin thing didn't work, then.'

'No, but I do go back regularly, to see Luca. Except, you know that, don't you? Having just seen him yourself.'

I winced. 'I . . . happened to be passing.'

'Really? Portia's very fragile, you nearly unhinged her.'

'Yeah, she seemed that sort.'

'She's always on edge, waiting for a former amour to turn up and spirit him off.'

'I would have done if I could. He's a catch.'

'Yuck. I forgot you always fancied him.'

'It was more girlish admiration.'

'You're too old for that.'

'I know. Back to the play thing . . .'

She brushed it aside with a wave of her hand. 'I'm done with that analogy. Can I go now?'

'No, you haven't answered all of my questions.'

'But I don't want to answer them. There's no point.'

'Why not?'

She paused, stroking Mabel's ears, and then said, sadly. 'It's too late.' For a second, she seemed tearful, but then squared her shoulders. 'And besides,' she pushed the dog's head off her knee and prepared to stand up. 'I'm allergic to this animal.'

'Holly Griffiths thought you were working as a dog walker in Edgbaston.' This was said in a panic, to pique her interest.

Izzy's eye's widened. 'Intriguing theory.'

'But I knew you weren't, because of your allergy. Erica Stanley said you'd married a laird in Inverness, AND that you'd moved to Brighton.'

She screwed up her face. 'Never liked her, smug cow.'

'She hasn't changed. Chloe said you were in rehab, which was the craziest theory of all.' I paused, to let her deny it, but she just hugged herself, avoiding my gaze.

'I've been looking for you, these past few weeks, and I was thinking about you before that, all these years. And I know I probably did some stuff or said some stuff that didn't help, but I really don't know why you went off like that, and I did try to find you, at first, but then . . . everything got in the way, and I just let it slide. And I'm sorry about that, but you seem to be pissed off with me for leaving you alone, and for *not* leaving you alone, so I can't win, can I?'

Izzy sat down again. Mabel put her head back on her knee. 'Nice speech,' she said. 'Such eloquence. You give Charlotte Brontë a run for her money.'

'I'm Jane Eyre-head.'

She bit her lip again, but this time she was trying not to smile.

'Please don't go,' I pleaded. 'Stay, and tell me what I did wrong. I want to understand.'

'Like I said, I don't think there's much point now.' She stood up again, this time with an air of finality, holding her plate in its towel, and Mabel collapsed on the floor with a disappointed huff. 'It was nice to see you again, but . . . let's leave it at that, hey?'

'No. I . . . just . . .' She started to move away and in desperation I grabbed the plate, pulling it, and her, back. 'Stop acting like there's this great big mystery that I'm not grown-up enough to know! Just *tell* me!'

'I already did!' she shot back. 'And you didn't *want* to know!'

In our tussle, the plate slipped out of the towel, fell to the floor and smashed. The pub went quiet. Selwyn stepped in.

'Now, now, ladies,' he boomed from behind the bar. 'Do I need to alert security? Can't you two girls behave yourselves? Take your little catfight outside – and I'll sell tickets!'

'Oh, fuck off, Al Murray,' I shouted.

Izzy whirled around and ran away, the swing doors slamming behind her. Grabbing Mabel's lead, I prepared to embark on a hot pursuit.

'Hang on, sunshine, who's going to clear that up?' Selwyn pointed at the china daggers littering his floor.

'Don't touch it,' I said. 'I'll be back.'

46

Outside, it was dark and I couldn't see where Isabella had gone. I was about to give up and stomp home to moan about it all to Angus, but then Mabel cocked her ears and started pulling in the direction of the park. She did this occasionally when she'd smelled something particularly noxious that she wanted to roll in, so I wasn't inclined to follow, and tried to drag her back. But she was determined, nose down, gunning for the Stray, and then along the tree-lined road that bordered its edge, until the street lamps illuminated a figure slumped on one of the benches.

Isabella had her head in her hands; as we approached, I could hear smothered sobs – when she looked up, alerted by the dog's whining, her cheeks were wet. Mabel surged forward and shoved her equally wet nose into Izzy's lap, nuzzling and snuffling; Izzy gave a choked laugh and fondled the dog's ears. Then she sneezed. In the darkness, it was like a foghorn.

'I told you I was allergic,' she said, snottily.

'And I told you I already knew that.' I produced a tissue from my pocket and handed it over. After tying the dog's lead to the seat's arm, I sat down next to Izzy, and for a while we just sat in the gloom, silent apart from Izzy's occasional sniffle, and the soft rustle of the trees above our heads. Lowry could have painted us that way, tucked on our Stray stall, two women who didn't know how to reconnect. *Man Lying on a Wall. Women Sitting on a Bench.*

'A few years ago, I lost my job,' I said, eventually. 'I was quite senior by then, managing various accounts, in charge of a team, earning pretty well. I wouldn't say it was my *dream* job, but it was a proper career – I was busy and productive and could buy a Mulberry handbag if I felt like it. It was just about doable with the kids. But then, out of the blue, I got made redundant.'

'I'm sorry,' said Izzy. 'That must have been hard.'

'Afterwards, I found out that another guy on the team, less experienced than me, was given my job – with a different bullshit title – and a higher salary. So it wasn't that my position was redundant; it was that *I* was.'

'*Cazzo*,' murmured Izzy, and although it wasn't in my Italian lexicon, I appreciated the sentiment.

'I tried to get another job, but no one seemed very interested. Kept asking how old my children were and why I didn't want to work full time. So ever since, I've been . . . drifting. Aimless. Waiting for something to do. And for some reason, I decided you were that thing.'

'That's ridiculous,' said Izzy.

'I know.'

She sat up straighter, dropping the tissue, thoroughly roused. 'I mean, what a stupid, self-indulgent thing to focus on. Poncing round restaurants asking if anyone had seen me? Going to *Rome*? You know, I saw you outside Da Mario's yesterday, hanging about, eating pastries? That's why I decided to come and find you. To tell you to pack it in.'

'You saw me? You were there? Why didn't you just speak to me then?'

I heard her sharp intake of breath. 'It was such a shock seeing you, I ran away – I wasn't ready. But this morning something happened at my office that made me realize it had gone too far. It's been building for a while – Alaric told me you'd visited; so did Madison James.'

'I don't like her.'

'Neither do I, but she's useful.'

'Why did you go to see her, before you went off? Who were you looking for?'

'Like I said, it's a long story, but I haven't finished telling you off yet. OK, you lacked direction, self-esteem, whatever. You're not the first person to be in that position. It's not a *tragedy*. Go and volunteer for a charity, get a hobby, sue the agency that made you redundant, do something useful! Don't make *me* your purpose.'

I sagged on the bench, winded. 'I'm sorry.'

She was right. Totally and completely right. I was a waste of space. A useless, entitled, self-serving vacuum. An owl hooted in the trees above us, agreeing with my conclusion. Under the bench, Mabel yawned; she knew all this already. Her disdain for me was well founded.

I thought of the last few weeks, racketing round willy-nilly, harassing people, roping them in to my absurd quest, without a thought for the consequences. Poor Jackson DeLantro and Garth, giving up their time and expertise to help me with my wild goose chase. Poor Alaric, giving up his precious correspondence. Poor Lixin, folding his napkins while I opened up old wounds. Poor Richard Spencer, invisible to me until he had something I wanted. Poor Min, patiently absorbing my blatherings about my absent friend, when she was right there all along. Poor Angus, waiting for his deranged wife to come to her senses. My poor children, neglected and ignored. Poor Morag . . . no, not poor Morag; Morag could do one.

'I'm sorry,' I said again, and now it was my turn to cry, delving back in my pocket for another nose-rag. I always had one handy – the mother of three boys would never be without wipes – and it was put to good use as I sobbed tears of pity, still tinged with self-pity. 'The thing is,' I mumbled. 'I really do miss you.'

I really, really did. I missed our chats, and our drinks, and our meals, and our adventures. I missed her getting the joke more than anyone else I knew. I missed her knowing everything about me, down to the tiniest, pettiest detail. I missed having a best mate. We talk about single people, about not having a partner or significant other, but there was no word for that platonic state – not having a best friend, the first person you turn to, to tell your good news, share your woes; someone to bitch with, and compliment, and tease, and comfort. And I knew that it was wildly self-indulgent, as a fifty-three-year-old married mother, to bemoan that, and yet I did. I missed her.

'Oh, Mortimer,' Izzy sighed, and somehow, on that dark bench, her hand found mine.

'What happened to you?' I mumbled thickly, through my tissue. 'Why did you go?'

'It's a long story.'

'I've got time. I'm listening.'

And so, at last, she began.

47

Since she was little, Izzy always felt she was being watched. She was a paranoid child, constantly looking over her shoulder, needled by a sense of unease. As she grew older, this apprehension only increased, but it wasn't a huge, spiking fear – more a low-level disquiet. Something was up – an axe hovering above, waiting to fall. Was it the burglaries in Ecclesall – the ones that made the Harris family move to Hathersage – that made her feel that way? Izzy had been traumatized by those robberies – the feeling that someone had infiltrated and violated their home. She was waiting for the next intruder to strike. Well, maybe it was that – or maybe it was something else entirely.

She felt as if eyes were always on her. Spying. She walked quickly home from the bus stop, ran round corners, mixed up her routes. It was ridiculous, but she lived as though she was being tailed, taking comfort in the precautions.

And then, when she was at university, it started. Postcards sent to her address in Edinburgh. Nothing in particular: 'Hope you're well!' 'Thinking of you!' 'See you soon!' At first, she barely noticed, assuming it was a friend or random acquaintance. She never even got round to investigating who they were from; it didn't really matter – just a few friendly cards. After university, when she moved to Manchester, it carried on, at her new address. Occasionally she would get a delivery of something she didn't order, but she didn't think too much of it – the sort of thing that happens to everyone once in a while.

Later on, she started to get emails, which were a new thing then. Like the cards, they were anonymous, from addresses made up of random numbers and characters. At first, this was another thing she didn't really notice – in those days you barely checked your email at all as it was too much of a faff to get online. Besides, they were initially friendly, chatty, as if sent by a close acquaintance. Except this 'friend' clearly knew nothing about her, and would refer to moments between them that hadn't happened. Izzy replied 'Hi! Sorry, who are you?' but got no reply – just another gossipy email. They were signed 'X', which could have been a kiss, but somehow seemed more disturbing without a name. Izzy mentioned it to a few friends and they all reacted in the same way – wide eyes, 'That's strange!' followed by near-instant distraction. An oddity, but not a worry. Everyone had so much going on – who cared about a few weird emails? Probably just Junk, spam, or a mistake, sent in error. Izzy could have changed her address, shut down that account, but she was trying to get a new job, attempting to make connections in the big wide world, and she worried she'd miss that vital interview, commission or offer. So she ignored them. Or tried to.

But of course, she couldn't resist reading them and gradually, insidiously, the emails got nastier. And sometimes the sender would refer to things that *had* happened, that only somebody who knew her could know, like saying her new haircut didn't suit her, or that she needed to reconsider her jogging route for her own safety. The axe hadn't fallen, but it kept getting nearer, edging towards her, ever so slowly. She was never *sure*; never sure enough to say anything or really do anything. And what action could she take anyway? She couldn't block the emails because they were always from a different address. So she just existed, in that vague state of unease, waiting for the next message.

It wasn't clear if the sender was male or female. Sometimes the gossipy-ness of them indicated a woman, but occasionally the jealous tone suggested a man. She felt it was a man, and that was scarier, but really it was the anonymity that spooked her. The not-knowing. Eventually, she got sick of speculating and decided to change her email. This time she was more cautious, releasing the new address to small groups in stages – that way, she'd know, if and when the messages came, which pool it had come from.

It did work, and it didn't work. For a while, the messages stopped entirely, and she almost began to breathe normally again, but one day, when the group of people who knew her new address was huge and varied, she got a deadly missive: 'Where've you been? Anyone would think you were avoiding me!'

At various points during all of this, Izzy became aware she was being followed. *Maybe.* Maybe not. Occasionally when she was walking home, or on the bus, she'd have that feeling of being watched. But perhaps she was imagining it. She'd been imagining it for so long, hadn't she? Picturing the Ecclesall burglar, or whatever ogre lurked in her subconsciousness. It was a figment of her imagination. Probably. She was never sure. Sometimes she heard footsteps, or thought she saw someone in the shadows behind her, but again she couldn't tell if it was a man or woman, couldn't tell if it was anyone at all, really. She never told anyone about it because it was just too embarrassing, narcissistic: 'I'm being followed!' Don't be so silly.

When Alaric introduced Izzy to the famous reviewer Jean-Luc Riche in Paris, and the London job opportunity came through, she was thrilled for two reasons. One: her career could really take off, and two: maybe the move could draw a line under all this. Whoever was or wasn't following her must be Manchester-based. It was ludicrous to imagine they could hound her all the way to London. She could kill two birds with one stone. This was a new beginning.

But it turned out Izzy was the bird. When she moved, she felt homesick and alone, far from her parents and friends, vulnerable. London was so big, anyone could get lost, including her, but it also meant that a lurker could blend in as well. There were so many potential suspects –

it could be anyone in the crowd. Her new job was great – a dream – opening up all sorts of opportunities, but outside work, Izzy closed down. She didn't try to make friends – what if one of the people she met was her watcher, inveigling his or her way into her life? She was wary of a romantic entanglement, didn't want to go to bars on her own, socially, where someone might slip something into her drink, or follow her on the way home.

The emails still came, occasionally – whenever she let her guard down. When one of her reviews appeared online, it was often bombarded with comments; mostly good, but some . . . not. She found some of the replies disturbing, unnecessarily personal. Her employers were delighted – any engagement, however hostile, was great as far as they were concerned. She was hitting her targets, sparking debate, stirring things up. Don't worry about a few troublemakers!

Izzy continued to sign up for things – dance classes, interesting exhibitions, the odd Outward Bound course. She felt the spontaneity made it safe. She would leave it until the last minute, then just set off on her little adventure or expedition, without telling anyone. She carried on camping, impetuously, when the mood took her. When she was off-grid, she could relax – no one knew where she was, no one was watching. She could still find fun in life.

Then the parcels started arriving, at her new flat in London. Stuff she didn't order. A useful domestic gadget that she already had, a book she wasn't interested in reading, treats for the cat she didn't have. Sometimes she'd get a bunch of flowers, or a box of delicately iced biscuits. When winter was approaching, she got a cashmere scarf. She mentioned it to colleagues, and they said: *Brilliant! Free stuff! Don't complain.*

Maybe the 'gifts' weren't related to everything else. Maybe they were a genuine mistake. She was making connections that weren't there. Keep calm and carry on. She didn't tell her parents about any of this as she didn't want to worry them. Luca mostly brushed it off, and it was hard to talk to him about it properly when he was so far away. With close friends, she still felt embarrassed; this had been going on for so long – *how* long exactly? – and she didn't know how to bring it up. When she did mention it, Izzy found herself making a joke of it, referencing her 'mystery benefactor' in passing, lightly, and having dismissed it publicly, she couldn't find a way back to saying: *This worries me. I think about it all the time. What should I do?* It felt both humiliating and self-aggrandizing to say the word . . .

Stalker. She had a stalker. Maybe. Surely not. That was a thing that happened to celebrities, Hollywood actresses. Not ordinary people.

Then her flat got broken into. Another burglary, one of her worst fears. Except, *was* it? Burglaries happened all the time, didn't they? Unfortunate, nasty, but not sinister. She was just unlucky. Wasn't she? There was no sign of a break-in, but someone came in while she was out, made a mess, took some jewellery. All totally normal, as burglaries go.

Except the jewellery came back in the post. Gradually, in dribs and drabs. Every time, Izzy reported it to the police and every time they said they would investigate, but she heard nothing. The first package, a necklace, just came in an envelope, but later on, things would arrive beautifully wrapped, like a gift. An old pair of earrings in a mesh bag, a bracelet in a cute little display case. *Not* a bracelet – the shiny silver bangle given to her by her grandmother for her twenty-first birthday. So, although her instinct was to get rid of it, she couldn't. Again, Izzy felt awkward and ashamed. Stalkers were ex-boyfriends breaking in with knives – they were the kind the police paid attention to. Not her generous, assiduous well-wisher, returning her possessions, one by one. Izzy's stalker was a cut above, beyond reproach. Certainly beyond proper investigation. She was on her own. She put all the jewellery she received in a box. Couldn't bear to throw it away, but also couldn't bear to wear it or even look at it. Couldn't bear to touch it.

In the end, she moved back to Manchester. Back to her family, back to her friends, who could protect her. Except none of them really knew about any of this – she'd never found a way to tell anyone, not properly. And now, everyone had families of their own, were wrapped up in romances, kids, busy jobs, paying the bills, trying to carve out five minutes for themselves. No one wanted to hear about how she got spooked walking home alone from the bus stop. Or how, one night, a fire engine turned up at her flat, on a tip-off, the call traced to a phone box nearby. A teenage prank, no doubt. Or how the police once came round, saying they'd heard reports of an intruder. Probably just officious neighbours. Or how the *Scoop* office received flowers addressed to her – a funeral wreath of lilies. A mix-up, surely?

Izzy found herself listening to her friends' problems, unable to talk about her own. She'd waited too long, and now she was struck dumb by it. She couldn't believe her life had turned out this way, so many years nagged by this stupid, shameful situation. She was a successful food writer, owned two flats, in London and Manchester, had a circle of friends, hobbies, a good income. It wasn't broke, was it? Why did she want to fix it?

But she did. So much about her life should have brought her contentment, but she couldn't find it because of this *thing* that ruined it. She wanted to fix it, and the only way she could think of was to disappear. To cut herself off, go off-grid permanently. It was a ridiculous idea, she knew – Luca thought she was insane – but it felt like the only option. To draw a line under it all, to draw a line around *herself*, that no one would be able to penetrate.

Izzy made careful plans. She saved up. She set up new accounts. She let out her flats via a big faceless company. She told her work contacts that she would be unavailable for a while. She paid a tech guy to take her off the internet. She planned a leave of absence. It would be a long one. She wasn't sure she'd ever come back from it.

One of the last things she did was try to sound out people she knew, a last-ditch effort to unmask the villain, or to see if her friends could be trusted to know of her new existence. She tried. She met Richard Spencer in Derby. An old boyfriend seemed a likely place to start in the search, but she knew almost immediately that it couldn't be him – she felt it in her bones, just like she knew when someone was watching her. She moved on, leaving him baffled and bereft.

She went to her main editor, Madison James, told her she was taking a sabbatical and asked Madison to let her know if anyone asked after her. Anyone at all. Madison, a seasoned hack, loved the intrigue and willingly agreed. Izzy knew it was pretty stupid, and a long shot, but maybe it would draw someone out.

And then, she had dinner with me, that night in June 2009, the last time I saw her. As Izzy recounted that fateful evening, the fragments fell into place, and I remembered everything. Everything she said, everything I said, everything she didn't say, everything I missed.

Listening to Izzy's halting speech, the catches in her breath, the faint sounds of sirens in the distance, I relived that night and saw the precise moment that a decades-old friendship fell to its death.

48

I'm in the kitchen of our house in Didsbury, the cramped terrace we've now grown out of. Sam is screaming and I'm frantically pumping milk, ready to dump it all on Angus and get out of the house. I'm sick of it all. The sick. The breastfeeding, which is no easier this time, the endless washing, the sleepless nights, the whingeing from a jealous Liam, pushing prams and playgrounds and playdates, that crushing feeling of 'are we back here AGAIN?' For the second time, locked in the mad merry-go-round of babyhood.

It's not that I regret having Sam – *of course not; never* – and at least I knew what to expect this time round, but I forgot how *hard* and relentless it is, and now we're doing it with a toddler too, and I'm juggling part-time work with childcare, and for some inexplicable reason still trying to breastfeed, even though he's happily chugged the odd bottle of formula we've given him. In short, I am a mess, and don't want to go out this evening – oh, but I *do*. I want to go out, and get drunk, and gossip, and *forget* for a few hours. Stop being Mrs Stewart, wife and mother of two, and regress to Mortimer, Adrian Mole, Gwennie – Izzy's best friend. I can't wait.

Shoving the bottle and a muslin at my husband, I throw on some heels – I hate wearing them, but it's the principle of it – grab my bag and hurtle out the door before anyone can stop me. We're meeting at a little Italian place Izzy's found near Chorlton – nice enough, and neutral. She doesn't want to be analysing the wine list or thinking up adjectives for a puttanesca sauce.

It's only fifteen minutes on the bus and a short walk to get there, but by the time I arrive, breathless, with pinched feet, Izzy is already sitting waiting. I promised her I wouldn't be late. She's been stressed recently – something to do with work – and I've been distracted, cutting short phone conversations because of crying children, forgetting to reply to emails, moaning a bit too much. It's like those films where there's a main character and a sidekick, and the sidekick only exists to provide emotional support to the central figure. They don't exist in their own right. I know, deep down, that I've been a bit of a main character recently. It's time to let Izzy have the limelight. I'll do that. I will.

'Sorry, sorry,' I gasp, sinking into the chair opposite and swooping on the glass of wine she's ordered for me. 'Nightmare getting out the house. God, I need this.' I glug like Sam with his milk bottle. 'Angus is so useless, not knowing where anything is. I left a packet of pasta out for his dinner but even that will be beyond him; he'll order pizza again.'

Mustn't bitch about Angus. Not classy to complain about having a husband to someone without one. Not that I think Izzy cares about being single. Does she? She never seems to, and I don't like to bring it up just in case it's becoming a sore point. Maybe that's why she wants to meet. She postponed a few times, then suddenly contacted me suggesting tonight. Maybe she's met someone! I guzzle my wine and prepare to be enthusiastic about her new man. My phone buzzes and I can't resist looking at it, just in case Angus has dropped Sam and set the house on fire. Nope, he just wants to know where the dummy is.

Next to the dish drainer, I jab back furiously. The dummy.

'Anyway,' I chuck my phone in my bag and face my friend, beaming. 'Cheers!' I lift my glass and she clinks it, but something is off, I can tell. She's pale, hair scraped back, and she won't meet my eyes, picking at the bread basket, her nails chipped and the cuticles red-raw. *What's going on?* In my anxiety, I start to rabbit.

'Sam wouldn't nap this afternoon, too hot probably, which means he's been really fussy and Liam weirdly slept for three hours, which means he won't go down tonight, but luckily that's not my problem, or won't be until later. Honestly, though, sometimes Angus is the biggest child of all – I caught him moaning on the phone to Morag earlier, saying he just wanted a bit of peace. Peace! He slept for six hours last night. Anyway, enough about me, tell me your news.'

Izzy smiles wanly, and sips her drink. 'It's complicated.'

Shit. Is she ill? 'I love complicated. I spent the morning watching eight episodes of *Peppa Pig* and had to have a bacon sandwich for lunch as a fuck-you.' I also spent the morning trying to finish a presentation I'm due to give at work next week, and ended up falling asleep over it, jerking awake to hear Peppa squealing 'Daddy!' just as a weary Angus came in from the park with a wailing Liam. Lordy, this wine is going down a treat. I gaze at Izzy expectantly.

'Um . . . I don't quite know how to say this . . .' begins Izzy, fiddling with her napkin, as I immediately concoct disaster scenarios. She's been diagnosed with something, she's moving to Paris, becoming a nun, running off to—

'Are you ladies ready to order?'

In a harassed way, we both hum and haw over the menu. I don't care what I eat as long as I'm drinking, and when Izzy's not working, she doesn't really mind either, but for some reason we're both dithering, delaying the moment when we have to face each other again. Frankly, I don't want to know what she's got to say; I just want to sit here and switch off until I'm sucked back into the clattering drum cycle of childcare.

'The thing is . . .' Izzy pauses, as the waiter whisks himself away. Her hands are shaking. They're actually shaking. Is she dying? Oh God, I don't want to know. I can't cope with that sort of thing right now. Or ever. We're now in a Schrödinger's cat moment – Schrödinger's chat – where I don't know the bad thing yet and if I defer it forever I will never know and it might not happen.

'Shall we get another of these?' I wiggle my empty glass, summoning the waiter again, pretending not to notice the flicker of irritation pass across Izzy's face. The wine is taking effect and I'm feeling pleasantly numb, but unpleasantly tense, at the same time. 'I know I shouldn't drink when I'm breastfeeding but I pumped earlier and actually I read this article that said you'd have to drink like a whole bottle of vodka for it to make any difference to the milk and—'

'I'm . . . er . . . thinking of moving back to London,' says Izzy abruptly, as the waiter sets down our glasses.

I choke on my bread. 'What?'

She's gone from pale to flushed, dabbing at a drop of wine with a napkin so she doesn't have to look at me. 'Like I said, it's complicated, but . . . I think it might be good for me. For my career and my . . . me.' She picks up her glass and raises it defiantly. 'Cheers.'

The way she redelivers my own toast riles me beyond belief. There's no joy in it, just a mix of misery and defeat and dampened-down rage. I blink, against sudden tears, and tiredness, and the tail-end of conjunctivitis I picked up a few weeks ago from Liam. There's too much going on and I can't make sense of it all.

'Why?' I have many questions but that's the main one. Why on earth, why the fuck, why why why would she do this? When she did it already and it didn't work out. When she's back and re-established and everything's good – well, not *good*, exactly – not right now. I'm a basket case but that'll pass, and I know Izzy's been stressed and evasive recently, but I just assumed it was work stuff that would die down eventually. Why is she doing this, why is she announcing it out of the blue, why would she want to go and leave me festering in nappies and puree, abandon me for the brighter lights of the capital? *Again*. For so long, Izzy has felt like an escape route – from work, from married life, from motherhood, from *me*. She takes me out of myself, encourages me to be the fun, adventurous version of Gwen – *Mortimer* – and without her I don't see how I can be anything but the dull husk I've become. With her I'm the butterfly; without her I'm the chrysalis.

'Because . . .' Izzy pauses, regarding me steadily like she's weighing something up. Weighing *me* up, perhaps. 'Because . . . well, I never sold my London flat and I was thinking a change of scenery might do me good, and I could probably do with making a few more connections down there, and . . . I don't know . . .'

'I didn't know you still had your London flat. I assumed you'd sold it.' She's just bought a flat in Chorlton. *Two* properties? An empire!

She nods. 'I was going to, but then I realized it's such a great investment . . .' She trails off, aware that it's a crass thing to say. I've told her several times that Angus and I are saving to buy a house. Our place in Didsbury is rented and we desperately need something bigger. My parents can't afford to help and Morag's being her usual mad self – whenever Angus hints at a contribution, she starts sobbing about being a poor widow, or announcing

334

that she's thinking about buying a chateau in Provence and running a B&B with her friend Sophia.

Our property ladder is still on its side in the shed, but here's Izzy several rungs up, debating where to live with the same nonchalance that we browsed the menu earlier. *Ooooh, Manchester or London, which will I pick?!* I gulp my wine resentfully. I'll miss her so much if she goes.

'Well, if you feel like it would be a good move for you, then . . .' I can't get any further, can't perjure myself. 'Have you met someone?'

'Why would you think that?' She's frowning at me, vexed, and I'm vexed at myself. It was a stupid thing to say, and I only said it because I'd run out of supportive steam and it occurred to me that there is something else in play here – something bigger and more significant than Izzy idly dithering over which city to live in. Something is pushing her; maybe it's a man.

'You mentioned someone last month . . .'

She screws up her face. 'That was just Richard.'

'Yes, Richard. Who's he?'

'Richard.' She eyes me impatiently. 'Richard! From school?'

'Oh!' Realization dawns. 'Dickie! Why didn't you say so?'

Her lips thin. 'I did.'

I don't remember. Another sleepless night, another day blanketed by brain fog. 'Why did you see him? Are you getting back together?' I mean it as a joke, but I'm so tired and tipsy that it comes out wrong.

'No. Obviously not.' Her voice is clipped; I realize I've pissed her off, and part of me is glad because it's mutual. The hubbub of the restaurant is building and even as I'm relishing my mild inebriation, there's a tension headache pressing at my temples. I rub them distractedly as the waiter brings our food – pasta for Izzy; pizza for me. Angus is probably having the same at home – I wonder if the boys are OK, if Liam has finally gone down, if Sam has deigned to take his bottle.

But this is Izzy's and my night out: I've got to do better. 'Why did you see Richard?'

'Just catching up.' Izzy's tone is dismissive as she twirls spaghetti round her fork. I can barely remember her old boyfriend; he always seemed very reserved and I can't imagine why she would want to reconnect.

I try once more. 'So, London!' And promptly run out of steam again. I can't think of anything good to say about London, and it's so loud in here; the acoustics are terrible. My wine is nice though – I take refuge in it as Izzy swallows and pats her mouth with a napkin.

'I need to get away,' she says, and again there's that note of defeat, with a tinge of defiance, and I finally respond to my cue.

'What's wrong?' There's a lull in the racket around us and our eyes meet for the first time.

She takes a deep breath. 'For a long time now I've had a bit of a problem.'

'A problem?'

'It's hard to describe. I . . . have a kind of . . .' She grimaces. 'Someone is harassing me.'

'What?' The noise levels have risen again and I can't be sure I've heard her correctly.

She hesitates, toying with her fork. 'There's someone who contacts me. Who sends me things. Follows me. Maybe.'

'Who *what?*' This curveball is so random and unexpected that I wonder if I'm drunker than I thought. Have I fallen asleep? Is this all a dream?

Izzy smiles, or tries to. 'It's embarrassing. Ridiculous! But sometimes it gets to me a bit. I don't know what to do about it. Thought another move might help.'

'Who is it?'

'I don't know.' Her eyelids flicker; that look of irritation again – I'm not getting it, not working hard enough. 'He's anonymous. Sorry, that sounds so dramatic!'

'But you know it's a man?'

She shrugs. 'No, not really. I just assume . . . or am afraid . . . that it's a man.'

'What does he say?'

'Nothing much. Chatty emails. But it makes me . . . uncomfortable.'

'Maybe it's a mistake? He thinks you're someone else?' The room is spinning now, but when the waiter passes, I mouth at him and he goes off to get yet another glass. Izzy's eyelid twitches.

'No, I don't think so. Anyway, enough about that.' Izzy squares her shoulders and resumes her meal.

'Maybe an ex? Whatshisname? Poor Lee? Bent on revenge after you turned him down?' I'm bringing too much levity to this moment – I know it, but can't seem to stop myself. I'm feeling so inadequate right now, for so many reasons. As a mother, as a wife, as an employee, as a friend. And as a drinker. The waiter brings my third glass and I'm in no fit state but take a sip anyway. I hardly ever drink nowadays. My tolerance is low, my spirits high. The hum of the restaurant is now a cacophony.

Izzy shakes her head, dismissing Poor Lee and me. 'Don't be silly.'

'What?'

'DON'T BE SILLY,' she snaps.

It's a fair accusation, but I'm hurt all the same, particularly by the volume, even though it was necessary. 'I was only trying to help.'

'No one can help.' For a second she looks completely haunted, desperate, and then the moment passes, her face wiped so clean I can't be sure the previous expression was ever there. '*I'm* the one being silly. Ignore me.'

I do. 'I can't believe you haven't told me any of this. I thought we were friends.'

'Just forget it.'

'Dessert, ladies?'

'I'll have the tiramisu.' At least I don't need to worry about calories while I'm breastfeeding.

Izzy shakes her head at the waiter, and he departs. I feel peeved with her for not having anything, like I'm not worthy of her indulging in pudding. What were we talking about? It's such a din in here.

'When are you moving back to London then?'

'I'm not sure. Haven't decided yet.' That abrasive tone again.

'Well, let me know, when you . . . *decide.*' I can't help the bitterness creeping into my voice. I'll miss her so much. My best friend. Gone again. God, are my boobs leaking? I glance down at my top to check. Nothing yet, but my nipples are tweaking painfully and I know it's only a matter of time. I can pump again when I get home but will the milk be any good or will I have to throw it away? What a waste. My eyes fill with tears. I'm so tired. I miss my boys. I even miss Angus, who's no doubt currently asleep in front of *The Wire.* I've still got that presentation to finish. Must. Concentrate.

With a supreme effort, I focus on Izzy. Try to say something nice, positive, bolstering. Be there for my friend. Who's going through a rough time. Who needs me. Round and round goes the restaurant. Boom boom boom goes the room. I squint at my friend; the one constant.

'You can talk to me, you know. If you're worried . . . about anything.'

Izzy's expression softens, and she reaches across the table. My phone buzzes in my bag, and I knock a spoon on the floor in my rush to get to it. Her hand retreats as I peer at the screen.

'Bloody idiot.' I type in a frenzy of annoyance:

Binky's hanging on the dryer.

Putting the phone down, I turn back to Izzy. 'What were you saying?'

'Nothing,' she said. 'Actually, you know, I have to get back . . . Got an early start tomorrow.'

I re-focus the full force of my Angus-aggravation on her. 'Cool, cool. Yes, I know you have more important things to do. Flats to choose between, contacts to make. You must get on.'

She stands, her face flinty. Opening her purse, she peels off two twenty-pound notes and throws them on the table.

'That should cover my share,' she says, coldly.

My rage immediately dissipates, and I feel worn to shreds, like Liam's beloved Binky. 'That's too much,' I say, feebly. 'I had more to drink than you.'

She looks at me steadily, something more sympathetic edging into her gaze. Sympathetic and . . . resigned? Like it's done now, and there's nothing she can do.

'I have a feeling you need it more than me,' she says. 'Goodbye, Gwen. Take care.'

And then she leaves, and I drink the rest of the wine, and eat the tiramisu, on my own. Not Mortimer, or Adrian, or even Gwennie. Just Gwen.

49

Izzy gave up. She was angry and upset and frustrated and embarrassed and totally at sea. And she was scared. She didn't know who was harassing her, and she didn't know what to do about it, and she didn't know which of her friends she could trust, and no one was taking her seriously, and all she wanted to do was escape. So she put the plan in motion, and went to ground.

And it worked.

Izzy cut herself off from all but her closest family and a couple of professional associates – who she kept at a strict distance. First, she went to Positano, where her family had always holidayed. A little apartment, high up in the town, with views over the sea. If anyone was coming, Izzy could see them. She rested, and for the first time in years, she relaxed. She had no emails to check, no post to collect, nowhere to be. Then she went to stay with Luca, who still thought she was mad, but showed her a good time in Rome, took her to the best restaurants and escorted her home after. She got a temporary job translating at the publishing house where he was working, and she was so good at it that she actually helped Luca with his own career progression – everyone was impressed that he'd recruited his friend 'Rosa'. She felt valued there, and free to enjoy her success, rather than being brought down by a mysterious lurking figure.

Eventually though, she felt she had to find her own life, rather than squatting in Luca's. She moved back to England, to Oxford, where she'd lived as a child, before all this started. Feeling slightly more secure, she made tentative enquiries with contacts, always under an assumed name, and started re-establishing a career. It was normal for restaurant reviewers to adopt a pseudonym, and her employers were intrigued and amused by how far she took it. True dedication! The fan mail started to come in again, this time always positive, for 'Arthur Nicholls' (Charlotte Brontë's husband) and 'Charles Wellesley'. Charles seemed to have a better hit rate, perhaps because he sounded posh. Isabella enjoyed being a man – it was an easier, smoother path to success. People appeared to resent you less for it. Certainly, it seemed like a man was much less likely to have a stalker. She'd managed to kill off Isabella Harris; now she was Charles Wellesley. Having been terrified by someone else's anonymity, she relished her own.

Throughout all this, she did miss her old life. She missed her friends. She missed me. She thought about contacting me occasionally, and even sent a card when Fred was born. She'd set up a false account on Facebook and become friends with me – blithely unaware of any of the risks, I'd accepted her friendship, assuming she was a schoolfriend

I'd forgotten. Izzy saw the baby photos and felt a terrible pang that this was a child she'd never babysit, never buy ice cream for, never read *Phoebe and the Hot Water Bottles* to. But another part of her resented me – I'd never tried hard enough to grab at the ties of our friendship. Maybe it was for the best that it was allowed to lapse.

And it was a small price to pay for freedom. It wasn't worth opening up again, because once you started, where did you stop? Best to keep the hatches battened. Izzy kept moving, kept renting around the country, but found she was gradually circling the north-west, haunting her old haunts. She was drawn to home, regularly visiting her parents, who knew about the situation but not how much it had worried her, who accepted her decision unquestioningly, who were always there with their newspapers and sherry.

And then on a jaunt down south, she met Miles. There was a restaurant opening in Croydon, not a particularly trendy area, but a chef Izzy had long admired. Everyone was excited that the great Charles Wellesley was rumoured to be visiting, never suspecting that Isabella Harris, the muted, elegant woman in the corner, was the one they should be watching. Izzy loved that – no one noticed her any more. *No one* was watching.

Apart from Miles, their sommelier, who was so attentive and polite, and knowledgeable. The management was fussing over every man, in case it was Charles, but Miles was the only one who fussed over her. After so many years of semi-anxiety, Izzy trusted her gut, and now her gut was telling her this was a good guy. When he told her his surname, she knew for sure.

Mr and Mrs Braithwaite married in Positano, watched by their families and a couple of Miles' old friends. When they exchanged rings, Izzy remembered throwing the coins in the fountain in Rome, and realized that I was right – it would have been extortionate to fly *everyone* out. But I was the one she missed – I should have been there making a sour but funny speech, doing formation dancing, lying with her on the ground looking up at the stars. She wrote to Alaric to tell him about it: *we must be satisfied with tranquillity!* Mostly, she was, as it was preferable to the alternative. He wrote back, to an email address that only he knew, that he was told never to pass on – CB1816, Charlotte's birthdate – saying that at his age, tranquillity was all he could hope for, but at hers, she should aim for a little more spice.

After the wedding, Miles and Izzy moved back to Manchester. Miles' brother was there, and Izzy felt that enough time had passed for it to be safe. After all these years, who would remember or recognize her? After renting for a bit, they bought a house in Chorlton, a familiar area that felt like home. They built a new life together. Izzy had a baby. It was an accident, and she worried she was too old, at forty-six, but it all went well, and she had a little girl – Shirley Braithwaite – who was the apple of her eye. Shirley – or Sisi, as she was known – was extremely bright, and already spoke Italian. Apart from Alaric, Izzy didn't see any of her old friends, but she'd made a few new ones – always keeping them at arm's length until she could be sure. Sometimes she still felt a spike of rage, that she'd been forced to shrink her sphere in this way; to confine herself so completely. Mostly she just felt relief that she could at least exist without looking over her shoulder. They lived quietly, because that was her habit now, but it was a good life – an unmolested one, as Mrs Rosamund Braithwaite. Until earlier this year . . .

In March, Izzy's parents received a card addressed to her. It was from Holly Griffiths, inviting her to a school reunion weekend in the Lake District. Of course, Izzy ignored it, never replied, but it unnerved her nonetheless. She assumed everyone had forgotten about her, and yet, here they were, reminding her that there were parts of her life that were still accessible. It was a shot in the dark from Holly, of course, since she would have no idea if Julian and Coco still lived there. She probably thought it was worth a try.

And then one of Izzy's many email addresses – R_Braithwaite – started receiving odd messages. It was an account she used for Shirley's school correspondence, so she assumed another parent must have got hold of it and passed it on. At first, it sounded like another mum from her daughter's class, asking about play dates and school trips, but there was something in the tone that was off . . . Izzy quickly shut down that account, but her antennae were out, spinning wildly. Something was up.

Once again, she started feeling that someone was watching her. Following her. This time, she had Miles on hand, but she also had Shirley to protect. It couldn't be the same person, could it? But then, who was unlucky enough to have *two* stalkers? Why had it started up again?

As the weeks went on, she realized that I was also looking for her, blundering round asking questions, making no attempt to cover my trail. She wasn't threatened by me, but she was worried about what would happen if I tracked her down. Who else might be piggybacking on the search? What can of worms might I open?

Just after she'd received my email, to CurrerB@pronto. com, she got another, from an unfamiliar address: *It's been a long time . . . X*

Then, this morning, there was a delivery to the offices of *Mancunium* magazine, where she worked. It was a box of iced biscuits, addressed to Isabella Harris c/o Charles Wellesley.

She'd known it was a risk, moving back to Chorlton. Someone else had discovered her pseudonym, maybe someone had seen her around, maybe someone recognized her at the school gates, maybe someone had seen her at a restaurant and put two and two together . . . Maybe it was time to move on again.

* * *

As the darkness deepened around us, Izzy's voice rose to a rattle and her grip on my hand tightened.

As she began telling me this story, there was a part of me that thought she sounded dramatic, even neurotic. A part of me that felt her reaction was disproportionate. It was all a bit over the top, surely? Whoever was circling hadn't actually done anything properly dangerous or threatening, had they? OK, the burglary was weird, but who cared about a few biscuits? Had Izzy created a storm in a teacup?

But as she carried on talking, it became clearer: none of it had happened to me, but these things – all of these things, so small by themselves and so insurmountable collectively – *had* happened to Izzy. Who was I to say how it felt to be the target of some nameless person's obsession for so long? This drip-fed, faceless intimidation. Who was I to make a judgement on taking things too far? It was her life, and her fear, and her decision. Too many women had tried to ignore it, hoped it would go away, and had learned the hard way that one day it would come for you. Izzy did what she felt was right.

And another part of me felt desperately sad, that her whole life had been blighted by this one thing – so much of her joy and achievement undermined by a weaselly menace. Izzy never deserved this. She deserved to live loudly and proudly, not to skulk around jumping at shadows.

Throughout her story, I remained completely silent, just holding her hand and listening, listening, listening. I heard everything, and believed everything, and sympathized so strongly I couldn't speak, just squeezed her hand and listened with every fibre of my being. And when she'd finished, I still didn't say anything, just sat there in silence, still holding her hand as the owl hooted, and Mabel panted, and the trees rustled. Just those sounds. In that moment, it was all she needed.

50

'And then what happened?' murmured Angus.

'Nothing. She went back to her hotel. Wouldn't even tell me which one it was.'

We were home, in bed, with Mabel snoring between us.

'West Park's the best bet.' Nearby, and stylish, it was the obvious choice.

'Yeah. So she'll probably be elsewhere.' Now, I understood that Izzy would never go for the straightforward, easy option. She'd be somewhere unexpected, tucked away.

'Are you going to see her again?'

'I don't know.' Izzy didn't promise anything, but I gave her my mobile number and while she wouldn't give me hers, she did give me a new email address – rosa_caruso, which was the Italian name she'd used when she stayed in Rome. I looked forward to agonizing about what to say when I contacted her. Our tentative reconnection needed fostering before it fizzled out; before she got spooked and scarpered. *Scappo.*

'So, how does it feel now your quest is complete? Isabella's not dead, you've found her, and you know why she left. That's it, isn't it?' He knew it wasn't true, but wanted reassurance, that I wasn't going to dash off again, distract myself with another mission imbecile.

'Yes,' I said. 'That's it.' Of course, it wasn't. I might have found her – or rather, she might have found me – but we weren't friends. We weren't Adrian and Pandora, Izzy and Mortimer, the old double act. And I wasn't sure I could rest until we'd regained some semblance of that relationship. Now she was within arm's reach, it felt wrong not to try to salvage something. But I didn't know where to begin.

* * *

I began by getting rid of my parents and mother-in-law. The next morning, I found them all at the kitchen table squinting at our cereal selection and indulging in a bit of idle one-upmanship about who had the most dead friends. Marching up to my father, I handed him a Post-it note.

'This is the number of a highly recommended builder in Buxton who can underpin your kitchen and sort out the garden. He's very reasonable and available to start next week.'

My parents' collapsing network of underground tunnels very much resembled my own interior life at present, and I was eager to fix it, both as a metaphor, and a practical way of getting them out of my house. Amanda Simmons – via her possibly-soon-to-be-ex-husband – had provided me with excellent recommendations from the construction industry. With an array of reliable builders available to me, I was considering my own kitchen revamp and bin room refurb. It was time to Get Shit Done.

My mother and father immediately began their protestations – it was too soon, the upheaval of builders in the house, they'd have to buy Hobnobs for them all, how would Brock 1 and Brock 2 react to this breach of their habitat? . . . Leaving them to fret, I turned my attention to Morag.

'And here's a reputable, Edinburgh-based painter and decorator for *you*,' I said, handing her another Post-it. 'I have it on good authority that he is young and attractive.' Morag clutched the note to her bosom in ecstasy – knowing my mother-in-law, it wasn't just her flat that would get a once-over.

My guests thus dispatched, I packed Liam back off to Nottingham with a bag of clean clothes and the assurance that one day his heart would heal, but that in the meantime, he should get back in the romance ring. I didn't explicitly say 'shag your way out of it', but my meaning was clear.

Fred's new friends Jonny and Amos came round that afternoon and were provided with a bucket of snacks to accompany their screen action. Sam, as far as I was aware, was putting the finishing touches to whatever he was editing, which was definitely not porn, Angus was recording in his studio, and the house was clear and quiet. It was time to email Izzy.

From: Gwendolyn Mortimer <GMortimer@haremail.com>
Sent: 01 June 2024 14.27
To: rosa_caruso@pronto.com
Subject: Hello

Hi,

I hope you got home OK. It was really nice to see you. Could we maybe meet up again sometime? Wherever suits you is fine.

I'm so sorry about what happened, but glad you told me. I hope you are too.

Gwen

I put an X at the end and then deleted it because that might trigger her. Obviously, I wanted to say more, but there was a degree of formality between us now, and it felt unwise to rush things or be over-familiar. We had to get to know each other again, catch up, pick up the threads of our friendship, take it slowly. Maybe I could offer to babysit Shirley – Sisi – and return the decades-old favour, take ice cream and a storybook. Perhaps I should invite them all – Izzy, Miles and Sisi – over for a Sunday roast? Was tomorrow too soon? If I showed her photos of the kayaking holiday, might she be tempted?

* * *

It had been at least three-quarters of an hour – why hadn't she replied?

351

51

From: rosa_caruso@pronto.com
Sent: 06 June 2024 20.45
To: Gwendolyn Mortimer <GMortimer@haremail.
com>
Subject: Re: Hello

Hi,

Thank you, I got home OK. It was good to talk. Give my best
to Angus and the kids.

R

That was it? That was *it*? Fifteen years and an in-depth
heart-to-heart and that was all she could manage?
'*Give my best . . .*' Talk about a dismissal. Well, fine.
Two could play at that game. I was off to Hebden
Bridge for a few days to find some pottery for Dippy's
frame. Busy, busy, busy. See how *she* liked not hearing
from *me*.

From: Gwendolyn Mortimer <GMortimer@haremail.com>
Sent: 06 June 2024 22.57
To: rosa_caruso@pronto.com
Subject: Re: Re: Hello

Hi there,

I'll be in Hebden Bridge next week if you feel like a jaunt. A work thing, but plenty of time for play!

Gwen X

From: Gwendolyn Mortimer <GMortimer@haremail.com>
Sent: 06 June 2024 23.22
To: rosa_caruso@pronto.com
Subject: Re: Re: Hello

God, sorry about the X. And the gabbling generally.

From: rosa_caruso@pronto.com
Sent: 09 June 2024 19.21
To: Gwendolyn Mortimer <GMortimer@haremail.com>
Subject: Please stop

Hi,

I think we might have got crossed wires somewhere along the line, and I don't want to mislead you. I can't go back. It's been too long, and I'm in a different place now, a different person. Don't get me wrong, it was a huge relief to tell you everything – cathartic – but at the same time, it's made me anxious all over again. I find it difficult to let people in, and worry about the consequences of opening up. So I'm afraid I'm not in the market for cosy restaurant get-togethers and shopping trips.

I also feel like this is more about you, and where you are, than it is about me. Your job issues, and your kids growing up, and feeling rudderless – I can't fix any of it. That's up to you.

Given what you now know about my situation, I'd appreciate it if you let me know if anyone seems unduly interested in my business, in the hope that one day I might find out who 'X' is. But otherwise, I think it's best if you don't contact me.

I wish you well, and will always cherish the friendship we had. But it's in the past, and we should both move on as best we can.

With best wishes,
R

From: Gwendolyn Mortimer <GMortimer@haremail.com>
Sent: 10 June 2024 06.17

To: rosa_caruso@pronto.com
Subject: Re: Please stop

Sure thing!

All the best,
G

Fuck you, Gwen, you massive loser. Sort yourself out. When I'd finished crying, I went back to my tiling. Could always rely on the grout float to restore order. By the end of the day, I'd done a whole splashback in the downstairs toilet. Rudderless? We'd see about that.

52

With tremendous self-restraint and medicinal levels of alcohol, I managed to put former friendships out of my mind, and enjoyed my expedition to Hebden Bridge. I browsed the shops, strolled along the canal that Dippy had painted, had coffee on a lovely terrace that overlooked it, enjoyed a slap-up lunch at a country pub, and then hiked up the punishing Buttress – the steep cobbled path to Heptonstall – to visit Sylvia Plath's grave.

Paying my respects, as Dippy had requested, I laid a bunch of tulips by her headstone, which read *Even amidst fierce flames the golden lotus can be planted*. It was an unremarkable monument, with remarkable objects strewn before it – that day, I saw a collection of pens, a notebook, shells, and a potted azalea. The pot was ceramic, and I briefly considered pinching it, before deciding that Dippy would not want me desecrating Sylvia Plath's grave to make a frame for her painting. I felt like Sylvia would have enjoyed that though. On the headstone, someone had daubed over the name 'Hughes', erasing Ted, a desecration Dippy definitely *would* have appreciated.

That night, I stayed with Bhavini Gupta and her wife Freya, who lived in a gorgeous barn conversion on the edge of town. Over good red wine and lashings of spaghetti, we bitched about people we knew and recalled from school, speculated about the state of Amanda Simmons's marriage, discussed the upcoming election and exchanged tips on intermittent fasting. It was a thoroughly enjoyable evening, and the next morning, after serving scrambled eggs and hash browns, Bhavini pointed me in the direction of a pottery studio near the old Gibson Mill, telling me to speak to someone called Sage.

Walking along the canal, it struck me that Dippy was quite right about this view – there was nothing shut-in or sodden or dreary about it. On this bright summer's day, it was just as lush and vivid and beautiful as her painting, the colourful barges standing out like punctuation points along the line of the water, sunlight making dappled patterns along the surface.

At the studio, I found a group of pottery students solemnly moulding their creations, overseen by an individual who seemed to be dressed as a medieval wizard. This turned out to be Sage, who was so zen they gave Jacob Levy a run for his money. Softly spoken and slow-moving, Sage offered me a Fat Rascal rock cake while they listened to my request with great patience, then kindly directed me out back, where I hit the jackpot. Several crates of rejected or faulty pots, plates, bowls and mugs of all shapes, sizes and colours. Inspired by my visit to Sylvia's resting place, an idea was taking root, and I rummaged through this treasure trove for items that were red, orange or black.

Sage gave me a lift back to Hebden Bridge, where I visited various antique and second-hand shops until I found exactly what I was looking for – a box of old porcelain tableware, chipped and cracked, for a tenner, every piece with a golden rim. Perfect. I bought the lot, and loaded it into the car along with my studio finds, ready for the trip home.

Driving back to Harrogate, I felt lucky that we lived in such a serenely beautiful, replete part of the world. Who needed the Spanish Steps when you had the Buttress? Who needed the River Tiber when you had the Rochdale Canal? Who needed *cornetti* when you had Fat Rascals? And when you had *cornetti* at Da Mario's in Chorlton? Dammit, I was back there again. And I was doing so well . . .

I'd managed not to check my email at all while I'd been away, but when I'd got back home, been ignored by the dog, had unpacked, eaten a slapdash dinner made by my husband and settled on the sofa with a box of After Eights left by my parents as a thank you for their stay, I opened up my messages, not sure exactly what I was waiting for. An apology? A recant? Mocked by a bare inbox, I slapped my laptop shut, and distracted myself from the frustration by covering my teeth in the black paper chocolate wrappers, and doing witchy grins for an appalled and disgusted Fred. With achy legs from the walk up to Heptonstall, I decided to turn in early and plan my frame design in bed. Propped up on pillows with my notebook and pen, I began to sketch out the idea I'd had, occasionally googling images on my phone for inspiration. Was I artistic enough to pull this off? It was more ambitious than anything I'd attempted before, but I had the feeling Dippy would like it . . .

My eyelids drooping, the pencil fell to the duvet as I leaned back drowsily, Sage's oatmeal robes, the rich sienna of Bhavini's spaghetti sauce, the scarlet barges, the black of the After Eight papers, and the golden rims of my broken tableware, all coming together in a flickering mosaic . . .

My phone pinged, waking me, and I groped for it clumsily. An unknown number, the text swirling and rearranging itself until I could see it clearly.

X is back. Someone is checking your emails. Don't contact me again, under any circumstances.

The mobile fell from my hand as I let the guilty fire consume me. X was back, and it was my fault. Once again, I'd let my friend down.

53

'So, I have a very special invitation for you, and wanted to present it in person.'

It was a blazing day in July, and Min and I were in our favourite York tapas place, gorging on patatas bravas and doing a lot of signing because it was unusually busy and noisy. The sign for 'invite' was petite and precise, using your thumb and forefinger to pluck an envelope out of thin air.

'Oooh!' said Min. 'Is it a party?' The gesture for 'party' was to raise your hands either side of your head, with thumbs and index fingers extended, and move them forwards and backwards in a mini-rave.

'Sort of.' I 'raved' back at Min. 'My friend Dippy got her exhibition.' I had to admit, I was excited about this event. It had been a long time coming, and was thoroughly deserved. Moreover, I had a part in it, one I was proud of, so I intended to make the most of it.

Finally, Serendipity Holt had found someone as mad as her – an outrageous and exuberant gallery owner in Leeds who'd taken a punt on a young, hot, crazy painter. Dippy's new backer was called Mo Masham – four feet tall, stinking rich from several good marriages, and a passionate patron of the arts. Dippy thought she might have to perform sexual favours in return for the launch, and was thoroughly aroused by the idea. Me? I was just chuffed that picture frames I'd made were going to be hung in a cool Victorian warehouse in Holbeck.

'I'm inviting all the Harlots,' I told Min. 'Because there'll be something there I think they might like.'

'What?' demanded Min, spearing a chunk of chorizo.

I shook my head. 'It's a secret. There'll be a big reveal.' There was my picture frame for Dippy's canal barge, but also something else; another surround for a picture that I knew the Harlots would be interested in.

'No!' she whined. 'I demand prior knowledge!'

Min loved knowing things. She was full of questions, because she was always interested in the answers. She was a gossip, in the benign sense, and of course she would love to know the whole Isabella story, and yet I held back, not because I didn't trust her, but because it wasn't really my story to share. And maybe Isabella was right – the more people knew about it, the more difficult it became to contain. So I didn't tell her, and more to the point she didn't ask, as if she intuitively understood there were some things she wasn't meant to know. One day when I grew up, I wanted to be as wise and sensitive as Min.

'Just put on your glad rags and turn up here on Friday the twenty-third of August.' I handed her a card with the details. 'I'm going to organize a dinner after.'

'Yes, do,' replied Min, staring at the invite. 'Can I bring Oliver? He might be useful.'

'Oh my God, that's a great idea!' I'd totally forgotten Min's boyfriend was an art dealer. 'Dippy can be his next discovery.'

'I can't promise anything, but he can probably introduce her to a few people. Are you making her more frames?'

'Yes.' Previously a lacklustre enterprise, Mortimosaic had taken off, thanks to this new direction. I'd made Dippy two frames for her exhibition, with more planned, and had already been contacted by other artists and art lovers in the area who were interested in the same service. With help from one of Amanda Simmons' tradesmen, I'd reorganized our spare 'bin' room and now this serene and clutter-free space served as a little gallery displaying my work. 'It's more of a hobby though. A lucrative, fun one, but not a proper job.'

I had to face it – mosaics were a stopgap. A way to fill in the holes in my existence while I waited for something more substantial to come along. Only it hadn't, yet.

'About that,' said Min. 'I have a suggestion.' The sign for 'suggestion' was to tap your temple with your forefinger and then pull it away from your head as if you were literally dragging out an idea.

There was one *croqueta* left, which I decided was destined for my mouth. 'What?'

She signed something without saying anything. Because I was used to following signs along with speech, I didn't understand at first. 'Do that again?'

Min repeated the movement, her palms out flat and facing each other, circling, and then chopping into each other.

'Signing . . . occupation?' I said, doubtfully.

'You're really good at it. You know that, don't you?'

I blushed harder than when Dippy had seen my first frame. 'Am I?'

She nodded. 'You were always good at it, at school, I remember. It was one of the reasons I liked you. But now . . . It's not enough just to sign. You have to really watch, and listen, and respect every little detail. I think you'd be great at it, and there are loads of jobs you can get as an interpreter. You'd have to train, of course, and it's hard. But it could be a really interesting career. And obviously, I have all sorts of contacts. I can keep my ear to the ground!' She grinned. 'Deaf joke.'

So here it was, the fifth coin in the fountain. Not what I'd expected at all.

The idea churned around in my head. It would mean effectively going back to school, slogging away at something, learning something new. But, sitting there, stunned into sign-less silence, I realized that was exactly what I wanted. Exactly what I was ready for. A project. A challenge. Something to get my teeth into.

'I don't know what to say,' I said eventually. 'But . . .' Putting my fingertips to my chin, I signed 'thank you'.

'Think about it,' Min said. 'Let me know.'

'OK,' I said. 'And because I'm so overwhelmed by all that, I'm going to let you in on the secret and tell you what to expect at the exhibition next month. But you have to promise not to tell any of the others.'

'Swear to die!' said Min, and so I told her what I'd done. The full picture they should expect, and the frame that I would put around it.

But beyond that, and this was something I was keeping to myself, I had a weird sixth sense that Dippy's exhibition was going to show more than just her – and my – creations. I had a feeling that, like Susan Lavery laying out her tarot cards, a truth was about to be revealed . . .

* * *

From: Gwendolyn Mortimer <GMortimer@haremail. com>
Sent: 26 July 2024 10.17
To: Gwendolyn Mortimer <GMortimer@haremail.com>
Subject: SAVE THE DATE

Hi guys,

I've spoken to some of you already, but please find attached the official invite to the launch of Serendipity Holt's

'Goddess's Own County' exhibition on Friday, 23rd August. I would love you all to come and see the big unveiling of something quite special, that the Harpur Harlots might appreciate! Dinner's booked after at the Holbeck Grill, and you're v welcome to join.

Full Press!
Gwen x

I'd changed my email password as soon as I received Isabella's text, and deleted all our correspondence, feeling deeply uncomfortable at the idea of someone – the mysterious and menacing X – reading my messages and using the information to their own ends. Although I longed to send an invite to Izzy, I knew it wasn't an option. How on earth had someone hacked into my account? How was that even possible? I felt guilty, and responsible, having inadvertently made my friend vulnerable again. At Izzy's request, I was listening, respecting every little detail – she said do nothing, say nothing, and I obeyed, but somehow felt it was all wrong.

Izzy's instinct was to shut down, close herself off, like the Hermit. But increasingly I felt the opposite tactic was required – tell everyone, shout about it, share it, bring it all out into the open. 'Full press' was a hockey term – an aggressive play where all the team work together to push the opposition into a mistake. You don't try to get the ball – you force them to give the ball to you.

We could be more aggressive. We could be cleverer about this.

But there was no 'we'. Izzy wanted it that way, and I had to listen to her.

54

'Harlots in da house!'

This time it was me saying it, without a shred of shame. Masham Temple, Mo's gallery, was spectacularly lit for the occasion, pulsing with music far too trendy for the reunion of a fifty-something hockey team. We were all wildly overexcited and wildly overdressed. I'd bought a black lace number with a bustle, which possibly made me look like a wizened Wednesday Addams, but who cared? This was my night. Well, actually it was Dippy's night, but I was hijacking it.

The gallery was a huge warehouse space with massive iron girders across the ceiling, from which hung a series of extraordinary light fittings, probably artworks in their own right. In the entrance, a sign on an easel read 'GODDESS'S OWN COUNTY', with a moody-looking photo portrait of the artist. Dippy, the actual belle of the ball, was going crazy in the corner. Dressed in a hot pink silk sheath, her dreadlocks threaded with gold ribbon, she looked a million dollars, but had overdosed on her

ADHD medication so was busy rearranging the buffet Mo had provided, shifting around plates of mini Yorkshire puddings, Wensleydale and parkin. Waiters sailed around carrying glasses of champagne, which my middle son was busy downing. My eldest, Liam, had rocked up with a lovely looking girl on his arm who definitely wasn't called Anna, which had already made my night. Angus, dressed in a kilt, was chatting jovially with other guests, fending off questions about what he was wearing under it. Jacob Levy, my wood-sculpting workshop-mate, in an exquisite three-piece suit, was already deep in conversation with Mo Masham, who appeared to be decked out as an Edwardian dowager, with an ostrich feather springing gaily from her head.

I was surrounded by my friends, who were offering a series of toasts.

'To Amanda! May her divorce settlement be generous!'

'To Gracie! May her twins stop getting nits!'

'To Chloe! May she tell a story that's actually true!'

'To Gwen! May she tell us why the fuck we're here!'

'Hang on, do you not appreciate being invited to a culturally enriching evening?' I demanded. 'This is a hot ticket.'

'I appreciate the free champagne,' said Rachel. 'But when are you going to do this big reveal?'

'Well, since you're all so impatient, we'd better get on with it,' I replied, bowing and sweeping my arm. 'If you wouldn't mind following me . . .'

I led them through the crowds, swiping a glass of champagne along the way. The bare brick walls were lined with Dippy's paintings, some large, some small, some in between. Almost all of them depicted Yorkshire scenes – mills, moors, reservoirs, a viaduct, a derelict farmhouse, a cobbled street in York. One of the odder images was of a litter bin in front of the Minster – I'd made a frame for it which consisted of rubbish I'd found in the city centre. Each painting had some word, phrase or quote scrawled across it – so as we marched through the masses, the walls screamed at us. 'BONE-CLINIC WHITENESS', 'TIME'S WINGED CHARIOT', 'COMMON PEOPLE' 'ALLELUJAH!' 'SHUT-IN SODDEN DREARINESS', 'CHEAT FOR THE SAKE OF BEAUTY', 'OLD BRAG OF MY HEART'. Heckled by the county's finest.

'This was my first effort,' I said, when we arrived at the Rochdale Canal painting.

'Now, that's cool,' said Holly. 'Very, very cool.'

Up in Hebden Bridge, I'd been inspired by the inscription on Sylvia Plath's grave: *Even amidst fierce flames the golden lotus can be planted.* So I'd assembled that image in Yorkshire crockery, using red, orange and black shards from Sage's pottery studio to create a burning frame. Along the bottom, a glinting water lily emerged, made from the golden rims of the antique shop's broken tableware, nestling in the conflagration. The whole effect was fiery and magnificent – a crackling, seething rebuke to the Ted Hughes dreariness quote that was scrawled across the painting. Dippy had been utterly delighted.

'And through here is my latest effort,' I said, heading towards a smaller room that led off the main gallery.

The Inner Temple, as it was known, was quieter, though just as splendidly lit, and featured one large painting on the far wall. On the floor, a half-circle had been marked out in white in front of it. A striking circle, as it's known in field hockey. The Harlots stopped, contemplating the vision before them.

'Fucking hell,' said Rachel, softly. 'It's us.'

During my conversations with Dippy and Jacob about Izzy, I'd shown them the old photo of the Harlots team, taken circa 1986 after a match on the outskirts of Sheffield. I remembered that day so well – breathless and dishevelled, assembling on the edge of the pitch as our coach, Miss Edwards, got her camera out, yelling at us to squash in. We were all high from the victory – 3–1 to the Harlots – which was especially satisfying because the clash was against a private girls' school who thought they were a cut above. Izzy and I were on the end of the row, heads back, laughing at Holly's unrepentant crows of triumph. It was a good moment, a sweet snapshot in time.

Dippy's mind was blown by the antiquity of the photo (a scan of the original), which was to her a daguerreotype, dizzyingly bygone. She asked me to send it to her, and would occasionally query me about a detail in the image. Why was one of the girls holding a stuffed bear? That was our mascot, Granville. Why was he called that? Granville was a character in a sitcom called *Open All Hours*. Why was that other girl making a peace sign? She was doing an impression of Neil in *The Young Ones*. What was that? Neil? *The Young Ones*?? Oh, come on . . .

After she finished her Rochdale Canal painting, Dippy started a new piece, painting in a frenzy. Every time I went to our workshop she'd be there, covered in splotches, face set in concentration, but she wouldn't let me see what she was working on. Of course, she had to show me eventually, because she wanted me to make her another frame . . .

The painting, large and compelling against its stark white wall setting, was a direct copy of the original photo, except Dippy had given it her own twist, her pointillism technique picking out the little details – our flushed cheeks, Granville's wonky stitched ear, Rachel's ripped bib from a dirty tackle, Bhavini resting her arm on Holly's shoulder to do the peace sign, Erica's sharp profile as she looked down the line towards me and Izzy, the mud splattered up our legs – our lithe, ruddy, slim legs that bore no signs of stretch marks, nor varicose veins, nor cellulite. Our teenage legs. Nearly forty years ago.

Yet here we were, most of that team, gathered to gaze at ourselves, celebrate past and present, and rejoice in the words that flowed across the sky above us: 'KEEP IN GOOD HEALTH'. A proper toast, from a proper Yorkshire woman. And to complete this epic work, I'd made a frame for it, buying a load of vintage hockey sticks online, getting Jacob to cut them into pieces and arranging them in a wooden surround that faintly retained the old patterns, nicks and brand names.

'It's brilliant,' said Rachel.

'A masterpiece,' said Chloe.

'Sexy,' said Holly.

'But you know what?' said Bhavini. 'We've got a secret too . . .' She hoicked an enormous bag from around her shoulder and unzipped it, revealing a tangle of intact hockey sticks.

'I told them everything,' said Min. 'Sorry not sorry.'

I gave her a mock glare. 'You cannot keep your mouth shut.'

'We thought we'd do a recreation,' grinned Holly. 'Young Us, Now Us.'

'Oh God,' I groaned, thrilled. 'It'll be such a hideous contrast.'

'You bet,' said Min.

And so, we posed beneath the old images of us, wielding our sticks, giggling like schoolgirls, as Oliver, Min's partner, took photos on his phone, directing us into the correct positions and speculating who might buy such an unusual piece. Several of Dippy's paintings had red dots on them, signalling that they were already sold, and I'd briefly considered bidding for this one, but concluded we didn't have enough wall space and, even with Angus's socking great income, we probably didn't have enough money either.

'To old friends!' toasted Amanda, raising her hockey stick.

'To old friends!' we shouted, waving our sticks.

By the time I finally got back to the main room, it was even busier, crammed with people eager to meet this gorgeous, kooky new artist the legendary Mo Masham had found. Drunk and happy, I headed for the buffet to soak up all the champagne I'd necked, before I rounded up my errant sons. Dippy was still there, frantically rearranging.

'Someone brought these,' she moaned, pushing a tray backwards and forwards. 'They won't fit.'

Smiling, I looked down, ready to reassure her that the food didn't matter, that everyone was interested in what was on the walls, not what was on the table. But my smile faded as I saw what was on the tray. They were out of place amongst the hearty servings of Yorkshire pudding, rough chunks of Wensleydale, fat squares of parkin. They were delicate, dainty, elegant, and, in this setting, they were supremely sinister. They intruded on the buffet. They were definitely not invited.

Iced biscuits.

What was it Jackson DeLantro said in one of his first emails? 'Go back to the hockey team – one of them knows something, even if they don't know they know.'

It turned out it was me who knew, even though I didn't understand fully until that moment. All at once, in the buzz of the gallery, I put two and two and two and two together, arriving at a number that chilled me to my core, made me look back on everything and wonder how I'd been so oblivious, so stupid, so blasé. Of course, that was how it happened, and of course, that was who it was. It was so obvious. I'd felt it in my bones all along, but didn't listen to them.

To old friends . . .

X was right here. And had been right there all along. For forty years.

55

There was so much about my past that was a blur – lost in the frantic caper of family life and work and childcare and sleeplessness and drunkenness and time. It was odd, though, the things that stood out, that pierced the fog. Not necessarily the things you thought you would remember, or should remember. Little details, seemingly inconsequential, that lingered in your subconscious, ready to surface when you least expected it.

I found her upstairs, on a terrace that overlooked the street, her hockey stick propped against the balcony. She turned as I approached and smiled thinly, seeing my thunderous expression.

'Did you know this was an old flax mill?' she said. 'Spinning yarn, like Chloe.'

'Like you,' I said.

'I never liked you,' said Erica.

'The feeling is mutual,' I replied. 'But you like Izzy, don't you? A bit too much, one might say.'

When Izzy mentioned the iced biscuits, I pictured those ones you ordered from a bakery, professionally mass-produced at vast expense, but the ones at the buffet, although neat and pretty, were clearly home-made. And there was only one of us who liked baking that much, who turned up with carrot cake, who yakked about her sourdough starter. And I recalled Sue Lavery saying that the person who came to the Edinburgh flat asking about Izzy brought shortbread, and the 'neighbour' who knocked at the Chorlton flat brought cookies. And I imagined Erica, slaving away in her kitchen, carefully daubing her creations with that sweet sugar paste before packaging them up and sending them off to Izzy . . . Such a wholesome, honeyed offering, laced with such malice.

And I pictured that hockey team photo, blown up and emphasized by Dippy's tiny dots. Erica, looking down the row at me and Izzy, something in her expression that spoke of resentment, repressed bile. And I remembered, once, Izzy, Min and I signing something to each other in school, catching sight of Erica's baffled and aggrieved reaction – because unlike the rest of us, she never really learned any BSL to help out Min, and was always irritated when she didn't understand what we were saying to each other. She was always on the outside, looking in. It got to be a habit.

'In fact,' I continued, 'one might almost say that you're obsessed with her.'

'Pot calling the kettle black, sweetie.'

'What do you mean?'

Erica looked completely relaxed, leaning against the stone balustrade. 'Well, you've got the same problem, haven't you? Texting us all asking if we know where Izzy is? Getting a private investigator on board, booking those train tickets to Edinburgh? And flights to *Rome*? Isn't that taking things a bit far? One might say that . . . *you* are the one who's obsessed.'

I was silent for two reasons. One, I was trying to work out how she knew all this, and two . . . was she right? Was I as bad as she was? Looking back on that summer, was that all-consuming desire to find Izzy, whatever the cost, digging into every part of her past to track her down . . . creepy? Had I been . . . *stalking* her?

I shook my head, tried to focus. 'Bullshit. Why'd you do it?'

She shrugged. 'Why does anyone do anything? She annoyed me. Stuff always seemed to be happening for her. Everyone liked her. Success on a plate – literally.'

'That's not true,' I said, ignoring the fact that sometimes I'd felt that way too. 'And besides, it's no excuse for making someone's life a misery.'

'That's a bit dramatic. What's a few messages, a few little gifts?'

In a way, it was true. Other people might have been able to shrug that sort of thing off, not let it get to them. It was a quirk of fate that Erica had chosen someone intensely private to fixate on; someone fiercely self-contained, who crumbled when her protective shell was breached.

'You've been reading *my* emails. How?'

Erica's nostrils flared, her tone exultant. 'The lobby at the Lever Club. Couldn't believe my luck. I saw you type in your password. So easy! 'AdrianM1' – I bet you haven't changed it in years, have you? You really should be more careful.'

Adrian Mole, my alter ego since my teens. When I logged onto that iPad in the hotel, it never occurred to me that someone might be reading over my shoulder, just as it never occurred to me to worry when I accepted Facebook friendship requests from people I didn't really recognize or remember. Unlike Izzy, I'd never felt the need to be wary about that, never had to fret that I'd inadvertently made myself vulnerable. So Erica had seen my emails to Jackson DeLantro, seen my booking confirmations for train tickets, plane tickets and hotel rooms, seen my note to Alaric Irving asking to meet him; seen everything. Crucially, she'd read my first message to Izzy's CurrerB address, and then the others I'd sent to Rosa_Caruso. She'd intercepted Jackson's email revealing Izzy's professional pseudonym. I'd provided Erica with a handy trail of breadcrumbs, and she'd used them to send her confections.

I felt horribly guilty: I'd blundered around, the bull in the china shop, smashing Izzy's scrupulously disguised existence to smithereens. But I was also fucking livid. Erica Stanley, that smug two-faced cow, putting the idea into Holly's head to arrange the Harlots' forty-year reunion, pushing that planchette on the Ouija board to stir things up, putting Izzy's name uppermost in our minds, seeing who took the bait. She planted the seed, and of course it was me, Adrian to Izzy's Pandora, who obligingly watered it for her.

'Yes...' Erica wagged a finger, enjoying my dumbfounded reaction. 'You really should be more careful.'

'Well, so should you. You screwed up bringing those shitty biscuits tonight,' I spat. 'May as well have signed your name on those emails to Izzy, rather than "X".'

'So, because I bought some gingerbread to a party, I stand accused? Seems a bit of a stretch.' She presented me with an innocent face. 'I just wanted to contribute to my old friend's big event. Why does that have anything to do with Izzy?'

She was going for extreme denial. I had to appreciate that as a strategy, but it added fuel to the flames of my fury.

'Oh, I don't need to prove anything,' I assured her. 'I just need to tell Izzy who's been looking over *her* shoulder all these years. The thing that always frightened her the most was the fact that she didn't know who it was. When she finds out it was . . . y*ou*' – I gestured dismissively towards Erica – 'she'll feel very differently.'

A flicker of unease, quickly banished. 'And you think she'll believe you? You're not exactly close at the moment. What makes you think she'll listen to anything you have to say?'

I bore down on her. 'You said we're the same, but we're not. I won't deny I went a bit mad this summer, but you know what makes us different? You're "X" – that's all you are. Faceless, anonymous, a nobody. You're nothing. And you know what I am? Yes, you know because you know my old password – I'm Adrian. I'm Mortimer. Sometimes I was Gwennie, when she was teasing me. I was her *buona amica*, her plus-one, her best friend. And you don't get to erase any of that.' It was true. In the smouldering remains of our friendship, this was my lotus. 'So, yes, she'll listen, and yes, she'll believe me. You're done.'

She was flushed now, trembling with rage and consternation. 'You still don't have proof,' she said, stonily. 'This is all just speculation. Because you're crazy, mad she's not your friend any more. There's no proof I did anything.'

'Susan Lavery.'

'Who?'

'The daughter of Izzy's old landlady in Edinburgh. She said someone came round looking for her. Brought shortbread. What if I sent her a photo of you? Do you think she'd recognize you?' I already knew she probably wouldn't, but Erica didn't know that.

'So?' Erica shrugged. 'I was just looking up an old friend. Happened to be in the area.'

Shit. I'd have to do better. All that churning anger had rearranged the fractured images in my head. What was it Min said about signing? *You have to really watch, and listen, and respect every little detail* . . . When Izzy told me her story that night on the park bench, I watched her face, and listened to her words, and respected every tiny article she included, and now I remembered something that glittered and sparkled as I held it up to the light.

380

'Izzy's bangle,' I said.

Erica looked confused. 'What?'

'You might not remember it, but you should. I remember it. It's silver, quite wide. She got it on her twenty-first birthday.'

'What's Izzy's bracelet got to do with me?'

'Now, you're not listening to me. I said "bangle" not "bracelet". Bracelets are flexible but bangles are rigid.'

Erica shook her head. 'You're not making any sense.'

'Oh, but I am. You see, after Izzy's London flat was burgled . . . I'm sure you don't know anything at all about that burglary, do you? I thought not . . . anyway, after her flat was burgled, someone started sending the stolen jewellery back to her, piece by piece. How did you get into her flat, Erica?'

'I'm not saying I *did* . . . but . . . people always leave a key somewhere. Usually with an obliging neighbour who doesn't question you when you say you're feeding her cat.' A ghost of a smile flitted across Erica's face, no doubt reliving one of her finest moments.

'Izzy reported it to the police but they weren't very helpful. She put all the jewellery she received in a box. Couldn't bear to throw it away, but also couldn't bear to wear it or even look at it. Couldn't bear to touch it.'

'So?'

I smiled kindly at her, like she was a child. 'So it's still there, in the box. What if we were to get out that rigid, shiny bangle, and . . . take it to the police station? See if there are any fingerprints on it?'

Morag was absolutely right. This *was* a murder investigation, and I was fucking Poirot. Erica was stock-still, silver-stiff, and I was ready to punch the air and take out an advert in the *Manchester Evening News*, notifying everyone of my genius. Madison James would probably give me a freebie.

Erica took a deep breath. 'Go ahead,' she said. 'I don't know what it proves. I once admired her bangle? We've been friends for years . . .'

Bloody hell, she was impossible. Maybe I could just punch her in the face until she capitulated. I couldn't see any way of penetrating that smug veneer, making her crumble like Izzy had crumbled, finding the gap in her armour.

'Why start up again, after all these years?' I asked. 'Izzy disappeared, you couldn't find her. Why didn't you just leave it?'

Her lips twisted. 'Back in January, I saw her one day, outside a school in Chorlton. Gossiping with the other mums, the life and soul. I couldn't believe after all that time she was just *there*, right in front of me. Not a care in the world. I waited till she'd gone and then got chatting to the group – it wasn't hard to get her email address. People are stupid, thoughtless.' She dragged a nail along the ledge of the balcony. 'I was bored, at a loose end. Thought it would be interesting to . . . poke the nest.'

'Because you were *bored*?' Izzy's life had been blown up because Erica didn't have much going on?

Her intake of breath was a hiss. 'Have you never felt that? At our age? That sense that you're just . . . *done*? That nothing matters any more and you may as well do just what the hell you like – act on a whim, stir things up, do something crazy without thinking about the consequences – to *feel* something, to break the monotony? Otherwise it's just . . . baking bread and hoovering clean floors.'

Or grouting kitchen tiles. I shivered. We were different, but we also weren't. The realization made me deeply uncomfortable.

'But why did you have to direct that at *Izzy*?' I asked. 'Couldn't you have just . . . found a hobby? One that didn't involve harassing people?'

She laughed; a short, joyless crack. 'Like I said – a few emails, a few deliveries. Where's the harm?'

'You knew where the harm was,' I said. 'She disappeared. You made her disappear.'

'Yes.' Erica gazed at me, her eyes wide, alight. 'I was surprised it worked so well.'

I stared at her, more in sorrow than in anger. She was . . . not insane, but certainly on the spectrum. Maybe we all were, but at least most of us were benignly mad. Erica Stanley was full-on malignant, and I realized I felt sorry for her, crafting her barbed emails, packaging up her spiteful little parcels. Such petty, pathetic pastimes. But equally, the evil cow needed to be shown the red card.

'You should go now,' I told her. 'And if I ever, ever hear of you approaching Izzy again, in any form, I will finish you. She gets so much as a sniff of cinnamon in the post, and I will come down on you like a ton of bricks, do you hear me?'

Erica sneered at me. 'What are you going to do, write to the newspapers?'

'YOU MIGHT NOT HEAR *HER* BUT DO YOU HEAR *ME*?'

Min's voice came out of nowhere, booming across the terrace. We both whirled around. There she was, scowling in her flaming-red party dress. And behind her were the rest of the Harlots, looking every mixture of shocked, enraged and appalled. Rachel's arms were folded like she was in an army recruitment photo, Holly flanking her, Bhavini menacingly wielding her hockey stick. Chloe stepped forward, swinging her handbag, show-pony hair mussed up, pleasingly manic.

'You mess with them?' she snarled at Erica. 'You mess with Izzy? You mess with Gwen? You mess with *us*.'

'We will fucking *crush* you,' rasped Amanda. She turned, and hurled her empty champagne glass at the wall, where it shattered into a thousand pieces, the shards scattering across the terrace floor like tiny diamonds. The awed silence afterwards was golden – a lotus blooming in a blaze. After all these years, it felt good to be part of a team again. I relished it for a second, then turned back to Erica, who was as pale as a gravestone, outnumbered and unmasked at last.

'So,' I said, finally. 'I'll ask you again. Do you hear me?'

She said nothing, her lips pursed.

'DO YOU HEAR ME?' I repeated, my circle of friends crowding behind me, urging me on.

Erica nodded, her eyes burning.

'Good girl. Now, off you fuck. We've got a party to get back to.'

And as she stalked off, my old hockey team swept me into a victory pile-on, like we were sixteen again, the Young Us and Now Us coming together in a gloriously messy, noisy huddle. I wished Izzy could have been there to see it.

56

Squinting, I rubbed a last fleck of dried grouting off a sliver of china, carrying on until the porcelain shone.

'There,' I said, satisfied. 'I think it's done.'

Together, Dippy and I surveyed her latest work, and my latest frame.

'It looks good,' said Dippy. 'You were lucky to get it all back.'

'Yep,' I said. 'Every last piece.' I picked up the painting and started covering it in bubble wrap. 'Thank you for doing this,' I said. 'You know I would have been happy to pay for it.'

She shrugged, popping a piece of chewing gum in her mouth. 'My latest painting sold for seven thousand quid. I can afford to throw you a bone.'

'Oof. You're a big cheese now.'

She grinned, grinding away. 'I can tell you, I'm getting a much better class of cock.'

'For God's sake, give it a rest.' I loaded my package in my rucksack. 'Right, I'd better get on.'

'You around next week?'

'Nope – next week, I start my signing course!' I was studying for my BSL Level 1 at a school near Harrogate and wanted to do some swotting up in advance, make sure I was top of the class. 'OK, I'm off. Got a train to catch.'

'Have you told your bloke where you're going this time?'

'Left him a Post-it note.'

'Bon voyage, then. Hope she likes it.'

I was on the train by midday, and used the fifteen-minute wait at York to buy myself a sandwich. My next train left promptly, arriving at its destination in time for me to check into my room and change into something a little less travel-dishevelled. Leaving the hotel, I strolled down Princes Street, feeling the autumn tang in the air, the sky already darkening as I turned towards Queen Street Gardens. Feeling apprehensive, I continued towards Nelson Street, until I saw the warm, welcoming lights of Cosa Bolle.

It was 24th September. Izzy's birthday. I knew she would be there because Alaric told me so. He'd been very helpful, eager to spice things up for his favourite former student. 'Tranquillity is for *i vecchi*,' he wrote. 'Young folk need storms.' But I hoped I wasn't heading towards one now.

Walking through the entrance vestibule, I found my heart was hammering, my legs suddenly weak. It was mad, what I was about to do. Worse than doorstepping her parents or arriving unannounced at her brother's office.

Even if my motives were pure, perhaps I should have done this in a more . . . hands-off way. But it was too late now.

They were having drinks in the bar area. Izzy's mother Coco caught sight of me first, raising her eyebrows as she sipped a glass of red wine, then whispering to Julian, who turned and nodded like he expected to see me there. There was a pretty little girl between them who must be their granddaughter, Sisi. Alaric, leaning heavily on a walking stick, caught my eye and immediately turned his back like he had nothing to do with any of it, the *vecchi* bastard. Izzy was standing with a tall, suave-looking man who must be her Mr Braithwaite, laughing at something he was whispering to her. The weight of my rucksack pulled on my shoulders, making them ache. I slipped it off, carefully, and held it, waiting.

As if aware of my presence, Izzy turned and surveyed the room, before fixing on me. A number of expressions chased their way across her face – dismay, confusion, irritation, but maybe . . . a glimmer of pleasure? A tiny spark of welcome? I stepped forward, awkwardly holding my bag in front of me as a shield.

'I'm not staying,' I assured her as she approached. 'I just wanted to say something.'

'How did you . . .?' She shook her head, to dismiss the question. 'Of course. You were busy this summer. What are you doing here?'

'I came to bring you a present,' I said. 'Two presents, actually. The first is this.' I pulled the bubble-wrapped package from my bag, brushing off the protective plastic to reveal Dippy's painting. 'Happy Birthday.'

It was a cut-down version of the Harlots photo painted in Dippy's pointillism style – just me and Izzy at the end of the row, laughing together. Without the others, we looked like we were in our own world, cocooned in the joke, young and carefree. Across the top, Dippy had written 'OLD WOMAN'S CACKLE', a quote from Charlotte Brontë's *Shirley*. Izzy always had an old woman's cackle, even when she was a teenager. It was one of the things I loved about her.

The frame had been made by me. After sweeping up the smashed pieces of the plate we'd broken in The Stray Dog, I painstakingly put them back together, so that along the top, you could see the quote picked out: 'Keep in good health.' Fragments of Charlotte's portrait decorated the rest of the surround, the blue of the old rim complementing the azure Sheffield sky above the hockey field.

'It's an original Serendipity Holt,' I said. 'Plus an original Mortimosaic frame. One day, it'll be a collector's item.'

'Thank you, it's lovely,' observed Izzy, gazing at the painting. 'Strange, but lovely.'

'That's Dippy,' I agreed.

'You said two presents.' Izzy looked up. 'Is one the painting, and the other the frame?'

'No.' I took a deep breath. 'The other is that I found X and she won't be bothering you any more.'

Izzy went very still, clutching the painting, eyes never leaving my face.

'It was Erica,' I explained. 'Erica Stanley.'

'*Erica?*' she breathed. 'But I barely had anything to do with her. Why did she . . . what . . .?'

'I still don't really understand,' I said. 'But it was her, and she won't come anywhere near you ever again.'

'How did you . . .?' Izzy seemed to be at a loss for words. Watching us, her husband raised his eyebrows as if to ask if she was OK, and she nodded distractedly, raking a hand through her hair. She tried again. 'How do you know it was her?'

'She gave herself away with her iced biscuits, the dumb bitch. We had a little talk. And now she's gone.'

'I . . . I don't know what to say. Thank you. Thank you.' Izzy smiled, and all at once her face looked ironed out, as young as the one she was holding. She turned to Miles, and I could see she wanted to tell him straight away, tell him that this huge weight had lifted, and I knew that was my cue to go.

'I must be off. But I just wanted to say one more thing.'

Izzy turned to me, her eyes alight.

'You were right about us not being able to go back. Too much water under the bridge, as my mum would say. But . . . we could go forward. When I started searching for you, I wanted to be friends again for my sake, because there was something lacking in my life and I thought it might be you. But now . . . I think we should be friends for your sake as well. And I don't mean *best* friends, or plus-ones, or anything like that. I mean let's just stay in touch, catch up occasionally. Because I think everyone needs a support network, as big as you can make it – people who know you of old, who've got your back, who get your stupid jokes. People you trust. I could be one of those people. I'd like to be. But it's up to you.'

I backed off, picking up my rucksack, and walked away, leaving her standing there with the painting in her hands, tears in her eyes. I walked away, my legs still trembling as I wrenched open the door to leave, and I walked away, wiping my own tears as I emerged on Nelson Street and turned towards my hotel.

I was still walking away when I heard the shout, and it took a while to make my marching, shaking legs turn around so I could face Izzy, who had come running after me, her face flushed and triumphant, as if she'd just scored a goal for the Harpur Harlots.

'Braithwaite,' she said, holding out her hand. 'Pandora Braithwaite. And you are?'

Harrogate's Hip New Hotel Is a Hit

Our resident food guru Isabella Harris is impressed by the spa town's latest opening

What better time to launch a hotel restaurant than Christmas, when festive greenery and twinkling fairy lights make everything cosy and inviting? That's what renowned hotelier Lixin Lee told me, when he welcomed us to a brand-new branch of Manchester's beloved Lever Club. The restaurant's name, Fontibus, is a nod to Harrogate's Latin motto, *Arx celebris fontibus* – 'a citadel famous for its springs' – and I suspect that this new establishment will become as popular in the spa town as the waters.

My guests for the evening were long-time associates Gwen and Min, who kindly joined me to celebrate this illustrious event in Gwen's hometown. She was eager to point out several artworks in situ, painted by celebrated local artist Serendipity Holt, and their bold, intriguing quality adds spice to the elegance of the eating space.

Fontibus aims to provide contemporary fine dining in a relaxed setting, and as such, is dog-friendly. Gwen brought her Labrador along to enjoy the experience, and Mabel appeared to appreciate her (spring?) water and bone-shaped treats. The human menu is short but thoughtful, celebrating local, seasonal produce, sustainably sourced, with a twist. Lee has brought in the supremely talented young chef Ayo Okoro, and she brings her own signature style, putting a new spin on traditional dishes like Shepherd's Pie and Toad in the Hole. My cauliflower tart starter, laced with Kirk Jagger goat's cheese, was fresh and zesty – the ideal appetizer – and it was followed by an equally well-judged plate of salt-aged Yorkshire lamb, the meat sweet, nutty and mellow. I concluded with a Blackberry Vacherin, the feather-light, airy meringue topped with a silky vanilla cream. We were told the fruit came from within spitting distance – 'not that anyone would spit in here,' assured our waiter. Mabel begged to differ – she was not the most refined of diners – but Fontibus is an accommodating place.

It was lucky my fellow tasters are fluent in British Sign Language, because their mouths were frequently too full to talk. When we reached the end of our meal, I asked them how they would rate Harrogate's hippest new destination. Both joined their thumb and forefinger in a circle, and I didn't need to be well-versed in BSL to know what they meant.

Perfetto!

Acknowledgements

This fourth book of mine, possibly closest to my heart so far, came out in a rush after watching *The Banshees of Inisherin* and wanting to tell my own tale of broken friendship. It feels fitting, then, firstly to thank my friends, to whom this book is dedicated. In ways big and small, they've enriched, supported, comforted and amused me, and I'm grateful to every one of them:

- Schoolfriends, some of whom bought and read my books on the basis that we shared a classroom decades ago, some of whom sent me incredibly cheering messages of congratulation, some of whom even turned up to my events. Alex, who I played badminton with aged eleven, exchanges WhatsApp messages with me almost daily – mostly Rightmove links and photos of our pets. It's lovely to have long-standing friends who, as Gwen would say, 'know you of old'. Cheers to the Old Mannerians.

- University friends, many of whom I see very regularly indeed, some of whom live within a minute of me, all of whom are brilliant, funny, creative and captivating people. It's amazing that those brief three years in college have had such a huge influence on my friendship group, and I'm very glad that they did.

- TV friends. There were lots of great things about working in telly (lots of annoying things too) but the best thing was the people. Telly folk are the sharpest, darkest, wittiest, quickest and often drunkest people, and I'm lucky that despite having left the business, I still run into my old comrades at parties and dinners (and the odd book launch, because there's some crossover). They continue to dazzle me.

- Dog friends. They were the muses for a whole book! My debut, *Saving Missy*, was inspired by the eclectic, entrancing pack I met in the park while walking my beloved Polly. Now I've got Phoebe and Peggy, and continue to meet sociable, engaging, interesting locals who make standing in a wet field more bearable. I'm delighted to live in such a vibrant and friendly community, where it's impossible to get around without stopping for a gossip.

- Mum & Dad friends. When our eldest started school, the era of the Parent WhatsApp Group dawned. I'm now a member of about fifty such groups, mostly concerned with lice outbreaks, but a great circle of parent-friends has come out of it. I go for coffee with them, attend the provocatively named 'Orgy Admin' book group with them, occasionally sing karaoke with them, even go camping with them. Sharing the highs and lows of parenthood with these fellow sleep-deprived, multi-tasking mums and dads has been very special, and I'd like to raise an overflowing glass in their direction.

- Swimming friends. Anyone who follows me on social media will know that a passion of mine is getting into extremely cold water, like a massive middle-aged dryrobed cliché. But, in case monsters of the deep attack, I like to take a dip in company, and am privileged to have the most delightful coterie of fellow idiots who also love freezing their arses off. A doffed silicone cap to Mamma Swim, and the Friday morning brigade.

- Writing friends. I had many dreams about what writing a book would involve, but to be honest, I didn't think about the other people writing books. I was clueless about a lot of things, and one of the unexpected joys of becoming an author was meeting other people in the publishing world. A fantastic online group, the Savvy Writers' Snug, spawned the sanity-saving spin-off Debut 20, a gaggle of debut authors who got me through Covid and the ensuing fallout. In the years since I was first published, I've met so many wonderful, supportive and extremely talented writers who are always there to share their stories, put things into perspective and occasionally join me for Drinks of Despair. It's extremely exciting to see your name on the cover of a book – it's also exciting to see the names of people you know. Bravo, all of you.

Some more specific chums and experts who helped with the creation of this book include renowned food writer Kathy Slack, who looked over Isabella's reviews with a critical eye, providing delectable advice about what constitutes an acceptable culinary adjective. Thanks also to Jerome Smith, who was never a spy but was maybe once able to fax one, for giving me a droll and fascinating glimpse into the world of espionage.

I asked two authenticity readers to check my work, and was hugely grateful to both of them for their diligent and intuitive feedback. Thanks to Steve Day for offering the invaluable perspective of a deaf reader, and to Claudia Spadoni for correcting my Italian and giving excellent notes on my Roman chapters – *grazie mille*.

As ever, hearty applause for my publishing teams in the UK and US who are so encouraging and enterprising, and whose myriad of talents come together to create and sell a book. Sales and marketing dynamos, design and audio teams, eagled-eyed copy editors, proof readers and hardworking assistants – an intricate and beautiful publishing mosaic; this book would be scattered fragments without them. To my brilliant editors, Martha Ashby and Tara Singh-Carlson: thanks for pushing me and cheering me on – I always feel a spark of joy when I see an approving comment in the markup notes! And then my amazing agent, Madeleine Milburn, her assistant, Saskia Arthur, and the incredible team at the MM Agency: I'm so grateful for their patience, wisdom and enthusiasm, and feel proud and privileged to be a member of their bookish club.

Last but not least, thanks to my sons Wilfred and Edmund, and their friends Jonny, Keir, Sonny and Oliver, for schooling me in Generation Alpha slang and mocking my attempts to be cool. Luv 4 dat, yung G.

Finally, to my family: I can offer no higher compliment than to say that if we weren't related, or married, or related by marriage, then I hope we'd be friends anyway. *Cin-cin!*

If you enjoyed *Isabella's Not Dead*,
read on for an extract from *Lucky Day*,
the uplifting, life-affirming novel from
Sunday Times bestseller
Beth Morrey . . .

One day. No rules. What would you do?

Lucky Day

'Funny, inspiring, uplifting'
Nina Stibbe

'Will leave you squealing and cheering'
Lizzy Dent

SUNDAY TIMES BESTSELLING AUTHOR
BETH MORREY

Available now

1

Today started like any other, but then . . . veered off course. It all derailed pretty quickly, to be honest. Little things snowballing, building up to an avalanche. Like that poem about the horseshoe nail: 'For want of a nail . . .' I can't remember it now – God, brain fog again – but it starts small and before you know it a whole kingdom is lost and you're screwed. All for the want of a tiny nail. On Thursday, 16th June, I should have been in my office looking online for nice places in Padstow, but for various reasons I called my boss a prick and had some sort of episode, and here we are.

A headache came on last night, creeping up the side of my face like a dark force, prodding me awake. Ordinary painkillers do nothing, and I've long given up asking the doctor for something stronger. Last time, as I hunched, whimpering, on a vinyl chair that reeked of disinfectant, he suggested I try meditating, and turned away to tap something on his computer. I panicked it would be one of those coded notes medics use, calling me malingering or making sure I didn't get any more sleeping tablets, so I backed out, saying I'd download the Calm app. I did download it, but the sound of rain made me fret that the leak in the loft dormer had opened up again, so it didn't really work.

Unable to get back to sleep, I got up early and pottered round finishing jobs from the night before, folding washing, reloading the machine, blinking as the colours danced in front of my eyes. Scraping dried tomato off the base of the casserole dish, fetching lamb out the freezer for later, mentally adding naan bread to my shopping list, giving Grizelda her breakfast, which she lapped at fastidiously. The fridge door was a seething mass of Post-it note reminders, scrawled by me, ignored by my family: *Cancel milk, Call roofer, Hima's birthday, Jonathan's birthday, Dry-cleaning Tuesday, Cat flea treatment, Ethan inhaler, Order garden waste bags, Book smear, Fix landing light, Pay Lottie, BDD WRAP??* ☹

Those booming capitals reminded me, as they were supposed to. I started checking emails and got sucked into one about the work party later, a viewing of a show we'd made. I had nothing to do with it, didn't want to go, didn't want to be involved, but Vince, my boss, had insisted we all turn up. Now Imogen, Vince's PA, was sending me guest lists and asking me to check in case anyone on it was someone he hated: Clover, You're a Life-Saver!!!! Not even 6 a.m., and I found myself scrolling down a list of names to see if they'd included a commissioner Vince had offended or a former employee with a grudge.

Names, names, mostly unfamiliar, one I recognized

here and there, and then a particular selection of letters seemed to balloon and scatter in front of my eyes until the pain took over and I couldn't look any more. I slapped the laptop shut, pressing my hands to my face to push away the ache, banish it. Who cared who was going to the party, I certainly wasn't, so it didn't matter either way, just forget it, put it out of my mind, none of my business. After pinching the bridge of my nose for a second, trying and failing to do some mindful breathing, I decided to get on with the day, to see if ignoring it would make it go away.

My head was still pounding as I unloaded the dishwasher. Robbie always loads it wrong, fork prongs down, probably to make sure it remains my job. I mean, I pretend I can't understand council tax for the same reason, but the balance of things we both pretend we can't do seems unfairly uneven. When everything was sorted and put away, I rooted about in the ceramic chicken that lives on the windowsill in the kitchen. It's supposed to hold eggs, but who decants eggs? Instead, it's a repository for random tablets – indigestion, constipation, congestion – you name the 'tion' and we've got a tablet for it in the chicken. I like to be ready for any development – steeling myself for disaster, Robbie says.

There they were: two leftover Vicodin pills, the last of a packet he brought back from a work trip to the US where he wrenched his shoulder getting his bag down from an overhead locker. Robbie said they made him high for a week, and he had to stop taking them because he was starting to enjoy it too much. He dropped the last two into the chicken, saying 'These are not to be taken, under any circumstances,' and I said 'Why are you putting them in there then?' and he said 'As insurance against those circumstances.' Like, if they were there, no one would need them. But I did need them, and they were bound to be out of date, so I was doing everyone a favour by getting rid of them. It was basically tidying up, hoovering pharmaceuticals, being useful. But there was also a hint of rebellion there, consuming forbidden fruit – fruit forbidden by my husband, whose loading of the dishwasher should be criminalized. I took them with a swig of tea, and immediately felt better. Well, I felt much the same physically, but had the sated feeling I get after decluttering. Pills, with added jam.

Except . . . what if I was allergic to Vicodin? It's American; they put different substances in stuff over there, like chlorine and pesticides. I pulled up my sleeves to check for hives, the beginnings of anaphylactic shock, then noticed ancient antihistamines nestling at the bottom of the hen – bingo. I took three to finish the blister packet, and chucked it in the bin, figuring that at the very least, this medicinal mix should achieve some degree of numbness. Those letters, that name, still dancing in front of my eyes, stabbing at my skull . . . I needed the drugs to delete them.

That done, I started laying out breakfast things; the cereal library the twins require every morning to get them up and running, a cafetière for Robbie's coffee, which he mainlines as soon as he gets out of bed. I love coffee, but it makes me twitchy as hell so I gave it up in favour of tamer tea-caffeine. Seems lately I react to everything one way or another. Bloated after carbs, queasy after meat, gassy after vegetables. Can't even drink a sip of water without peeing every five minutes. Sometimes I drink wine in the evenings just to dehydrate myself, so I won't be up every hour in the night, heading to the bathroom, quaking in the dark at the sighs and grinds of our creaky old house. But wine gives me a headache. In my twenties, I could sink a bottle and come up smiling the next morning; nowadays I can feel my brow tighten just looking at the glass. An anticipation of undoing. The older you get, the more things stop being fun and just become a chore. Music festivals, flights abroad, wrap parties – someone always has to prepare for eventualities, deal with the mess.

The headache had receded by the time Robbie came down just after seven, in his MAMIL gear, ready to cycle to work. No point in telling him about the drugs, he probably forgot they even existed, it would only cause a fuss. For the same reason, I didn't mention the forks, or the plates thrown in every which way so that they came out flecked with bolognese. My husband began making his coffee with the concentration and precision of a lab technician studying embryos, while I put another tea bag in a cup and picked up my book. I've been reading *The Blind Assassin* for about eleven years and have never got past page 48. Sure enough, as the words blurred before my still-prickling eyes, the washing machine beeped. I got to my feet.

'Don't worry, I'll do it,' said Robbie. He pressed the plunger down slowly, focused on the rolling granules. We both knew he had no intention of emptying the washing machine. I prefer to do it myself, since he once took the wet clothes out and left them in a pile gathering crumbs on the kitchen table, while he went off to fetch the *New European* from the front doormat. He didn't come back.

My husband isn't deliberately unhelpful, or one of those men who thinks it's a woman's job. Just absent-minded, and better – probably deliberately – at other things. He tends to favour building shelves in seventeenth-century nooks, and fixing the constantly-on-the-blink boiler, leaving me to take care of . . . well, everything else. You tend to settle into these roles without either of you meaning to – the school calls the mother when the child is sick, the plumber tells the man the valve is faulty. It can grind you down, but there are bigger battles to fight, like getting Robbie to agree to book a nice cottage in Cornwall for our October half-term holiday, rather than some dodgy Airbnb in Athens so he can visit the Parthenon. On some level, though, the prongs of those forks were needling, reminding me it was my job to put them the right way up so they got properly clean.

After breakfast, the usual hassle of getting everyone up and out, hauling Ethan out of bed, telling Hazel to switch off her GHD irons, wiping down worktops, dashing upstairs to slap on some semblance of a face, despairing at the eye bags, age spots at my temples, thread veins around my nose. Downstairs again, grabbing an overstuffed tote, shouting at everyone to get a move on. Of course, as soon as the front door closed, I had to go back to check the straighteners were off. I have to do this every day – we live in a lovely old farmhouse and I really don't want it to burn down. The ancient wiring worries me enough as it is.

It's the morning dance routine of a million households, we're nothing special. No exceptional circumstances here, unless you count twins, and that's only one in two hundred and fifty. Or is that two in two hundred and fifty? Whatever. The four of us were out of the house by ten past eight, and I was on a train to Bristol by eight-thirty. For a while after we went back to the office, post-pandemic, everyone had staggered starting times, but somehow it all fell away, Vincent began scheduling 9 a.m. meetings again and no one, least of all me, raised any objections. Like the Fire of London. After it razed everything to the ground, they said they were going to rebuild the city better, get rid of that higgledy-piggledy layout and plot big wide streets in grids, but in the end, they just built the roads where they'd always been, same as before. That pretty much went for everything, really. All this talk of making everything better, greener, fairer, came to nothing. Back to how it was, waiting for the next fire to strike.

On the train I was trying to read my book again but felt dozy and distracted, probably because of the pills kicking in, those letters still scrambling under my lids, so let it fall to my lap, as a thousand and one abstract concerns crowded my brain, vying for attention. Shopping lists and guest lists; cleaning tasks and sorting out mess; nails, emails and migraines; eye bags and emotional baggage. So much to do, so many people to placate, circling, jabbing at me like the prongs of the forks. I closed my eyes, then opened them, staring into space, vision swimming and refocusing.

That was when I saw the case. The case with the bomb in it.